ASCENDING MAGE 1: CHANGELING JUSTICE

FRANK & RAELEA HURT

CONTENTS

1

A REAL CHANGELING

Summer 1998
Lancashire, United Kingdom

"Don't lose him! The Transmute Spell is nearly worn off."

Ember wordlessly obeyed the directive from her new partner and kept running as fast as her aching legs could carry her. She feared losing the suspect they pursued—or maybe worse, catching up to him after the spell wore off.

She tapped the rush of adrenaline to give her lungs greater capacity, her legs greater span—even as the voice in her head screamed at her, warned her of the menace she knowingly ran toward. *Bloody changelings. Why are they always so fast, even in human form?*

The Transmute Spell could only block a changeling from shifting for a short time. Even such a spell cast from someone as powerful as The Legend—as her partner tolerated being called—even *that* would only briefly contain a changeling as aggressive as the one they chased. If this one was allowed to shift into his animal form, there was nothing stopping the beast from tearing both Investigators to pieces.

Ember inwardly shuddered at the thought.

She watched her partner race past her. Wallace Livingston may have been 174 years old, but the Senior Investigator had no trouble outpacing younger mages. Especially when it came to catching criminals. *There's a reason they call him The Legend.*

The dark trench coat flew ahead like the wings of a demon. His wide-brim hat sheltered his face from view and from the light English rain that drizzled down, shrouding the night sky and making the stone pavers dangerously slick to run on.

The flying coat crossed between two pillars abutting a wrought iron fence enveloping the Blackburn Old Cemetery. "Go left!" Wallace ordered.

Before Ember could acknowledge, the coat, hat, and the man within, all disappeared between headstones into the cemetery.

Ember's lungs burned. Her blonde locks were plastered against her face and neck. After the long chase through the evening mist, there was no way of knowing whether it was rain or sweat condensing down her back. *It's not enough that the bloody changeling makes us chase him. At night. In the rain. Now through a cemetery, too?*

Into the poorly-lit graveyard, Ember pursued her quarry.

Despite *knowing* that the changeling was guilty, they would continue referring to him as a suspect until a confession was given or extracted. This suspect was guilty of breaking one of the oldest of the Old Laws; he was accused of shifting into his animal form in the presence of NonDruws—in front of non-magic humans.

Wallace and Ember cleaned up the aftermath, though it wasn't easy. It was one of their first cases together as partners and no small case at that. They had to track down each of the NonDruws who witnessed the changeling's crime, interrogate them, and then give them each a Memory Wash before setting them free. It was an exhausting task, and they had to be thorough about it. It was for everyone's benefit that nobody would remember the events but for the Investigators assigned to the case.

It was then for the Druw High Council at Malvern Hills to decide what Brevar's punishment would be. If the suspect was particularly lucky, he might get lifelong imprisonment. If he attempted to harm either her or Wallace, the changeling would likely be executed. But there were worse punishments than dying.

As harsh as the sentence would be, the changeling's action was inexcusable. Their kind—the Druw—were so few and spread so thin around the world, far outnumbered by NonDruws. The only thing that kept them safe—kept them *alive*—was by remaining hidden.

Ember's flat-soled shoes slapped against wet pavers lining the path weaving through the cemetery. Three times, she slipped but caught herself. She wasn't so lucky the fourth time, as she stubbed her toe against an uneven stone and momentarily went airborne—for all of one second.

"Bollocks!" Ember hissed. She reached down and touched her elbow where it connected with the soggy earth. Her fingers squished a smattering of slimy moss and mud, which she initially mistook for blood. She pulled her knees up to the slippery surface to find her footing. *At least nothing's broken.*

An aged lamppost illuminated the headstone in front of her. She gripped the mossy stone and used it to pull herself up out of the muddy turf. *Typical for me to trip where there's actually some form of light.*

Her thumb ran across the markings etched into her borrowed handhold:

Frederick Kempster, 1862-1942

Ember spoke to the stone as she found her footing. "Quite sorry for disturbing you, Mister Kempster, but I don't suppose you've seen a wayward changeling running through your graveyard, perchance?"

She stood up beneath the lamp and peered into the night, letting the light bathe her backside as her eyes adjusted. "Barring that, if you would have a torch I could borrow, that would be brilliant."

Movement in her periphery caught her attention. If she wasn't so soaked, the hairs on the back of her neck would have surely stood. Mustering what confidence she could, Ember said, "Hold it! You, there!"

A sharply-dressed man stepped out from behind an old oak tree. He wore a dark suit and a thin, black tie over a white collared shirt. Ember blinked as her head tilted back to look upon the man's towering figure. She never knew someone could be so tall. *Good God, he's nearly three feet taller than me! This one must be approaching eight feet!*

The giant of a man seemed as surprised to see her as she was to see him. She could sense that he wasn't a Druw, but he didn't quite feel like a NonDruw, either. Ember's voice was lost for a moment, and she realized her mouth was agape.

"I am sorry if I startled you, Miss," the towering man said. "I could not help but overhear you talking. I admit I did not expect anyone to see me tonight." The man adjusted his tie and furrowed his brow. "You *do* see me, Miss?"

A dozen questions ran through Ember's head. *What is this man doing wandering a cemetery at night? Where is his peculiar accent from? And what kind of absurd riddle is he telling?*

There was no time for any of that, not now. "I'm looking for a man, a tall man—well, not as tall as you. He ran through here just a moment ago. I don't suppose you saw him?"

"Why, indeed I did!" The man sounded amused. "Is he some sort of a criminal, I suppose?"

Ember tried to maintain patience with the stranger, but she knew the Transmute Spell was growing weaker by the minute. "Yes, yes. I'm a member of law enforcement. Now, which way did he run, if you please?"

If the tall stranger was at all troubled by Ember's brusque tone, he didn't let on. "The gentleman is no longer running, Miss. He is crouched, hiding behind the big, headless angel statue." The man clicked his tongue and shook his head as he pointed up the wet path. "Such a desecration, and in a sacred place, no less. So little respect."

"Brilliant!" Ember resumed running up the path, only belatedly remembering to thank the odd stranger.

The statue was easy enough to find, even in the dim light offered by the sparsely-placed lampposts. The granite angel's wings were wide and proud—and its head was indeed missing. Some part of Ember's subconscious thought that the decapitation may have been intentional, as though by design. *Macabre design that would be.*

She carefully picked her way through the grounds between grave markers, attempting to remain stealthy. The dampness of the night made the grass spongy and her shoes made audible squishing noises. Everything about this place smelled of wet leaves and decay.

"I think he hears you, Miss." It was the giant of a man, leaning down as he spoke to her.

Ember caught the exclamation in her throat before it could betray her position. She whispered, "What the bloody hell! How did you sneak up on me?"

The man shrugged apologetically and then waved one of his dinnerplate-size hands toward the beheaded statue. "I believe your quarry is meaning to ambush you, Miss. Your partner is not far off; perhaps he could be of assistance?"

"How do you know that?" Ember whispered into the drizzling rain. She swept clinging, soaked hair from her face and peered into the night, trying to see what the tall stranger was seeing. She saw only more grave markers, statues, and mature trees.

"Your partner is behind the shrubs, over there." A large hand gestured. "He is making his way here as we speak. Begging your pardon, but your partner moves quickly and gracefully, Miss."

Ember grumbled beneath her breath, but then she saw it, saw the movement—the shape of a man wearing a wide-brim hat and a trench coat picking his way through the shrubs. She knew she couldn't take the changeling on her own, so she had to act—and quickly. She had to warn Wallace, to alert him.

Ember stayed crouched, cupped her muddy hands to the side of her mouth and shouted, "Brevar! We know you're behind the headless angel statue! We have you surrounded!"

She was answered with a throaty, deep roar from behind the winged, granite figure. The changeling was transforming—the Transmute Spell had worn off. A huge silhouette stepped out from hiding and began lumbering on four legs, away from Ember's position.

"He's shifting, Wallace!"

Ember chased after the roaring creature, unsure what she could possibly do if she caught up with it, but unwilling to let her partner face this changeling alone. The beast moved too quickly though, and its roaring form ran toward the shrubs—straight for Wallace. *Oh no! I've just got The Legend killed.*

"Head's up! He's coming your way!" Ember yelled desperately as she ran, slipping on the wet grass and mud.

Another angry roar rang out through the cemetery, followed by a brief flash of yellow light.

Ember charged into the shrubs to find Wallace, bent over and panting to catch his breath. Before them was a humongous polar bear, wrapped tightly in a shiny, gold Containment Net. The net glowed, writhing and moving as though alive. Wallace's net shrunk itself around the body of the bear, unbreakable and secure.

The bear gave one more roar, though this time it sounded like one of frustration.

Wallace stepped over to the trapped bear, clapped his hands together once, and then uttered "Sleep." The moment his hand touched the beast, the bear went silent. Its head dropped and it stopped struggling.

Ember stared at the Senior Investigator with admiration and made a silent vow. *Indeed, there's a reason they call him "The Legend." Someday, I'll inspire others the way this man inspires me.*

Her partner returned the gaze, though he frowned at the mud and grass smeared on her knees and arms. "Cheers, Ember. But...are you alright?"

Ember shrugged self-consciously and looked down at her messy clothes. "Nothing's broken."

A gasping voice from above and behind made Ember turn. It was the tall stranger.

"My word!" The well-dressed giant looked with wonder at the netted polar bear. "A real changeling, could it be? That would make you both...Malverns, wouldn't it? How delightful! I had heard stories about changelings and mages during my time, but I always dismissed them as mythology. My word!"

It was a pity this helpful stranger would enjoy his discovery for only a moment longer. Ember knew Wallace would make her cast a Memory Wash upon this NonDruw. The three Druws would return to obscurity and the NonDruw would be back to...wandering through the cemetery or whatever it was that he was doing when she found him.

Ember looked up at the awe-struck man. "Yeah, so...about this bear."

"Ember...who are you talking to?" Wallace said between breaths.

Ember felt her neck and cheeks grow heated as she began to explain. "Wallace, I'm so sorry, I know I bumbled this. This fellow—I know I should not have allowed a NonDruw to get involved—but you see, he knew Brevar was waiting for me."

"Ember. Who. Are you. Talking to?" Wallace's voice was calm and firm between deep breaths. His words held no mirth. It made Ember feel uneasy.

"Um, well, yes," Ember turned back to the stranger, "I suppose I never caught your name."

"Ah, yes. I am Fred, Fred Kempster. At your service." The towering man placed a hand on his stomach and bowed.

Ember looked back at her partner sheepishly. "As I said, Fred helped me—helped us, Wallace."

Wallace shook his head, his focus never leaving her. "Ember, when you slipped, did you hit your head? Are you sure you're alright?"

"Why do you keep asking me that? Of course, I'm alright!"

Ember looked back at Fred. "Not that you'll remember this

conversation in a few minutes, but if you wouldn't mind telling Wallace what you told me, that might be helpful."

The tall man looked down at Ember, his expression transforming from excitement to something resembling sadness. "Miss, I do not believe your friend can see me."

"What the bloody hell are you going on about? He would have to be blind *not* to see you!" Ember waved her hands with exasperation.

Fred sighed and shook his head. He said, "until you, I have not known a living person who *could* see me, much less speak with me."

Cold realization seeped into Ember's consciousness just as Frederick Kempster fed her the explanation.

"Dear Miss, that was *my* headstone you read from."

2

BLINDIN' US WITH SHADOWS

THE MAN'S DEEP-SET EYES FIXED A GLARE BENEATH A protruded brow. Dried, mossy-smelling mud flaked from his muscled arms when he flexed. He seemed wholly unimpressed with his captors, and over the past five hours he made a point of sharing his assessment with them.

Even in human form, shackled by his wrists to a heavy steel table and injected with a Transmute Inhibitor serum, Brevar cut an imposing figure. The changeling had been administered a triple-dose of the serum when he was brought in overnight by the Malvern Hills Department of Investigation. Nobody was interested in seeing a belligerent polar bear appear in the office building. All the same, he probably could overturn the table and pin one of the Investigators against the wall before the security detail outside could respond.

If he was at all concerned, Wallace didn't show it. The Senior Investigator casually unfolded his legs from beneath his chair. His handlebar mustache twitched whenever his gravelly voice drawled. "Let me ask you one more time—"

"Ask me as many times as ye like," Brevar growled in a thick Scottish accent. "Mah answer's still gonna be th' same, ye fuckin' heartless knob."

Heartless. That was a new variation of the many colorful insults Brevar slung at his interrogators. Ember leaned against the wall-sized mirror as she watched her partner for a reaction. She wasn't surprised to see Wallace notice the same.

"Heartless, am I?" Wallace's lips teased a smile though his posture remained firm. "Why am I heartless now? Are you trying to tell me that you broke Council Law for love? You expect me to believe that?"

The reaction lasted less than a second, but Ember noticed it: Brevar's aura changed color, shifting to a rose-pink before returning to the deep red shade it had been all morning. She knew Wallace wouldn't see what she saw—as far as they both knew, she was the only mage who could see auras.

The scowl never left Brevar's face. "Aye, ye got me. Ah shifted in front o' those Mundies 'cause ah had tae protect mah burd."

"Your bird? You mean your girlfriend? Why are you telling us this now?" Wallace frowned. "Why the subterfuge, if what you say is true?"

"Aye, it's true," Brevar sighed. His hulking form leaned forward, his head slumping. "Ye lifted me 'n' brought me tae this midden. Nae rights tae a solicitor ye say. Well, ahm knackered. Ah tell ye th' truth, ah've git tae kip."

"We've been sitting here all morning, and this is the first you've mentioned a girlfriend." Wallace crossed his arms and studied the changeling's body language. "Why did you have to protect your girlfriend from NonDruws?"

"She an' ah were steamin' a few pints at a pub when some Mundie wanker tried talkin' mince tae my burd. When ah stepped up tae gie him a square go, four o' his buddies walloped me." Brevar shook his head, his gaze focused on the table's steel surface. "Ah was pissed an' didn't think. Ah just shifted an' threw 'em off me."

"Well, that was unfortunate. So your shifting was an accident, you're saying. Self-defense, but an accident." Wallace glanced at Ember and the mirror she leaned against.

Ember squinted at the changeling. As a Novice Investigator, she was supposed to stay silent and observe the interrogation. She was as surprised as anyone when she heard the words escape her lips. "He's lying, Wallace. Everything he just said is a lie."

Brevar looked up from the table and shot a menacing glare her direction. "Whit wid ye ken? Ye'r aff yer nut. Pure skyrocket, ye! Aye, ah heard ye talkin' tae yerself back at th' graveyard."

"I wasn't talking to myself, I was talking to—" Ember's jaw snapped shut as she realized what she was about to say. She blinked and shook her head, her blonde hair sweeping against the glass behind her. "Don't try diverting the topic. You're lying to us. What're you trying to cover up?"

"Investigator Wright, that's enough." Wallace's tone had an edge.

Ember pointed at Brevar. "But he's lying!"

"Ye think ahm lyin'?" Brevar roared. The short chain

connecting his wrist shackles clattered against the steel table. “Hoi, doll, ye’ve been lied tae yer whole life. We’ve all been lied tae! Ye have no idea how many lies we’re bein’ told. There’s mages practicin’ dark magic, darker than anything any o’ ye dobbers know. They’re th’ puppet masters, blindin’ us with shadows, makin’ us dance. An ye say *ahm* lyin’!”

The door to the interrogation room whipped open, and two members of security rushed in, wielding Tasers. Behind them, the station supervisor stood in the doorway. “I think it’s time we press pause on this little show, don’t you agree?”

“I want to hear what he has to say,” Ember admitted as she watched the two security officers step to either side of Brevar.

Wallace nodded at the supervisor. “Good call, Philip. I think it’s time for a smoke break.”

Ember frowned. “But neither of us smoke.”

“We’ll be back in five minutes.” Wallace’s voice was calm, but his stern expression left no room for negotiation. He led her down the hall, through the offices, and past the elevator. He swung a door open, propping it against his foot.

“You know how I feel about stairs, Wallace.” Her gaze flitted at the cement-and-steel stairwell and then back at her partner.

He held his index finger vertically to his lips, shaking his head slightly. The mage leaned over the railing, looking down the descending well as he listened.

Ember filled her lungs with musty air and held it. The only sounds she detected were emanating from the offices beyond the now-closed steel door.

Wallace pivoted on his heel to lean against the gunmetal grey railing. He crossed his arms and stared at Ember with eyes the color of highland fog. "You're on thin ice, Ember."

"If this is about me interrupting in there, I'm sorry, but—"

"You were to *observe*, not participate."

"Yes, but he was *lying* to you." Ember ran her fingers through her hair.

"So he has been all morning," Wallace frowned. Those bushy, silver eyebrows shaded his eyes from the dim light filtering in from the window above the stairs. "There's a process we need to follow. One which you need to respect, especially when others are watching."

Ember chewed on her bottom lip. "I know. I'm sorry. I lost my cool in there, yeah?"

"You did." Wallace groomed his handlebar mustache with a thumb. "Tell me, what did you make of his outburst at the end?"

She thought for a moment before answering. "You know how I've told you that when I focus, I can see a person's aura, right?"

He nodded once.

"While you were talking to him, I watched Brevar's aura... change." Ember touched her palm to the rough plaster wall. "I don't know how to explain it, other than it looked different when he was spinning tall tales."

"He was lying about the girlfriend." Wallace nodded again.

Ember blinked. "He was. But...you knew?"

"I may not be able to read auras, but there are plenty of other signs I can read. You forget I've been interviewing liars for a whole lot longer than you've been alive." The elder Malvern raised a bushy eyebrow. "You didn't answer my question, though. What of the changeling's outburst?"

"He sounded mental. I mean, dark magic and mages making us dance like puppets? That's the rambling of a bloke who's cracked." Ember glanced at the door, in the direction where Brevar waited in the interrogation room. "What do *you* think?"

Wallace didn't answer right away. He groomed his mustache and stared at the lone window. Particles of dust floated in the late-morning sunlight. "I'm not sure. I think we need to let our suspect explain himself. And you're going to *listen* in there."

"Right." Ember pushed herself away from the rough-plaster wall. She walked alongside the Senior Investigator as they meandered around the desks of the Department of Investigation.

The station supervisor, Philip, stood in front of his office, shaking hands with an elderly Malvern who Ember didn't know. The leathery old mage peered at Wallace, a hint of recognition in his eyes. He then turned and slowly walked away. His spine was bent with a stoop, as though his back was unable to straighten under the weight of so many years. His ivory-handled cane tapped an uneven staccato on the tile floor as he shuffled toward the elevator.

As the visitor departed, Philip noticed the two Investigators approaching. "Smoke break over already? I was just about to fetch a spot of tea. Care to join me?"

"We've got work to do," Wallace answered without slowing.

"Right. Of course." Philip walked alongside with his hands behind his back, one hand holding the wrist of the other, as though joined by invisible handcuffs. "Livingston, I trust your experience, though this particular suspect doesn't seem willing to budge. Do you think you're making progress with the changeling? I wonder if we shouldn't pause and discuss strategy. He seemed rather agitated and rambling like a lunatic."

Wallace made a noise which sounded like the hybrid of a scoff and a sigh. "That tells me we're getting close to something."

"Close to something? You mean a confession, yeah?"

"That, and something else. Give us another hour with the man and I'll tell you what it is. What's this now?" The Senior Investigator stopped so abruptly, Ember nearly walked into him.

A short, bald man with a hooked nose was backing out of the interrogation room, drawing the door closed behind him. When he heard Wallace's voice, he stopped and flashed an insincere smile. "Oi! Finally, you're back. This one's quite a handful."

Wallace growled, "what were you doing in there with my suspect?" His tone chilled further when he looked in on Brevar. "What the bloody hell did you just do, Lawrence?"

Ember saw it, too: the changeling stared listlessly at a wall, his unfocused eyes glazed over. Drool pooled at the corner of his mouth.

"He was going mental, Livingston. The arsehole was

babbling nonsense—a whole lot of drek." Lawrence shrugged. Perspiration beaded on his forehead and acrid sweat saturated through the sleeves at his armpits.

"Did you just perform a Memory Wash on this man?" Wallace spun around and grabbed the bald man by his jacket, shoving him against the wall with a thud.

"Oi! Ye—yeah, I did, Livingston. Just a little, to get him to calm down." The man shrugged again and licked his lips as they turned up into a sheepish grin. "I mi—might've gone too deep. My mistake."

The station supervisor shook his head. "Of all the incompetent nincompoops to walk through this office, you, James Lawrence, win the pennant. This is going in your file, you can be sure."

"In his *file,* Philip?" Wallace slammed the bald man against the wall for emphasis.

"Alright, let's just settle down, Livingston." Philip held a palm up. "Why don't you and your partner resume the interrogation while I go and reprimand Investigator Lawrence in my office."

"Interrogation?" Wallace spat the word. "This changeling's a drooling idiot now. Brevar will be lucky to remember his own name after this."

"You and Wright have been working on no sleep," Philip Pender said. "Why don't you both go home, get some rest, and let cooler heads prevail. I'll transfer your suspect to lockup. He'll be ready for you to continue working the case tomorrow."

Wallace's handlebar mustache lifted in a snarl, but he

released his grip on the bald mage's shirt. His voice resumed its calm drawl without losing any of its tension. "Case? This little wanker just destroyed my case. Now Brevar's fate is in the High Council's hands. Whatever he might've been able to tell us is lost."

Ember silently followed her partner through the offices, down the elevator and outside. The low clouds provided just enough cover to shield her weary eyes from the bright midday sun when she looked up at him.

Her mind swirled with questions, with one finding its way to her lips. "Wallace? I've never seen you angry before. I hope I'm not out of line asking you this, in a car park of all places—"

The Legend grumbled, "stop chewing and spit it out."

"It wasn't an accident, was it? Investigator Lawrence's Memory Wash."

Wallace stopped walking. He looked around the array of parked automobiles before he focused on his junior partner. "I've known James Lawrence for many years. He's a proper wanker, but whatever he is, he's not incompetent."

Ember spoke sotto voce. "It's quite a coincidence that someone would wipe Brevar's memory when he was about to tell us the truth about something."

"Coincidence indeed." Wallace matched her hushed tone. "Did you notice that pensioner talking to Philip?"

She nodded. "The one with the cane? Who was he?"

"He's a very old Malvern—one of the oldest, in fact. Richard Longbow is his name. He's a member of the Druw High

Council. I believe he was watching our interrogation of Brevar."

Ember frowned. "Why would a member of the High Council be interested in a simple case like this? Do you think Brevar actually knew something about mages practicing dark magic? He said something strangely poetic. Something about 'blinding us with shadows.' What do you suppose that means?"

"I'm skeptical, but there are too many coincidences aligning today. With his memory washed, we might never know." Wallace adjusted his wide-brimmed hat as he surveyed the parking lot again. "Just as I wonder if it's mere coincidence that our suspect finally began telling the truth only when you spoke to him. This, the same day when you discover that you're able to speak with ghosts."

She ran her fingers through her hair and muttered, "there's got to be something we can do. Someone we can tell."

His gaze met her fire-blue eyes. "It's been a dozen years, but do you remember when we met? Do you remember what I told you?"

3

YOU MAY NOT RISE TO PROMINENCE

Summer 1989
(twelve years earlier)

The girl and her room were both uncharacteristically tidy. She was at that transitory age where her bedroom was still decorated with once-loved childhood toys that were no longer played with. The aged, wide-eyed stuffed animals were witnesses, ready to offer testimony to the innocence of their owner.

All her books were on their shelves, in their proper places and not stacked on the nightstand or cluttering the desk as they usually were. All the books, that is, save one large tome. *Primer of the Arcane* was an obvious recent immigrant, out of place in its dusty, leather-bound cover and its faded yellow pages. That book sat open atop the girl's vanity, reflected in the freshly-cleaned mirror.

Ember stood above the opened book and stared at the

stranger in the mirror. This girl barely resembled her usual self; her light blonde hair was neatly curled, her lips were painted a faint purple hue, she wore a puffy lavender dress with matching shoes. Ember felt like she was wearing someone else's skin.

Her mother's insistence, all of it, as was the importance of this day pressed upon Ember despite the anxiety it caused her. *I'd rather be running through the woods around Malvern Hills like a wild animal than pretending to be someone I'm not—someone proper and refined. Maybe they wouldn't notice if I ran away and lived in a tree. At least squirrels don't have to dress up and be tested by a stranger.*

"First impressions are paramount," her mother told her earlier. "The Investigator may wish to see your room, darling. When I was tested, the Investigator spent the better part of a day observing and making notes. It's all part of the process."

"What if I don't *want* to be tested?" Ember spoke aloud to the mirror, uttering what she didn't dare say to her mother.

Her parents had such high hopes for their children. Cynthia had already been through this a few years ago when she herself was 13 years old. Cyn was eager to be tested, to prove herself. The irony was that the need for a test was all but unnecessary for her sister; she had already proven herself artistically gifted.

Not so with Ember. She attempted to play instruments, to sing, to sketch and paint. Her parents had given her Cynthia's old easel and paint set. They let her try various instruments. Mr. and Mrs. Wright even sent her to countless instructors. The obvious conclusion was that Ember could safely rule out the Art Track.

Her mother, the accomplished Healer, had shown signs of adeptness when she was an adolescent. She had—in the sixty or so years since—cultivated her skills to become known as one of the most sought-after Healers of mind-body energy in Europe, if not the world. Druwish people with ailments other Healers could not reach would schedule appointments to see the gifted Benedette Wright at her private practice in western England.

Ember one time summoned her energy to connect with an injured finch that the family's tabby brought in. She cradled the helpless creature in her hands as her mother instructed, but the quivering bird died anyway. She had no desire to feel such angst again and never tried after that.

Her father, the Analytic, showed early promise as evidenced by his skill in math through primary school. His position as a career financial manager within the Druwish Government was secure.

Oliver Wright's youngest daughter, on the other hand, was an average student on the best of days. Certainly not a candidate for the Analytic Track. Ember was fine with that, as the thought of being a career bureaucrat or financial advisor such as her father bored her to tears.

Ember's parents didn't outright *say* they were disappointed in her, but they didn't exactly have to. She sensed their dismay, their frustration. She imagined them voicing their concerns in hushed whispers to one another, "at least one of our children will contribute to the Druw community."

Ember sighed. She looked down at the open book and

decided to practice one of the Elemental spells she read about in the *Primer of the Arcane* that every self-respecting Malvern family seemed to have in their home library. She read the instructions for a basic telekinesis gesture. *Seems simple enough.*

First, Ember squeezed out a satisfying dollop of canary yellow paint onto Cynthia's well-used palette. The acrylic fumes met her nostrils, tempting her to sneeze. She set up a blank sheet of poster board on the easel and stood back. She straightened the ruffles in her new dress and stared at the brush laying next to the palette. Her index and middle finger of both hands were pressed against her temples, exactly as the old book instructed. She focused intensely and visualized the brush lifting into the air, dabbing a sample of paint into a neat swirl across the boar hair bristles, and then finally drawing a simple circle onto the poster board.

At least that was what was *supposed* to happen.

She detected a hint of movement—did she imagine that? She focused, closing her eyes and concentrating. Then came a crash. When she opened her eyes, the easel was knocked over, and the palette had been flung onto her—bright, yellow paint on her new lavender dress.

Her parents had gotten used to Ember's clumsiness over the years. "Nothing's broken" became her weary announcement whenever she tripped down stairs or knocked something over, or otherwise demonstrated her lack of gracefulness.

She couldn't make that claim this time, however.

Her mother rushed into the room. "Oh, Emberly Wright,

you've ruined your dress! The Investigator is to arrive any moment! What were you *thinking*?"

Ember was instructed to change into her next-best dress, which was a gaudy mint green number that didn't quite fit. As her mother fretted and tsked, Ember felt her emotions burn.

"Mummy, I don't *want* to be tested!" The words crawled out of her throat in a pathetic sob.

Once she found her voice, Ember couldn't control the outburst which followed. "Please don't make me do this. I just want to live my life. I don't want to be groomed into something special like Cyn. I know I'm not talented like you or Daddy or sis. I'm sorry I'm so disappointing."

Her mother's posture softened almost immediately. She sat down on the bench at the foot of Ember's bed and said nothing at first. Ember knew her mother to be compassionate—as most Healers are—but she was more used to seeing that compassion second hand. Her parents were loving but expressed that love in indirect, sometimes distant ways.

Ember recalled the last time she remembered her mother focusing her healing energy on her. She was learning how to ride a bike and had just fallen off her bicycle, skinning both her knees. Ember was hysterical and afraid to go near her bike. Her mother calmed her down and focused her healing touch to repair both the physical damage and her emotional bruising. Ember didn't know that her mother was channeling her healing magic at that time, but she recognized it now.

Her mother patiently talked her through the rite of passage

all young Malverns go through in undergoing the test when they reached puberty. "True, there are some Mage Tracks which are perhaps more desirable in our culture—more respected, even. Analytics, Arts, Healing. These are at the core of what makes our people special from other humans. But even if you were to test highly as an Investigation or Elemental track, that doesn't mean you aren't an important part of Druw society."

"But..." Ember swallowed. "But what if I don't test highly in *any* of the five tracks?"

"You may not rise to prominence, but you will not be a disappointment, not to me nor to your father." Mrs. Wright seemed to choose her words carefully. Even as she pronounced them, though, Ember could tell that her mother was lying.

That's when the guest arrived.

4

YOU ARE THE MURDERER

THE SENIOR INVESTIGATOR WHO WAS ASSIGNED TO INTERVIEW and test Ember was not at all what she was expecting. Judging by her parents' reactions, they were expecting something else, too.

Wallace Livingston was a tall, lanky old man with a handlebar mustache and scuffed, black boots. His car was the very definition of a jalopy, clanking and whining as it rolled across the pavers, oily smoke belching from its tailpipe. When he had to slam the door of his weathered sedan a second time to get the door to stay, the hinges groaned in rusty protest.

Ember's father huffed and murmured. "This is the man you insisted on, Bennie?"

"It's not as though I had ever met him before, Olly." Ember's mother spoke through gritted teeth. "He's supposedly called 'Legend' by those in the know."

"He certainly doesn't look like anyone legendary. Though I suppose that rust bucket of his may qualify."

Ember warmed up to this stranger the more she observed her parents' disapproval of the superficial aspects. Here was a man who did not meet their expectations of class and societal distinction. They wanted and expected only the best for their family. She couldn't help but find amusement in the fact that her parents had called in favors among their bureaucrat friends to have this specific Investigator assigned to test their daughter.

When tea was served, Wallace sipped noisily. Biscuit crumbs remained in his mustache, letting loose onto his faded grey jacket when he spoke.

Ember snickered as she watched her mother try to keep calm and act as though it didn't bother her. Mr. Wright sat stoically, but Ember could see that he was agitated—she always could pick up on subtle cues. He was nervous, anxious. Not for the subtle low manners of their guest—Mr. Wright was never too concerned with such things. No, Ember figured that the anxiety that her father was trying not to show was out of concern for his daughter. She imagined him thinking the same thought as she had fixated on: "what if she tests poorly in *all* Mage Tracks?"

Ember watched her mother and imagined her thought process centered around Ember rating highly in one of the more respectable tracks—those which would yield increased status for the family. She imagined her mother bragging up the youngest daughter in the same way she bragged up Cyn at dinner parties. She had a difficult time believing that scenario.

The small talk continued, and Ember noticed Wallace watching her. She got the feeling that he was appraising her, even when she was just sitting there saying nothing.

"Do you read much, Miss Wright?"

"Oh, she constantly has her nose in a book." Her mother answered before Ember had a chance to speak.

"I love reading. Mostly westerns from America." Ember knew that her mother wouldn't appreciate her admission. Pulp fiction wasn't considered classy reading material, after all.

"She reads the classics too, of course." Benedette Wright chuckled nervously. "Shakespeare of course. James Joyce, as well. CS Lewis is probably her favorite author."

Ember could see the look of incredulity on the Senior Investigator's face, though he didn't say anything. She had barely heard of Joyce, much less read anything of his. She saw no point in lying to an Investigator. "Actually, Louis L'Amour would have to be my favorite. Especially his Sackett series."

"Ah, an American. Yes, I'm familiar with his work." Wallace stroked the crumbs out of his mustache with a thumb. "What is it that you like about the Western genre?"

Ember thought for a moment before answering. "I suppose it's the conflict between good and bad. And that the good guy almost always wins."

Benedette started to speak until Wallace set his teacup down and said that he would like to proceed with the test. He asked if they had a garden where he could walk with their daughter (they did). He picked up his oversized brief-case and followed Ember out into the back garden.

Wallace and Ember strolled in silence for a while. A gazebo surrounded by manicured hedges was where they stopped. He gestured for her to sit, which she found somewhat strange, as it was her own home, her own family's gazebo.

"I would imagine you are wondering when the test would ever begin," Wallace said as he sat the briefcase on a small table next to him and released its latches.

"Something tells me that your test began the moment you arrived at our home."

Wallace blinked with surprise and a smile appeared in his eyes, though he didn't allow it to reach his lips.

This man isn't used to being surprised, I see.

Wallace unwound an unnecessarily long string from a coffee-colored folder. Within were sets of documents, on which he began to check boxes and write notes.

"You don't have an affinity to social mores, do you, Miss Wright?"

"Hmmm, I don't quite understand the question."

"Tea and chat. Small talk in the foyer. 'How're the children. What do you think of this weather?' and all that."

Ember shook her head vigorously. "I don't, no. I never know what to say in such situations, and...and it bores me."

"I know exactly what you mean." Wallace nodded slightly. "I don't think you appreciate being lied to either, is that correct, Miss Wright?"

"Just Ember, if it pleases you, Mr. Livingston. And no, I don't. Are there people who *do* appreciate being lied to?"

"Just Wallace, if it pleases *you*, Ember. And yes, you would be surprised at the lies people embrace. Lies they are told, lies they tell themselves."

Ember thought on Wallace's words and felt as though she understood what he meant. She told him such.

Wallace glanced at the form in the folder and read aloud. "Two men are stranded, alone in a boat in the North Sea. They are slowly starving to death. One man decides to kill the other and then eat him. He throws the remains overboard for the sharks. He never tells anyone about his dark deed. Which man was the murderer?"

Ember furrowed her brow. She hated riddles. Cynthia warned her that the test was strange, unknowable questions and puzzles. Ember was about to admit that she didn't know the answer. Instead, she blurted out. "Why you are, Wallace. You are the murderer. How else could you know this story?"

The Investigator did not react, but jotted down a note, checked another box.

Wallace produced a set of cards with colorful patterns on one side and plain numbers on the back. He proceeded to show them to Ember and asked her to tell him what she saw in each one. A sort of Rorschach Test. To each card and response, he jotted something down in the column on the form. There were many such cards, and Ember was exasperated. She didn't know if she was answering correctly. She suspected there *was* no correct answer.

As she stared at the sixth or seventh card and was about to provide a response (she thought it looked like a purple giraffe wearing a flowered hat), Wallace suddenly spoke up.

"Quickly now: Mr. Montgomery was killed on Sunday afternoon. His wife said she was reading a book. The butler said he was taking a shower. The chef said he was making breakfast. The maid said she was folding clothes, and the gardener said he was planting tomatoes. Who did it?"

Without hesitation, Ember answered, "I suspect the chef is lying, but that doesn't mean he's the murderer."

"Interesting answer. Why do you say this?"

"His alibi is that he was making breakfast, but you said the victim was killed in the afternoon."

Wallace nodded. "So, then the chef is the murderer."

"Is he though? I wouldn't be so quick to pass judgment without further details."

"You *do* realize it's just a riddle, don't you Ember?" Wallace raised an eyebrow.

"So you say, but how can I trust the words of a confessed cannibal and murderer such as yourself?"

Ember detected the hint of mirth in his voice, though his face remained stoic, professional. "Quite right, Ember. Quite right."

"It's a purple giraffe wearing a flowered hat."

"Hmm, what now?"

"This card. Purple giraffe wearing a flowered hat." Ember handed the card to Wallace.

He scribbled some more notes down. *Everything* was interesting to this man, it seemed. Ember supposed every response, every reaction—even the *timing* of her reactions probably held some sort of significance in this test.

After another dozen or so cards were reviewed, Wallace proceeded to show Ember a series of photos of people. They were average-looking humans of various ages, both male and female, different skin tones and ethnic backgrounds.

"Tell me what you see."

Ember started to describe the people in the photos, but then stopped and looked up. "They are all smiling."

Wallace gave an imperceptible nod and wrote something down. He reached for the photos, but Ember didn't hand them back.

"But they *aren't* all smiling."

Wallace leaned back in his chair. "What do you mean? You said they're all smiling."

"Yes, but...the smiles on some are real. The smiles on others are faked."

"Show me."

Ember went through each photo and declared some "real" and others "fake" as she did.

Wallace made a note for each response she gave, his brows tight together as he wrote.

"Time for something different," Wallace announced as he collected the photographs back from Ember. He produced a silver thermos—the kind one would use to transport hot tea. He unscrewed the lid and tipped it upside down on the table, lifting the cup from the lid. A single ice cube sat atop the lid.

"Please melt this ice."

Ember wasn't expecting this but surmised that it was to test her Elemental powers. Elementalists were the rarest of mages. One with the power of pyrokinesis would have no trouble melting the ice.

Ember placed her fingers onto her temples, recalling the lesson in *Primer of the Arcane* which instructed on channeling one's thoughts into projected power. She closed her eyes and imagined heat, fire...anything that could further melt the small piece of ice in front of her. Her fingertips felt slippery on her right hand, and her focus dissipated. When she pulled her fingers away and looked at them, they were smeared with bright yellow paint. She had been wearing paint splatter on her forehead the entire time.

Ember gritted her teeth in frustration, reached out to the block of ice and held it in both hands. Soon, it was dripping between her fingers.

Wallace scribbled something in his notes, checked another box, wrote something else down. Ember felt embarrassed.

He handed a small towel for her to dry her hands. When he did, his fingers contacted Ember's wrist. Instantly, she felt a tingling sensation. She saw a sheen of energy pass from Wallace over the top of her hand, traveling up her arm. She snapped back her hand and stood up, knocking her chair over. "What did you just do?"

"What do you mean? Did you feel something, Ember?"

"Yes, a tingling, as though a hundred little needle points were laid against my wrist like a bracelet."

"Needles, really?" Wallace scribbled notes. This was interesting to him, it seemed.

Almost as an afterthought, Ember added, "and the...the blanket of...of energy."

The writing stopped. Wallace peered at Ember above the rim of his spectacles. The look he gave Ember gave her goosebumps. "Tell me *exactly* what you saw."

As she gave her description, Wallace muttered something, remaining outwardly stoic but she could see he was becoming animated. His breathing was rapid, his eyelids were opening wider as she talked, and his lips parted ever so slightly. "That's mana you're describing, Ember. It's not unusual for mages to feel magic energy, but you shouldn't be able to see it. Nobody can *see* mana."

"But I can see it. This means something to you, doesn't it?" Ember already knew the answer before she asked the question.

5

DON'T SHOW YOUR TRUE STRENGTH

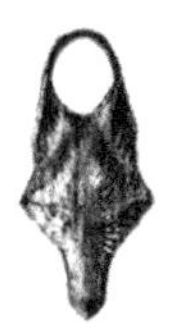

"VERY GOOD, EMBER. WE'RE DONE HERE." WALLACE SAT back. He avoided her question, as though she had not said anything. "Congratulations, you made it through testing."

"Really?" She felt relief. "We're done?"

He shuffled the paperwork and tucked them back into the large briefcase. "We are, yes. How are you feeling about the testing?"

He snapped the clasps closed, his gaze monitoring Ember. She had the impression that he was still taking measure of her, despite his pronouncement.

"I'll need to return to the office to tabulate the results of the various tests and to provide a scorecard for each of the five mage traits. In each, you'll be rated from Weak, Capable, Moderate, or Strong."

"Pft." She waved her hand and played along. If the Investigator wasn't going to answer her question, she decided she wouldn't let that bother her. Much. "Much to Mum's dismay,

I'm fairly certain I'm ranking Weak in Healing. She has been trying to teach me since I was little." An image of the dead bird she couldn't save invaded her thoughts momentarily.

"Well, you're quite right. Healing was Weak, though you don't lack in empathy." Wallace nodded. "Did I miss any talents you've hidden away?"

Ember crossed her arms. "No hidden talents here. None that I've discovered, anyway." She gave him a wry smile, "You really should see all my failures in the Arts before you go. They're more a comedy of errors, but they'll make you laugh. Or cry. Depending on your love of the Arts." She rubbed the yellow paint now crusted on her forehead. "And music. God save us all if I am ever again handed another musical instrument."

Wallace only smiled.

"Poor Father tried to get me interested in Analytics. But, numbers and statistics bore me to tears. So, Wallace, is there any good news?" She felt butterflies dance in her stomach.

"You're right. You rank Weak to Capable in each of the five Mage Tracks – except one."

"Really?" She squeaked in delight. "What is it?"

"The Investigation Track. You rate Strong. Indeed, *very* Strong, Ember."

"Oh." She glanced at the house where her parents watched from the window, "They'll be disappointed."

Wallace's brow furrowed. "How so?"

"Investigators don't rise to high society." She remembered to whom she was speaking: one of the top-ranking Investigators of Druw society. "Sorry, no offense."

"Ah. Well, as I've no ambitions of high society, none taken." She could sense that he truly wasn't offended.

"I realize the Investigator Track has only three levels—as opposed to all the others having six—but the work we do, carrying out the Council's Justice, is essential to Druw society," Wallace spoke with conviction.

Something settled in Ember as his words resonated in her mind. She held the assessment, 'very strong.' She was eager to tell her parents that she excelled in something—she was not a complete disappointment, even if she could never meet their highest hopes for her.

"Ember, there is something you need to know. I'll be officially reporting that you are only of Moderate skill in Investigation." His face cast a grim expression.

"But, why?" Her momentary excitement was suddenly slapped away, replaced with confusion. She felt like something very important was being taken away from her.

"I have reasons for keeping your impressive potential a secret. I promise you, I'll tell you about it someday when I figure out how to keep you safe. But, for now, you need to downplay your abilities."

"But—"

"You will need to practice. Read everything you can get your hands on. I will check in on you from time to time until I figure out how to best cultivate your abilities without attracting attention. Develop your instincts. Train hard, but keep it secret—certainly, don't let on that you can *see* mana.

Don't show your true strength. Not even to your parents or your sister."

"When can I tell them?" Ember's eyes were stinging. She felt a tear trickle down her cheek. She scrubbed it away, angrily.

The man known among his peers as The Legend spoke with earnest. "I don't know. Possibly never. Ember, I do not say this lightly: keep your true talents secret. This is for your own safety."

6

MISS BY-THE-BOOK

Spring 2010

Ember knew she shouldn't do it. The payoff would be minimal and the risks would be great if she was caught using magic in public, in plain view of NonDruw folk. That she was even entertaining the notion of doing this underscored just how irritated she was.

The now all-too-familiar vodka-laced voice invaded once again. "It's a generational thing, I tell ya. Your generation just doesn't know how good they have it. Civilization is collapsing and all you kids want to do is take yourself some selfies and put them on your my-facebook-space."

Ember nodded and kept the fake smile affixed to her lips. She had given up on attempting to participate in the conversation a half hour ago. The progressively inebriated woman beside her had no trouble maintaining a conversation solo.

"I know because my grandkids are the worst of them all. I flew all the way to Indianapolis to see them, and you think they cared to talk with lil' ol' Granny? Not even long enough to look up from their phones and their my-facebook-space, no they didn't! The Rudest Generation, that's what these kids are!"

The source of Ember's irritation: an older woman who had been pontificating since they boarded the plane in Minneapolis. The lady wore heavy makeup and an increasingly slurring tongue to augment her cynical outlook. To this woman's perspective, the whole world was "going to hell in a handbasket"—whatever *that* meant. The shortest leg of Ember's exhausting intercontinental flight was proving to be the most tedious, thanks to this one person.

Ember made the mistake of acknowledging her seatmate after they boarded. Somewhere between the second and third cocktail, the stranger began to interpret Ember's smiles as proof of a receptive audience. Never mind Ember's polite attempts to excuse herself from the conversation. This lady was undeterred. *I'm beginning to understand why some Druws refer to NonDruws as "Mundanes." This one is a specimen of "Mundane" if ever there was.*

Ember chastised herself for even thinking such ugly, prejudicial thoughts. Still, she had never met a person who had driven her patience to such limits that she actually was contemplating bending the rules. Until now, that is. Emberly Wright, Miss By-The-Book; that's what her sister Cynthia teasingly used to call her.

She looked around the crowded Delta flight. The persistent hum of the jetliner's turbines whined softly in the background. Everyone else was either napping, reading, or watching TV, headphones isolating them from their surroundings. The closest flight attendant was talking with a passenger toward the front of the small plane. *It would be so easy to end this headache right now, and nobody would possibly notice.*

"Are you even listening to me, young lady?" The older woman's shrill voice bit into her thoughts.

Ember reacted without even thinking. She brought her palms together to form a quiet clap. The heat of mana rose instantaneously from her viscera and flowed through her in a pulse. At just the right moment, Ember reached out for the old woman's wrist, touching it lightly as she whispered, "Sleep."

The old woman's glassy eyes lost their focus, and her eyelids dropped closed. Her head fell back against the soft headrest, and she immediately began snoring lightly, her mouth agape. Ember barely managed to catch the half-empty cocktail glass before the fingers wrapped around it released.

Oh bloody hell, what did I just do?

The Sleep Spell she learned from her mentor twelve years ago was just as effective on belligerent polar bears as it was on incorrigible old ladies. The woman would wake feeling rested and probably even halfway sober. No harm, no foul—so long as Ember didn't get caught. *Miss By-The-Book indeed.*

Ember was just starting to feel pleased with herself for the ensuing peace she conjured by putting her seatmate to sleep. That is until the man across the aisle spoke up.

"Oh, thank God. I thought she would *never* shut up!"

Ember's eyes grew wide and she whipped her head around

to meet the man's gaze. Her gold locks were still settling against her shoulders when she said, "Excuse me?"

The portly man wore a dark goatee and a business-casual sports jacket. He was grinning. "The old nag. I've been wishing she would pass out ever since she started talking. I guess her drinks finally caught up with her metabolism. Oh, I'm sorry—she's not your grandmother, I hope?"

Not missing a beat, Ember said, "Yes. Yes, she is my dear old Grandmum. She's the sweetest little lady, you see. I'd thank you to not be so insulting."

The man's cheeks turned red and he started to apologize. As he was stumbling over his words, Ember allowed her lips to form a smirk and she winked at the man.

He stopped mid-sentence and his face turned even more flush. "She's not *really* your grandmother, then?"

Ember simply shook her head. "Indeed, not remotely someone I know or would wish to know. But seeing your reaction was worth the charade."

"Dammit, you just about gave me a heart attack!" The man clutched his chest comedically. "You're a dangerous woman, you know that?"

"So, I've been told." Ember had never been told that she was dangerous. It was delicious to pretend otherwise.

The man extended his hand across the narrow aisle. "Cooper. Cooper Severson."

Ember slid her hand into his much larger grip. She grasped it tightly, and instinctively allowed a tiny wisp of her mana to pass into and then over Cooper. It was a simple technique that any novice mage knew. For one who practiced regularly such as she did, the recipient would be none the wiser. Not that a NonDruw would even be capable of detecting mana, anyway.

As their conversation progressed, that tiny piece of mana would form a sheen around this man that would be visible only to Ember. By reading the sheen's hues and shades, the opacity and brightness, Ember would be able to read the veracity of a NonDruw's aura just about as well as she could that of a Druwish person's.

"A pleasure to meet you, Mr. Severson. I'm Ember Wright." She smiled at the man.

"Oh, just Cooper, please. Or Coop, as some of my buddies call me." He seemed mildly reluctant to release her hand. He gestured at the pamphlets on her lap. "Tourist, are you?"

Ember chuckled and brought the travel brochures to bear, pointing at the headline. "Minot, the Magic City. Marvelous, isn't it?"

"I like to think so. Minot's my hometown, born and raised. I've moved away but couldn't stay away."

"So...Coop. Why do they call Minot the Magic City?"

Cooper opened his mouth but no words immediately emerged. His brow furrowed. "You know...I hate to admit it, but I don't really know. I mean, the high school sports teams are 'the Magicians', so many of the businesses like to call themselves 'Magic City' something-or-'nother. I've lived there my whole life and I cannot honestly say why Minot's got that nickname. Now that's going to bother me until I find out."

The glimmering sheen around Cooper's aura told Ember that he wasn't lying. This man was bemusedly troubled that he didn't have an answer for the tourist.

"My innocent inquiry isn't going to give you a coronary," Ember flashed her smirk again. "Is it?"

The man shook his head, but Ember could see that he wasn't as dismissive as he feigned. "No, it's just that I'm not someone who likes to leave questions unanswered. I'm going to have to research this until I have an answer for you."

"We're not so different in that respect."

"Oh yeah?" Cooper's aura shifted suddenly. "Is that what brings an English woman to such a far-flung destination as North Dakota? Your accent *is* English, isn't it?"

Ember took measure of the man's aura and found genuine curiosity—no sense of malcontent. Still, he was a little too intuitive—much more than most people tended to be. She had to choose her words carefully. "Actually, I'm here for work; I'm a massage therapist. The Magic City Spa—one of those namesake entities in your hometown."

"That's a long way to travel for a massage therapy job, isn't it?"

"Well, that job will be paying the bills while I'm visiting. In my spare time, I've been nominated by my family to track down relatives from lost branches of our family tree for a genealogy project." The lie emerged so easily. Ember could see that Cooper bought it.

"Ah, in that case, if you really want a tour of the Magic City, I can show you all sorts of sights which you won't find in the brochure." Cooper gestured again at the papers in Ember's hand. "Wait—that sounded kind of creepy, didn't it?"

He put his hands up to show her his palms. "No strings attached, I just love my hometown. I'm actually a police officer. Not that *that* means I'm not a stranger. Or that you should necessarily trust me just because I happen to have a badge. I really should stop talking, shouldn't I? Why am I still talking? Is it *really* warm in here?"

Ember couldn't help but smile at Cooper as his face grew flush again. He was speaking the truth to her. If there was even a hint of insincerity in the man, she would be able to detect it, like any Malvern Investigator with any talent could —and even for her young age, Ember was particularly talented.

Cooper produced a simple business card, on which he scrawled a number with his clickable ballpoint pen before passing it to her. "That's my cell phone number. When you get settled in, give me a call and I'll have an answer for you as to why Minot is called the Magic City."

She was charmed by his confidence and accepted the card, which declared Cooper Severson as a Detective in the Minot Police Department. "Oh, you are sure we will be talking to one another again?"

The man shrugged, "We pretty much *have* to. If I'm not able to answer your question it will drive me bonkers."

"Bonkers, really?" Ember couldn't help but laugh.

"Truly it would," Cooper insisted. "And if you need help tracking down a long-lost relative, I might be able to run a check on our computer system for you. Maybe one or two—

I'm not going to abuse my privileges *too* much, even for a pretty lady with an exotic accent."

Ember raised an eyebrow. "Exotic, is it? Yet I am supposedly the dangerous one here?"

Cooper held up his hands again. He said, "Hey, I'm harmless!"

With that declaration, Ember detected Cooper's first lie to her.

7

NOT ROSIE

THE JUNE SUNSET PROVIDED A CAPTIVATING IMPRESSION AS the plane approached Minot International Airport. The last rays of sunlight were diffused against distant dust in the western prairie horizon, turning the fading light a burnt orange hue.

Ember would have appreciated the sunset better if she wouldn't have been so exhausted. The conversation with Cooper helped whittle away the final leg of her journey, but it didn't entirely compensate for the sheer length of the transcontinental flight. When the plane touched down, Ember felt the weight of those hours sink in. All she could think of was a hot shower and a soft bed.

Cooper offered—twice, in fact—to give her a ride into town, but Ember declined as she knew she had a fellow investigator from the embassy arriving to pick her up. She told him that it was a coworker from the Magic City Spa who would be waiting for her. It wasn't entirely a lie, as the spa was a legitimate business—a legitimate business which formed the public front for the incognito Druwish colonial embassy.

"I think I see your chauffeur, my lady." Cooper's poor attempt at an English accent earned a tired chuckle from Ember.

Cooper pointed to a hand-lettered tagboard which read "E. Wright." Holding the sign was a stout Malvern woman with a square jaw and short, spiked hair. Her unenthusiastic expression and bored, beady eyes scanned the crowd. Even the woman's aura appeared unhealthy and dirty to Ember's assessment. *Or maybe I'm having mild hallucinations—chalk that up to jet lag.*

Ember closed the distance and extended her hand, "Hello! I believe I'm the Wright you're looking for. Ember, that is."

The woman studied Ember and then looked expressionlessly at Cooper. Ember stood awkwardly, her hand extended and her carry-on bag biting into her shoulder. The woman finally accepted Ember's hand with a firm, single pump. She said, "I'm Roseanne. Not Rose. Not Rosie. Not Anne. Roseanne. Get your stuff and follow me."

Roseanne spun on her heel and began walking briskly to the luggage carousel.

Ember felt heat rise up her neck and her face reddened. *So much for a happy welcome.*

Cooper's eyebrows were both raised. He extended his hand into the air and moved it up and down. "Hi, I'm Cooper, nice to meet you, Rosie." Roseanne was already ten yards away and Cooper's comedy was lost in the bustling crowd of weary fellow travelers. He looked at Ember and smiled. "She seems nice."

A grin found its way onto Ember's lips and she shook her head. "The unwelcoming committee has arrived."

Cooper and Ember shook hands at the carousel and parted ways with their respective luggage. Cooper waved and shouted across the expanse. "I'll have an answer for you when you call me."

Ember smiled and waved back at Cooper, but said nothing. She pulled her wheeled Rimowa suitcase across the tile floor and followed Roseanne as quickly as she could; her coworker didn't check her pace. She didn't even glance back.

Roseanne escorted Ember wordlessly through the warm evening air of the brightly-lit parking lot. A gentle breeze tussled Ember's hair. If she would have been by herself, Ember would have found a quiet place to stop, close her eyes, and drink in the spaciousness of the prairie. *As it is, this friendly Roseanne would probably leave me here if I don't catch up with her.*

Roseanne unlocked the hatchback of a silver Subaru Forester. She crossed her bulging arms at her chest and waited impatiently for Ember to catch up. Ember was sure that the woman was moments away from tapping her foot.

"Terribly sorry, Roseanne. My bags weigh nearly as much as I do, I fear!"

Roseanne rolled her eyes and scoffed. She walked over to Ember, lifted the heavy suitcase as though it was filled with feathers, and hefted it into the back of the Subaru. Ember's carry-on followed.

"You're a strong one." Ember winced at her own banal observation immediately after making it.

Roseanne was unaffected. "You're not going to expect me to get the door for you, too, are you?"

Ember blinked. "Get the...no, no of course not." She scurried to the right side of the car. *Opposite of home, I'll need to get used to that.*

When they were both in the vehicle, Roseanne turned to Ember and said, "Who was that man—that *Mundane*? I don't know how they do things at Malvern Hills, but here, relationships with Mundanes are discouraged."

"Coop—I mean Cooper? He's not anybody. He's just a fellow passenger—a local who was friendly to me." Ember was exhausted and was caught off-guard by the racist outburst. She was surprised and annoyed that she was being pushed to defensiveness by her coworker. She shifted in her seat and realized her shoes were sticking to the vinyl floor mat. Recently-spilled cola formed an adhesive bond beneath her soles, announcing itself whenever she lifted her foot from the tacky surface.

Roseanne rolled her eyes. "You will be filing with the Department of External Relations first thing in the morning, I presume?"

"I—well, I hadn't expected to. I'm not exactly in any sort of relationship with Cooper. Really, Roseanne, we only just visited on the pl—"

Roseanne interrupted. "As *ranking* Associate Investigator, I will not hesitate to report any infractions I observe during your visit to Minot."

Ember was flabbergasted and momentarily lost for words. Too much was riding on this mission for her to start having a conflict with the other Investigators literally on Day One. "Roseanne...if I said something to offend you, I sincerely apologize. I would really like to have a positive relationship with my coworkers while I perform my duty here. Can you tell me what's bothering you?"

Roseanne didn't hesitate. "Yeah, I'll tell you what bothers me. I know all about you, Ember Wright. You've just been promoted to Associate Investigator—the youngest ever to reach this rank, just ten years after you became a Novice Investigator, so I've heard. I know that you were sent here by the Druw High Council to audit our census records—like we quaint colonials aren't capable of counting heads. Instead of serving as an assistant to a Senior Investigator, somehow you've managed to climb rank in half the usual time and then land this cushy solo job."

Roseanne started the car but continued her lecture as she exited the airport parking lot. "I also know that you come from an old family—a noble family. Maybe that means something in Europe, but over here we have to *earn* our ranks—we can't just inherit them. Not everyone can have a paid vacation given to them just because they have the right last name."

Ember swallowed. The initial cold shock transformed into burning anger as Roseanne vented her litany of grievances. *So much for a friendly start. Holiday, indeed.*

Her first impulse was to lash out, to defend herself against this judgmental stranger. Sure, it was true that Ember was promoted sooner than any other Associate Investigator on record, but she had to pass the tests just like everyone else.

Her family connections may have opened the door for her to meet The Legend, but he would not have offered his mentorship to her if she hadn't demonstrated a natural talent for the profession. It was Ember's career ambitions, her single-minded obsessiveness to pursue justice, and her deep belief in the Investigator's Creed which got her to where she is. *Wasn't it?*

The pursuit of justice. That is what she had to focus on here. She could defend herself, argue with this woman with the inexplicably ugly aura. But Ember could see that Roseanne's mind was made up, and winning an argument with her—if that was even possible—would be fruitless.

Worse, unnecessary confrontation could derail her mission —the *real* reason Wallace hand-picked Ember to travel solo to the Minot colony. The census audit task was just one more cover story—another layer of lies. Just like the massage therapy job and genealogy research hobby were meant as public cover for NonDruw, Ember's assignment as census auditor would get her closer to her real purpose. Much more was at stake than hurt feelings—especially her own.

She swallowed her pride. "I'm sorry you feel that way, Roseanne," Ember said it as timidly as she could. She kept her feet in place, lest the sound of the tacky floor mat would sabotage her theatrical performance.

They didn't say anything more to one another as Roseanne guided the Subaru into Minot. Ember blinked away a burning tear and chastised herself for being so weak, so susceptible. She could blame it on exhaustion, but there would be no excuse if she stumbled on this mission. There was no backup, either. She couldn't trust *anyone* here—

Wallace made that very clear to her. After being his protégé and partner for ten years, Ember was now truly alone.

Just take me to my hotel. Let me fall into bed. Let me sleep.

She had to shift her attention, to focus on something else lest the tears start flowing. She stared out the window and looked upon Minot, North Dakota. The Magic City. Population of 40,000, and home to the secret Druw Viceroyalty of North America. All the 2,000 or so Malverns and changelings which called North America home were centered around this innocent-looking town on the northern prairie in the center of the continent.

The street they drove on appeared to be "Broadway Street" and it was bustling with traffic and summer evening activity. They drove past several hotels. Each time they did, Ember felt her hopes get deflated a little more, as she fixated on turning in for the night.

Broadway passed over a dark, curving waterway—though the sign said "Mouse River," it was labeled as the Souris River on maps Ember earlier studied in her packet. Another little mystery to unravel. Soon after, Roseanne turned left onto Central Avenue and into downtown Minot. They stopped in front of an old eight-story brick building which bore a vertical sign proclaiming it as "The Parker Suites."

Ember silently groaned; she was expecting a hotel room, not the embassy building. "I don't mean to whinge, but I was rather hoping to bathe and get some shut-eye before coming in to work."

Roseanne grunted and parked the car. "I don't know what a 'winch' means to you, but I was given orders to show you where you'll be working. That *is* why you are here, isn't it? This isn't just a vacation for you I hope."

Ember clenched her jaw and held her tongue.

Through glass doors they walked, entering a contemporary lobby with verdant foliage. Ember's shoes carried residue of floormat soda, causing her soles to tear at the floor as she walked. The reception area was empty but for a young woman with bright hazel eyes, dark skin, and even darker hair sitting behind the front desk. "Welcome to the Magic City Spa—oooh, you must be Emberly! I'm Ami. Welcome to Minot."

Ember smiled at the girl. "Just Ember is fine. It's so nice to see a friendly face, thank you. You keep quite a lovely reception area, Ami."

Ami beamed back at Ember. Her aura, Ember could see, was bright but thin; Ami was only half Druw. She would have been vetted to work in the public front of the spa but likely not allowed clearance to visit the embassy offices in the upper floors. Ember wondered what this bubbly young woman's parents were like, whether it was her mother or her father who dared to challenge the age-old taboo of procreating with a NonDruw human.

"Moving right along with the tour," Roseanne grumbled. She stood in one place and pointed over her shoulder. "Through that door is the chiropractor and massage therapy offices where you'll be working as part of your public-facing job. The exercise equipment is in the 24-hour fitness center over there, and over this other way are the elevators which will take us to the upper floors of the building where the offices are. You'll be assigned a key card to gain access to the elevators and the stairwell from the main floor. Everything from floors 2 through 8 along with the basement and sub-basement is off limits to NonDruw and any Druw lacking clearance."

Roseanne proceeded to call the elevator with her key card. Just then, a neatly-dressed woman with dark, curly hair and espresso brown eyes came walking down the hall. She was holding a blue and white motorcycle helmet beneath her arm.

"I was just closing out the books for the day before heading home. Did I hear correctly that you're my new massage therapist?" The woman smiled and held out her hand. "I'm Josette Hanson. I'm the office manager for the spa."

"I'm Ember Wright, just landed and taking the tour through your lovely facilities now." Ember shook Josette's hand. The woman had an admirable iron grip. Hers was an authentic, confident handshake. *This woman is no weakling, despite her lithe figure.*

"Oh, I just love your accent! We get visitors from Malvern Hills from time to time, but not too often." Josette's aura matched her enthusiasm—and Ember could see that this one, too, was another half-Druw. "How do you like your new apartment? I set it up for you myself."

"My apartment?"

Roseanne seemed irritated. She grumbled and said, "we haven't been by the apartment yet. Tour first."

Josette still clasped Ember's hand. "But dear, you must be pooped! No offense, but you look like you haven't slept in a day."

Ember nearly whimpered when she admitted that she hadn't. She shrugged and said, "Roseanne was given orders to give me the tour first."

"Given orders? Really, Roseanne, would you stop hazing Ember, please, and get the poor girl to her apartment so she can get settled in? Can't you see she's exhausted? There will be plenty of time to show her around tomorrow."

Then to Ember she said, "when you come in tomorrow, you be sure to stop by and see me. I'll make sure you get situated with anything you need. I tried to make your new place cozy, but anything you need while you're visiting us, just you let me know, ok?"

Ember felt like crying right then, hearing the sincerity in Josette's voice. The office manager's aura wasn't as strong as a pure-blooded Druw's, but her energy surged with empathy. Ember nodded and patted Josette's hand. "Thank you so very much, Josette. I'll be so delighted to work with you."

The drive to the apartment building was just a few city blocks. Ember was too blustery-eyed to make more than a cursory note of the route she would be taking to work. She was likewise unobservant of the building she would be calling home for the next few months, but for the fact that it was three stories and her apartment was unfortunately on the top floor.

When Roseanne led her to an elevator, Ember said a silent prayer of thanks to whichever deity was listening. *Though I'm so tired right now, I probably wouldn't even have enough energy to spare for my stair-phobia.*

Roseanne's tour guide skills were on display once again as she stood on the threshold of apartment Number 302's doorway and pointed. Some corner of Ember's weary mind superimposed a flight attendant gesturing during their pre-flight checklist. "Kitchen. Living Room. Bedroom. Bathroom."

The uninspired tour guide dropped a set of keys into Ember's hand. "You've got a Honda Pilot in the parking lot. The license plate number is on the key ring. You have been provided a cell phone, which is on the kitchen table, along with your key card for the elevators at The Parker." Roseanne stepped out of the apartment. "The Department of Investigation offices are on the third floor. You will be expected at eight o'clock, sharp. Unless you think that punctuality doesn't apply to you."

Roseanne didn't wait for a response. The apartment door closed behind her and Ember was alone.

Ember blinked and rubbed her eyes. There was something troubling about Roseanne, and it wasn't just her unfriendly demeanor. It was the woman's aura. Ember had seen it at the airport and dismissed what she saw as merely a jet lag induced hallucination. She saw it again though, more clearly in the apartment just now when Roseanne was talking.

Typically, a person's aura has a light shimmer to it, infused with colors that change depending on emotions and attitudes. Roseanne's aura looked different; her aura looked like a shadow or a dark smudge was surrounding her entire body.

Ember clicked the deadbolt to the door. Only then did she notice her hand was trembling. *That smudged aura was no hallucination. What in the bloody hell did I just get myself into?*

8

CONFORMITY IS OVERRATED

EMBER'S NOSE AWOKE BEFORE THE REST OF HER DID. SHE WAS having an odd dream (as dreams so often are) that she was being chased down a flight of stairs. She tripped and tumbled, falling into a human-sized pie pan. Flour, sugar, and water were each poured over her and the Ember-pie was placed into an industrial oven.

She thought she was still dreaming when she caught the scent of baking bread. When her sight and the rest of her senses joined the realm of consciousness, though, she realized she was in her new apartment. The aroma of baking bread persisted.

Ember glanced at the clock—it was just past 4:30 am, which meant that she slept solidly for all of four hours. Recalling the unsettling sight of Roseanne's blemished aura gave Ember an involuntary shudder. She held out hope that she was just hallucinating, just imagining that sight. She wasn't convincing herself.

The subdued light was already starting to provide a hint of

dawn's pending arrival through her third-floor windows. Streetlights were still on and the rest of Minot seemed to be asleep.

She hadn't unpacked before collapsing into her bed, so Ember dug through her luggage to find and slip into her black yoga pants, well-worn sweatshirt, and trusty running shoes. The familiar aroma of home wafted out from the Rimowa, as invisible stowaways only her nose could detect. She zipped the luggage shut, lest those molecules escape.

Stepping into the hallway, Ember glanced back at the number on her apartment door—302—and pulled the door shut behind her, careful not to disturb her neighbors who had the good sense to be sleeping at this hour.

The source of the baking scent was quickly discovered. The ground floor of her red brick apartment building featured two commercial properties: one was a dance studio, the other a bakery. "Sweet & Flour" the illuminated sign announced. Though the smaller signage in the window had not yet been swapped from "CLOSED," workers were already inside getting donuts and muffins prepared.

Wallace warned that her mission could be potentially dangerous. Somehow, she didn't think he was referring to the Sirens' call of having such easy access to fresh baked goods.

Exploring downtown Minot on foot in the crisp, early morning air gave Ember an appreciation for the quiet, small town known as the Magic City. Most of the buildings were aged but cared for. Nothing was nearly so old as the typical buildings of her home country, but there was a similar sort of charm to them. There was history in this community.

Upscale restaurants were interspersed with dive bars, professional offices, and light industrial businesses. A railroad ran along the river and beneath a bridge. The traffic lights flashed a cautionary yellow—she noted the signals differed from home in that respect, where the red and yellow lights were displayed simultaneously.

As she jogged, she found The Parker Building easily—it was one of the tallest buildings downtown, even though it was a mere eight stories in height. Her workplace was conveniently just a few short blocks from her apartment.

Further away from the downtown district, larger retail businesses, shopping malls, and suburbia-style houses appeared. Minot was a sprawling little urban forest, surrounded by farmland as far as she could see.

Traffic was beginning to increase by the time she neared the end of her route and found her way back. She noticed that far more drivers were in large pickup trucks and sport utility vehicles than what she observed in Great Britain. She began to understand why the streets were so wide, the garages so big.

In some ways, the Magic City resembled home—with constant reminders that it was anything but.

"YOU'RE NEW." THE ABRUPT MAN WHO JOINED HER IN THE elevator of the Parker Building had a nasal voice and pale skin. His chin was host to a pointy goatee, which only served to amplify his triangular face. "You're the new investigator from England, sent to audit our census?"

Ember forced a smile. "Correct. I'm Ember Wright."

The man glanced at Ember's chest, flashed an insincere smile, and then looked away.

Ember felt her skin grow flush. *Did this bloke just look at my boobs?* She did what was socially expected: she pretended not to notice. "I'm sorry, I didn't catch your name?"

"Neal Page." The man looked straight ahead at her reflection in the stainless-steel elevator doors. He didn't even bother to make eye contact with her. The elevator hummed quietly and nothing more was said.

When the LED display illuminated "3" followed by an audible ping, Neal took a step forward. The doors hadn't even fully opened before he exited and walked away.

Ember stood back a moment, attempting to make sense of the rude exchange. Neal couldn't distance himself from her quickly enough, it seemed. She touched her nose to her shoulder and sniffed. *I did shower this morning after my run, didn't I?*

"Good morning, how may I help you?"

Before Ember registered that it was her that the question was being directed to, the cheerful voice spoke again. "Oh, you must be Ember, right? Hey, I just realized that sounds like your full name, 'Ember Wright.' You've been expected. I'm Joy. Welcome to Minot, and welcome to the Department of Investigation."

The energetic words streamed rapidly from a young changeling woman. Her perky, brown ponytail swished like a pendulum as she skittered around the receptionist desk. A steel filing cabinet was opened, papers were rustled, and a manila folder was produced.

"Ah. Yes. Good morning?" Ember hadn't intended to frame her response as a question, but she was struck by the whirlwind of energy that this cheerful woman exuded, especially following the awkward interaction with Neal.

"Oh, what a cool accent! I wish I had one. You can tell most people who're from 'round here by how they talk, don'tcha know? Oh, you have some crumbs on your blouse. What a lovely top! I love bright colors, but I can't wear synthetic fabrics."

Ember stared at Joy for a moment as she processed the succession of syllables. She glanced down at herself and embarrassedly swept the remnants of lemon poppy seed muffin from her clothes. She had resisted only so long before she succumbed to the Sweet & Flour prior to leaving for work. She justified the freshly-baked treat as a reward for the miles she trod as most of Minot slept.

"It was worth it," Ember muttered.

As the young changeling woman rifled through a cabinet, Ember closed her eyes and focused. Immediately, Joy's aura shined brightly against the inside of Ember's eyelids. It was a skill that Ember taught herself—one which allowed her to see beyond surface aura to reveal the animal form contained within a changeling.

Joy's animal form was unusual: a small, furtive rodent. Ember didn't know what species it was, and the Investigator in her couldn't allow a mystery to exist. Yet, she could never reveal to anyone that she was able to see a Druw's aura—much less the animal form hidden within changelings. To the extent of the combined knowledge of herself and Wallace, no living mage had this ability—except Ember.

"Pardon me for inquiring," Ember said as she opened her eyes, "but are you a changeling?"

Joy grinned broadly. "Yep! How'd you guess? Oh, I suppose you had a fifty-fifty chance. It was either changeling or Malvern. Or I guess 33% since I could've been half Druw—but half-Druws aren't allowed to work upstairs since they aren't able to get the security clearance. So fifty-fifty chance. But yes, I'm a changeling—my animal form is a sugar glider."

Ember got as far as opening her mouth before Joy continued, breathlessly. "I know what you're gonna say, 'oh my god, what's a sugar glider?' am I right? Well, I'll tell ya. Sugar gliders are energetic little critters that act and look kind of like flying squirrels but they aren't related to squirrels. They're marsupials. Aussies, which is funny because I've never been down under. 'Oz,' I've heard it called, I guess because it's so far away? I dunno. My parents weren't at all surprised when I reached my Manifestation Day and 'boop!' I ended up changing into a tiny rodent. I guess you could say all the signs were there that I'd be a little different. But I don't mind being different. In fact, I prefer it."

Ember canted her head and chuckled. "Conformity is overrated."

Joy's eyes lit up. "I like that! Conformity is overrated. I'm gonna steal that line. I'm not asking to borrow it, I'm just sayin' right up front, I'm stealing it. Done. Stolen." She jangled a set of keys she retrieved from the cabinet, as though they were ceremonial bells. "There. Trademarked by Joy."

Ember was still processing the flurry of statements as the changeling started walking. Joy was already five paces down the hall when she waved her hand. "Come on, I'll introduce you to the rest of the crew."

Ember hastened to keep up with the bouncing ponytail, which led to the room where Neal had disappeared. It was a common area—a break room—within which four mages were gathered. Each had coffee cups in hand, in various stages of consumption.

"Hi, everyone. The new Associate Investigator has arrived. This is Ember Wright. She has the coolest accent."

Ember once more forced a smile. She felt her neck flush as the attention of gathered strangers focused on her. Two of them were people she'd met. The other two were new to her. Not one face smiled back at her. "Good morning, everybody. It'll be a pleasure to work with you, I'm sure."

"So, I guess you met Neal in the elevator. And Roseanne picked you up from the airport." Joy pointed with the manila folder in her hand. "So, there's Jackie Roberts, the other Associate Investigator. And Duncan Heywood, the Senior Investigator—our supervisor in this department."

Ember blinked with surprise as she focused on each person in the room. Where Joy's aura was healthy and normal—sugar glider subform notwithstanding—the four Investigators each had dirty smudges where their auras should have been. Ember hadn't noticed Neal's marred aura in the elevator, so flustered as she was by the conversation that she hadn't focused her sight. Here, though, it was as blatant as

Roseanne's dirty aura was. As Jackie's and Duncan's both were too, for that matter. The hairs on the back of her neck stood and her mouth felt dry. *What the bloody hell is going on around here?*

She realized, belatedly, that everyone was wordlessly staring at her, so Ember turned her attention to the objective—her whole reason for being sent to the Magic City by special mission from Wallace.

"Mr. Heywood, it's a privilege to meet you, sir." Ember extended her hand as she stepped toward the man. "I had the honor of serving as junior partner to Wallace Livingston prior to his elevation to Druw High Council. I understand you and he came up through the academy together. I'd love to hear any stories you have on The Legend sometime if you're willing?"

Duncan remained seated. He shook Ember's hand stiffly before dropping it as if it were a hot potato. His expression was of annoyance. He cleared his throat and said, "Oh, I don't know about that. It would be a little unseemly, don't you think? In any case, I don't expect you'll be in Minot long enough to warrant much small talk. This census audit is just a formality, I'm sure, but you will find everything you need to complete your task by asking any of my Associate Investigators. I hope you won't expect preferential treatment just because you were Wallace's...assistant."

The Senior Investigator stood, refilled his coffee, and left for his office.

Ember felt her lips move, but she produced no words. Her throat was dry and she felt lightheaded. Her entire mission was to get Duncan Heywood alone, to talk to him. To find out what was wrong—why he had left Wallace a disturbing partial message and then went silent. She expected to find a man similar to Wallace—an accomplished Senior Investigator who commanded respect and deserved every bit of it.

The fire-maned Jackie exhaled a sigh and offered her first words to Ember. "Look, golden girl, I'm sure you're real popular back in England, but here we 'provincial folk' have to earn our own dang way. We all got our positions by working hard, not by relying on our family name and social contacts."

Ember clenched her jaw until her teeth hurt. It was the only way she could suppress the stinging in her eyes, to keep tears from forming. She wanted to defend herself. She wanted to set the record straight. She knew, though, that if she spoke at that moment she might undermine her entire mission—or at the very least start crying in front of these strangers. These unnecessarily rude, bitter strangers.

It was the changeling girl who rescued her. Joy cleared her throat—a poor mimic of Duncan, if that was what she was attempting—and deadpanned, "So...well that was...odd. Um...alrighty then. Maybe we'll try that again later? How 'bout you follow me, Ember. We made some space for you in a supply room. I'll show you to your office."

Ember nodded, not daring to say anything. She avoided looking at the other Investigators—her supposed peers and coworkers. Roseanne didn't even bother to wait until Ember was out of the room before she started snickering. Three coffee cups cheerfully clinked together as a toast.

For her part, Joy was noticeably subdued. She made a couple of wisecracks when she unlocked the door to the supply room that would serve as Ember's makeshift office. The walls were lined with steel shelves, overflowing with boxes, reams of paper, ink cartridges, and old computer hardware of every variety.

Joy handed the file folder to Ember. "Here's the list of personnel and phone extensions. You've been given access to all the raw census data, including the computer system for the Minot Embassy, as well as summarized data. If you need anything you can ask any of the Associate Investigators." Joy glanced down the hall to the break room. "Or... maybe you can just ask me. I'm marked on your phone as 'Front Desk.'

Ember forced a smile but said nothing as Joy left. She looked around the windowless room that would serve as her office for the duration of her time in North Dakota. On the grey, steel desk next to the phone was a form with a header stating, "Department of External Relations." A yellow sticky note was affixed, with handwritten scrawl:

For your convenience, here's the required paperwork. No thanks expected. –Roseanne.

Ember spent the rest of the morning alone in her office, pacing as she ran the conversation with Duncan through her mind. He had no reason to be so rude to her—or did he? Was it possible that Duncan was just putting on a ruse, as a cover in sight of the other Investigators? Was he being blackmailed by one of them, or spied on by someone?

No scenario she could imagine would explain the smudged auras that she was witnessing. No mage was even supposed to be able to *see* auras, much less differentiate between ones that looked normal versus ones which were...contaminated. Contaminated. Could that be it—could there be some sort of epidemic that's infecting the auras of Malvern people? It might explain the change in personality that Duncan apparently suffered or the heightened rudeness from those infected.

She needed to eliminate scenarios, but she needed to do so under the cover of her census audit. If the infection hypothesis was disproved, she couldn't risk showing her hand to malicious actors—assuming there even was something nefarious behind the infected auras.

With access to the Minot colony's census database, Ember logged into her assigned computer. She began running queries to the server which was located in the same building, but four floors above where she now sat. She searched for any abnormalities in the population. Economic behaviors, crime statistics, changes in migration—she wasn't even sure what she was looking for. She hoped she would know when she found it.

Lunch came and went—Ember had no appetite and no desire to take a break. She found a couple case files of crimes, but nothing noteworthy. She worked her way backward through the years until she stumbled upon one that had a curious name:

Incident at Mandaree

"Incident? That's sufficiently vague," Ember said aloud as she pulled up the dossier's summary.

Mandaree, North Dakota, it turned out, was a small town near the Missouri River, something like 100 miles southwest of Minot. Details on whatever the incident was were unhelpful and nondescript, which made Ember even more curious.

Public news searches online provided another layer of information. The media described what was popularly called "The Mandaree Incident" as some sort of industrial accident which released a poisonous gas cloud. The cloud persisted for the better part of a year. A quarantine zone had been in place, but there were few casualties reported.

Ember cross-referenced dates and names and discovered that there were ten changelings associated with this case file —with this Incident at Mandaree.

She pulled up the case files for each of the changelings and noticed another coincidence: all ten were marked as "emotionally disabled"—and all acquired that designation in September 2001.

She couldn't put her finger on it, but something felt important about this case. Not even sure what she was going to do with the information, Ember jotted down the personnel numbers for each of the disabled changelings onto a legal pad. She slipped the sheet of paper into her leather satchel.

Ember was reading the personnel file of one disabled changeling—an Arnold Schmitt—when she saw Duncan walk past her office door. This was her chance. She grabbed her notepad and hurried into the hallway.

"Duncan! I'm sorry to pester you, but I really do need to ask you something."

Duncan had his briefcase in his hand and glanced at his

watch. "It's 5:00. I'm calling it a day and so should you. Whatever it is can wait for tomorrow."

Ember hadn't realized how late it was—she had remained cooped up in the windowless supply closet, pulling countless database queries. She rubbed her eyes. "It will only take a moment. I just needed some information on a couple case files and then I'll leave you alone."

The man sighed, but to her surprise he relented. "Alright, I'll pull the information you need, but then you had better not bother me anymore. I have three Associate Investigators who would be more than happy to help you out, after all."

Somehow, Ember doubted the "more than happy" assessment. Her goal was just to get Duncan alone, to talk with him away from anyone else. She needed to get a read on this man who was once a close friend of Wallace. She would need to be subtle, careful.

She followed him into his office, where he pressed the power button on his desktop computer. The machine beeped and cooling fans whirred to life as he settled into his chair with a sigh.

"Alright, give me the case files and I'll punch them in."

Case files. Ember scrambled to jot down the series of numbers from her notes. She purposely placed the case number for the Incident at Mandaree on the bottom. She wasn't expecting much, but she was hoping that while he was distracted entering in numbers, she could get a read on his aura. She prepared to pry.

"These are old cases." Duncan furrowed his brow. "I can see

by the numbers that they are maybe, what, nine years old? Are you really going back that far with your audit?"

Now was her chance. "I need to ask you something. Wallace had mentioned something about a call you made to him a few months ago." Ember's voice trickled off as she saw the dark smudge on Duncan's aura come to life and swirl around him. His aura was reacting to her words, and unless she was mistaken it appeared angry.

"I don't know what you're talking about." The man's face was placid. "I thought you wanted to know about these case files?"

It was a strange sight: Duncan didn't seem to be lying to her. He was genuinely confused. And yet...and yet his aura—his contaminated aura—reacted angrily. It was unsettling. She decided to let the subject sleep until she could think of another way to broach it. She would consult with Wallace and maybe he would have an idea.

"No, you're right. My mistake. Yes, please, these case files." Ember pointed at the paper now in Duncan's hand.

Duncan studied her for a moment with his olive drab eyes—probably trying to detect the untruth in her statement. Ember hoped she was hiding her lie adequately. She must have, as he turned his attention back to the flickering computer monitor and began punching in numbers on the keyboard.

"Oh, right. I remember this one. It's been closed for some time." He scribbled a note. "I'll pull the hard copy and sign off on it." He entered the second case code and studied his screen. "Oh, yes. Same with this one. Another family squabble." Another scribble was added to the first.

He entered the case number for the Incident at Mandaree, pulling up the digital file on his computer. "This, too. This one is closed." Duncan's voice sounded ordinary, even bored. In contrast, the smudged aura surrounding him swirled violently. It pulsed and grew larger, the darkness seeming to snuff out the light in the room, to envelope Ember.

Ember interrogated murderers before. She interviewed sociopaths, rapists, even child molesters. Their auras were ugly and left her disgusted, feeling unclean just for the proximity of such imbalanced energy forces. Until now, she had never been even a little scared of a person's aura. It was, after all, just a reflection of its host. What appeared in a mirror might be ugly, but to be afraid of the mirror itself would be unreasonable.

Now, though, Ember was terrified.

Duncan crumpled up the paper she had handed him. He tossed it into the trash and steepled his fingers. While his aura raged around him, his expression was bored, his voice tired. "Are you satisfied now, Ember?"

Ember's chest tightened. Her heart threatened to burst through her rib cage and flee if she couldn't will her legs to move. She opened her mouth but quickly snapped it shut. *Is this how the infection spreads? Am I about to be contaminated?*

She didn't remember what she said—maybe Ember said nothing at all—but she finally willed herself to look away from the dark tempest forming around her. When she wasn't looking directly at it, she thought she saw Duncan reaching out—crying in silent desperation. She glanced back to see the man sitting stoically, his shadowy aura raging as before.

Breathing was becoming difficult. Ember didn't remember leaving Duncan's office. At some point, she grabbed her satchel and ran past the front desk and into the waiting elevator. She punched the button to close the doors. Sweat dripped down her back. She felt nauseous.

Ember braced herself against a corner and tried to keep her knees from buckling. She distantly heard a cheerful Joy wish her a pleasant evening as the elevator doors closed.

9

SO MUCH IS WRONG

Ember's arms windmilled in an unsuccessful effort to stop her sudden descent. She tumbled into a short hedge parallel to the sidewalk, landing on her satchel.

"Are you okay, ma'am?"

She looked up to see two boys—both teenagers, NonDruws—rushing to her aid. She accepted their help, brushed herself off, and uttered a half-hearted excuse for her clumsiness. Ember walked another block before she realized she hadn't even thanked the two strangers.

She had been running aimlessly, recklessly from The Parker and the people within that building. Her mind was a distracted beehive of incoherent thoughts. To her knowledge, auras couldn't grow, block light, or surround someone like that. *So, if that wasn't Duncan's aura, what was that? Am I infected by whatever that thing was?*

Ember focused on herself, looking at her arms, her legs. No shadowy smudge to be seen.

"Touch wood for that." Ember reached for the trunk of an ash tree planted in the boulevard. A bird sang to her from somewhere up in the canopy. Even that modest reminder of nature in the midst of bustling downtown Minot helped settle her panic. *Now if my heart would stop pounding and I could somehow teleport back to England, that would be the bee's knees.*

She closed her eyes and thought of home—of Great Malvern in western England. The namesake hills surrounding the community which formed the seat of power for Druwish people the world over was a place of ancient beauty. It was where a ley line approached the surface and was why the ancient Celtic people were drawn to it. It was why later peoples would build monasteries and churches, and people later still built healing spas.

When Ember opened her eyes, she was still in Minot.

Her introspective moment was enough to provide a hint of clarity. She would call home. The cell phone given by the colonial government wouldn't do, though; it could be bugged for all she knew. She gave her apartment a wide berth for the same reason.

Perspiration beaded on her forehead, and her forearms were scratched from hugging the hedge that broke her fall. Without warning, a sob broke through her paper-thin defenses and shattered what little calm she'd managed to collect. Ember pressed the back of a clammy hand against her mouth to muffle the sound as she looked around for a place to hide her imminent breakdown.

Roosevelt Park

The unadorned sign announcing the entrance to Roosevelt Park beckoned. Ember couldn't see anyone on the pathway so she stumbled forward. Whimpers fought free. She chastised herself to maintain composure, to keep it together.

A high-pitched scream stopped Ember's meltdown. She froze, looking around for its source.

Another scream, followed by laughter. Children's laughter. Her gaze flitted over the set of brightly-colored equipment which comprised a waterpark. Ember sagged with relief.

She exhaled, unaware that she had been holding her breath. All around her, parents and their children were enjoying the early summer evening. Nobody was even paying attention to her—nobody seemed to notice the blonde woman experiencing a meltdown in public.

Near a building which contained public restrooms was a blue-and-white steel sign of a telephone handset. It looked different from its equivalent in her homeland, but Ember recognized it as a payphone. She followed the directions for entering her credit card and then dialed a number rooted in her memory from childhood.

"Hello, Wright residence." Sleep deepened the voice that Ember wanted so badly to hear.

"Hello, Mummy." Ember choked, unable to say more. Her shoulders shook with suppressed sobs as homesickness crashed through her emotional shell, like water eroding the shoreline.

"Hello, darling. We expected you to call, just not so late. Is everything fine?"

Her mother's voice opened the floodgates. Ember covered

her mouth with a shaky hand. Her throat felt constricted. She squeezed her eyelids shut, evicting tears. Her voice was weak, quavering when she whispered. "Nothing's broken."

"Darling, whatever is wrong?"

Ember heard a rustling of fabric. Her mother murmured behind a semi-cupped phone receiver. Her father's voice in the background completely undid the young woman. Ember leaned against the frame of the payphone, the handset pressed flat to her ear as she cradled it with both hands like something precious, fragile. She wanted so badly to tell her mother everything.

"Emberly, what is happening? What's wrong?" There was a taste of evolving alarm in Benedette's voice.

Her mother's concern, curiously, helped Ember gain some form of control over her runaway panic attack. She took the phone away from her face and held it against her chest as she took a deep breath. She willed her next words to sound calmer than she felt. "I'm just...I'm just feeling homesick, I think."

"Mm." Her mother didn't sound convinced. "Sweetheart, you've been away longer than this. Perhaps not alone, but this is something more. I can't help you if you don't tell me." When Benedette Wright used *that tone,* nobody stood a chance.

"I'm sorry, Mummy." Fabricating such a simple lie to her mother shouldn't have made her feel so guilty. She had experience covering up the truth for years, after all; she heeded Wallace's warning on her Test Day and never divulged her true skills, not even to her parents. For all they knew, she was just a run-of-the-mill Investigator, of no exceptional note beyond being their second daughter.

Ember doubled down on her story. For a dish of dishonesty to be palatable, the right blend of sincere spices must be added. "I guess I'm just exhausted. I'm working on too little sleep and too many pastries, I suppose. The staff at the embassy aren't being very warm to someone from another country sent to audit their work."

"Mmhmm." Ember's mother sounded doubtful as she parsed the admission. "I'm not the Analytic in the family, but it sounds like you're trying to tell me that the kids in school are being mean to you. Something tells me that there are a fair few more things to it, but I won't jostle you."

Ember nodded against the phone, daring not to say anything. The breeze shifted, and her nostrils flared as molecules of chlorine burned her sinuses.

Ember heard the muffled voices of her parents before her mother came back on the line. "Your father said to remind you that your room is always available whenever you wish to come home. Never believe you must stay where you're not wanted—or where you don't wish to stay, darling."

"Thank you, Mummy. Tell Daddy, too. I love you both. I'll call again in a couple days. Goodnight."

She gently slipped the phone's handset back into its hook. The braided steel line swayed, waving goodbye. Ember sniffled as she composed herself for the second number she knew she needed to dial.

The phone rang several times. A clamor followed as the phone on the other end was picked up, dropped against a table, and then retrieved. “Livingston,” the gruff voice finally answered.

“Hey, Wallace. It’s Ember.”

“Ember, did you forget about the time difference? It’s...it’s after midnight sometime here.”

“I know. I’m sorry.” Ember sucked in a breath of air and exhaled slowly. “This is one report that can’t be sent by email though.”

His voice was gentler this time. “Something’s wrong. Did you make contact with Duncan yet?”

“Something’s wrong. Now that’s an understatement.” Ember laughed humorlessly. “God, Wallace, so much is wrong here. There’s something heavy happening here. I’m freaking out and I’m not too proud to say it.”

“Wait—where are you calling me from?”

She cradled the receiver between her ear and hunched shoulder so she could massage her throbbing temples. “I’m not in the office, nor using the mobile they gave me. Don’t worry. I’m at a public phone at a park.”

“We have to be careful.”

“I know.”

“I want you to get another mobile before you check in again. Can you do that?” His voice was tighter than usual, stressed.

Ember swallowed. “Yes, I can do that. I’ll figure it out.”

“What can you tell me about my friend?”

“We met. God, Wallace, there’s nothing right here.” She

began recalling her conversation with Duncan. The darkness that surrounded her. She shivered, standing in the evening sunlight.

"Ember, I need you to calm down. Are you safe?"

"I'm not sure. I think so, for now."

"Tell me what you know." His voice was lower, injected with a measure of calm—whether it was real or forced. The clink of ice cubes falling into a glass served as notification that he was pouring himself a scotch. He would soon be pacing in his study as they talked.

"It started last night when one of the Associates dropped me off at my apartment." A whimper snuck out as she remembered Roseanne, despite her will to stop it. "Have you ever encountered a...a disease that encases a person's aura in a... in a shadow?"

"What? Can you say that again? You know nobody literally sees the energy auras. It's just a sense, a feeling." Though he knew that Ember had the unique ability to visualize auras, Wallace was careful not to say it outright. He was always cautious.

"Everyone in the office has this dark smudge on their aura. At least, the Investigators."

"Even Heywood?"

"God, yes. Especially Heywood." Ember shuddered. "I can't even begin to describe it. He wouldn't even talk to me at first. I had to formulate a reason to single him out. I had him look up some old case files under the auspices of the audit. When he got to one of the cases, his aura got...well it got violent, Wallace."

"Violent? Heywood? That doesn't sound like him."

"No, not Heywood. He didn't get violent. His aura did. Or some sort of shadow surrounding his aura, at least. The shadow surged and blotted the light in the room." Ember closed her eyes, remembering. "When I looked in my periphery, I thought I saw him reach for me, through the shadow."

"It did *what*? That doesn't make any sense." Wallace sipped his whiskey. "You mentioned a case. What sort of case was it?"

"It was an odd one, but quite interesting, of what I had access to read in the summation, anyway. It concerned ten changelings who had become disabled in 2001. I came across it by chance, but it gnawed on me, so I kept digging. This case coincided with an industrial accident that occurred around that same time."

Silence, but for the tinkling of ice against glass. Finally, he said, "I don't know if it means anything or not, but since being elevated to the High Council I've done some digging on past reports from the colony. As best I can tell, the tenor of the reports began to change sometime after 2001. You may have intuitively come across a vital piece of that puzzle. That's top-shelf investigative work, Ember."

"Thank you, sir. But honestly, Wallace, it was sheer luck. Good or bad, I've not decided."

"You know that we create our own luck. It's not pure happenstance."

Ember bit her lip and nodded silently against the phone.

Wallace continued. "I'm still troubled by Duncan's voicemail message that prompted me to send you there. He sounded like he was drunk or choking, I don't know. But, he cut off his message mid-word. Not mid-sentence, mid-word. When I called him back the next day, he claimed to have no knowledge of any phone call. He's not returned my calls ever since. I thought that he might have been in some sort of trouble—blackmail of some sort."

"Something is wrong here, Wallace, but I don't think that it's blackmail. This friend of yours...whatever he was before, he's not that man now. He is rude and standoffish. All of the Investigators are rude and standoffish, for that matter."

"There is more going on over there than I had thought. I knew something was wrong but had no idea it was this bad." Melting ice shifted in his glass.

"Wallace," Ember summoned the courage to articulate her question. "This is all too big for me—for any one person to handle. I don't think I can do this."

"I would go there myself were it not for my duties with the Druw High Council. I don't mean to shame you into staying, and I see the folly now in sending you there by yourself. Even so, I have every confidence in your abilities, Ember. I trust no other Investigator like I trust you. With your skills, hell, I know of no other Investigator as bloody competent as you are. I need—"

"I wish I had never agreed to this assignment. If I knew then what I know now, I would never have come here." Her thoughts given voice, there was no going back now. "I can't stay, Wallace. I just can't."

More silence, and then his voice was quiet, the disappointment unmistakable. "Alright, Ember. I'll bring you home if that's what you wish."

She hesitated a moment as the relief made her knees weak. "I'm sorry, Wallace. I'm sorry. Please, yes."

"Give me a few days so I can figure out who I can send out to relieve you."

Ember closed her eyes, pinching the bridge of her nose between two fingers. "A few days?"

"I need to find someone I can trust who can replace you out there. You can't expect me to just drop an investigation because an agent can't handle it." Wallace's words stung.

"A few days. Brilliant." Ember swallowed. "I'm really sorry, Wallace."

She didn't know which hurt worse—the sound of her former partner's disappointment, or the fact that he hung up without saying goodbye.

10

A SHARK'S GRIN

A SCREAM STARTLED EMBER AWAKE.

Her eyelids snapped open. She cautiously scanned the darkened, unfamiliar apartment as consciousness returned. Her throat was painfully dry when she swallowed—evidence that the scream she had just emitted in her sleep was real.

Awareness trickled slowly like a leaky faucet. She was drenched in sweat, her hair plastered to her face and her favorite pajamas clinging to her damp skin.

"Bloody hell." Ember groaned into her hands as the echo of her nightmare lingered. "I can't do this. How am I going to keep it together for a few more days?"

She willed herself out of bed, glancing at the digital clock. It assured Ember that she had plenty of time for a morning run before work. Neither jogging nor returning to the embassy held any appeal to her.

The small kitchen table retained evidence of the night's stress eating. She had wiped out her precious supply of

Marmite from home—both small jars eaten in one sitting. It was a new personal gluttony record, and she was feeling it. There was no point in rationing the treat, not when she would be returning to England soon.

She ran the water scalding hot in her shower. Standing beneath the torrent, she imagined the water cleansing her mind of the troubling dream of a shadowy figure chasing her down a hallway. Thinking about it only served to reinforce the mental image. She stood and thought of home, of being away from whatever disease was plaguing the Magic City. Mysteries be damned, it wasn't worth contracting whatever that shadow was.

Feeling some semblance of being refreshed following the shower, her stomach started to rumble. *You'd think I wouldn't be so hungry after pilfering the cupboards last night.*

The Sweet & Flour would be open for business soon, and it was just too convenient to pass up. She had just a couple more days to enjoy their fresh offerings, so she reasoned that she should enjoy them while she could.

On the way out of her apartment and to the elevator, she noticed a newspaper and a small package outside her neighbor's door. The items must have been delivered overnight, as neither had been there the night before. Always too curious, Ember peered at the address label. *M. Anderle. Are you Druwish, I wonder? Man, or woman? Did I wake you with my scream? You must think your new neighbor is a nutter.*

When she returned ten minutes later clinging to a bag of pastries, the package and newspaper were already gone.

It was still too early when Ember drew the courage to walk to The Parker building. She intended on lingering in the Magic City Spa, hoping to visit with Josette. She was desperate to see a friendly face without an infected aura.

Ember waved to the receptionist in the lobby. "Hello, Ami. I don't suppose Josette is in yet?"

The dark-skinned girl wore her hair differently than the last time Ember had seen her. The girl narrowed her eyes and held out her index finger. "Let's see...English accent, asking for the manager. You wouldn't happen to be Emberly, by chance?"

Ember blinked. *Is this some sort of jest? We already met!*

"Um...yes." Ember spoke slowly. "I'm fairly sure we've already met. It was two nights ago."

Ami shrugged, "Sorry if that's so. We get a lot of people coming through here. I'm sure I would have remembered if we had. Anyway, I'll show you to Josette's office."

The general manager's office was cramped. One wall was covered by a whiteboard with dry erase notes scrawled across. Yellow sticky notes clung to the edges of Josette's computer monitor, forming a cheerful border.

"Oy! Honey, you look even worse than when you got in." Josette's espresso brown eyes narrowed with worry. "Are you doing alright?"

Ember offered a reluctant smile. "It's been a rough 24 hours I guess."

"I guess!" Josette echoed. "No offense, but you look like you were out all night. Are you getting into the party scene or something? Never mind, that's your business. Oh, honey, you missed a button on your blouse. A couple buttons."

Ember blushed and fumbled to fix her attire. "I didn't really look in the mirror yet today, I suppose."

"How's the apartment working out for you? Did you notice that there's a bakery in the same building?"

"It's been brilliant, thank you." Ember held up the takeout bag from the bakery. "I've been enjoying their products perhaps a little too much."

Josette grinned. "Aren't they the best? I just love their kolaches. Have you tried them yet?"

"Kolaches? No, I don't know what they are, but I will ask for them next time. I've been gorging on their muffins. In fact, why don't you take this from me. You would be doing me a favor."

The curly-haired woman needed no convincing. She dug into the bag and mumbled her gratitude around a mouthful of cake.

Ember sunk into the one available visitor's chair in the small office. A shiny blue-and-white helmet occupied the other chair—the same helmet Josette was cradling when they met. "What sort of motorbike do you own?"

Josette became animated. "I've got a 2005 Harley Softtail Deluxe. It's sort of my pride and joy. Do you ride?"

"Oh, no! I would absolutely kill myself. I already have a problem with stairs. I think I'd be pressing my luck driving anything that didn't come with an airbag and safety belts."

"Honey, you never know until you try! If you ever feel like you want to try it, give me a holler. It's a great way to travel."

"I'll have to take your word for it."

"So, I know you're just working as a massage therapist in the spa as your cover job, but I'm really eager to get you in here." Josette brushed crumbs from her desk and into the wastebasket. "We do accept NonDruw clients, but of course the real draw is for Druws. As with all Druwish spas the world over, we're built atop a Ley Line, and the mana it produces has some wonderful healing benefits."

"Where is the Ley Line for this spa, exactly?"

"Oh, that's down in the subbasement, but it's off-limits, other than to the upper-level mucky-mucks and security personnel. When we need Leystones charged, we send them down with someone from security. Every crystal has to be accounted for since they are so valuable. Of course, if there's dire need for intensive healing we can appeal to Higginbotham."

"I don't believe I know that name," Ember admitted.

"He's the Director of Wellness for the colony. I do hope you will get a chance to meet him. He's such a nice guy, always so helpful and supportive."

Helpful and supportive. That would be an exception among Malverns around here. Ember wondered if he might be able to provide information about the Mandaree case. "Brilliant. I'll be sure to give him a call today."

Josette grinned. "Brilliant. Well, I've got to make my rounds before things get too crazy around here. Thank you for the cupcake."

The elevator ride was solo, which afforded Ember a chance to give herself a pep talk. "Just a bloody few more days to work the assignment. You can do this."

"'Ello, Guv'ner!" The bubbly third-floor front desk receptionist waved with such enthusiasm, Ember almost took a step back into the elevator. "How was that for matching your accent? Pretty close, huh? I've been working on it since last night. I think my true calling is to be a voice actor. You know, those cartoon voices for, like, cartoons and stuff? 'Ello, Guv'ner!' And 'top O' the mornin' to you, lassie!' I guess that was a little bit Irish that time. I probably need to practice a little more. Or, oh, a wee bit more, as you might say."

Ember waited for a pause in Joy's stream-of-conscious monologue. Seeing none, she finally interrupted. "That's brilliant, Joy. But keep practicing, yeah?"

Joy beamed. "You really think so? Oh, I will! I will."

"Oh, Joy, I have a favor to ask, if you would be so kind? Could you put a call in to the Director of Wellness for me, please? I would like to set up a meeting with him at his earliest convenience. Anytime in the next couple days would be lovely."

"That would be Director Higginbotham. He's such a nice man! You will just love him, I'm sure. Everyone does. His office is on the Sixth Floor." Joy picked up the phone and began rapidly punching numbers. She held her hand over the receiver and adopted her crude parody of an English accent. "I'll set the meeting up right away, Guv'ner. It'll be just two shakes of a squirrel's tail."

"Thanks. Let me know what you find out, please. 'Two shakes of a squirrel's tail.' I'm stealing that one, just so you know." Ember shook her head and chuckled as she walked to her office, avoiding the break room where the other Investigators gathered. The pure silliness of the changeling girl's manner helped lift the mood and there was no need to have it dampened by facing those people again.

If she could make it through the next few days with minimal time around the other Investigators, that would be for the best. Ember powered up the embassy-provided desktop computer on the grey steel desk in her makeshift office. If she could find an excuse to stay away from the office while still pursuing the Mandaree Incident case, that would be ideal. She began formulating a plan to do just that.

She would need to pull from the database the names and addresses of the ten changelings designated as disabled in 2001. She would then meet with them—at their homes, away from the embassy—and interview them. She could do all this under the auspices of the census audit. Nobody would be the wiser.

Ember logged into the embassy system and began searching the records in 2001 for all references to Mandaree. Her screen displayed:

ACCESS RESTRICTED: PERMISSION DENIED

"What the bloody hell?" Ember performed additional queries. She could bring up personnel records for recent years, but nothing older than three years, and nothing at all related to disability status nor anything containing the term "Mandaree."

Cold realization set in. Someone had pulled her clearance to access the files she needed. *Duncan. It had to be Duncan.*

If there was one certain way to rile the anger of Ember Wright, Associate Investigator, it would be to stand in the way of her sense of justice. She couldn't be sure what happened with the industrial accident at Mandaree in 2001, but she had a hunch that the disabled changelings were connected to it. That the Senior Investigator was preventing her from finding out raised serious red flags. Duncan might as well have set up a neon sign: "clues found here."

Wallace needed to be informed immediately. Ember logged out of the computer and reached for her satchel just as someone knocked on her office door.

"Ms. Wright?" The sizable Malvern man at the door stood over six feet tall. His hair was receding, grey with some hint of black and a salt-and-pepper mustache to match. His skin was uniformly tanned, though it bore no freckles or spots. The pale suit looked striking against his toned skin. The thing that Ember noticed first was his aura, though: bright, powerful, and unblemished by any shadow. This man was a Level Six mage, and a strong one at that.

"I'm Ember, yes." Ember blinked at the man's bright aura. She had never met someone with such a strong presence. It was overwhelming her senses.

"I'm Elton Higginbotham, Director of Wellness. I was told you wanted to meet me?" The man leaned against the frame of the door, his figure seeming to barely fit. His voice was high and cheerful. The mouthful of bright, white teeth looked nearly fluorescent when he smiled. "I see they stuck you in a corner office. Downright lavish quarters, these."

It took Ember a moment to realize that the man was making

a joke. "Oh, these...well, yes. I suppose an interim auditor doesn't quite warrant something posh."

Elton pressed his lips tightly together and crossed his arms. His face formed a charming expression that could have been stolen from Rob Lowe. "Posh. Now there's a word we don't use around here very often. How are you settling in? They treating you okay around here?"

Unsure how much she could—or should—reveal, Ember hesitated before answering. Though the director had no smudge over his aura, she couldn't trust too readily. "It's... okay, as you say. I can't blame anyone for being less-than-thrilled to have an external auditor roaming the halls."

Elton laughed, loud enough that it startled Ember. She hoped he hadn't noticed.

"Speaking of, how is the census audit going, anyway?"

Ember glanced at her computer screen before saying, "It's early yet. Just getting started."

"Well if you need anything, you just let me know. Will you?"

"That's quite kind of you, sir. Actually...there is something I wonder if you might be able to help me figure out?"

The director uncrossed his arms, revealing the glint of a sparkling tie pin. "If it's in my power, then I am at your service. What can I do for you, Ember?"

"As I said, I'm just now starting the audit, but I noticed that between yesterday and today, my access to the government database has been restricted."

He furrowed his brow. "Mmhmm, I see. Restricted how?"

"Yesterday, I was looking through files from 2001, for example." Ember pointed at her monitor, though she had already logged off. She hastily added, "Just random personnel files. Standard process for these audits. This morning, those same queries are resulting in 'access denied' messages."

"I'm sure it's just a computer glitch. Sometimes these systems can be all kinds of cockamamie like that. Even the servers know that the weather is beautiful outside and they have trouble focusing." He laughed loudly at his own joke.

Ember smiled politely. She watched Elton laugh and made a mental note that his piercing, icy blue eyes never left her. His gregarious laughter, his toothy, bright smiles—but, his eyes told her that his lighthearted demeanor was superficial. The man was lying to her. *His is a shark's grin.*

"But seriously, Ember, as I said I'm in charge of the Department of Wellness. You need to talk to the boys one floor above me, in the Department of Information. They can get you sorted out, okay?"

She nodded, hiding her disappointment. "Of course. Thank you for clarifying. I'm sorry you had to come downstairs for nothing."

"Not at all! I wanted to meet our guest regardless. But the offer does stand: if there's anything I can do to help, you just let me know. Tech support notwithstanding, that is." He extended his large hand and stepped forward.

Elton Higginbotham was as charming as a politician, attractive as any actor, and his aura was more vibrant than any she had ever seen. Her hand disappeared within his palm. He closed his tanned fingers, adorned with oversized, bejeweled rings. She smiled and looked up at his eyes. Such icy blue eyes, to match his periwinkle gemstone tie pin. The shark smile beneath his mustache broadened, and his grip tightened around hers.

Ember felt lightheaded, then nauseous. *I should never have eaten so many pastries this morning.*

When the director released her hand, Ember leaned against her desk. She brought her hand up to the side of her head.

"Are you alright, Ember?" Elton's voice sounded cloudy, as though he was talking to her from a distance rather than right next to her.

"I'm...yes, I'm just knackered. I think I didn't get enough rest last night, that's all. Jet lag, you know."

The foggy voice said, "Of course, of course. Why don't you take an early lunch and go take a nap? That will freshen you right up."

"That sounds like a good idea." Ember collected her purse and satchel before exiting.

"It was nice meeting you, Ember." The foggy voice laughed.

Ember walked past the front desk and called the elevator.

Joy chirped, "Oh, your meeting is over! Isn't Director Higginbotham such a nice man? See, I knew you'd like him!"

Ember nodded without looking back at Joy. She wanted to say something, but she couldn't think of an appropriate response. She walked back toward her apartment, and the nausea seemed to subside. At one of the crosswalks, she noticed a crow perched atop the traffic lights. She closed her eyes and now she saw an adult man sitting on the traffic light. When she opened them, there was the crow, again. *Why am I bothering looking at a silly bird?*

A subconscious thought tugged at her, but she couldn't focus enough to make sense of it. When she arrived at her apartment building, she unlocked the door to the embassy-provided car. *Opposite side. This is going to be an unusual driving experience.*

The Honda started, and Ember maneuvered down the unfamiliar streets. She headed south on the main thoroughfare. She glanced at her satchel and recalled the notes she had written yesterday. She struggled to make sense of what she was doing, where she was going. She felt disconnected from herself. It was as though someone else was controlling her actions.

No, that's not quite right. It feels like I'm watching myself. Like I'm watching myself on television. Like I'm not quite here.

Ember glanced in her rearview mirror before making a lane change. She did a double-take when she saw it: a shadow surrounding her face.

Her blood chilled and she struggled to regain her focus lest she crash the SUV. She was outside of the city limits now, where the land quickly transitioned to suburbs and then open fields. Ember turned off and parked on the shoulder of a gravel road. A cloud of dust billowed around her.

Gripping the rearview mirror with both hands, she looked at herself, wild-eyed through a dirty shadow which seemed to roil and move around her. She felt the nausea return with a vengeance.

The queasy woman barely got out of her car before the

contents of her stomach began to force their way out. She retched painfully, squeezing her eyes shut as she vomited onto the gravel road. She fumbled for the side of the car for support, slipped, and landed hard on her knees. The world seemed to swirl around her as another wave of bile emerged.

Her nostrils stung and her throat burned from stomach acid. Another wave of retching. It felt like she'd just been kicked in the abdomen.

"Bloody hell," Ember groaned. Tears dripped from her cheeks. She opened her eyes to see black vapors rising from the dispelled contents. She scrambled to back away from the unholy steam.

Ember shook her head and blinked, trying to focus on her arms, her legs. A vise loosened from her temples, and she could feel as well as see the smudge dissipate from her aura. She struggled to her feet and looked in the mirror again. *If I didn't look like hell before, I sure do now.*

But, her aura was clean again. The shadow was gone.

Ember sat hunched in her car, her feet still on the rough gravel road surface. Her thoughts became her own again as clarity returned.

She grimaced at the memory of Elton Higginbotham's strong handshake. He was so charming, his aura so bright and strong. She failed to recognize when his spell seeped into her, taking over almost immediately. She wasn't sure what it was that he spelled her with, nor how she managed to counter it. *This thing that's infecting everyone is no disease at all. It's a spell. A powerful, ugly spell.*

Ember leaned out and spat, attempting to clear her mouth of the foul taste. The road dust was settling now. In the fields around her, she heard pheasants call and meadowlarks sing. A crow perched on a barbed wire fence, almost as if it was watching her.

A crow watching me. Why am I feeling a sense of déjà vu?

She looked again at the crow, then closed her eyes. Inside her eyelids, a man appeared where the crow was; this bird was a changeling. It was the same changeling that was watching her from the streets of Minot.

Ember was being followed.

11

HOW FAST CAN A BLOODY CROW FLY

THE HONDA RACED DOWN THE ROAD AS QUICKLY AS EMBER dared to drive. She was pushing her luck, driving 80 miles per hour in a 70 mile-per-hour zone—in an unfamiliar vehicle, on the "wrong" side of the road, no less.

"How fast can a bloody crow fly, anyway?" Ember thought aloud. "Supposing he can see a lot farther and he can get way up high, how far until I lose the arsehole?"

There was no way to know for sure who the changeling was working for, but it was a safe bet that it was Director Higginbotham. He would want to keep an eye on Ember, to make sure his spell—whatever it was—took root. She would need to lose this tail without tipping her hand; Elton had to believe that his spell was a success, or she would blow her cover.

Elton. Ember practically spit when she thought of the man and his dark, nauseating spell. *A Healer is supposed to help people, not harm them. How bloody dare he!* She gritted her teeth and hit her fist against the steering wheel. If Elton's aim was to discourage her from investigating his dubious activities, he couldn't have done worse. What was little more than an assignment had now become personal. She burned with righteous anger.

The state roadmap laid partially unfurled on the center console beneath Ember's right arm. She glanced down at it. She said to herself, "Highway 83, heading south. I need to watch for Highway 23."

Mere minutes passed since she emptied her stomach on the side of the road, ridding herself of the shadowy spell that clouded her mind. She thought about turning back for Minot, to call Wallace and update him on this turn of events. Ember would do that eventually, but first, she had more pressing business gnawing on her mind. She needed to know what Elton didn't want her to see.

Without access to the database, she had only the case number itself as her sole tangible proof of the Mandaree Incident's existence in the Viceroyalty's computer system. That wouldn't be enough to put together this cover-up that the Director of Wellness was orchestrating. She needed to know more.

A name and a place stood out among all others in her memory: one Arnold Schmitt, from Plaza, North Dakota. By coincidence, she realized she was heading in the right direction when she came out of the spell the director had cast on her.

When she took the right turn at Junction 23, Ember peered out her window, scanning the sky for any sign of the crow. It was impossible to make out what would be a tiny, dark speck in the otherwise open sky. She would continue to Plaza, regardless.

The drive was long enough for a plan to form. To the tune of the Pilot's rubber rolling along Highway 23's miles of straight asphalt, Ember hoped her extemporaneous plan would work.

Plaza registered more as a village than a proper town—but then, so many settlements in this expansive prairie fit that definition. A total of 167 individuals called Plaza home, according to the chart on her 2009/2010 North Dakota road map. With a population so small, Ember hoped that she could find someone who could point her to where Arnold Schmitt lived.

On the edge of town, along the main road near the public school, a tidy, grand two-story cottage stood proudly. The charming abode was painted yellow, with white trim. It looked like something straight out of a children's storybook, except for the fact that a pair of American flags flew in the yard. Red and blue bunting clung to a white picket fence encircling the property.

The other houses sprinkled around Plaza ranged from old farmhouses to newer trailer houses. Some yards were well cared for, while others had junked out vehicles parked on unkempt lawns. If there was a covenant or homeowner's association, it wasn't apparent. This was a town which seemed populated by individualists.

Ember slowly maneuvered the SUV down the narrow, rough streets of the small town. She intended to find someone out in their yard, working their garden on this bright summer day.

She practiced her introduction aloud. "Hello, I'm Ember, how do you do? I'm doing research for my family's genealogy, and I have a distant cousin in town here. Do you perchance know where Arnold Schmitt lives?"

It didn't take long to find the center of town, where a tan building housed Plaza's only bar: the "Grub and Pub." It was as good a place to start as any. She pulled into the small parking lot, next to a rusting Chevy pickup.

Two off-shift oilfield workers sat at a table, tipping back bottles of beer in silence. Tall stools lined an empty bar. Ember climbed onto one of the stools, which swiveled as she pushed her feet against the base.

The country song on the jukebox was in its chorus:

Indian Summer,

The wonder,

The hunger,

And the sound of distant thunder.

Indian Summer.

The barmaid approached, and Ember ordered a bottle of water—something to wash the foul taste from her mouth. She took a long swallow before she asked, "Is it safe to assume that you're a local?"

The barmaid studied her customer. She was several inches taller than Ember and outweighed her by at least twenty pounds—most of it muscle. She was a full-figured woman who wore her dark blonde hair in a braid down the middle of her back. Her eyes were dusky with a wary intelligence. She had a peculiar habit of looking for a second before her head turned to follow her gaze. She gave Ember a hint of a smile to go with her nod. "It's safe to assume you're not."

Ember mirrored the smirk. "Fair guess." She tried to appear nonchalant as she tipped her bottle of water back for another swig. She managed to spill half a mouthful down her shirt.

"I'm Anna," the woman behind the bar said between chuckles. She handed Ember a napkin. "I hope you don't mind my saying, but I think you might have a drinking problem."

The jukebox blared, *I wonder where we'd be if I never scored that last touchdown.*

Ember sighed with embarrassment as she dabbed with the napkin. "What do you mean? This is how we consume beverages back where I come from. I'm Ember, by the way. I'm here working on a family tree project. I wonder if you might happen to know my distant cousin?"

"If she's from around here, then yeah, I probably would."

"Brilliant! It's a he, actually. My cousin's name is Arnold Schmitt."

Anna's smile melted into a frown. She leaned over the bar menacingly.

Ember's eyes went wide. "I'm sorry if I—"

"Cut the crap, Malvern." Anna hissed. "What do you want with my brother Arnie?"

"Your brother?" Ember closed her eyes. Before her, a magnificent golden eagle appeared, its predatory glare inimitable. When she opened her eyes, she noticed Anna's aura. In the dim light of the bar, she missed that telltale sign earlier. *Ace situational awareness, Ember. The Legend would be so proud.*

"You're a changeling," Ember whispered. The twang of the jukebox gave cover, but Ember whispered anyway. "And Arnold Schmitt's sister. Small world."

"Yeah, no shit, Sherlock. Small *town*." Anna glowered. "So again, what do you want with Arnie? He's been through enough already from you people."

"Anna, I don't know what happened with Arnie. That's exactly why I'm here. I want to help."

There was no humor in Anna's laugh. "So, you're telling me you're not from the embassy?"

"No. Well, I am, but only by way of the High Council." Ember looked around to make sure nobody was listening. The Indian Summer song reached its conclusion, and another song had taken over. "Something happened in 2001, and I think it involved Arnold—Arnie—somehow. I'm trying to figure out what happened, but I need to talk to him."

Anna's expression became pained, and she looked away, her head turning a moment later to follow her focus. "I can't talk about that, here. It...it just hurts too much. You'll need to talk with my other brother, Rik."

"Rik? Where can I find him?"

"Alarik," Anna said as she clicked a ballpoint pen and began sketching lines onto the back of a disposable coaster. "He's our big brother. He's the one you should talk to. I'll call ahead so he knows to expect you. He'll be working at his farm today." She slid the map into Ember's hand.

Ember accepted the coaster without looking down. She met Anna's eyes and saw barely-contained grief. As curious as she was, Ember knew not to make any further inquiries here. She said, "thank you, Anna. I can't pretend to know what's going on, but I promise you I won't stop until justice is served."

Anna's fierce, dusky raptor eyes met Ember's. "You'd better be telling the truth, mage. Our family's been through enough misery already." Anna turned away, wiped the back of a calloused hand over her cheek and said no more.

ALARIK SCHMITT'S SMALL FARMSTEAD WAS ABOUT A HALF-dozen miles north of Plaza, just as Anna's sketched map promised. Rows of aging elm and pine formed the shelter-belt to the north and west, protecting an old red-and-white gambrel barn from the prairie's prevailing winds. Gravel crunched in protest beneath Ember's SUV as she turned into the yard.

She approached the front door of the farmhouse. Its roof had a steep pitch, clad in modern shingles. The siding and windows looked newer too—a modern facelift over old bones. Aside from the updates, the house looked to be a contemporary to the old barn. Both structures were much older than the other outbuildings. She imagined the early homesteaders working their small patch of land, planting seedlings that would cast shadows for future generations they would never meet.

Ember curled her hand into a fist and reached for the door. Before she could knock, a man's voice startled her.

“Over here.” The voice belonged to a lean figure, tall with broad shoulders. His square jaw was coated with stubble, slightly darker than the shaggy, brown hair on his head. A narrow band across his forehead was the only clean patch on him.

Ember blinked to reveal the changeling’s subform: a coyote. “I’m Ember Wright. You must be Alarik Schmitt?”

The man lifted his chin, his nostrils flaring as he smelled the air. He pulled off a pair of leather elbow-length gauntlets that may have once been beige. His grimy sleeves were peppered with tiny burn holes. “Anna called. You want to know about Arnie?”

As she walked toward him, the acrid scent of burnt flux and smoke wafted off Alarik. The unfamiliar medley tickled her nose. Ember quickly turned away and sneezed.

It was only a moment, but when she closed her eyes to sneeze, she saw him: a man standing nearby on a narrow fence post, watching her. With her eyes open, a crow took its place. *Not just any crow.*

Ember pretended not to notice the spy. She felt sure that she had lost him, but clearly, she hadn’t.

“Ember?” Alarik’s head was canted, his brow furrowed.

“Huh? Yeah, sorry.” Ember swept a lock of blonde hair from her face as she shook her head. “I must be allergic to you. Were you playing with fireworks or something?”

The man grunted. “Or something. My brother and I own a welding truck. We’re doing a lot of oilfield work now that drilling around the Williston Basin is picking back up. Arnie used to run his own truck, but now he just helps me out when he can. He's not exactly functioning at full capacity anymore since he breathed in…whatever those chemicals were."

"I see." Ember glanced at the crow. *That arsehole is listening.*

"I'm sorry," Alarik said. "I thought you wanted to talk about my brother's disability?"

"What? No, no. I'm just here for an audit of the census. You and your brother just came up as part of a random sample. I just need to ask a few questions to verify your place of residence."

The man frowned, "That's not what you told—"

Ember interrupted. "You know, I'm so sorry, I think I ate something undercooked for breakfast. I'm feeling unwell, like I might have to chunder. Could I use your loo?"

"My loo?"

"Your…washroom? Bathroom?"

"Oh. Right. Uh…yeah, sure. It's just inside, off the living room to the left."

"Brilliant." Ember turned toward the house, then turned back. "Would you mind terribly if you showed me? I don't much feel comfortable wandering around your house unattended."

Now Alarik seemed annoyed, but he shrugged and held the door open for her. As soon as the front door closed behind him, Ember spun around.

"Listen, I know this won't make any sense, but you need to trust me. We're being watched."

The white band of clean skin on Alarik's forehead formed ridges as he frowned. He sniffed the air and began to glance out the window.

"No! Don't look now. It's a crow on your fence. He's a changeling, and he has been following me since Minot. He's spying for someone. Someone bad."

"How can you be sure—"

"I'm sorry, I just don't have time to explain right now." Ember looked up at a skeptical Alarik. She knew she had to give him something. *I'm asking him to trust me, but how much can I trust him?*

"Okay." Ember inhaled deeply. She ran her fingers through her hair as she paced down the hallway, away from the window. "What I'm about to tell you cannot leave this room, understand? The census audit is just my cover story. I was sent by a member of the Druw High Council to solve a mystery. In so doing, I've stumbled upon some sort of cover-up."

She locked eyes with the man. "All I can tell you—all I know right now, really—is that I suspect your brother's disability is somehow connected to an industrial accident that happened in 2001."

"Yeah, and tell me something I don't know." Alarik glared and crossed his arms. In that moment, the resemblance to his sister was uncanny.

"Wait—you're aware of what caused your brother's disability?"

"Somewhat." Alarik shrugged, his arms still crossed. He glanced up at the ceiling as though he was drawing memories from an invisible shelf. "All we know is that when that whole gas leak happened around Mandaree in late 2000, Arnie was hired along with some other changelings to slip past law enforcement to check it out. He was told that it was important. Vitally important. It was for the sake of the whole Druwish colony, all that bullshit. The only reason I know any of this is because Arnie confided in me before he left. The whole thing was all hush-hush."

"Told by who? Who asked him to do all this?" Ember suspected she knew.

"I don't know. Some asshole Malvern from the embassy in Minot is my guess. What do they care about changeling lives." He scowled.

"So, what happened to Arnie?"

Alarik's jaw clenched. His dark umber eyes glared at Ember. "He disappeared for nine months. My brother's head has been fucking scrambled ever since. Nobody will tell us what happened, or how we can help him. My little brother has a wife, two little kids. He used to be ambitious and happy. But now...he's practically a zombie now."

Ember spoke softly, choosing her words with care. "I'm guessing the Department of Wellness hasn't been very helpful?"

Alarik laughed mirthlessly. He hit his fist against the wall with a dull thud. "They tell us that there's nothing they can do for him. They won't even give him treatments at the spa anymore. Like giving my brother temporary relief is a big waste of time or precious Leystones."

It was Ember's turn to frown. "They can't deny Arnie access

to treatment. That's a right of all Druws, to recharge at a Ley Line facility whenever they wish. That's guaranteed in Druwish Law."

"Not around here it isn't," he growled. "Not if you're someone who asks too many questions. Not if you're a changeling."

"That's wrong of them. I'll look into that, I promise you. Now I'd really like to meet Arnie, if I may?"

Alarik slowly tilted his head back, and then forward. His appraising gaze never left her. "Alright, but not today. He and his family are living with my folks. Anna and I are going to be there when you talk to him."

"That's understandable. Thank you, Rik. Can we do this tomorrow afternoon, please? Sooner is better."

Alarik agreed. He wrote an address on the back of a Schmitt Brothers Welding business card. He paused before opening the door for her and growled low. "You'd better not be jerking my family around."

The crow was still outside, still watching when Ember returned to her car. She patted her satchel and called out with as much feigned cheer as she could muster. "On behalf of the Viceroyalty, thank you for completing this census survey, Mr. Schmitt."

"THIS IS ALL VERY TROUBLING," WALLACE MURMURED ON THE other end of the telephone line. "Very troubling. So, am I correct in guessing that this means that you're staying in Minot, after all?"

Ember held the cheap pay-as-you-go cell phone against her right ear. The cord for the charger was plugged into her Honda's power port beneath the dash, keeping the fresh battery alive for its maiden use. Along with some groceries in the back seat, these gadgets were among her purchases from the southside Walmart in Minot. She had just finished recapping the day's events to Wallace as she sat in the car.

She didn't hesitate to answer. "I know I made a fuss about wanting to come home, but I need to stay. I need to find out what's going on. I need to help these people find justice. I'll admit that I'm still scared, but...I don't think I could leave even if I was ordered to."

Wallace's words were slow, measured. "You can't begin to know how grateful I am to hear that, Ember."

"It's just so many coincidences, Wallace." Ember kept glancing around the Walmart parking lot, expecting at any point to see a crow looking back at her. She could smell her own body odor heating up after the intense day. She didn't dare crack a window to let in the cool evening air, lest her conversation was overheard. "It's a coincidence, how I accidentally came across the Incident at Mandaree case file, or how I stumbled across and then remembered Arnold Schmitt's name before my access to the database was culled. Running into his sister as the very first person I talked to in Plaza. Or, bloody hell, the fact that I was already heading toward Plaza when I came out of his spell; it was like my subconscious was taking over because the rest of me was all loopy."

Ember sighed, closing her eyes as she scanned the parking lot again. "I'm just glad Higginbotham was sloppy with his spell, whatever it was. If it would have taken root properly, I probably wouldn't even be talking with you right now. I'd be another rude drone like Duncan and the others."

"I'm not so sure." Wallace sounded contemplative. "Elton Higginbotham is no novice. He's a Level Six Healer, one of the few to exist in the world."

"So why do you suppose his spell wore off so quickly?"

"I'm given to suspect that *you* were the reason it wore off so quickly, Ember."

She didn't know how to respond, so the woman allowed silence to linger.

"It's no mere coincidence that you pulled that file, Ember. Nor that some part of you knew to follow that particular lead, even with whatever dark magic you were fighting through. You've got Investigator's Instinct. It's common among high-level Investigators. How do you think I earned that silly nickname: The Legend? I have a knack for discovering coincidences that become patterns which I'm in turn able to recognize and piece together to solve cases. I don't always know where a case will take me, but I know when I'm on the right path. It's an intangible sense."

"Yeah, except I'm not high-level; I'm just an Associate. Level Two."

"Ember, that's merely what you've tested for. What you're capable of is far beyond your current rank. You have to know this, don't you?"

Some part of her did. Ember knew, after all, that she was able to visualize auras in ways that no other Druw could. Changelings could sense other Druws—the way Anna back at the bar had identified Ember as a Malvern—but they couldn't outright see auras. Likewise, nobody but her could see the subform of a changeling.

Wallace continued. "I'm going to tell you something that I've known since the day I met you. I think you need to hear this now. Do you recall the day we met, Ember?"

"Of course I remember, Wallace. I'd just turned 13 all those, what, 21 years ago. My Test Day. You pointed out how terrible I was at all the other tracks but Investigation."

Wallace snorted.

Ember combed her fingers through her hair as she reminisced. "That day changed my life. Your findings gave me a sense of purpose in the world."

"Do you remember that I told you how you rated in the other Magic Tracks?

"Yes. Poorly, as I recall."

"When we test young Malverns, the scale we use to measure each level is logarithmic; approximately doubling with each new level. Almost every mage scores at least a couple points in each Track. Level One is one to three points, Level Two is four to nine points, Level Three is nine to eighteen points. That's where the Investigation Track ends, though the other Mage Tracks continue through Level Six, which tops out at about 150 points."

Ember nodded as she quietly listened.

"Bearing in mind this just measures *potential* capabilities among candidates, as each Malvern must prove themselves by passing a test to proceed through each level, as you know."

Ember wasn't sure where he was going with this, but she indulged him. "I remember. It's been twelve years since I became a Novice Investigator, but it was only a few months ago when I was allowed to take the Level Two test to become an Associate Investigator."

"Indeed." Papers rustled on Wallace's end of the conversation. "And even this was half as many years as usually is allowed for that test to be offered. We have to be careful."

Ember smiled. "I know. You remind me of that often."

"With good reason. Do you remember on your Test Day when I told you that you had to be careful, that you had to keep your skills secret?"

"I remember you said that I rated higher than you were officially reporting. Later, you told me that when you had found other children who tested as high as I did, that they disappeared—that you suspected someone was eliminating high-rated Investigators before they could get trained in. That's why I've had to keep my skills a secret even from my parents, to this day."

"You've got that mostly correct Ember. The part I never told you is that I could never say what your true rating is." Wallace tapped his fingers against his desk. He murmured, "You'd think that after all these years, I would have thought of the perfect way to tell you this."

"As you always tell me," Ember shifted her voice down to a cartoonishly low octave to mimic his. "Ember, stop chewing and spit it out."

Wallace snorted again. "Fair enough. The Investigation Track ends at Level Three. When I tested over a century ago,

I rated at the upper end of the scale: something like 18 points, if I recall. I don't tell people that, because it sounds too much like boasting, as I'm one of the highest-rated Investigators in the world."

"That doesn't surprise me. There's a reason you're called The Legend."

"Yes, that silly nickname. Well, my point here is that whatever my rating is, it pales in comparison to yours."

"What do you mean?" Ember's heart rate suddenly doubled.

"I mean that I can't tell you what your true rating is because our scale doesn't go that high. You literally tested off the charts."

12

NOT A WHOLE CLAN

"'Ello, Guv'ner!" Joy's wide smile greeted Ember before she even stepped off the elevator. Her chosen dialect this morning was a sordid bastardization of exaggerated Cockney and Pidgin. "I'm a'fearin' there won't be time fer wee chit chat, 'cause you'll be wantin' by the boss, see?"

"Morning, Joy." Ember shook her head and continued walking to her office. She couldn't muster an appreciation for the young woman's antics. Too much was on her mind, and too little time to spare.

"Um, sorry. You're wanted by the boss. Duncan. He said to tell you to come to his office right away when I see you."

Ember bypassed her office, walking straight to the Senior Investigator's. She wondered if he was about to deal her in on the game that was being played by Director Higginbotham. For all they knew, after all, she was still under the effects of Elton's spell. She would act the part, and in so doing become privy to the dark doings. As nervous as she was to see Duncan again, she couldn't help but feel a hint of excitement. *Today is the day I blow this whole cover-up wide open.*

Brown, crew-cut hair capped six-and-a-half feet of muscle standing outside of the Senior Investigator's office. The changeling man's full beard was dark but couldn't hide his grim expression. Ember blinked to reveal his badger subform. His aura was clean, with no hint of shadow.

"Ah, good. Come in, come in." Duncan stood up from his desk, pulling a pair of reading glasses off and tossing them onto a calendar pad. "It seems someone had a little oversight that needs fixing. I'll be needing your car keys."

"Oh? Under what grounds?" Ember wasn't sure she liked where this conversation was heading. *I don't need two guesses as to who ordered this.*

"Yes. So, you know the embassy provided you with a loaner car, but apparently, we failed to realize that you do not have a valid North Dakota driver's license. Since you won't be here more than—what, a couple months—it doesn't make sense to waste time trying to arrange for you to take the necessary test and all that." Duncan waved his hand dismissively at his desk.

"As part of my external audit, I was told I would be afforded the means to travel." She knew she had to moderate her tone. She was, after all, supposedly still under the Director's dark spell. "How can I get around town, around the countryside to interview citizens if I have no car?"

"A fine point. Not to worry, as we have you covered." Duncan snapped his fingers once. The imposing changeling stepped into the office. From her angle, Ember didn't see much clearance between the door's head and the man's. "This is

Dennis. He normally works in Security, but he will serve as your driver for the rest of your time here in the Magic City. Anywhere you need to go, Dennis will take you. Service with a smile."

Dennis grunted, his grim expression unchanged.

"Brilliant. Will that be all, sir?" Ember hoped she was hiding her true emotions well enough.

Duncan's smirk was replaced with a hint of disappointment. "That about sums it up. Oh, just the keys, please." His upturned palm extended toward Ember.

Dennis was more than just a driver; he followed her everywhere. As she settled into her cramped supply closet-turned-office, he squatted on a box of copy paper against a shelf. She was surprised it supported his mass.

"Is it really necessary for you to be in here?" Her annoyance was hard to contain. "There's a lovely break room, you know."

The man's huge shoulders shrugged. "I was instructed to stay with you at all times during office hours."

Ember narrowed her gaze. "Is that so. I need to make a few calls if you'll excuse me."

"Then make them." Dennis shrugged again. "I've got my crossword puzzle book. I don't mind."

Ember silently cursed her situation. She needed to call Alarik, to cancel their afternoon meeting. She couldn't just *not* show up; the Schmitts would lump her in with all the other government employees who have failed them over the years. *Just another Malvern, looking down at changelings.*

"I need to use the loo. Or do you need to follow me in there, too?"

Dennis grunted. He pulled a tattered booklet from a thigh pocket of his khaki cargo pants and stole a pencil from Ember's desk. "Just don't leave this floor without telling me."

She grabbed her purse and hastened for the women's restroom. Within the faintly bleach-scented room, she peered beneath the stalls to verify she was alone. *I need to make this quick before someone walks in.*

Ember found her new cell phone and dialed the phone number on the Schmitt Brothers Welding business card. The display on the phone brightly announced, "NO SERVICE."

Bloody hell!

She checked the cell phone provided by the embassy. It, too, failed to detect a signal. *I'm either too deep within the walls of this old building, or they are blocking mobile signals.*

Back at her desk, she nonchalantly checked the embassy cell phone again. *Still no signal. I'll need to find another way to reach him. I need to get outside this building so I can make the call.*

Ember logged into her computer and made a few quick queries to the personnel database to find local retirees. From there, she called two Druw residents—one changeling, and one Malvern—living in the Magic City and informed them that they had been randomly selected to participate in the census audit. She scheduled both appointments for later that morning.

"Looks like you're up, driver." Ember acted as cheerful as she could.

Dennis folded up his crossword puzzle, tucked the stolen pencil between his ear and scalp, and grunted.

The interviews were uneventful. She asked the standard, boring census questions and acted interested. She did make a mental note that both citizens' auras were clean from any shadowy spell.

Ember intended on finding a chance to make a quick phone call within the interviewees' homes. Unfortunately, Dennis didn't wait in the car like she hoped. *Time for Plan B.*

They were both walking back to his white GMC Suburban when she said, "Next stop: Plaza."

Dennis looked over his shoulder but kept walking to the left side of the SUV. "You mean the little Podunk town?"

"Podunk," Ember repeated. "I don't know that term. I think we're probably talking about the same place though. I've got an afternoon appointment there. Do you know where it is?"

Dennis swung his door shut and grunted.

With a grumbling badger changeling as traveling companion, the drive to Plaza seemed infinitely long. Ember considered sending a text message to Alarik, but she couldn't take the chance that Dennis would notice. She gave up trying to make conversation with the brute after his third grunted response to her questions. He cranked his stereo up, filling the cabin with 80's heavy metal. Ozzy Osbourne's *Crazy Train* blared as the Investigator relegated herself to studying the passing landscape and hoping her backup plan would work.

She didn't mind the music by any means, though it seemed disjointed for the pleasant landscape of rural North Dakota.

Flat plains morphed into rolling hills peppered with wind farms. Fields of brilliant, yellow canola formed hundreds of acres of broad canvases framed by verdant, narrow strips of lush grass. Crops of young sunflowers turned to face the sun as it moved across the sky.

Vast prairie potholes served as basins in which the spring rains collected with nowhere to escape. Those cattail-lined ponds were magnets for countless geese, ducks, gulls, and pelicans.

Ember got excited when she saw buffalo grazing in a pasture along Highway 23 and pointed them out to Dennis. He was far less enthused by her finding than she was.

"Where to now?" Her driver growled.

Ember glanced at the digital readout on his dash. "We have another 45 minutes before the scheduled meeting. I could fancy a bite, how about you?"

He muttered, "There's a café."

"Oh, I don't know about you, but I wouldn't mind an adult beverage with lunch." Ember acted apathetic. "Looks like there's a bar right over there."

Dennis said nothing, but the Suburban turned towards the bar.

Now, to get a message to Alarik by way of Anna.

After 45 minutes of blaring classic metal riffs in an enclosed vehicle, it was an abrupt transition to the twangy country-western sound in the bar. The Grub and Pub was notably empty, except for the bartender—a bartender who was not Anna.

Ember chose a seat, but Dennis continued walking. "Gotta go drain the dragon," he explained.

"Delightful."

The bartender wandered over to her table. "What can I get you?"

"Menus, please. And, I don't see Anna." Ember surveyed the room. "Is she in back somewhere?"

"Anna? Oh, no she had to take the afternoon off." The man scratched his stubbled chin with the edge of a small, laminated menu before setting it down on the table. "I'm filling in for her. She had some sort of family thing she had to deal with."

Bloody hell. Time to adapt. Ember took a quick glance at the menu. "You know what, I'll just have a bottle of water and a plate of chips, please. I guess I'm not that hungry after all. I'll be right back."

Ember quickly left the bar, pulling out the burner cell phone from her purse as she did. She redialed Alarik's number and squinted at the bright sunshine as the line rang softly in her ear. The prairie wind tugged at her hair and blew dust in her face. Her eyes watered as she unblinkingly watched the front door, expecting Dennis to emerge at any moment.

Her call went to Alarik's voicemail.

"Shite. Um, this is Ember. Ember Wright. I'm in Plaza, but

I'm not alone. They've sent someone to babysit me. We'll have to—"

The bar's door opened. Ember quickly snapped the phone shut and stuffed it into her purse.

"What're you doing out here?" Dennis growled.

Ember blinked in the sunlight and could see the changeling's badger subform was irritated. "I just needed to get some air. And...um...to get away from that music for a moment. Honestly, I don't know how anyone can listen to such depressing songs."

Dennis simply shrugged. He held the door open for her, though she suspected it wasn't out of newfound courteousness.

He washed a greasy burger and onion rings down with a pint of tap beer while she nursed her bottled water and a small bag of Ruffles, served to her on a ceramic plate. *I ask for chips, he brings me crisps.*

They were back in the SUV when he asked, "Where's your appointment?"

"It's just outside of town. A...let's see..." Ember pulled the legal pad from her satchel. She made a show of flipping through her notes until she found what she was looking for. "A Ronald and Muriel Schmitt. Changelings." She gave him directions as he drove. *We're committed now.*

The wind seemed ever brisker as they drove into the Schmitt family farm. Several pickups were parked in a row in front of the house. An American flag whipped and snapped noisily on an aluminum flagpole surrounded by freshly mowed mixed prairie grass. Several puddles of mud were in varying states of evaporation throughout the yard.

"Is it always this windy here?" Ember repurposed a rubber band from her census packet, using it to keep her blonde mane in a hasty ponytail.

Dennis snorted. "What, this little breeze? It's nothing."

As they exited the SUV, a large German Shepherd ran up, barking loudly. Ember closed her eyes and realized it was simply a dog—not a changeling. She wasn't sure why this surprised her, but it did. She shifted her satchel to her back so she could lean down to pet the animal, digging her fingers into its deep coat. She cooed, "Oh, you're a pretty baby. Yes, you are! What's your name?"

"She's Lucky." A familiar voice answered. "And who are you?"

Ember looked up to see Alarik watching Dennis from the porch. His thumbs were hooked in the front pockets of his blue jeans, which he wore overtop brown leather cowboy boots. The sleeves of his collared plaid shirt were rolled up above his elbows. She resisted the impulse to whistle. *He cleans up nice.*

Without missing a beat, Ember extended her hand and a wink, hoping he would catch it. "I'm Ember Wright, and this is my driver, Smiley."

Alarik shook Ember's hand, studying her briefly. "Nice to meet you. I'm Rik." He then glanced at Dennis, who didn't need to walk up the last porch step to match Alarik's height.

"Dennis," the man said simply as he shook Alarik's hand.

Lucky let out a bark as she leaped up the stairs and forced herself between Alarik and Dennis. The dog bared her teeth at the bearded man and growled low.

"Lucky! Down, girl." This new voice belonged to an older version of Alarik. The same square jaw, dark steely eyes, weather-worn face. He had less hair and it was greyer, but there was no doubt that this was the patriarch of the family.

Ember blinked and identified him as a changeling grey wolf. She couldn't help but notice that the man's wolf subform had the same distrustful expression as Lucky showed toward Dennis. *I'm liking this family already.*

The dog stepped back obediently, but she never took her eyes off Dennis. The low rumble in her chest didn't cease, either.

"I'm Ronald. You needed a driver to find us?" The elder Schmitt raised an eyebrow.

"Special circumstances," Dennis grinned. "She's a blonde, and a woman, *and* from England to boot. She'd get lost trying to find her way out of a parking lot. Am I right?"

Ember was surprised when Dennis answered with more than a grunt. Unfortunately, she wasn't surprised by the content of his response. Neither of the Schmitts so much as cracked a smile at Dennis's misogynistic joke, but that didn't stop him from laughing loudly.

"Hmm. Right." Ronald exchanged a look with Alarik, then glanced at Ember. "Well, everyone's waiting inside." He held the door open for her and stood back.

Ember gripped her satchel and smiled at Ronald. "Thank you. Um...but...everyone?"

She soon discovered who "everyone" was: Anna and Alarik of course, but also Muriel (Ronald's wife, a grizzly bear changeling), Boniface (Ronald's brother, whose subform was a red fox), Stephanie (Arnold's wife, a mink), and her twin children, Maxim and Marta (who at ten years old had not yet reached their Manifestation Day). It was a veritable Schmitt family gathering, it seemed.

But no Arnold Schmitt.

"I thought this was supposed to be an interview with Ronald and Muriel," Dennis folded his arms as he stood in the doorway of the living room. "Not a whole clan."

Ember shot a glare at Dennis. "And I thought that I was the one doing the interview, not my driver. So, I guess that means we're both disappointed today."

"Cute. Have you two been married long?" Boniface and his fox subform grinned in unison.

Dennis snorted. "Me? To *her?* Never in a million years."

Ember rolled her eyes, "Oh come now, sweetheart. I know I'm repugnant, but let's not make a scene."

Chuckles emerged from the Schmitt family, evolving into full laughter when Dennis scowled.

He may be a mountain, but his ego is fragile. Ember smiled at the family as she pulled the binder and legal pad from her satchel. "Since you're all here, I will take advantage and include each of you in my census audit. That is if you don't mind?"

They didn't mind. Stephanie sent Maxim and Marta outside to play. Ember asked the same boring boilerplate set of questions as she had during the two interviews in Minot earlier that day. Dennis sat against the wall and worked on his crossword puzzle, a scowl affixed to his face.

The Schmitts indulged Ember's charade, much to her relief. Still, she kept wondering when Arnold would walk in so she could meet him. Barring that, she tried to think of a way to get her babysitter to leave the room so she could just ask about Arnold.

"I should go check on the kids," Anna announced. The woman glanced at Ember, her head turning to match her gaze a moment later. Ember thought she noticed Anna's eagle subform wink at her. A short while later, Anna returned. "I'm sorry to interrupt you—Ember, is it? Can I borrow your driver for a second? The kids were throwing mud at each other, and your windshield is all splattered. I'll hook up the garden hose and help you wash it off."

Dennis left in a huff. After he stormed past Anna, she looked straight at Ember and gave a wink. There was no mistaking it this time.

As soon as Dennis and Anna were out of the house, Ember blurted out, "I'm so sorry about this guy. I don't know how much Rik has told you, but I'm more convinced than ever that someone at the embassy is trying to keep me from discovering the truth."

Ember met each family member's gaze as she talked. She had to convince them of her sincerity.

It was Ronald who spoke. "He's told us everything. And for better or worse, we believe you. I don't know how much you'll be able to do for my boy, but it's nice to meet a mage who actually gives a damn about us."

"I don't know how much time we have," Ember admitted as she pointed a thumb over her shoulder. "I'd really like to meet Arnie now."

Alarik directed his question to Stephanie. "Do you mind if I take her upstairs to show her?"

Stephanie bit her lip and nodded twice. She looked like she was doing all she could to keep from crying. "Just...just keep it quick."

Ember followed Alarik down a hall adorned with family portraits and up carpeted stairs to the second floor. The man walked with an easy lope, lighter on his feet than his size would suggest. Beneath her feet, on the other hand, the floorboards creaked with each step she took.

"He has good days when he can get outside. He'll ride along with me to well sites and help me with projects." Alarik's voice got quieter as they approached a closed bedroom door. "Then he has...shitty days. Where he refuses to get out of bed and he just sleeps."

Alarik placed his hand on the door handle and whispered. "He's having one of those days."

Ember wasn't sure what she would see when she followed Alarik into the dim bedroom. The curtains were closed, letting only a hint of the bright sunlight in. A man laid on his side, clutching a pillow against his chest.

"Arnie," Alarik whispered. "Arnie, there's someone who wants to meet you."

A pathetic whimper left Arnold's throat, but he rolled over to face them. His face was pale, his hair was thin, and he trembled constantly. The look in his eyes revealed that he was in a state of incredible misery. Arnold's aura was weak and twisted, distorted into itself like knots in a rope.

She had never seen anyone so sad, so pitiable. Ember looked away and was ashamed for it. When she looked back, she closed her eyes and focused on Arnold's subform so she could gauge its health, though she suspected that it would as pained and sorrowful as the changeling's human form.

Try as she may, Ember could not see Arnold's subform. It was as though the changeling's animal side was stripped away from him completely.

13

CASUAL INTERROGATIONS

It was early evening when Dennis dropped Ember off at her apartment building. The wind had waned, making for a pleasant early summer evening to wrap up the hectic day.

As she rode the elevator up to the third floor, Ember couldn't help but replay the sight of Arnold Schmitt's twisted aura. She'd never seen anything like it. The fact that his animal subform didn't even exist—that it was somehow taken from him—explained a lot in the way of why he was having trouble functioning in everyday life.

"He hasn't been able to change since he was recovered from the Mandaree fog. It's tearing him up." Alarik told her in the hallway after introducing her to his tormented brother. "His animal form is a coyote. Same as mine. He says it's run away and he can't call it back."

She recalled how Alarik winced with that admission. He had swallowed hard and looked at her with wet eyes when he asked, "Can you help him?"

"I don't know. But I'll try." Ember whispered the promise to herself as the elevator doors opened.

Her neighbor, M. Anderle, had another package waiting in front of his apartment door. This time, it was a bulky envelope with no return address. Her Investigator's curiosity had her wondering what her neighbor was like and when she would see him. That incessant curiosity had earned her the nickname "Miss Doosinspect" from her Year Four teacher, Mrs. Oderman. *Early signs of an Investigator in the making, I suppose.*

In her own apartment, she rifled through the refrigerator and then the cabinets. Though she had purchased groceries, there was one critical item she couldn't find in the store: her comfort food.

"What kind of place doesn't stock Marmite? Uncivilized, that's what it is," she complained to her fridge. When It didn't answer, she swung the door shut and reached for the embassy-provided cell phone in her purse. She needed to make an emergency call.

"Wright residence."

"Mummy. I hope I didn't wake you."

"Darling, not at all. Your father and I have only returned from a little outing with friends." Her father's voice rose in the background, followed by her mother's muffled response. "I don't know, Olly. She hasn't said, and I haven't asked yet."

"Asked what?" Ember balanced the cell phone with a shrugged shoulder as she filled a Styrofoam container with tap water. It was one of the containers of microwaveable ramen noodles she bought yesterday. Though it was labeled with a foreign name, it was essentially the same flavored Pot Noodles that she lived on back home.

"Your father wants to know if you're still planning on coming home?"

"About that." Ember gave the gaping maw of the microwave an offering: the Styrofoam cup with its paper lid peeled back. She closed the door and tapped the keypad, its high-pitched chime betraying her culinary actions.

"Emberly, are you eating those horrible noodle cups again?" Her mom scolded, "You know you can't live on those things. You'll positively atrophy."

Ember couldn't help but smile at the familiar chiding. "Yes, Mum. And they're Pot Noodles. Food of the gods, really. Anyway, I decided to stay in the colony a bit longer. I was just a little stressed and homesick when I phoned last. I've got a job to do, and I will see it through."

"Very good, darling." Benedette repeated the conversation to Oliver. "I told your father that you'd probably change your mind after a day or two. It's not you to flee trouble, after all."

"Yes, Mum. You know me well." The microwave beeped happily, announcing that the offering was ready. "I've got to go, but there was another reason I rang you. I have a favor to ask. It's vitally important. Critical, really."

Benedette grew serious. "I'm listening, Emberly."

"Would you please send me a box of Marmite, post haste? If I'm to stay, I'll need my victuals. The people at the grocer didn't even know what I was talking about when I asked them. Can you believe such nonsense?"

Her mother sighed. "You can be such a dramatic brat, daughter."

"Yes, I suppose that's true. Does that mean you'll help me with this vital procurement?"

"I'll pass along your request for procurement from the resident bureaucrat."

"Oh goody! Please tell Daddy 'cheers and kisses' from me."

"Goodnight, Emberly."

Ember smiled at the feigned exasperation she heard in her mother's voice. When Benedette Wright trotted out the faux formalities, Ember knew she could expect her wish to be granted.

"And now, it's your turn." Ember licked her lips and stirred in the packet of flavoring. It may not have been her Pot Noodles, but this imposter would do just fine after an exhausting day.

While she messily slurped her feast, Ember dug through her purse, cleaning out a couple convenience store receipts, paperclips, and a candy wrapper. She found a business card and smiled at it.

Her phone was still warm from the previous conversation. She dialed the number penned on the back of the business card.

The phone rang just twice before a man answered. "This is Coop."

"Hello, Cooper." Ember smiled then, a game forming in her head. "This is Cooper Severson?"

"It is, yes. Who am I speaking with?"

"Cooper Severson, Detective with the Minot Police Department?" Ember read the card with a formal tone.

"The same." Cooper's voice sounded slightly less friendly. "Who's calling?"

"Oh, I just have one question for you. One terribly important question." She could almost feel him holding his breath. Ember spoke now like a TV game show announcer. "Detective Cooper, for one *million* dollars, why is Minot called the Magic City?"

He hesitated for a few seconds, then blurted, "Ember? Is that you?"

A giggle erupted from her throat before she could suppress it. *Great, now I sound like a schoolgirl.*

"Ember, you little shit. You had me going there."

"Little shit! Really, manners Coop." Ember grinned through her lecture.

"In 1886, the Great Northern Railroad stopped in what was to be Minot." Cooper spoke as though he had been practicing this for days, which Ember supposed he probably had. "A tent town sprung up, almost overnight. Like magic. That's when the nickname formed, and 'Magic City' persists to this day."

She laughed. "Have you been going mad, holding that in, yeah?" *The Druws who discovered the Ley Line here were nothing if not blindingly clever in creating this cover story.*

"Well...yes. It's about time you called. I don't know if I could have lasted much longer. I'm probably going to get a brain tumor from all the stress you've put me through. How are you finding the Magic City, speaking of which? Everyone treating you well at your new job?"

It took Ember a moment to realize he was referring to the spa. "Oh, yeah. Yes, it's all been fine. Lovely people there, really. It's quite a nice facility. Very posh."

"Posh," he repeated, then chuckled. "Sounds like just the sort of place I probably wouldn't visit. So, to what do I owe this call, lovely lady?"

"I just wanted to hear a friendly voice, I suppose." She dropped the empty Styrofoam container in the trash and stretched out on the sofa, laying on her back. "In addition to learning the answer to that million-dollar question, naturally."

"Naturally. So, when can I expect the check for one *million* dollars?" He emphasized the word, just as she had.

"How do they say it? 'The check is in the mail?' Yeah, so if it doesn't arrive, do blame the post."

They talked for the better part of an hour. Ember's cheeks began to grow sore from the constant smiling, the banter between them.

It seemed too soon when he said, "I hate to end this chat, but I've got a place I need to be in a few minutes. I would be tempted to invite you along, but it wouldn't be an appropriate first date. It's a get together with some buddies. It's for a friend of ours, who passed a couple years ago."

First date. Ember blushed, just hearing him make such a pronouncement. She admonished herself for latching on to that part of his statement. "I'm so sorry to hear of your loss, Coop."

"Thanks. It's been a while, but Jacob touched a lot of lives. He was my partner when I first made grade. I learned more from my brief time working with him than from the academy, any workshops, or conferences before or since. It was a big loss to the department—hell, the whole community of Minot."

Ember sat up on the couch and shifted the phone to her other ear. "What did he die from, if you don't mind my asking?"

Cooper exhaled. "It was a cancer. Pancreatic. Moved quickly, and there's no cure I guess."

"That's pretty rough."

"Yeah, it is." Cooper sighed. "Jacob was so good at interviewing suspects. He called them 'casual interrogations' where he would make the suspect feel so at ease with him, they started thinking of him as their friend. Before they knew it, they had hung themselves—metaphorically, of course. Defense attorneys hated him."

"That's a skill that's hard to teach." Ember quickly added, "I mean, I assume."

"It is. There are cases to this day where I find myself wishing I could just ask Jacob for his advice. Just to ask him for guidance on the hard cases. You know, like...if I could just talk to his ghost."

Ember felt like a lightning bolt just shot through the ceiling of her apartment and grounded with her. She felt her pulse quicken. She stood up at once, the cell phone nearly slipping from her grip. *Brilliant!*

SHE COULDN'T BE SURE SHE WASN'T BEING WATCHED, THOUGH she made a point of closing her eyes and scanning every bird, cat, and dog she jogged past. *So far, so good.*

The toil of the long day had her both physically and emotionally exhausted. Dusk was settling in, and she had initially planned for a hot shower and her warm bed. Yet, now she was running with vigor, reenergized by the inspired suggestion her NonDruw friend had unknowingly instilled in her.

She returned a friendly wave from a young couple walking a Beagle on a leash. Beneath the overhead lamps lining the paved walking path, she could see their warm smiles. The man offered an obvious observation, "Gorgeous evening for a run!"

"Gorgeous. Right." She managed to agree between breaths before she was out of earshot.

The nearest graveyard was about a mile south of her apartment, and she soon arrived. The well-kept grounds of Rosehill Cemetery were enclosed by a low chain-link perimeter fence, separated by stone gate columns facing the street. Cottonwood, ash, and spruce trees grew in copses throughout the acreage. Straight, paved lanes formed a grid throughout the 50-acre parcel.

"Now to test my luck," Ember exhaled as she slowed to a walk.

She paced up and down each neat row, softly calling out as her hand contacted each headstone just briefly. “I’m calling for a Malvern. Any Malvern will do, please. Is there a Malvern here?”

If anyone living saw her, they might be forgiven for thinking that they were watching an obsessive-compulsive person. Ember walked between each headstone, touching two at a time when she could, as she called out. *I’m not actually crazy, but I must sure look the part.*

She recalled the first time she talked with a ghost. It was shortly after she began working with Wallace as a Novice Investigator, on one of their first cases in fact. She had accidentally called upon one Frederick Kempster, who she later learned was famous for being the tallest man alive—or rather, who once was alive. Even in that accidental call, that giant’s ghost proved helpful all those dozen years ago.

Wallace was never one to allow a latent talent to go to waste. They didn’t have many homicide cases, but when they did, her ability to call upon the deceased was utterly invaluable. They still had to form a proper chain of evidence to cover the fact that they had a “cheat code” in Ember, but it wasn’t so difficult to work backward and find tangible clues when you’ve got the victim helping you out.

Ember was at the last row of grave markers in the third cluster she searched, still with no spirit answering to her call for a mage. If she didn’t find one tonight, she would need to go to the next cemetery on the map. Just then, a familiar, faint shimmer formed in the air near an old stone cross. The temperature dropped appreciably, and goosebumps formed on Ember’s skin.

The ghost's form was faint, and its voice was a hoarse whisper. The halting whisper it offered was like nails on a chalkboard. "Who...disturbs...the dead?"

Ember winced. Calling on the ghost of someone who was recently deceased felt different than when the ghost was long since buried. With the latter, the experience was so much more unpleasant. There was a sort of temporal disconnect, she surmised, with the passing ages. *I suppose if I was dead a long time, I'd be confused too.*

"I do. I call you." Ember tried to sound more confident than she was. "Are you a Malvern?"

"Let...the dead...rest." The ghost hissed its advice.

The hair on the back of her neck stood, but that might have been from the chilling air temperature. Ember hugged herself and wished she would have thought to bring a jacket. "You will answer my question. All of my questions."

The ghost hissed its acquiescence. "Malvern...yes."

"Brilliant. I'm looking to speak with a deceased Investigator. Preferably one which was high-ranking when he or she was alive. A Senior Investigator, if you please. Do you know where one might be buried?"

The ghost's form was less abstract now. It began to coalesce into a form resembling something humanoid. Ember glanced at its headstone and saw the name:

Dr. Rufus James Corwin
1832-1901

Ember knew that the birth date was likely fake; this mage

was probably closer to 200 years old when he died, assuming he died of natural causes. It wouldn't do to let that truth be etched in stone, however—not where NonDruws would see it.

"Investigator?" The ghost of Dr. Rufus James Corwin hissed. "Not...an Inquisitor?"

"An Inquisitor? I'm not sure what you're going on about, Rufus James Corwin." Ember purposely used the ghost's name. Doing so always seemed to help spirits gather themselves to the present. *Or future, from their perspective.*

The ghost's form materialized further. She could see his face, the turn-of-the-century suit he was buried in. The vacant, lifeless eyes made her shudder, though she'd seen it countless times before.

"Please answer me, Rufus James Corwin." Ember kept her arms crossed and she tapped her ASICS running shoes against the stone cross, as though that would somehow encourage the spirit to comply.

"Inquisitor. Someone...higher ranked. As...you asked." The ghost of Rufus Corwin spoke in halting hisses, though his mouth never moved.

Ember tapped the fingers of her right hand against her forehead, the percussion knocking loose the line of questions she needed to ask this stubborn spirit. "OK, fine. Inquisitor. I suppose that's what you called Investigators in your day? No matter. Tell me who was the most senior...Inquisitor, as you say, buried in the Magic City."

"Grand...Inquisitor...Barnaby...Harrison. Not...in Minot. His remains...were in...Surrey. Died...a few years...before me. His was...a tragic...construction...accident."

Ember frowned. *Grand Inquisitor? Was that what they called Senior Investigators back in Rufus's time?* "Barnaby Harrison. Brilliant. I don't know where Surrey is, but I will find it. I hope he will prove worth the trouble of tracking down."

The ghost stared at her with vacant eyes.

"Thank you for your assistance." Ember waved farewell at the spirit. "Rest now, Rufus James Corwin."

The ghost of Rufus James Corwin sighed. Its periwinkle translucent form faded until it disappeared. Where his silhouette was, dozens of fireflies flickered, briefly forming the shape of a man. Then their lights went out and Ember stood alone in the dark graveyard.

14

JEST WITH THE DEAD

It was a new one, this spy following Ember. A second changeling spy.

She was out for her early morning jog, after yet another rough night of poor sleep. Ember needed to work through her options, especially since she no longer had a car of her own to use—not to mention the fact that she was being watched, constantly.

Case in point: the appearance of a not-too-subtle turkey vulture in downtown Minot. The large bird had an impressive wingspan which made it impossible to hide when it lifted off. The vulture had done just that when she was doing her stretches in the parking lot. A quick blink was all she needed to confirm that it was a changeling. She supposed the buzzard thought it was being clever by circling high above her on unseen thermals as she jogged.

Ember should have been insulted by the lack of subtlety. Director Elton Higginbotham was having her tailed so overtly, choosing such a changeling as this. *He still thinks I'm under his spell, so there's no need to be so cautious with his spies.*

Yet, the man clearly had enough foresight to keep tabs on her, despite believing his spell had taken root. She made a mental note not to underestimate her foe.

The burner phone was tucked inside her fanny-pack, and she intended on using it away from her apartment—which could well be bugged. She just needed to figure out who she was going to call.

Since the chilly meeting with the ghost of Rufus James Corwin last night, Ember had been formulating her next move. It was an inconvenience that this Barnaby Harrison was buried in a small town ten miles outside of Minot. It didn't help that she had no car.

She thought about jogging there, but she would be spotted and followed for a certainty. This morning's spy affirmed that suspicion.

She could rent a car, but that, too, would be difficult to conceal from Higginbotham's spies. She wasn't even entirely sure she would be eligible to rent a vehicle without an American driver's license.

So, that left her with the unattractive choice of calling in someone to help ferry her around. There was Cooper Severson; Coop knew the local area well, and he had already hinted at wanting to spend time with her. Maybe she could frame the request as a date?

But, Coop was a detective and a NonDruw at that. She couldn't take the chance that he would figure out that she was hiding something from him. No, Coop was not an option.

Ember thought about the other helpful local who had shown an eagerness to help: the manager at the Magic City Spa. Josette was privy to the Druwish world as she was a halfling herself. *That doesn't mean she can be trusted, though.*

She jogged through the windy riverfront trails of Oak Park. She wasn't the only runner enjoying the crisp summer morning, but she was reasonably sure that she was the only Druw in the tidy, green park nestled in the oxbows of the Souris River. The jogging trail weaved between cottonwood and elm trees, and she inhaled the pleasant scent of morning dew. She realized then that she was beneath a dense canopy, and that she couldn't see the circling buzzard high above her—and that he could not see her. *Time to make a quick call.*

Ember chose a massive Y-shaped cottonwood away from the path, where she could keep watch while she made her call. She flipped the burner phone open, and almost without thinking redialed a recent number. *I guess I choose you.*

Alarik picked up on the third ring.

"It's Ember. I hope I didn't wake you?"

"Oh, hi. No, I get up at 4:30." Alarik cleared his throat. "What can I do for you, Ember?"

The way he said her name made Ember close her eyes. An involuntary smile formed on her lips. She imagined him on the other end, perhaps sipping coffee as he made himself breakfast of eggs and bacon. She had to shake her head to remind herself that she couldn't risk a lengthy call—not when she knew she was being followed. "I have a huge favor to ask of you, Rik. They took my ride, and I'm being followed and watched constantly. But, I need to get to Surrey to meet a contact. Someone who might be able to help with your brother's case."

It was rotten to lie to him, but Ember didn't know how much she could trust Alarik. Certainly, she couldn't tell him that she was intending on talking with a man who had been dead for over a century. *The less he knows, the better for us both.*

"When?"

Ember stepped around the tree's trunk, surveying the park, looking for signs that the buzzard may have landed. "Tonight, if at all possible."

Alarik cleared his throat again. After a moment, he said, "Okay. I'll pick you up at six tonight."

"Thank you. Oh, and we can't meet at my apartment, or we'll be followed. I was thinking I could go for an evening run, and meet you someplace where we might lose my spy?"

"You're staying at one of the apartments that the Viceroyalty owns, right? The building with the bakery downstairs?"

"Yes, in Number 302. But—"

"I know how I can get you out of there." Alarik sounded confident. "Just trust me."

EMBER SPENT THE MORNING IN HER OFFICE AT THE EMBASSY, trying to appear busy as she waited for the day to end.

Dennis interrupted her thoughts from time to time to ask for hints to the crossword he was working on. She would offer the answer when she had it. He would grunt his appreciation.

It was Josette who once more came to the rescue, however unintentionally. The phone on Ember's desk rang, and it was the spa manager on the other end.

"I know you're probably super busy today," Josette said. "But is there any chance I could get you to come into the spa today? I'm already short-handed, and I had a massage therapist call in sick at the last minute. We've got clients scheduled."

The prospect of breaking up her day—and being away from Dennis for that matter—appealed greatly. "Sure, I can help."

"You're sure? I'm not taking you away from anything pressing?"

Ember chuckled, "Nothing that can't wait. When do you need me?"

"Honestly, in a half hour if you could?" Josette's voice breathed with relief. "I really owe you."

Downstairs, Dennis insisted that he needed to follow Ember into the spa, but it was Josette who stood up to the bearded mountain. "You are not going to be anywhere near clients. You can wait in the lobby if you insist on being such a pest. I'd better not hear that you are bothering Ami, either. Jesus, I mean really, is Ember a prisoner or something?"

In the end, Josette got her way, and Dennis sulked in the lobby's reception area. Ember couldn't help but feel smug. *Whatever disturbing games the powerful Elton Higginbotham was playing throughout the rest of the building, on this floor at least it was Josette Hanson who called the shots.*

Ember spent the rest of the day working on clients. Though she had to concentrate on muscle groups and at times carry on conversations with the chattier sort of customers, for the most part, she could let her mind relax while her upper body worked.

Most of her day's clients were NonDruws, paying to have their muscle tension eased either by order of their chiropractor or as a treat to themselves.

Ember did have one Druw client though; a Malvern artist who had injured her arm while unloading crates of her paintings. The injury was significant enough that if it would have happened to a NonDruw, they would have been forced to undergo surgery and follow up therapy. As a Druw, however, the woman was eligible for special treatment.

As the woman sat reclined in a padded chair, Ember slipped on a ring. The ring was too large, made in a universal size, but its purpose was the large gem attached to it. It was an icy blue Leystone, fully charged from the Ley Line deep in the subbasement of the building. With its power and a simple trapezius and deltoid muscle massage, Ember helped the Malvern woman heal from her injury within minutes.

"Like new again," Ember smiled at the artist.

"You're a wonderful healer." The woman returned the smile, though she was looking at her arm as she flexed the repaired muscles.

"Thank you, but I'm no Healer." Ember wiggled her fingers, displaying the crystal held in the prongs. The Leystone's blue hue was slightly diminished from what it was minutes earlier—evidence of its power discharge. "It's all about the mana."

"I wish I could just wear one of those all the time." The woman continued smiling and flexing as she stood up. "I think I'd be invincible if I did!"

Ember pulled the ring off and placed it back in its numbered case for Security to retrieve. Though she hadn't been sleeping and she had felt drained after calling up the ghost last night, she now felt fully refreshed. *I think I'll ask Josette to put me on the schedule more often.*

ALARIK ARRIVED A QUARTER TO SIX. THOUGH SHE WAS expecting him, the knock on the door startled Ember.

"I'm a little anxious," Ember explained as she let him into her apartment.

He appraised the apartment from just inside the doorway, lifting his head as he breathed in. "Nice place. Roomy. How many people are living here?"

"How many? This is my apartment alone. Whatever makes you think I have flatmates?"

Alarik lifted his head once, using his chin to gesture toward the kitchen. "Stack of dishes in the sink, overflowing garbage can, laundry on the couch. Must be, oh, three or four people living here?"

Ember rolled her eyes and pushed on his chest with her hand. "Let's go."

"What, I don't get to meet your roommates?" Alarik grinned wolfishly as he stepped back into the hall, allowing himself to be pushed by the short woman. "Nice white lace bra, by the way."

"Excuse me?" Ember's jaw dropped.

"You had it hanging from the doorknob of your bathroom in there." He continued grinning. "I couldn't help but notice."

Ember clicked her apartment door shut behind them and shook her blonde mane. She marched toward the elevator.

"You're going the wrong way," Alarik said in a hushed tone. He led her to the stairwell. "This way."

Ember hesitated at the top of the stairs. The old staircase was narrow and steep, as was common over a hundred years ago for an old former industrial building as this once was. *Built for mountain goats.* She crossed her arms. "I'm not going down those bloody stairs."

Alarik stopped, already five steps down. He looked up at her, confused. "Why the hell not?"

"We've a perfectly good elevator."

"Yes, but I'm taking you to the basement," Alarik explained. "There's a passage beneath the streets where we can slip out unseen. The elevator needs a maintenance worker's key to go to the basement. Unless you have such a key?"

Ember shook her head.

"Well, then..." Alarik's voice trailed off purposely.

Ember clutched the handrail with both hands and stepped gingerly down the stairs.

The man watched with growing consternation. "Are you going to be alright?"

"I *hate* steep stairs. Especially going down bloody stairs." Ember glared at him. "I'm not the most graceful person if you must know. I have a habit of falling, and it would really be inconvenient if I twisted my ankle, yeah?"

Wordlessly, Alarik stood next to Ember. He gripped her arm firmly and guided her, one step at a time. She was perspiring by the time she reached the chilly basement.

"You really weren't shitting about being afraid of stairs."

"No...shitting...here." Ember breathed as she shook her head.

"Minot used to be known as Little Chicago, back during the Prohibition Era," Alarik explained as he led her by flashlight through a chilly subterranean tunnel. "These tunnels were used by bootleggers to get around the downtown area. I'd imagine in the winter it was especially handy."

"How do you know all this?"

"You remember meeting my Uncle Boni? At my folks' house? Well, he was a moonshiner back in the day. He made a decent living at it, too, for a while."

The musty tunnel forked a few hundred feet in. He chose the left passage. Ember had difficulty even sensing direction and realized it wouldn't be difficult to get disoriented underground. She shivered at the thought of being lost in this place. She shivered again when she saw mice running along the edge of the curved walls, fleeing the bright flashlight.

"Just a few steps upward now," Alarik said, glancing over his shoulder at her. The flashlight only partially illuminated his face, but she could see he was sincere when he asked if she was doing well.

"I am. Going up stairs doesn't bother me too much. I've only rarely fallen *up* stairs."

A yellow-painted door was partially ajar at the top of the set of stairs. The door's hinges squeaked loudly in protest.

Alarik whispered, "Shhhh! I'll feed you some squirrel piss next time."

"Bloody hell?" Ember frowned. "Please tell me you're not talking to me."

"No, no. I'm talking to the door."

"Oh, well that makes more sense." Ember scoffed. "What's squirrel piss supposed to be?"

"That's what my Uncle Boni likes to call WD-40."

"WD-40? Like, a lubricant?"

"Yup," Alarik said, his voice still hushed. "But between having to explain it to you and the way you say 'lubricant,' the joke isn't as funny."

Ember smiled. "You might consider that it wasn't too funny to start, yeah?"

They emerged in a large, unlit room. Rows of banquet tables were lined with steel folding chairs.

Alarik clicked his flashlight off and whispered, "Nobody should be here right now, but let's not take any chances." He took her hand and led her through the darkened building, up yet more narrow stairs, and finally through a steel door to the outside street. He seemed to have no trouble finding his way in the near-dark. The flashlight had been more for her benefit, given the superior night vision his canine eyes afforded him.

He unlocked and opened the door to a large Ford Super Duty pickup parked at the curb. The pickup's front end was mounted with the biggest grill guard Ember had ever seen. She accepted his help getting up into the pickup.

As he walked around to the driver's side, Ember glanced back at the building they had just exited. It was a large church, with a white-capped steeple barely visible from her angle.

"St. Leo's Catholic Church," he explained. "It'll be locked if we get back late, but I have a key. Are we going to be getting back late, you think?"

"I don't know. Probably, I suppose."

Surrey wasn't more than ten miles east of Minot, but she used the time to ask about him and his family. His was a farming family, and he seeded some acres of his own, along with helping his father and Uncle Boniface with their operations. Alarik never married ("no time," he explained). He spent most of his days building Schmitt Brothers Welding, plying his trade at job sites across northwestern North Dakota.

"I noticed that you had a different lorry with your welding tools," Ember said. "Business must be brisk to afford more than one?"

"Lorry?" Alarik scrunched up his nose and laughed. "We say, 'truck' here, Englishwoman. Or better still, 'pickup,' unless you're from the city. If you say 'lorry' you're talking about a woman."

"Mmhmm, I see. Just so we're reading from the same menu, you are lecturing an Englishwoman on...English? Is that about right?"

"Yup." He grinned wide, showing her his pearly white incisors. "Yup, that's about right."

She convinced Alarik to wait in his pickup a few hundred yards away from the cemetery's edge by telling him that she was meeting her contact for the first time. It wasn't a lie, not completely.

It would be a couple of hours before the sun set. She wouldn't have to call this particular ghost in the dark, nor be stuck communing with him in the same. Talking with dead people was one thing, but doing so while alone at night in a cemetery, that was something she preferred to avoid.

Ember found the headstone quickly enough. It was a prominent block of rock, framed by two junipers. The weathered, etched letters were rough but readable:

Barnaby Harrison
Died 1898

"Convenient that they left your birth date off, Mr. Harrison. No need to lie about it, this way." Ember traced the capitalized letters with her fingertips. She closed her eyes, breathed deeply, and muttered, "I hope you're easier to talk to than the last bloke. Please speak with me, Barnaby Harrison."

The first thing Ember noticed was the precipitous drop in

temperature. Though the evening sun still shone, it felt like she had just stepped into a walk-in freezer. She exhaled and saw her breath misting before her eyes. The golden-orange sunlight was joined by a shimmering blue-white fog around the grave site. Within the center of the fog, a man's silhouette formed.

"Tedious...girl." This ghost's voice was dismissive and unfriendly. If words could be formed by pouring coarse sand over a sheet of aluminum foil, this is what the spirit of Barnaby Harrison sounded like to Ember's ears.

"Mr. Harrison? Barnaby Harrison?" Ember cupped her sweating hands over her ears. *Bugger, it feels like my head is vibrating when he speaks.* "Barnaby Harrison, can you hear me, sir?"

"The dead...hear you...foolish girl. What right...have you... to call on me?" The lethargic voice had a bite to it, and it echoed in Ember's skull. The shimmering silhouette began to form details: a stout old man, dressed in a formal suit. His grey, woolen jacket was unbuttoned, revealing beneath it a brass-buttoned black vest to match his dress slacks. A necktie framed a white shirt, the collar which jutted up to meet the man's snowy mutton chops. His nose was prominent, and his brows formed a glare, though the man's eyes were completely transparent—she could see the trees behind him through those empty eye sockets. Topping Barnaby's head was a smart beaver skin hat with a pheasant feather tucked into its band.

Ember pressed her hands flat against her ears when he spoke. *This doesn't feel right. The power I feel from him. It's like he's in my bloody head.* "Oh, my god!" She hadn't intended to say that aloud.

"No, but...close enough, woman." Barnaby looked around the cemetery. "Where the hell...am I?"

Ember kept her hands over her ears, but she heard the metal-aggregate voice bounce across her eardrum just the same. *He's coalescing in form and voice much faster than Rufus did. All the more amazing for how long he has been dead.*

The ghost turned sharply to look at her. His voice boomed. "Little girl, do not...make me ask twice!"

"Surrey, sir!" Ember winced, and though she knew she was groveling, she couldn't help herself. "Surrey, North Dakota. You're in a cemetery, sir. You've been dead some 112 years."

The ghost looked then at his own grave marker. His transparent hand reached out for the stone. He did something then that in dozens—scores, even—of talks she had had with ghosts, Ember had never seen: he swept a leaf off the headstone with his fingers.

Ember's mouth was agape as she watched the translucent shape of a man walking casually around his grave site, inspecting the ground. He clapped his hands, and birds fled in response. It wasn't much, but the fact that he was able to directly interact with the physical world at all unsettled her greatly.

"Sir," Ember's mouth was dry and she had to swallow to form the words. "Mr. Harrison, sir, I really need your help."

The ghost swirled around and stepped up to her. The air grew colder still as he approached. Empty eye sockets glared down at her and the sound of pouring sand began again. "You! How dare you make demands of me, tart! Who taught you these parlor tricks? Answer me now!"

Ember shrank. She dropped her gaze and noticed his feet made impressions in the grass where he walked. She managed a hoarse whisper. "Nobody. Nobody taught me. I'm an Investigator. Please, sir, I need your help. I have no other Investigators I can trust. Not here, anyway."

The ghost's laughter echoed in Ember's head. "You really are a foolish little girl, if you confuse a Grand Inquisitor with a mere Investigator. The dead care not about the petty machinations of the living."

Ember looked up, forcing her eyes to meet his. She looked through the swirling fog where his eyes once were, mustered her courage, and said, "I care. And I need to ask you some questions."

The ghost grew with rage. Its frosty presence slammed into her. "Release me!"

She felt her eyes roll up into her head. A whimper forced its way from her lips. She stumbled backward, tripping against the uneven ground and falling onto her ass. She looked up to see the imposing ghost leering over her. Ember scrambled, crab-walking away from the enraged spirit. She backed up against the juniper's trunk. She rolled over and clung to the rough bark, breathing the tree's gin aroma as she involuntarily sobbed.

The fury of Barnaby's spirit spoke within her head. "You... will...release me, now!"

Ember opened her eyes and tears streamed down the side of her cheek. She looked over the cemetery, seeing the setting sun and wondering if it would be the last she would see. Far down the street, closer to the small town of Surrey, she saw the vehicle that delivered her to this hell. She thought of

Alarik, of his brother, and of their family and the nine other families affected by whatever happened to them nine years ago in Mandaree.

"No." She clutched the tree, using it to help steady her as her feet found purchase to stand. She said it louder now. "No, I will not release you, Barnaby Harrison."

The ghost screamed in her head. It swirled around her, its fury forming a whirlwind that transcended the plane of the dead to reach the physical dimension. Leaves and tiny, blue-grey berries blew off the juniper to rain over Ember's body. But she didn't back down. She didn't even blink.

"You will settle down now, Barnaby Harrison, and you will entertain my questions with honest answers. Do this, and I may release you. Fail, and I will keep you here, locked away from your eternal rest."

The ghost withdrew then with a shriek. "You wouldn't! You wouldn't curse one of your own to such a fate."

Ember canted her head. A resilient last tear dropped from her jaw when she said, "So we are peers now, is that right?"

The ghost's expression didn't change, but she was sure it scowled. "We are both Inquisitors, that much is undeniable."

"Good. That leads to my first question: why were Investigators called Inquisitors during your time."

The ghost canted his head and studied her. "You jest with the dead?"

"I won't jest with you, Barnaby. Serious inquiries only."

"There have always been Inquisitors. Three levels of Investigator, followed by Inquisitor, Grand Inquisitor, and Supreme Inquisitor. Only a Grand or higher can wake the dead." He peered at Ember and crossed his arms. "Especially one who has been dead for as long as I."

She combed her fingers through her hair, tugging twigs, needles, and juniper berries from her golden scalp. "There are only three ranks for Investigator, Barnaby."

The ghost scoffed. "Hogwash. You are beyond ill-informed, little girl."

"You're a very rude spirit." Ember flicked a juniper berry at the ghost. It sailed through the transparent form and ricocheted off his headstone. "Were you this rude when you were alive?"

"You call me rude? You, who breaks my eternal slumber, then threatens to imprison me?"

"Brilliant. Fair enough." Ember bit her lip and shrugged. "Moving right along. So, let's say there are six levels in the Investigator Track—"

"There are, little girl."

"If that were so, why has nobody heard of this?"

"Nobody living, perhaps," Barnaby growled. "In my time and back through history—back when the Druws descended from Celtic Druids in ancient times—always, all Mage Tracks had six levels. Tell me, little girl, why would it make more sense for the Investigator Track to have only three when all others have six?"

"I asked that of course when I was young. The answer is simple: Investigators work for the Druw High Council, serving the Council's Justice. The Investigator Track is not a fully-formed Mage Track as the Council collectively fills those roles."

The ghost laughed loudly. She knew only she could hear it, but that didn't stop her from looking around the cemetery, to be sure nobody else was listening.

"Lies. Whoever filled your pretty little skull with such lies is a buffoon." Barnaby walked through his headstone, waving his hands on either side, seemingly for his own amusement. "The Investigator Track is equal to all of the other Mage Tracks, combined. Inquisitors though...ah, Inquisitors serve nobody. We keep the balance of power, serving only justice. We seek out corruption and snuff it out before it takes root like a cancer."

Barnaby's empty eyes looked over to stare straight at Ember. "The Supreme Inquisitor sits at the head of the Druw High Council, keeping their power in check."

"No." Ember shook her head. "No, that can't be true. Investigators serve the High Council, enforcing its law for the good of Druwish people." Even as she uttered the common rationale, the words sounded hollow in her head. *Why haven't I questioned this with more insistence? Why hasn't anyone else?*

Night was settling in. Ember heard the songs of distant coyotes. *Coyotes. Alarik. Shite, he is still waiting for me!*

"I can't stay longer, Barnaby. I'm sorry that I will have to call upon you again soon. I have so many questions. More questions now than I had before."

Barnaby's growl was the sound of one piece of sandpaper slowly massaged against another.

"I know, I know," Ember sighed. "I will let you rest for now, but I will have to call you again. I'm sorry that you died in that construction accident. I wish you could somehow still be alive. I think things somehow might be different."

"Accident?" Barnaby leaned over Ember. "I died of no accident, little girl. I was pushed from a tall building. I know who pushed me, too."

15

IT WAS SUPPOSED TO BE ME

"EMBER, WHAT THE HELL?" ALARIK JUMPED OUT OF HIS PICKUP to meet her as she approached. "Are you okay? Did your contact beat you up?"

"I'm fine. Just...tired. Sorry it took so long." She could hear the weariness in her own voice. She was spent from the lengthy conversation with Barnaby. Calling on a spirit which had been at rest for 112 years took more mana than she had expected.

"Let's get you home." He didn't sound convinced by her explanation, but he didn't press, either.

Standing up to the ghost of a combative Inquisitor took everything Ember had. Her energy—both mana and physical—was drained. She laid her head against the tan leather headrest and stared out the side window.

"I suppose you won't tell me how it went?" Alarik drove west on Highway 2, his headlights illuminating the way. "Did you learn anything that can help my brother?"

Ember lolled her head lazily. "I'm sorry...I can't say. I'll have to meet with him again." She mentally went over the conversation with Barnaby, his declaration that he had been murdered. He couldn't remember the name of the man who killed him, but he remembered the man's face. It would come back to him, now that he was awakened. Barnaby declined to return his spirit to rest so that he could coalesce further and remember. Even in death, the Inquisitor was driven by the quest for justice.

It was just as well, as she would have needed to wake him when she visited him next. The act of calling upon a century-old spirit wasn't something she wanted to engage in any more than necessary. She hoped she would not need to speak with the ghost of Barnaby Harrison more than twice. *Rude old misogynistic bugger, that's what he is.*

"You're trembling, Ember." The concern in Alarik's observation was undeniable. "Let's stop to get something to eat before I take you home. Would that help?"

"I could eat," Ember admitted. "But I've got food at home."

He laughed. "Junk food, maybe. I saw your apartment, remember? Come on, my treat. Schatz's Crossroads is just up ahead to the left. It's a truck stop with a twenty-four-hour diner. It's rib-sticking good food."

"Something must be lost in translation, because rib-sticking doesn't sound terribly palatable, Rik."

She was hungrier than she thought, and the plate of hot food disappeared quickly. "Chicken fried steak" Alarik called it. *Whatever you want to call it, it made the trembling stop.*

Alarik sipped a ceramic mug of black coffee and watched her work on the mashed potatoes and gravy. "So, you can't tell me anything, huh? I'm just a chauffeur to you?"

Ember looked up, her mouth half stuffed. She shrugged apologetically and talked around her food. "Wish I could."

"So, why don't you? Don't you trust me?"

She swallowed. "I do. Sure. A little at a time. I trust you more today than I did yesterday. That's something, yeah?"

He shook his head and looked out at the brightly-lit parking lot, where semi-trucks lined up at the diesel fuel islands. "Unbelievable."

"Hey, you need to know that this thing...whatever it is...the less you know, the better. For you and for me."

"I want to help, Ember. I can do more than just drive you around." He lowered his voice and leaned toward the center of the table. "I know the other guys who were hired to go to Mandaree with Arnie."

"You do?"

He nodded once. "They know me, they trust me. A whole lot more than they would trust a cute Malvern stranger who wants to interrogate them with a bearded prick."

"Dennis was not my choice, you know that." Ember scraped the last of the mashed potatoes with the edge of her fork, blading them into a neat furrow. "But he truly is a bearded prick, you've got that part right."

Alarik continued his lobbying when they were back in his Ford. "All I'm saying is that you'd have a lot more luck getting face-to-face with these guys if I'm the one introducing you. He looked square at her before he started the vehicle. "I want to help."

Ember narrowed her gaze as she studied the man's aura. "Tell me why. Why do you want to help?"

"For my brother, of course." Alarik looked away from Ember's penetrating gaze and glanced at his dash as it lit up. The engine rumbled to life and the air conditioner kicked in with a soft hiss. "For Arnie."

Ember touched the back of his hand, stopping him as he prepared to pull the transmission out of Park. She said it quietly, hoping to reassure him. "Please tell me the truth, Rik."

He looked down at her hand, so small and soft against the back of his tanned, rough skin. "I'm telling you the truth."

"Not all of it. Or did you forget that I'm an Investigator?" She spoke so quietly, she wondered if he would even be able to hear her over the din of the beefy engine.

Alarik looked out his passenger window, opened his mouth, closed it. When he looked back at her, his eyes were wet. "Can we...can we just not right now? I'll get you home."

She briefly squeezed her hand around his wrist. "I need your help, Rik. But we need to trust one another if there's any chance of us helping Arnie."

He withdrew his hand from her grip and ran his fingers through his thick, shaggy hair. He said nothing for a full minute, but Ember knew to be patient. Finally, he said, "I've never told anyone this. The only one who knows is Arnie, and I don't even know that he remembers it."

Cool air blew softly from the pickup's round, silver-grey vents. It was fresh air chasing the cabin's trapped heat away.

Alarik breathed in deeply, held the air in his lungs, and then exhaled. He looked up at the headliner of his pickup's cabin, evidently unwilling to look at his confessor. "When the whole Mandaree Incident happened, it was all over the news. 'A toxic gas cloud,' they said. It made headlines all over the country throughout 2001. Nobody seemed to know what caused it, or if anyone was still alive beneath the cloud, or hell, whether it would spread. The whole area was quarantined off because anyone who tried to go in didn't come back out. Didn't matter if they wore hazmat suits or not. They just disappeared in the fog. This went on for a month or so."

"Then, sometime in February, someone from the Viceroyalty called me. Said they were looking for volunteers—changelings who were willing to earn some fast cash in service of the Druwish people. He rattled off some patriotic cheerleading speech, but wouldn't tell me anything more than that."

Alarik shook his head, remembering. "I was busy and wasn't interested, but I knew Arnie would be. He had two babies and a wife, and he was always short of cash. So, I gave the guy my brother's phone number."

"Who?" Ember felt goosebumps forming. "Who offered you this job?"

"I don't know," Alarik shook his head in frustration as he finally looked at her. His face was painted with grief. "I don't know, just some guy from the embassy I guess. But don't you get it? I need to help you, 'cause I need to make things right.

I was the one who he called, but I didn't go. I sent my brother instead."

"Arnie never should've gone." The man looked out the driver's side window, his focus lost in the beyond darkness. "It was supposed to be me."

16

WOKE UP IN SEPTEMBER

DROPLETS SPLASHED ON THE WINDOW'S SILL. EMBER OPENED all the windows in her apartment to invite the fresh scent and sounds of the gentle spring storm into her living quarters. The overcast weather reminded her of home, and she was taking full advantage of the setting to decompress from a rough first week. *God, could it really have only been a week since I arrived here? So much has happened, it's small wonder I'm so exhausted.*

On the coffee table, a mug steamed with freshly-brewed coffee flavored with a splash of cream. A packaged sampling of pastries from the Sweet and Flour were nibbled on, as though there was a curious rodent in the apartment eagerly consuming them. The young Malvern woman lounged on the couch, Kindle suspended in one hand and a warm almond bear claw in the other.

She was midway through one of her favorite novels—*The Lonesome Gods*—when the phone rang. It was the embassy-provided cell phone. She stared at it for three rings, trying to will it to cease, to leave her alone with Louis L'Amour so she could enjoy her relaxing, rainy Saturday morning. When that didn't work, she flipped the phone open and answered.

"Ember Wright? This is Bartholomew Samson with the Department of External Investigations."

"What can I do for you, Bartholomew?" Ember swallowed a sip of coffee and tried to sound calm, though her mind raced. *Why would they be calling me? On a Saturday, no less.*

"I need you to come down to the Parker at once, please. I have some questions we need to ask you."

She felt the blood drain from her face and her head felt light. If she wasn't sitting down, Ember might have fainted right then. She cleared her throat. "Questions? That...well that sounds serious. You can't ask me questions over the phone?"

"No, ma'am. I need you to come to my office right now. We're located on the Seventh Floor of the embassy. Unless you are refusing to comply?" The voice on the other end nearly sounded hopeful that Ember would refuse.

"This is just unusual, that's all." Ember rubbed her cheek with an open palm but feigned a confident tone. "Of course, I'll comply. I will be right there once I get changed."

There was little use stressing, but she stressed anyway. She was sure that she and Alarik had been careful when they slipped away to Surrey yesterday. Apparently, the little spies were more effective than she had given them credit.

Her Saturday relaxation plans were obliterated. Ember dressed, pulled on her jacket, and walked the four blocks to the embassy in the rain. She was thoroughly soaked when she arrived at The Parker Suites. She wished that she would have had enough foresight to buy an umbrella since it wasn't practical to bring one of hers from Great Malvern. *Honestly, Ember, you're an Englishwoman who doesn't own an umbrella. Have you no shame?*

Director Samson at least had the decency to offer her a towel to dry her matted hair. She hung her saturated jacket on the back of the chair next to her, letting it drip onto the Berber carpet in his office.

"As according to Druwish Law, it is requisite that you report any external relations with NonDruw people when they become or have the potential to become intimate." The man sniffed as he looked at his computer screen. He wore glasses on the tip of his nose, but he never seemed to look through the lenses. His gaze flitted between his monitor to Ember, always looking just above the rim of his wire spectacles.

Ember was studying the man right back. He was a mage, perhaps 120-140 years old. His aura looked clean and healthy—no sign of any shadow, no smudge. She wasn't sure if this meant he was working with Director Higginbotham, or if he was a completely innocent—if irritating—man just doing his job.

"I'm an Associate Investigator, Director Samson. I know Druwish Law as well as anybody, so you don't need to recite it line and section." Ember tried to keep her annoyance in check. Her clothes were sticking to her skin, soaked through as she was. "We're not intimate, not that it's any of your concern. Rik's a changeling, and last I checked I am under no obligation to report such a relationship."

The man furrowed his brow. He had a tuft of hair above the bridge of his nose, between his eyebrows, which Ember couldn't help but stare at. The ridges that formed on his forehead when he frowned elevated the furry copse. Bartholomew read from his computer monitor. "This inquiry concerns one NonDruw male, by the name of Cooper Severson. Do you deny knowing him?"

Ember silently cursed herself for volunteering information. She blamed her uncomfortable drenched state, but it was an amateur mistake to mention Alarik without his name being brought up by her interrogator.

"No, I admit to knowing Cooper, sure." Ember ran her fingers through matted hair, trying to untangle it. "We are simply casual friends, what of it?"

"If there is a potential for this relationship to...develop into intimacy, you need to file a report with this office, Miss Wright." The director gave her a judgmental look. "If you do elect to have an intimate relationship with a NonDruw, you will be obligated by law to have your mana suppressed. Failure to do so voluntarily will result in forcible—"

"As I said, I know Druwish Law well." Ember glared at the director as she interrupted. *Was he threatening me? Is this Director Higginbotham's doing, trying to intimidate me?*

"Very well." Director Samson and his proto-unibrow peered at her above his glasses. "Then tell me about this changeling, Rik. You are aware that procreating with a changeling would result in offspring with...diminished capacity. A coupling between Malvern and changeling can only produce changeling children."

Ember stood up abruptly, almost knocking her chair over. She placed her hands on the edge of the man's desk and leaned forward, letting wet tendrils of hair drip onto the assembled papers. She fixed her glare and said, "You judgmental, little man. How dare you suggest that a changeling child is somehow diminished when compared to a mage."

"Miss Wright! I never—"

"And furthermore, even if I *am* dating a changeling it's absolutely no business of the Department of External Relations. Last time I checked, changelings are Druws, ergo such relationships do not fall under the definition of 'external.' So, unless you have any further questions, I am going to leave you and your petty bigotry while I go out and enjoy what's left of my weekend."

Ember didn't wait for permission. She grabbed her jacket and marched out of his office, leaving a flabbergasted Bartholomew to salvage what he could of the papers soaking in the puddle on his desk.

The young Investigator was still fuming as she walked home. She paused on the sidewalk beneath a coffee shop's pent roof to make a call to Alarik.

"Rik? I know we agreed to set up interviews with the others this coming week." Ember chose her words cryptically. "By chance, might you get one or two in queue today?"

"Today? Well...yeah, I suppose I could." He sighed into the phone.

"Brilliant. And...would you mind picking me up, please?"

Alarik chuckled. "I guess, sure. Why not? It's only a 45-minute drive each way."

Ember ignored the sarcasm. "That'll give me time to shower and change—I'll explain on the drive. I know it's inconvenient, Rik. It is for me, too." She looked back at the tall building housing the embassy offices. Her gaze floated up to the windows of the Parker's seventh story. "Oh, and Rik? If anyone asks, you and I are officially dating."

ALARIK ARRANGED FOR HER TO MEET TWO DISABLED changelings at a residence in the town of Makoti. The drive from Minot through the steady rain had given Ember ample time to tell him about the morning's unexpected meeting, and how she hypothesized that it was little more than an intimidation tactic.

The house where they met belonged to one of the subjects, Peggy Barth. Though she was just 52 years old—typically prime physical age for a changeling—Peggy's hair was thin and completely grey. The skin around her eyes was dark from chronic fatigue, sagging as though the muscles beneath had atrophied. She placed a lit cigarette to her lips after Alarik made the introductions.

Seated next to Peggy at the weathered table in the cramped, poorly-lit kitchen was the other subject. Kenneth Newman looked no better off than Peggy. He looked twice his age at 40 years old. He was tall and thin to the point of emaciation. Ember studied their auras and found them to resemble Arnold Schmitt's: knotted, twisted, coiled. There was no sign whatsoever of their animal subforms.

Both explained that they were unable to focus for extended periods of time, had difficulty sleeping, and suffered from a range of medical issues. All of it, they said, started in 2001.

"Take me back to 2001. What happened?" Ember crossed

her legs and began scrawling on a yellow legal pad. "You were hired to explore the industrial accident south of Mandaree, yeah?"

"We were." Peggy took a drag of her cigarette. Her voice had the deep, rough growl consistent with someone who suffered from emphysema. "Kenny and me, we were part o' the second group to 'splore the fog."

"Second group? How many?" Ember drew a horizontal line in her notes. "Do you recall the names of those who were with you?"

"Sure. Let's see it was Paul Barkley from Stanley, Marv Richter from the Velva area, Roy...hell, what was his last name?" Peggy looked at Kenneth.

"Turner. Roland Turner." Kenneth fidgeted nervously in his seat. "Joseph Anyon, too. He's the other one."

"You betcha, Joe too." Peggy sucked on the shrinking, white stick. "He's a dog. Literally. Well, he was a dog I guess."

"So was I." Kenneth chewed on his fingernail, his eyes never looking up from the table. "Mine was a Blue Heeler. Joseph was a Black Lab though."

"Anyway," Peggy coughed loudly, twice. "The six of us were sent in after the first four didn't come back. We were selected 'cause we were all fast—our animal forms were, anyway. Mine was a pronghorn antelope, believe it or not."

Kenneth counted off on his fingers, the tips which seeped carmine with blood from his gnawing. "Paul was a White-tail, Marvin was a dog, too, and Roland was a big elk."

"Roy had one hell of a set of antlers, he did." Peggy smiled faintly as she remembered. Her few remaining teeth were mustard-colored. "He was a good lookin' young man."

"I'm sorry, you keep saying this in past tense." Ember suspected the explanation from witnessing Arnold's missing subform, but she needed to confirm. "Neither of you have been able to change into your animal form since the Mandaree Incident?"

"None of us. Right, Peg?" Kenneth resumed his nervous nibbling.

Peggy gave Kenneth's shoulder a squeeze. The fingernails on her leathery hand were long and yellow. "Yup, that's right. I know the first group—the four who went in before us—they're dealin' with the same shit. Ain't that so, Rik?"

"It's so." Alarik agreed. He sounded morose. "I know all ten of you, and the story's all the same."

"Okay. Please continue." Ember gestured with her right palm upward, ink pen tucked between her index and thumb. Her eyes began to sting and her nose tickled from the accumulating smoke in the small room.

The tip of the cigarette between Peggy's lips turned cherry red as she drew oxygen through it. She blew a lungful of smoke out the corner of her mouth, away from the table. "They had a theory, thems that hired us. They said that every human who went into the fog never came back out again, but wildlife was seen to come and go like no big deal. They figured that if we went into it in animal form, we'd be able to go in and out as we please, same as them critters."

"Do you know if the first four scouts went in, in their animal subform?" Ember resisted the urge to sneeze from the growing cloud of carcinogen. When both Peggy and Kenneth shrugged, she made a note to include that question when she interviewed the other changelings. "That's alright. So, tell me what happened when you visited the industrial site. Whatever you can remember."

Kenneth shifted his weight. He began nibbling on the fingernails of his left hand, though they were already pared back too far. "It's not much, the memory."

Peggy nodded. "We talked about it a lot over the years, tryin' to make sense of it all. The cloud o' gas looked like fog of any kind. We didn't have masks or nothin' but they told us that it didn't matter much, as we wouldn't be goin' in far. We were supposed to just go in about a hundred yards, turn 'round and come right back to report to them. We were gonna go deeper into the fog each time."

"Didn't get far." Kenneth sniffled.

"Nah, we didn't." Peggy flicked ash into a chipped coffee mug. "So, we all walked in together, in our animal forms. It was cold as fuck—February, remember—and the fog was chilly, too. Frost everywhere. Snow, ice. We went in just far 'nough that we couldn't see the pickups parked on the section line. Next thing you know, we're waking up in September."

Ember leaned forward and spoke quickly. "What do you mean, you woke up in September? You don't remember anything at all that happened in the eight months between? Nothing?"

"Nothing." Kenneth sniffed. "And we were in our human forms when we woke up, too."

"Right. All of us were." Peggy hunched her shoulders as she sighed. She tapped another menthol out of a moss-colored pack of Kools and lit it using the butt of her previous cigarette. "Ain't never been the same ever since."

"Do you remember anything at all from your time in the fog?" Ember suspended her pen over a blank line on her notepad. "Any sounds, smells? Did you see any people, any clue as to what was going on?"

"I remember a sound," Kenneth closed his eyes. "Like a...a buzzing, in my ears. And no smells, but my mouth tasted like copper. I have good hearing and taste buds. Or...at least I used to." He opened his eyes and resumed chewing on his thumbnail.

"It's like havin' a part of you fuckin' ripped away." Peggy looked at the dingy, tar-yellowed curtains in her kitchen window, though her eyes didn't seem to focus. "It's like losin' your identity. Like losin'—"

"Your soul," Kenneth whispered.

Peggy nodded imperceptibly. "It fuckin' sucks. I ain't gonna lie; every couple'a months I think about endin' it all. I even tasted the muzzle of my shotgun once—I got that close." She held a finger a few inches away from her cigarette. "But these goddamn things are gonna do it for me." The woman chuckled hoarsely. She brought the menthol back up to her lips, though she didn't take a drag.

Silence followed. Ember looked at Alarik, sitting next to her as he watched Kenneth. She wondered if Arnold had told him a similar encounter. She was feeling deep sympathy for these people, and the thought of having to bear these experiences for nine excruciating years—with no cure in sight—had to wear on their mental health.

"Arnie's subform was a coyote," Alarik said quietly, as though he was almost hearing her unspoken question. "Same as mine. He always wanted to be like me when we were growing up—wanted to be like his big brother. I hated how he followed me around all the time, mimicking me. When he reached his Manifestation Day, I prayed that he wouldn't be a coyote. I didn't care what he was, just so he wouldn't follow me in that, too."

Alarik slid his chair back and stepped over to the refrigerator, facing away from the others. He leaned his elbow against the edge of the fridge. "He has nightmares now, where he sees his coyote, trapped in quicksand, surrounded by fog." Alarik tipped his head forward to rest against his tanned forearm.

The lit cigarette stuck against Peggy's lower lip, the ash accumulating though she had yet to draw from it. It vibrated as she spoke, sending particles of burnt tobacco floating. "Me, too. I see my antelope in mud. Up to its neck."

Kenneth stopped chewing. He looked at Peggy and then at Alarik, who was looking over his shoulder now. "I can't sleep unless I take pills because when I don't, I see my Blue Heeler trapped in swampy mud. I wake myself up from the screaming."

"Wait, so..." Ember looked at each of the changelings. "You two are having the same recurring nightmares as each other? And Arnie is, too?"

All three nodded, their eyes wide as they looked at one

another. Alarik broke the silence. "What does that mean? Does it mean something?"

Ember ran her fingers through her blonde mane. "I don't know. Maybe. It might just be coincidence. You've seen Healers though?"

They both nodded. Kenneth said, "Several. They couldn't do anything for us. They told us to stop coming around because we were scaring off customers at the Magic City Spa."

Ember frowned. She had more questions—such as who was denying them access to the spa, who they were hired by, and who their handlers were when they were driven to the fog. She felt compelled to do something else, first.

"I'm not a Healer, admittedly, but my Mum is one of the best in the world. I learned some from her, and I recently learned that I have some...abilities...that I didn't know I had before." Ember thought of her conversation with Barnaby, and how he had declared her to be his peer—a so-called Inquisitor possessing unheard of abilities. She was feeling confident. "I would like to try something if you don't mind? Kenneth, let me see your hands."

Kenneth looked uncertainly at Peggy and Alarik. When neither of them said anything, he reluctantly brought his hands down on the table, palms up. His skin was so pale it was nearly translucent.

Ember sat her notepad aside and took his hands in hers. She studied him, but he kept his gaze affixed at their hands. Before she closed her eyes, she noticed the set of raised track marks inside his elbows.

Her eyes closed, she focused her attention to the changeling's twisted aura. She willed her own aura—vibrant and healthy—to slowly slide down from her arms, over and up his arms. Her energy shined, rich with mana only she could see. She imagined her energy coating his knotted, twisting aura, like thick paint pouring over rough wood.

She heard Kenneth sigh, and Ember's lips twitched into a satisfied smile. She knew she was no Healer, but she had a gift beyond what any living Investigator had. *I can help these people.*

Then she felt it awaken within Kenneth. He whimpered and fidgeted even as Ember saw the sickly, dark green slime seep to the surface of his knotted aura. It acted like a sentient infection made aware that its existence was being threatened. It felt like oil, viscous and foreign.

The slimy, alien presence oozed over the blanket of Ember's aura and began flowing up her arms. Ember tried to let go, tried to pull away, but she couldn't. Someone touched her, and her eyes snapped open.

Alarik was saying something, but all she could hear was a swarm of bees. His face was panicked and he was shaking her, yelling as he stared into her eyes. In those dark pools, Ember saw the reflection of a familiar blonde woman, paralyzed with terror.

17

SPARK OF JUSTICE

THE ROOF OF HER MOUTH TASTED METALLIC LIKE SHE HAD been sucking on dirty pennies. The headache was severe, to the point where the act of opening her eyes took effort.

Ember willed herself to look, despite the pain. She was in a stranger's bed, the overstuffed pillow cradling her head. A mason jar on the nightstand was half-filled with water and cut white and purple lilacs, greeting her with a strong floral aroma.

With effort, she swung herself out of the borrowed bed and shuffled along the carpeted floor. The door to the bedroom was unlocked. While the Investigator in her wanted to study the room, to search for clues to where she was, the only thought she would allow into her pounding skull was that of finding water. Anything to rinse the awful flavor from her taste buds.

One hand shielded her eyes from the bright morning light, the other felt along the plaster wall, as much for balance as a guide.

"Oh, thank god, you're awake!" A man said. "I was trying to decide how much longer I dare wait to take you to the hospital."

It took Ember a moment to associate a name with the voice. "Rik?"

"Yup. Here, sit down, sit down. Are you feeling okay?"

"Nothing's broken," she murmured. *At least I hope not.*

A padded, wooden chair slid up to her. A strong pair of hands gripped her shoulders and sat her down. She was given a glass of water, which she eagerly drank. The copper taste dissolved with each sip. Already, she was starting to feel better, the pressure on her sinuses decreasing. That's when she noticed she was barefoot. *Not only barefoot but pantsless.*

"Rik, what the bloody hell?"

"What?" He sounded befuddled. "Something wrong? The water's filtered, and I swear I washed the cup."

"Not that. Where are my clothes?" Ember tugged the oversized shirt forward, seeing chipped screen print that she couldn't read. "My pants! This isn't my shirt."

"Yeah, sorry about that. That's one of my old t-shirts." Alarik shrugged. "You can keep it if you like it. It looks better on you than me."

"You...you stripped me down?" Ember blinked at the bright sunlight. It was still difficult to focus.

"Only down to your underwear. You really don't remember?"

Ember frowned, then glared. "We...did we...I mean you—"

"What? You mean have sex? Oh god no! Jeez, of course not!" Alarik tilted his head back and released a laugh. He scratched his stubbled chin with his fingers and shook his head. "Are you kidding, I'd never do that!"

"Wow. Just keep piling insults on, why don't you." Ember continued glaring. She handed the drained water glass to Alarik. "My clothes, please. Where are they?"

"They're in the dryer. I had to wash them—I wasn't about to make you sleep in your own mess. You threw up all over yourself. A couple of times in my pickup, on the drive here from Makoti. You were speaking gibberish, murmuring. I tried to pay attention, but I couldn't make out a word of what you were saying. You scared the shit out of me, woman."

Ember looked down at the carpeted floor and began to remember thick cigarette smoke and murky slime. As the memory of the interview with the changelings came back to her, she closed her eyes and focused on her own aura. It was clean. Whatever that alien, oily energy was, she didn't seem to be contaminated with it. She held her head in both hands and trembled. "Oh, bloody hell, what was I thinking? I'm so stupid!"

Alarik crouched in front of her and placed his hands around her shoulders. He spoke quietly. "You're trying to help. You *are* helping."

"And Kenny?" Ember's fire-blue eyes met Alarik's dark pupils as she remembered her foolish attempt at healing the thin man. "Is he...is he fine?"

"He is. No change from before, but he's fine. He was a little rattled, no denying that." Alarik nodded. He released Ember from his partial embrace, though he stayed crouched at eye level with her. "Kenny and Peg were both more worried about you. They wanted to take you to Minot—to the spa for emergency treatment. That, or to Trinity—to the hospital. I decided to bring you here instead, to let you sleep it off. Whatever 'it' was."

Ember leaned back in the chair and looked around. The wood creaked as her weight shifted. "That was probably a good choice. Where is 'here,' anyway?"

"It's my place. North of Plaza, remember? It was nearby, and better than trying to unload and carry a passed-out blonde in downtown Minot at night." He glanced at the scorched, leather-banded Casio he wore on his left wrist. "You've been asleep for about fourteen hours."

Her thoughts were a jumble, but at least her head was feeling better. She said simply, "I'm hungry."

Alarik's face brightened into a grin. "I can help with that. You go ahead and take a shower and I'll get your stuff from the dryer. I'll take you out for brunch—the best place to eat in Mountrail County."

Lucky excitedly ran up to Alarik's pickup, collecting tribute in the form of pets from the driver before scrambling over to the passenger side for more.

Ember leaned down to pet the German Shepherd behind her ears. She looked uncertainly at Alarik. "Are you sure it's okay to bring me to your family's Sunday brunch? Won't this be awkward?"

He reassured her that it wouldn't be. But it was, at least initially.

Alarik introduced Ember to a pale man who she recognized as Arnie. She shook his hand only briefly; the prospect of risking contact with the alien energy made her wary. She hoped nobody confused her caution with rudeness.

The spread Alarik's mother made for the Schmitt Family's weekly brunch was glorious: peppered bacon, whole grain toast with homemade juneberry jelly, scrambled eggs topped by melted Colby-jack mixed with chopped onion and garlic over a bed of tater-tots. Ember's stomach eagerly grumbled its approval.

Alarik made room for Ember, seating her next to him along one long side of the table. Ronald Schmitt sat on one short end, with his brother Boniface at the other end. Muriel was to Ronald's left, and on his right was Anna.

Ember nibbled delicately, though she was so hungry she would have used a trowel if it would have been socially acceptable. She felt them watching her, could sense that the usual family conversation was censored due to the surprise guest.

When the food on the plates was half-consumed, Alarik said, "I've got an announcement to make. Ember and I are officially dating."

Ember froze mid-bite with a piece of jellied toast held to her mouth. Her eyes widened.

Everyone but the two children stopped eating. Anna and

her golden eagle subform gave Ember a predatory glare that made her feel like she was a tiny rabbit in an open field.

"I should explain." Alarik was grinning. He was enjoying this. "Yesterday, she got a surprise call from External Relations—"

"Rik, you really shouldn't." Ember pushed the bite of toast into her cheek so she could produce her muffled words. "Let's talk about this."

"You really shouldn't talk with your mouth full, sweetie. Besides, sooner or later they're going to find out that you spent the night at my place." Alarik winked at Ember as everyone else scowled.

Ember felt the collective wrath of the Schmitt Family burrowing into her. *Kill me now.*

The twins played with their food and squirmed in their chairs, oblivious to the tension among the adults at the table.

Alarik still wore his silly grin. "Come on, let me tell them."

She squinted at him but said nothing.

Interpreting her silence as acquiescence, the man sitting next to her told his family about yesterday's events. From her brush with Director Samson to the interview with Peggy and Kenneth. She involuntarily shuddered when he told them about how she took Kenneth's hands in hers in some ill-advised attempt at playing Healer. When Alarik pulled Ember away from Kenneth, she threw up all over Peg Barth's kitchen floor and acted drunk.

When he was done telling his story, everyone was silent for

a few minutes. Ember stared at her half-finished breakfast. Her cheek still puffed out from the piece of soggy toast stowed within.

Arnold's wife pushed her chair back and sat her cloth napkin on the table. She walked around the table to where Ember was seated and wrapped her arms around the Malvern woman, hugging the still-seated Ember from behind. Stephanie sniffled and said, "thank you for helping us."

Ember swallowed and finally looked up. Everyone else was still silent, but the mood had changed completely. Boniface raised his coffee mug as a salute to her. Muriel dabbed at her eyes with a napkin. Ronald watched, his elbows on the table and his fingers weaved together against his chin. Arnold's eyes were wet but held a faint smile.

Anna leaned back in her chair, the ferocity in her gaze replaced with an appraising expression. "Well, hell's bells, Ember. If you wanted the family's approval to date my brother, there are easier ways to go about it than to get those External Relations jerks involved. A case of beer would've been all we needed."

Alarik gave Ember a wink that she answered with a simper.

The rest of brunch was increasingly lighthearted. When everyone was done eating, Ember helped clear the table.

"Feel like taking a walk with me?" Anna asked as she finished loading the dishwasher.

"I would, thank you." Ember's smile felt permanently affixed.

Maxim and Marta joined them for part of the walk until the

twins got distracted and ran off into the rows of trees and shrubs which formed the protective shelterbelt. Lucky barked and chased after them, wagging her tail constantly. Anna led Ember to a clapboard-sided building with peeling white paint and green asphalt shingles.

"This is why I don't have a savings account, and why I still live with my parents." Anna opened the door to the building and flipped a toggle switch on. "And why I don't have time for a boyfriend."

Inside, the small building was cluttered with woodworking tools Ember couldn't identify. Anna proudly showed off her table saw, a bandsaw, router, planer, and a scroll saw. Stacks of repurposed wood filled shelves mounted to the wall. Beneath the window, her project sat half-assembled on the workbench.

Ember marveled at the details of the doll-sized barn, tracing the scroll work with her fingertips. She peered into the window of the unfinished building, noting feed troughs and stalls, a hayloft, and doors mounted on tiny brass hinges.

"This is positively brilliant, Anna!" Ember was careful not to tip over a closed can of red paint, in case the lid wasn't tight. "And you have other little buildings, too!"

Anna beamed with pride. "I make a full set: farmhouse, barn, grain bin, corrals, chicken coop, windmill. And then no farm is complete without these." Anna's dusky eagle eyes turned upward, and her chin raised shortly after. She opened a cabinet and pulled out a box. Within were dozens of farm animals, all hand-carved and painted.

"Oh, my! These are exquisite!" Ember brought a Jersey milk

cow up to her face for closer inspection. "How much do you sell these for?"

Anna laughed, "I don't. These are gifts. I made a set for Marta and Max. This one is going to some neighbor kids down the road."

"Anna, you *need* to sell these! The level of detail is amazing."

"Who would buy them?" Anna shrugged and stretched her neck, leaning her head on one shoulder and then the other. "You can buy plastic toys so cheaply. So many hours go into each set, I can't imagine anyone willing to pay enough to make it worth my time. No, it's just a hobby. An expensive hobby."

"You would be surprised." Ember traded the cow for a chicken. "You even carved its little toes! That's incredible. You could set up a website, market these to collectors. Not as children's toys, but as high-end collectibles."

Anna's lips quirked, unconvinced but basking in Ember's enthusiasm for her handiwork. She looked up at the rafters in a futile attempt at stretching her muscles. "Besides that, it's brutal on my neck and back, doing all this carving. So many hours crouched over a workbench is hell to pay."

Ember watched Anna stretch. "That's caused by poor ergonomics. You're overworking your trapezius and sternocleidomastoid."

The woman stopped stretching and looked at Ember bemusedly. "My whaty-whatius? Are you having a stroke? Do you smell burning toast?"

Ember laughed. "No, not today anyway. I became a licensed massage therapist as a cover job. You should stop by the

Magic City Spa and let me work you over. I'm legitimate and all, despite it being a part-time gig."

"Yeah. Maybe." The woman looked at Ember appraisingly. "You really do like helping people, don't you? Come on, we'd better get back to the house."

Most of the afternoon was spent on the porch, sipping cold drinks and swapping stories. Ember felt somewhat disappointed when Alarik finally declared that it was time for him to take her home. Part of her felt like she was already there.

Ronald Schmitt walked with Ember back to his son's pickup as Alarik gave his niece and nephew hugs.

"You have a really lovely place here, Mr. Schmitt. Thank you for letting me intrude on your Sunday."

"You call me Ronald, you hear? And you're welcome here anytime. You're no intrusion at all." He opened the passenger door and offered his leathery hand to help her climb in.

Ember accepted, feeling his rough calluses and strong grip. "That's really sweet of you, Ronald. Thank you for being so welcoming."

"I'm gonna tell you something, Ember. You made an impression here today, don't you think otherwise. Not too many Malverns go out of their way to break bread with changelings, you know. It's like we're animals to them."

Ember cast her gaze aside. "I know, and it's not right. It shouldn't be that way."

"No, it shouldn't. But that's the way it is." The elder Schmitt scratched his chin, the way his son tended to do. "I guess what I'm trying to tell you is that for a long time, we've been trying to find answers for Arnie. We've fought, we've complained, we've prayed. Nobody in the embassy showed any hint of giving a damn."

She swallowed, feeling the weight of his words. Ember looked back at him and said, "There's a lot working against us—a whole machine of bureaucracy in our way. I can't promise I'll be successful. I don't want to get anyone's hopes up."

He scratched his whiskers and cleared his throat. "You know, before I taught Rik and Arnie how to weld, long before they went off to Wahpeton to get certified as welders, I showed them how to break down iron using an acetylene torch. In a good day, the two of them could tear apart a 400-barrel steel tank and turn it into nice, neat sheets of scrap that could be loaded in a dump trailer and taken to town for recycling."

Ronald leveled his gaze at her. "I need you to know that whatever comes of this, you've given us the first spark of justice we've had for Arnie. Make no mind, I know it's nothing more than a spark. But you know, when you light a torch all it takes is a little spark."

18

EXPECT A LONELY EXISTENCE

THEY WERE NEARLY TO MINOT WHEN SHE ASKED HIM TO TAKE her to the Church of Brethren Cemetery instead of her apartment.'

"Haven't you had a long enough weekend yet?" Alarik asked. "I thought you'd be eager to get home."

She couldn't deny that she was exhausted, so she told the truth. "Your father told me a little story, right as we were leaving. I don't know if he intended it, but he reminded me of why I got involved in the first place. I have too many questions, which I hope my contact has some answers to."

"Your contact? The same I took you to meet last week, you're meeting him tonight? How did you manage to get a meeting scheduled with him? I've been with you this whole weekend."

"It's complicated. Look, Rik, there's a lot going on that I can't tell you, I'm sorry. We just need to learn to trust one another. Do you trust me?"

"More than yesterday." He grumbled. "But eventually, trust means letting me in on what's going on." He flipped the Ford's turn signal and prepared to drive east, toward the town of Surrey.

"You are telling me...that the changeling's aura was deformed, his subform was completely absent, and he was possessed by—what—an...evil spirit? Little girl, have you been sampling laudanum?"

Ember would never get comfortable with the ghost of Barnaby Harrison. It was difficult to know which was more abrasive: his sand-over-sheet-metal voice or his condescension towards her.

"Laudanum? I don't even know if they make that stuff anymore. You mean to ask if I'm hallucinating? I assure you, I'm not. I say this knowing full well how ironic it is that I'm talking to a ghost." She hugged herself against the chilled air and wished she had brought a jacket.

Barnaby puffed out his chest. "An Inquisitor talking to the dead may only seem ironic to the ignorant."

She would need to try a different tack if she was to glean answers from the ghost. "No, I get it. You've never seen what I'm describing, so it mustn't exist. Irony is *you* calling me ignorant. I don't know why I thought a Grand Inquisitor would be able to help me."

"Oh, your tart words bruise me so." Barnaby clutched his chest with a transparent right hand. "Or they might if your opinion was of any consequence to me."

"I'm sorry, I thought you might still care about serving justice." She tilted her head and narrowed her gaze as an idea emerged. "You know, I could help serve justice to your killer, whoever he was."

"Billy would be...long dead by now. It has been over a century since he pushed me from that ledge. He was not much younger than I was." Barnaby dragged his fingers across the inscription on his headstone. "1898. I was...only 193 years old."

"Billy? You've remembered your murderer's name, yeah?"

Barnaby continued gazing at his headstone. His rough voice was melancholy. "I have. Billy Colton. We were friends...or so I had wrongly convinced myself. I was foolish to think we could have been."

"Billy Colton. Even his name sounds villainous. Why did he kill you?"

"That, I cannot fathom."

She tapped her chin with an index finger. "Barnaby, I'll find out what became of this Colton bloke. If he did get away without being charged with your murder, I can at least be sure to set the records straight."

"You would? How would you do that?"

Ember shook her head. "I'm not sure yet. I'm resourceful. I'll figure something out. So, will you help me?"

"It might be best if you start from the beginning." The apparition propped his elbows against his headstone. "How did you encounter this...evil spirit, as you deem it?"

She told Barnaby of Wallace sending her to the Magic City

to check in on his friend, Duncan Heywood. Ember told him of how the Senior Investigator and the rest of the Investigators were all "infected" with a shadowy blight.

"It is a Deference Spell that you are describing. It is a...dark sort of magic, not generally taught. Strongly discouraged, in fact."

"What does it do?" She had some guesses.

"As implied; it allows the caster—this Director of Wellness as you named him—to control the actions of those under his spell. You said that you saw an image of the Senior Investigator, Heywood, reaching out...when you spoke to him?"

Ember shivered as she remembered. "Though Duncan simply sat in his office, the darkness around him grew and grew. It felt like the shadow was surrounding me, trying to bloody grab me."

Barnaby shook his head. "The Deference Spell was not interested in you, it...doesn't work that way. What you were witnessing was the spell fighting to contain Duncan's aura, his will, and his thoughts. He was trying, desperately it seems, to tell you something. The Deference Spell prevented him from doing so."

"He knows something about the Mandaree Incident." Ember's voice trailed off. She felt like light was starting to show through the cracks in this conspiracy, and she was splitting those cracks just a little bit wider. "Duncan knows something. He wanted to tell me. Elton Higginbotham is keeping the Investigators under his control, as they know the truth."

"If they don't already, they would be inclined to pursue the truth. It is what Investigators are born to do." Barnaby paced the cemetery grounds, leaving footprints in the prairie grass. "This Higginbotham fellow is a formidable mage if he is able to hold sway over so many at once without exhausting his mana."

"He can't be too formidable; he wasn't able to get me. He tried, but the spell wore off in a half hour or so."

Barnaby stopped pacing. "Higginbotham cast a Deference Spell on you?"

"He did. It made me sick, and I vomited it out. The spell came out of me when I chundered."

"You have it backward; the nausea, the vomiting...those are side effects of repulsion. You drew the spell out of yourself. If you had been properly trained, you would have been able to resist the Deference Spell altogether. Since you were not, you somehow managed to exorcise yourself. That is admirable, girl. This is more proof that you are indeed...an Inquisitor."

She grinned. "It almost sounds like you're proud of me. If I didn't know any better."

"I am not, and you do not. Proceed with your tale, if you are finished admiring your reflection."

Ember sighed. There was no point in arguing with him. She told him about Arnie, about the other changelings who were sent into scout the toxic cloud surrounding Mandaree in 2001. She outlined what they had told her, and how they were each suffering from the same nightmare and various medical issues.

"That brings us to when you came in contact with the...evil spirit? Describe it to me again, girl."

Ember described the sentient, alien presence she felt when she had tried healing Kenny, and how that oily slime responded to her with such malcontent.

Barnaby paced circles around his grave. "Truly, what you describe is foreign to me. I will admit it."

"I was really hoping you were holding out on me." Ember ran her fingers through her hair. A light mist was forming in the air, bringing a heavy dew with it. "I don't know how I'm going to help them."

"You were not even assigned the case for these changelings." It was no question.

"No, I wasn't. I don't even think there *is* a case. Not formally. It's more like, I don't know, I see how they are being mistreated, and I can't help but think I might be able to help. I can't just stand by—"

"While an injustice exists." Barnaby's empty eye sockets glowed as he spoke. "That is the hallmark of an Inquisitor. It is why we are trusted with such responsibility. Our authority is a burden to us because we would be driven mad rather than allow corruption to exist. It is why a lone Supreme Inquisitor has always been held as an equal counter-balance to the rest of the High Council; because he or she will not—can not—permit injustice to persist."

"Then that might explain why you were killed by Billy. And maybe all other Inquisitors were murdered, too?" It was Ember's turn to pace. "But how could an entire generation of Druws forget that Inquisitors even existed? It's like history has been rewritten to suit some vile aim."

"That may be exactly what happened." Barnaby conceded her theory with a nod. "I do not know how anyone could perform such a vast coup. It would take more than one evil-doer. Many more. Though you are young and naïve, you must trust your instincts. Your Investigator's Instinct... indeed, that is all you can trust."

"I trust Wallace. And others. I have friends who are helping." She thought of the man waiting patiently in his pickup for her.

"Perhaps. But likely not." Barnaby turned away from her and waved a hand dismissively as he walked another lap around his grave. "Trusting others can be dangerous—just look at how that worked for me. It is a lonely existence, to be an Inquisitor."

"It could just be how things were for you, Barnaby. Forgive me for pointing out the obvious, but you're not exactly a people person."

His sandpaper laugh etched its texture into her brain. "Little girl, your naivety is worse than I would have guessed. You, like me, are obsessive in the quest for justice to the point of alienating everyone around you. Inquisitors live solo lives—it should be a rule, it is so self-evident. It is one of those laws of nature, like gravity or death."

Barnaby pointed a bony, periwinkle finger in her direction. "You are an Inquisitor; therefore, you can expect a lonely existence. Best wrap your pretty head around that fact and move forward."

Ember thought of the Schmitt family, of how welcoming they were toward her. "Maybe that's how it once was, but I have friends, people who care about me, and I care about them."

He released another gritty laugh. "Behold, a little girl and her hubris! My mistake, but of course you are so special that you would be the one exception among millennia of Inquisitors. If you deny it long enough, you might someday convince yourself." Barnaby leaned forward and growled. "But we both know the truth, do we not?"

"I think I'm done talking to you. I'm tired, and I don't need to hear condescending crap from a dead man."

"Is that supposed to bother me? I could hardly care less about your fragile ego, little girl. You will bear the truth of my warning irrespective of what you wish."

"Go, rest now, Barnaby Harrison. I've had enough of you."

She turned her back to him and walked away, not caring to watch the apparition fade.

19

WITH PEOPLE LIKE YOU

SHE UPDATED WALLACE BY PHONE THE NEXT MORNING. EMBER told him everything that had happened since they last spoke, along with her conversation with the ghost of Barnaby Harrison. He was incredulous at first—not because he didn't believe her, but because what she was suggesting was just so much to process.

"If I wouldn't be seeing this with my own eyes, I'd have a grim time believing it was real, too." Ember closed her eyes, remembering the sensation. "I *felt* the entity—whatever it is—within that changeling. It's something bloody otherworldly. Alien, if you will."

The chair in Wallace's office creaked as he rocked back and forth. He itemized aloud, attempting to organize his thoughts. "The victims from the Mandaree Incident and surrounding cover-up by Director Higginbotham. The alleged existence of Inquisitors and subsequent eradication. The probable conspiracy then to rewrite our history and somehow convince entire generations of Malverns and changelings that a whole subset of the Investigation Track never even existed. In your estimation, are these things all related?"

"I don't know." Ember had been chewing on her lower lip while Wallace was speaking. Hearing the scale of events stated back to her was overwhelming. "I'm convinced that the Deference Spell and Higginbotham's involvement with the afflicted Mandaree Incident changelings are intertwined. Whether that's got anything to do with this bigger, historical conspiracy though..." She let her voice trail off.

Her mentor exhaled into the phone. "One of these injustices is huge. The other is utterly epic. Altogether, it would invite an Investigator to lose his bloody mind."

"I'm right there with you, Wallace. So where do I begin? Shall I focus on trying to help the disabled changelings, somehow? Should I gather evidence to unmask Director Higginbotham? What would you suggest as my next course of action?"

Wallace was silent long enough for Ember to glance at her burner phone, to be sure the call had not been disconnected. Finally, he answered. "No, I do not want you confronting this alone."

"Which part?"

"All of it. Any of it."

"But Wallace, I can't just stand by—"

"You will do exactly that. Just for now. Let me think on this for a few days, to consult a couple individuals whom I trust."

"Alright. In the interim, I'll interview the remaining changelings and—"

"Negative. Ember, I'm ordering you to stand down until you receive further instructions from me. Is that understood?"

"Wallace, each day we wait, people are suffering."

"Do you think I don't know that?" He snapped. He breathed into the phone again, returning to a calmer tone. "Ember, it doesn't do us any good to go into this half-cocked. You've only been in North Dakota for a bit over a week and you've already uncovered two possible conspiracies along with potentially deep corruption within the colonial government. Don't you think it would be wise not to potter about until I've had a chance to gather information on my end?"

She knew he was right to exercise caution, to be patient—neither which were her strong suits. "Fine. I'll do as you instruct, Wallace. I'll take no action until I hear otherwise from you."

For the rest of the week, Ember spent only part of her time in the closet-turned-office on the Third Floor of the Parker Building, going through the motions for the census audit while Dennis sat in the corner, working through his crossword puzzles and being a general hindrance to her sanity.

Most of her time was spent working in the spa. If she had to kill time, she could at least help others with her massage therapy skills. Ember also benefitted from working with the healing Leystones on clients who needed it; the weekend's excitement had exhausted her own energy so the secondary recharge brought relief.

The co-workers at the Magic City Spa were much more fun to be around than the Deference Spelled Investigators upstairs. The spa's manager, Josette, was delighted that

Ember was working more hours for her. Ember knew this, because Josette said as much to her, at least twice per day.

"We've just been so busy, and it's hard to find good help." Josette leaned in and lowered her voice since they were talking in a public area between the gym and chiropractor's office. "Especially good Druwish help. Not enough qualified therapists with the security clearance to handle Leystones."

Ember smiled. "You're quite welcome. You've created such a friendly environment here, and you've been so accommodating with my hours. In truth, I should be thanking you."

"Girlfriend, are you kidding me? You are doing *me* a favor by filling in. Though it would be nice if your babysitter didn't have to tag along. He's been sitting in the same corner of the lobby every day, like a big, dumb plant. If this keeps up, I think Ami is going to be tempted to start watering him along with the rest of the ferns in the reception area."

Ember chuckled. "Oh goodness, don't do that! We don't want him growing larger. I do hope Smiley isn't bothering Ami too much. She's a sweetheart, always so friendly. Though I think her memory isn't great. I greet her in the morning when I arrive, but when I leave in the evening she seems to forget that we even said 'hello' to one another earlier."

Josette was only half-listening, as her attention was focused on an employee in the gym. "I'm sorry, will you excuse me, Ember? I've got a new personal trainer who seems more interested in flirting with the girls than doing his job. I need to go give him an earful."

"He doesn't know what he's in for!"

"No, he doesn't." Josette marched into the gym and gestured at a young man in a tight t-shirt. He was in the middle of flexing his biceps in front of the wall mirror, in the line of sight of two attractive women on stair climbers.

Ember just shook her head and chuckled to herself before going back to work.

It was early on Thursday when Josette informed her that a client made an appointment with her for later that morning. "She requested you by name, Ember. Only a few days working here, and you're already gaining regulars. Good for you, lady."

Anna Schmitt appeared at the spa a few minutes before 11:00. "I decided I'd better take you up on your offer."

"I'm glad you did. Your neck and shoulders are still bothering you?"

"And my lower back. I guess I'm a wreck."

Ember performed a deep-tissue massage, kneading Anna's back muscles using her elbows. The changeling woman uttered satisfied moans.

"You are a magic-worker," Anna groaned into the horseshoe-shaped face cushion. "I mean literally. I think I might get addicted to this."

Ember applied more jojoba oil. She held the fluid in her palm for a few seconds to let it warm before dribbling the clear oil between her fingers over her client's upper spine. "It's not magic, just technique and a little empathy." She transitioned her attention to Anna's shoulders, working a series of widening circles with her thumbs, sliding easily over the warm oil. "Next time I visit your woodshop, I'll observe your posture while you work at the bench and give you advice on how you can improve your ergonomics."

"That would be nice, having you visit us again. You know, you're not half bad—I mean, for a snobby Malvern."

"Thanks. You and your family aren't too bad either—for a bunch of hillbilly changelings."

Ember finished working out the knotted muscles of her client's neck and shoulders. She blotted off any excess oils before providing Anna with a small glass of cucumber water and instructions to stretch and hydrate, lest the released lactic acid cause her muscles to cramp up again.

"Seriously, Ember, you know what you're doing. You made an impression on me. On my family. Most of all, on Rik."

"That's sweet of you to say. I'm just doing my job though."

"No, not just. What you're doing for us isn't just out of a sense of duty. I don't buy that. You know that Arnie's subform is a coyote?"

"I do know that, yeah. And so is Rik's."

"I made something for you." Anna pulled something out of her purse and placed it in Ember's hand.

It was a detailed wood carving of a coyote's face. A leather string was weaved through it with a pewter clasp fixing the ends of the leather into a loop.

"It's a necklace," Anna said. "But you don't have to wear it. I just wanted to show you my appreciation for all that you are doing for Arnie. For all of us."

"You made this for me? That's so sweet of you. It's beautiful,

Anna. Thank you. Not only will I wear this, but I'll do so every day." Ember slipped the necklace over her head, pulling her blonde hair through the loop so the leather could rest against her skin. The pewter clasp was slightly cold against the back of her neck, but the leather was smooth, its edges carefully beveled so it wouldn't scratch the wearer's skin.

"It's made of natural materials," Anna explained. "As you probably know, when a changeling shifts from human to animal form, what they are wearing reappears when they return to human form—so long as those clothes and accessories are not made of synthetic materials like plastic. I know that doesn't apply to you, but I wanted to make this necklace and pendant in the same fashion as I would for any of my people."

Ember held the pendant in her hand and looked down at the detail in the coyote's face. Its ears were pointed forward, its expression one of amused curiosity. She recognized that face; Alarik's subform looked the same whenever the man laughed. "You have amazing talent, Anna. I'm telling you, you need to go into business for yourself. You'd make gazillions of dollars."

Anna chuckled and shook her head. "If only the world was filled with people like you."

20

FRIDAY NIGHT PISS-UP

"TEN LETTERS, THIRD LETTER IS R. IT MEANS, 'HAPPENING BY chance'."

"Listen, Smiley." Ember squinted at the changeling sitting against the wall of her office. "I told you, if you insist on being in here while I'm working, you can at least have the courtesy to do your puzzles in silence."

Dennis grumbled. "Yeah, but I'm stuck on this one, and you always seem to know the answers."

"How about 'annoyance'."

He counted on his fingers. "That's only nine letters. And there's no R in it."

The ringing of a phone saved her; it was the embassy-provided cell.

She cleared her throat before answering. "Ember speaking."

"Hey-a Ember! Coop here."

"Coop? How did you get this number?"

"Uh...you called me last Thursday, remember?" He chuckled. "I promise I'm not stalking you, I just simply added you to my phone's contacts."

"Oh. Right. Of course." Ember thought back to her conversation with him, how she had dialed his number after hanging up with her mother. *I must've just used the same mobile. I really need to be more careful about which one I use.*

"I know this is last minute, but if you don't have any plans tonight, would you like to come to a party at my place? It'll just be some friends of mine."

"That sounds lovely. What's the occasion?"

"Most of my friends have to work over the holiday, so we're celebrating the Fourth of July early." Even over the phone, his grin was palpable. "It seems fitting to have at least one Redcoat present for Independence Day."

"I'm not sure I have any red coats, but I can belt out a brilliant rendition of 'God Save the King' if it helps the Yankee festivities."

Cooper laughed. "That'll be perfect. There'll be burgers and beer."

Ember smiled at the sound of his laughter. "With the week I've been having, I could use a proper Friday night piss-up."

Dennis had been frowning at his crossword puzzle, but his head lifted suddenly. He shot Ember a quizzical look.

A couple seconds of silence followed on the phone, before Cooper said uncertainly, "What did you just say? Ember, I don't know what kind of parties you're used to attending, but this is just a barbecue. I don't know what 'pissing' means over in the U.K. but over here it's associated with urination."

Ember stammered, "No I...of course. No, piss-up just means a party where pints are served. Beer. Not...not what you just said."

"You might want to keep that phrase tucked away when you stop over tonight, okay?"

"I'm so embarrassed." She covered her eyes with her hand. "I'll keep my lips zipped. Oh, but I don't know what I should wear? And should I bring something?"

Cooper chuckled. "It's casual, don't worry. Just bring your biting wit and charming personality."

"Brilliant. I'll see if I remembered to pack that in my luggage."

He recited his street address and told her to arrive anytime after 6:00.

By the time Ember flipped the phone shut, her flushed cheeks had just about returned to their normal hue.

Across the small office, Dennis was mumbling at the crossword puzzle as he gnawed on his pencil.

"Hey Smiley," she called out. "The word is 'fortuitous'."

It was just past 7:30 when Ember arrived at the driveway of Cooper Severson's house. She walked from her apartment, across town to the residential development where he lived. His was a modest split-level home with a double garage, the overhead doors of which were both open as people milled about.

When she was growing up back in Great Malvern, Ember's parents hosted parties regularly. Those were dinner parties, garden parties, and cocktail parties where the intellectual and political elite of Druwish society mingled. Attendees were well-groomed and well-heeled. A caterer and wait staff were sometimes hired, and she and her sister Cynthia were expected to act the part of proper children of the upper class. When she was a child, she shared her older sister's enthusiasm for the classy gatherings. As Ember developed her latent Investigator skills, however, she grew to dread those charades and the superficiality of the people who attended them.

Cooper's get-together couldn't have been more different from those upscale affairs. In his garage, two insulated plastic coolers sat open: one filled with bottles of beer, the other with cans of soda and bottled water. Crushed ice blanketed the contents of both, and guests served themselves. Laughter and conversation were accompanied by sounds coming from a satellite radio, which was tuned to a 90's rock station.

A tough-looking woman with tattoos on her forearms and a pierced nose was the first to greet her. The brunette pointed to the coolers. "You look thirsty. What can I get you: beer, soda?"

"Oh, a beer would be brilliant, thank you."

The woman fished out a long-neck, dark bottle. Before she handed it to Ember, she twisted off the bottle cap. "I don't think we've met. I'm Jolene."

"Ember. Coop's friend. Obviously." She smiled nervously and scanned the faces in the garage as the frigid bottle dripped melted ice onto her fingers. "Thanks. Sorry, I don't...really know anybody here. This *is* Coop's place, right?"

Jolene's smile broadened. She slapped a hand on Ember's shoulder, turning toward the assembled crowd. "Everyone!" Jolene had a voice that demanded attention, even with Nine Inch Nails blaring in the background. "This is Ember. Ember, this is everyone."

The strangers collectively raised their beverages toward Ember and simultaneously yelled, "Skol!" They couldn't have been more synchronized in their greeting.

"There you go, now we're not strangers." Jolene grinned. "Coop's out back, grilling. You just got here? Oh, you'd better grab something to eat before it gets put away. Come on, I'll walk you through the maze."

As Ember was led through the crowd, she made a mental note that all the individuals had the thin auras of NonDruws. Men slightly outnumbered women, and everyone was dressed casually. Several people greeted her as she meandered past.

Cooper wore a dark green apron and stood over a propane grill with tongs in one hand and a half-consumed bottle of Coors Light in the other. He was talking to a broad-shouldered man with a dark, wavy mullet, but he stopped mid-story to greet the new arrival. "Ember! I was beginning to think you weren't going to make it."

"Right. Sorry about that. Some things came up at work."

"Where do you work?" The man next to Cooper asked.

"I'm a massage therapist. At the Magic City Spa, downtown." She casually raised the bottle to her lips and took a sip of the bitter liquid.

"Ray-J, this is the woman I was telling you about." Cooper gestured at Ember.

"Oh, the one from the plane! I should've guessed from your accent." The man's hand shot out. "Ray Johnson. This shit-head insists on calling me Ray-J."

"Doesn't he look like a Ray-J? I mean, look at that fucking haircut! He's growing it out for his album cover photo." Cooper mockingly snapped his tongs over Ray's shoulder.

Ember shook the man's hand. "So, you're a musician, Ray?"

"I only sing in Coop's fantasies. Nah, I'm a fireman here in Minot. This asshat's just jealous of my magnificent 'do."

Jolene pointed at Ember's purse. "I think you're ringing."

Ember hadn't heard her cell phone's chime. "So, I am. Please excuse me one moment." She dug out the embassy-provided phone as she walked away from the crowd to a quieter corner of Cooper's backyard. Beneath a golden willow, she flipped the phone open. "Ember speaking."

"Emberly darling, I haven't heard from you all week. I thought perhaps your mobile had gone missing, or you'd forgotten our number."

Ember sighed, "Hello, Mum. I'm sorry I haven't called. It's been a busy week."

"I'm sure you're much too busy to call home. Your father was busy, too, but he found time to post his daughter a case of Marmite as you'd asked. How are things with my little girl?"

"Mum, I'm at a friend's house now, meeting people. Maybe I could call you back tomorrow?"

"Emberly, since when have you friends? When did this happen?"

"I'm going to hang up now. I'll call you back later, I promise."

"Your father and I shall wait with bated breath until then."

"Kisses to you and Daddy."

As she tucked her phone back into her purse, she noticed a black bird perched on a branch above. A blink confirmed her suspicion: it was the changeling spy. She resisted the impulse to throw her beer at the crow. *This is getting bloody ridiculous, spying on me even in social settings. I can't wait to see your face when I take you down someday.*

The evening was spent laughing and exchanging stories. Mostly, Ember just smiled and listened. She marveled at how unpretentious Cooper's friends were. They could veer onto the vulgar side at times, but even that had a certain charm, she found. Many of his friends were civil servants like him: police, firemen, paramedics. There was a camaraderie and familiarity among them which Ember admired.

As twilight set in, Cooper lit a fire pit in the backyard, and the crowd assembled plastic lawn chairs in a circle around the dancing flames.

"Did you see my bike yet?" Cooper asked her when the

crowd had begun to thin, sometime after 10:00. "It's in the garage."

She followed him in there, leaving the rest of the guests in the backyard as they shared work stories.

"Isn't she a beaut?" Cooper pulled a stitched canvas cover off the black-and-silver motorcycle. "Do you ride?"

Ember recognized the Harley-Davidson logo on the fuel tank and was reminded of a similar conversation she had recently with Josette. "Oh goodness, no. I'd bloody well destroy the motorbike and probably myself. I have a terrible sense of balance. Honestly, it's amazing that I can even walk upright. I might be the missing link with primates, you know."

Cooper grinned. His eyes were glassy, and his spirit was high. The man played host to his friends that night, plying them with beverages and food prepared from his grill. He obviously loved every moment of it. "Say, how's your project coming along?"

"My project?"

"Yeah, your family tree project. The genealogy research."

"Oh, right. It's been going brilliantly, thanks." Ember nodded. Her cheeks were sore from smiling so much throughout the evening. A thought sprang into her consciousness then. "Actually, I did run into a snag. I have a distant relative whose name I came across in my research, but I can't find any more information on him. He lived in Minot, around the turn of the century."

"Maybe I can help." Cooper seemed eager. "I am a detective, after all."

She thought of the database queries she performed on her computer in the office earlier in the week. With her access restricted, she came up empty.

"I haven't been able to find his death certificate, nor anything about his life for that matter." She shrugged, trying to seem indifferent. "But I wouldn't want to be a bother. It's not that important."

"It wouldn't be a bother at all. I can pull death certificates for anyone in the state of North Dakota. If that doesn't work, I can broaden the search nationwide. Just give me a name, and I'll get you whatever info I can find on him."

"Really, you could do that? His name was Billy Colton. That's all I know about him."

Cooper pulled a notepad and ink pen from his left chest pocket. He clicked the pen and scribbled. "Billy Colton. Got it. I'll call you with anything I find."

"You're such a dear. Thank you for helping me. And thank you for having me over tonight. Your friends are all so nice." Her gratitude was sincere.

A ringtone emitted from her purse again. Ember shook her head and smirked. "Wow, you're good. I didn't even see you dial me."

Cooper chuckled and squeezed her upper arm. "I'll let you take that call. I'll be back at the fire pit. Don't you dare take off without saying goodbye."

She flipped open the embassy phone, but the ringing didn't stop. It rang again before she realized that it was coming from the other phone in her purse.

Looking around to verify she was alone in the garage, she finally answered.

"Ember, we need to talk. Right now." The anxiety in Wallace's voice made the hair on the back of her neck stand up.

"What's wrong?" She hissed into the burner phone. "Wallace, are you okay? It must be four or five in the morning there."

"I'm fine, I'm fine. It's you I'm worried about. I've been making some inquiries, planning our next move. This thing...it's big, Ember. You're in danger. I'm getting you out of there."

21

DO RIGHT TO ALL MANNER OF PEOPLE

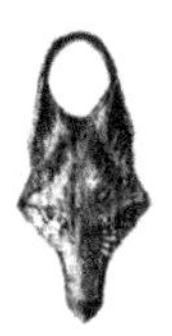

FROM THE FIRST TIME SHE MET WALLACE, HE ALWAYS reminded her of a character straight out of a Louis L'Amour western. He was consistently calm to the point of being stoic, a man of few words while commanding respect by his mere presence.

A few years later, the movie that would become her all-time favorite was released. The actor Sam Elliott was one of the stars of *Tombstone*, and the way he played the part of the lawman Virgil Earp practically mirrored the persona of Wallace Livingstone. As many times as she watched that film, Ember couldn't see it without imagining her mentor as that famous brother to Wyatt Earp.

So, it was all the more unnerving to hear the anxiety now percolating in her former partner's voice. "Are you somewhere safe right now?"

Ember was standing in Cooper's garage, alone. In the backyard, she could hear the host and his guests talking and laughing. She answered with a hushed volume. "I think so, yeah. You're starting to freak me out. Can you please tell me what's going on?"

"Where to begin?" He murmured. "Since we last talked, I've done a lot of thinking, some inquiring, and discovered a few things that lead me to believe that your ghost is telling the truth. That there was—and persists—a massive conspiracy ongoing. One which must reach the highest levels, including the Druw High Council."

Ember sucked in air. "How can you be sure?"

"In short, I cannot. At least not yet. Hear me out." Wallace's breath was rapid, shallow. "You have a set of skills which we know to be unique among Investigators: you can see the auras of Druw and NonDruw, and gauge the relative temperament of such. You see spells cast by others, not just your own like the rest of us do. You can see a changeling's animal subform—while even Senior Investigators can barely sense the difference between Druw and NonDruw, Malvern and changeling. You can call on the deceased and have conversations with them—nobody else can even see the spirits, much less converse with them."

He continued, "You and I have accepted that you are unique, but what if you aren't—or rather, wouldn't be if the natural order was left unmanipulated? You weren't the first highly-rated Investigator candidate I tested over the decades. You were simply the first that I could keep hidden. All the others—even ones I tried to hide after discovering you—all of those children died or disappeared completely."

Ember sat down on a stool in the garage. She felt the blood drain from her face as she realized what Wallace was piecing together.

Wallace breathed into the phone. "If Inquisitors once existed, as Barnaby suggested, then they have been eliminated entirely. They represented a powerful balancing force to the Druw Council and somebody wanted to remove that balance. To do so, they would have needed to move against Inquisitors the world over, in tandem. They have further managed to rewrite history, to somehow suppress the memories from everyone. It's not over, as they continue to eliminate potential Inquisitors before they have a chance to develop their skills."

"If this is all true," Wallace continued, "Then the full force of this global conspiracy would do anything to remove any threats to their order that they discover. That means you, Ember. That means me as well. That means anyone who knows about your powers. Anyone who is helping you. We can guess that these people would also do anything they can to hurt you, including targeting your family and anyone who you care about."

Ember held her head in her hands now. She whispered into the cell phone. "Then this goes way, way beyond the Director of Wellness and some changeling henchmen. So, you're saying even some High Council members may be party to this?"

"I'm saying *all* of the Council members might be, Ember." He breathed a weary sigh. "We can't be sure who to trust. It might be only you and me, for that matter."

"There are some who I met here—the families of the disabled changelings—who have been helping me. I haven't told them any more than I've needed to, but they've got skin in the game, too. They're hurting under this regime, and I need to help them."

"Do you care about these people, Ember?"

"I do."

"Then think about how involving them puts *them* at risk. They can be used to get to you."

Ember thought of the Schmitts. She thought of Maxim and Marta, the ten-year-old twin offspring of Arnie and Stephanie. She closed her eyes and recalled the mirth in their laughter as they chased the family dog through the trees. Ember whispered, "I can't abandon them, Wallace. I won't."

Wallace breathed into the phone for some seconds before he quietly responded. "I can't be there to help you, Ember. I'm more useful trying to pry from my end, within the Council. I have a few Investigator candidates who I trust, but none of them are ready yet. It will be months before I can send help to you."

"Until then, I will do what I can, alone."

"It might be wiser to keep a low profile," the man suggested. "To just focus on the census audit and keep away from the Mandaree Incident until we can know how deep this thing goes, until we have more suspects and we can find more people we can trust."

"These changelings don't have that much time, Wallace. I've seen the shape they are in. The ones who aren't suicidal are hanging on by a thread. Substance abuse, terrible health problems. After nine years of fighting their afflictions, they're starting to slip away."

"We have to think beyond them, Ember. This is much bigger than the lives of ten changelings."

Ember leaned forward and rested her elbows on her knees. "I know you're right. I know there's a big picture here to consider. But if we are willing to abandon justice for these people—for their families—then what is the point of all this? What's the point of pledging to the Investigator's Creed, if the line 'I will do right to all manner of people' is just a comforting piece of poetry?"

Wallace breathed into the phone. "I was afraid you would say that. You've always had an intensity for justice that borders on the obsessive. Maybe that, too, is a quality among Inquisitors."

"Maybe. What should I do next, boss?"

"I've thought of that, too. I think the best suspect we have right now is Elton Higginbotham. We need to find out what he is hiding, and why. We can't interrogate him directly, though, as he is likely just a lieutenant to those who have infiltrated the highest levels of the Council. We need to come at him sideways. See if this...Deference Spell...can be countered, in case he tries to hit you with it again."

"I'll talk to Barnaby."

"That was going to be my suggestion, yes." Wallace was breathing more evenly now. "Please be careful. We can't know who will turn on you if they find out what you really are."

Ember felt goosebumps at that pronouncement. Then the words flowed from her even as the thought formed. "Wallace, you knew I would refuse to back down."

"I'd hoped."

She disconnected the call and started walking home in the

dark. Ember was halfway to her apartment when she realized she hadn't said goodbye to Cooper.

SHE PACED IMPATIENTLY WITHIN THE UNLIT FOYER OF ST. Leo's Church, watching out the window for her ride. Ember called Alarik to come pick her up for another meeting with her "contact." He sounded like he had been sleeping. She hoped he didn't fall back asleep after they talked.

The return to her apartment building had been quick, as she ran the entire way. More than once, she stumbled on uneven sidewalks, made more harrowing by the uneven distribution of street lights. She assumed the changeling spy would be following her, so she needed to make a show of returning to her apartment building.

She fetched a flashlight and her heavier jacket from Number 302. She walked past the elevator to the stairwell which led to the basement and its hidden tunnel. Ember was only passing aware of the light peeking from beneath the door of her neighbor's apartment. *Anderle, are you, too, sleepless at two in the morning?*

She shook her head, dismissing the distraction. The sleep patterns of her mystery neighbor had no place in her consciousness, especially not when she was still trying to process what Wallace had told her.

Finally, the familiar Super Duty rumbled up to the curb. Ember hurried from the church, climbing up into the cab before the door to the church had even swung shut. "What took you so long?"

"Seriously?" Alarik gaped. "You wake me up at one in the morning, tell me that you need a ride to Surrey 'with immediate effect,' and then you have the gall to ask me what took so long?"

"Can we just drive, please?"

He frowned at her but pulled the shift lever into Drive.

She knew she should apologize to him, that he was doing her a favor. Ember thought of Barnaby's warning, of how the life of an Inquisitor is a solo existence. She began to understand why. Her obsession with the pursuit of justice far superseded any friendships. *If this is the price, I will gladly pay it.* She tried to convince herself that she really meant it, too.

"I need to meet this contact of yours," Alarik said as he turned off Highway 2 into Surrey. It was the first either of them had spoken during the drive.

"Now isn't a great time, Rik." Ember's blonde hair shook. "I can't expect you to understand, but I need you to wait in the pickup. Oh, and I may be a little longer this time."

Alarik grumbled. "Whatever you say, Miss Daisy."

She didn't understand his reference, nor did she care. Her body cried for sleep, but she was buzzing with adrenaline. The Malvern woman focused on her task, to the exclusion of everything else. Having sent Barnaby to rest, she would need to call upon him again, and that would cost mana. Holding the inevitably irritated apparition at bay would exhaust her further.

The yellow beam from her flashlight led the way as she walked across the graves in the Brethren Cemetery. She found Barnaby Harrison's headstone and was reaching for it when she saw movement in her periphery.

Instinctively, Ember clicked her flashlight off, reversing it in her grip to use as a weapon. As her eyes adjusted to the darkness, the movement became pronounced. A glimmering, transparent blue shape walked the edge of the cemetery, approaching her.

"The little girl...returns. Has she finished with her...temper tantrum, at last?"

"Barnaby?" Ember gasped. "How did you...how are you here? I...I sent you away. I released you. I sent you to rest."

His sandpaper laugh echoed in her skull. "So, you did. And I shall, when justice for my murderer has been served. You no longer hold sway over me."

"You can...you can choose not to return when I release you?" Ember felt sick to her stomach. "I didn't know."

"Indeed, you did not. Simply shocking, how ignorant you are. You do not even know what you do not know."

"I'm holding up my end of the deal. I've got a detective looking into Billy Colton."

"Very good, little girl." The spirit paced a circle around Ember. "This is why you are visiting me? A status report?"

"No. No, not entirely." She zipped up her jacket and hugged herself. The ghost's close presence made the night air even colder. "It seems that there *is* a conspiracy of some sort. Potential Inquisitors are being eliminated before they can become a problem to this upside-down order. There are suspicions that the parties involved include members of the Druw High Council."

"Troubling, indubitably." Barnaby stroked his mutton chops with transparent fingers. "How do you expect to combat this, if you are indeed the lone living Inquisitor?"

"With the help of a Grand Inquisitor." Ember focused her gaze on the glowing eye sockets of the ghost. "Tell me everything you know about lifting a Deference Spell."

Barnaby's face remained placid, but his gritty voice reverberated in her head. "Other than by the one who cast it, a Deference Spell can only be temporarily lifted."

"Okay, so a temporary lift. How long are we talking, days, weeks?"

"Seconds. Depending on the intensity of the spell and the strength of the Inquisitor, perhaps ten to fifteen seconds."

Ember felt her hopes sink. Her eyes began to sting with weary tears. She blinked them away and suppressed a sniffle. "Ten seconds. What is the use of lifting a spell for ten seconds."

"Admittedly, limited." Barnaby canted his head, the visor of his beaver skin hat hiding his eyes. When he raised his chin, the glowing eye sockets were fixed on Ember. "Unless you know how to use those seconds."

Ember contemplated before answering. "It's enough time for one question, and one answer."

"The girl guesses correctly."

"Will you teach me this, please? Teach me how to lift a Deference Spell, even temporarily?"

"I will." Barnaby stopped touching his face. "But know that if you attempt to counter a Deference Spell, it will be at great cost to you. You will be drained of mana, and perhaps worse. If the one who set the spell is strong, you may become immobilized."

Barnaby was remarkably patient in explaining the timing and actions needed to temporarily lift the spell. He explained how the use of a charged Leystone could be leveraged to increase the duration of the temporary lift, though only by seconds.

Ember practiced the gestures as her ghostly coach instructed. He was strict but Ember caught on quickly.

Midway through the tenth practice run, Barnaby stopped and extended his finger into the night beyond them. "We're not alone, girl. Behind you, a changeling lurks. It has been watching us."

22

FIND YOUR OWN WAY BACK

Ember thought she had been careful, thought she had taken the proper precautions. But somehow, one of the changeling spies managed to track her. She silently cursed her sloppiness.

"It is hiding behind that tree!" Barnaby's transparent finger pointed.

Reflexively, she called upon her mana, pulling it from her core and sending it down her arm, to her right fist as she spun around on her heel. The silhouette of an imposing man emerged from behind a mature maple tree, just as Ember moved her arm forward. She opened her fist, releasing a charge of bright orange light that only she could see.

The containment net widened as it shot toward the changeling. It connected with the man with such force, it knocked him to the ground. The man fell with a thud and began to struggle. The more he fought, the tighter the containment net shrunk. Soon his movements were restricted and futile.

Ember breathed in deeply, filling her lungs with the scent of cool morning dew. Though feeling triumphant, she approached her quarry warily.

Though the containment net prevented him from doing so, the changeling snarled and attempted to transform into his animal form. Ember's sense of accomplishment quickly faded when she blinked and saw what she had captured. The subform was a coyote. *Not just any coyote.*

She rushed to her prey, who continued to struggle and snarl. As she knelt and placed her hands on the strands of the golden net, Barnaby recognized what she was about to do.

"Do not release him!" The ghost effortlessly strode to her side. "At least interrogate him first. Can you not see he is trying to shift?"

"He's a friend." Ember glanced up at Barnaby before she returned her focus to the struggling man. "His name is Rik." She tucked her fingers into the strands of the glowing net and whispered, "Dissolve."

Tension fell slack in the containment net. The golden strands dissolved away within seconds.

Alarik struggled to his feet, his teeth back as he snarled.

A terrible thought teased at her consciousness: she feared that Alarik was going to shift into coyote form and lunge at her with his sharp teeth. Ember clambered to her feet and took a step back. "Easy. Easy. You're alright. You're safe." She wasn't sure which side she was speaking to: human or beast.

The man relaxed only slightly. His voice emerged as a low growl. "Why'd you attack me?"

"Attack you?" Ember crossed her arms. "How about I ask: why were you sneaking up on me? You were supposed to wait in the pickup."

"You've been out here for two hours. I was getting worried about you." He growled again. "I heard you talking to someone, but there's nobody else here. What kind of bullshit games are you playing?"

"It's not bullshit, Rik. I can't expect you to understand."

"No, how could I, when you continue lying to me." Alarik brushed grass off his blue jeans and started marching toward the road. "I'm leaving. You can find your own way back."

Ember glanced at Barnaby, who said nothing. She chased after Alarik, catching up with him just as he started his pickup. She opened the passenger door and managed to pull herself up into the cab as the Super Duty started to move. "You were seriously going to leave me here?" Her voice was shriller than she intended it.

"Why have you been making me drive you out here?" He growled at her as his foot stomped the accelerator pedal. The beefy Ford responded with squealing tires until tread found traction on the damp asphalt. "You're just out here practicing tai chi or some bullshit. There's no secret contact at all, is there. It's all just a lie."

"There *is* a contact. You just can't see him."

"Yeah, I'm sure there is. You won't show him to me because I'm just a dumb changeling. I'm just a sucker for trusting a mage. For trusting you. You don't really want to help us. You're just another in a long line of liars."

She returned his glare. She wished she would have had the maturity, the presence of mind to keep her mouth shut until his temper cooled down. Until *hers* cooled down. Instead, she blurted out, "Go ahead and act all high and mighty, Rik. We both know the real reason you're helping me isn't for your brother. It's for you and your guilt."

Ember immediately regretted her words, even as they spilled out of her mouth. For a moment, she thought that she had imagined those words and not given them voice. She wished for that to be so.

Alarik said nothing, as the miles melted behind them. The earliest rays of eastern sunlight chased the Ford into the Magic City. Before them, dark cumulonimbus clouds drifted from the west in the morning breeze. Sporadic lightning silently punctuated a lavender sky as sprinkles of rain arrived, beading and then streaming up the windshield.

As the vehicle found its way into downtown Minot, Ember finally found the courage to speak. "I'm sorry, Rik. I'm tired and under a lot of pressure, but that's no excuse. I should never have said that. Will you forgive me?"

He wouldn't even look at her. Even when he stopped in front of St. Leo's Church, he said nothing. The clouds opened and rain was falling heavily in sheets around them.

She persisted. "Rik—"

"Get. Out." The man and his coyote subform both growled the syllables.

If he would have punched her, it wouldn't have hurt as

much as the way he said those words. There was a finality to them.

Ember slid out of the tall pickup and onto the curb. Before she swung the passenger door shut, she stole one more look at his stubbled face, his mop of unkempt hair. He never even glanced at her.

She stood on the sidewalk while the cold dawn rain washed over her. As the taillights of Alarik's Ford disappeared down the street, she recalled Barnaby's words with a shiver. *An Inquisitor's life is a solo existence.*

23

TASTES LIKE COPPER

TIME MOVES MORE SLOWLY WHEN YOU'RE SUFFERING.

At least, that was the conclusion Ember reached in the days following the stormy argument with Alarik. She knew that she had begun to develop feelings for the man, but judging from her reaction to the way that they parted, those feelings were deeper than she had acknowledged.

She felt hollow, somehow. Wallace detected something to that end when they talked later Saturday to report what she had learned from Barnaby. She told her former partner about the fact that the Deference Spell could be lifted only with heroic effort—and even then, only for a few seconds.

"Then this will be of limited help to us." Wallace sighed. Then, his tone shifted. "You sound weary, Ember."

"I'm fine," she lied. "I'm just tired and disappointed that this might be a dead end. Lifting the Deference Spells could've been useful in recruiting the Investigators to our side."

"That would have been ideal." The Legend sighed again.

"We must be patient. You might lay low while we figure out our next move. Do nothing to arouse suspicion."

She spent the rest of the weekend locked up in her apartment, trying to ignore the gloomy mood she found herself in. She thought about calling in sick to work on Monday, but decided that the distraction might help.

Around noon on Thursday, Ember overheard the other Investigators in the office leave for lunch together. Dennis was in the break room, consuming a sub sandwich and soft drink. On a whim, she walked past the Senior Investigator's office.

Duncan wasn't in, but his office door was open, and the light was off. Ember glanced around and saw no movement down either hall. Impulsively, she stepped into the darkened office.

The computer monitor on Duncan's desk glowed brightly, betraying the fact that he was still logged into his system. *He hasn't left work, then. He would be returning any minute.*

Two inner voices lobbied for her attention: Caution screamed at her to leave before she was caught, while the other one said, "Just a little look won't hurt." Curiosity won the argument.

Ember approached the desk as she scrambled to think of what she would do with this opportunity. *I could access the entirety of the Mandaree Incident files. But then what? Send them to the printer? Email them to myself? Both could be bloody tracked.*

She hesitated as an alarming possibility announced itself.

What if the simple act of pulling a query on this case gets automatically flagged?

Her fingers hovered over the keyboard, ready to type. She looked away from the monitor, her gaze scanning Duncan's desk. Illuminated by the computer screen, she noticed a stack of envelopes. She picked them up and fanned them as she read: Montana-Dakota Utilities, SRT Communications, Midcontinent, City of Minot.

Bills. They're just his personal bills. Almost as an afterthought, she mentally noted his street address, committing it to memory.

Footsteps sounded off in the hallway. Someone was coming.

Ember thrust the stack of stuffed envelopes back where she had found them, then rushed out the office door. Her mind raced with excuses. *Oh, Duncan, what a coincidence; I was just coming to see you.*

Instead, as she rounded the corner, she ran into a mountain —a bearded mountain.

"What the—" Dennis started to speak.

Thinking quickly, Ember allowed momentum to carry her. She collided with the man, knocking the tall fountain soda from his hand. Dark amber fluid flew from the paper cup to splatter against the cream-colored wall.

She captured the moment. "Dammit, Smiley!" Ember scolded. "Can't you watch where you're going?"

"I...what were you—"

"Don't you try turning this on me, mister." She pointed at the cola, which dripped in sticky rivulets down the wall.

"Look at the mess you've made! What do you think Duncan will say when he gets back in and sees that you've made a feast for ants in front of his office door? This is exactly how you get ants, you know."

"Well, I—"

"The longer you stand there, bumbling, the more this stuff is going to dry. Have you ever tried cleaning dried Coca-Cola from painted plaster? I mean, really."

"It's Dr. Pepper." Dennis stammered. "Um, I'll go get some paper towels."

"Right. That's a good place to start." Ember watched the changeling run down the hall and into the break room. As satisfying as it was to make the burly security staffer nervous, she knew she had just dodged a bullet. She let out a long sigh, then quickly found a route to her office. *What was it Wallace said? "Do nothing to arouse suspicion." Yeah, brilliant, Ember.*

The corded landline phone on her desk was ringing when she returned to the supply closet. Ember picked up the receiver and was met with a flow of syllables, as though the person calling her was already mid-conversation.

"Don't you just hate it when everyone leaves but they don't tell you? I thought maybe you had gone to lunch with everyone else. Well, Mr. Heywood had gone upstairs, but it's still lunchtime. I should be taking my lunch, too, but then there would be nobody at the front desk if someone called. It's a good thing, too, because people do call."

"Hello, Joy. What do you need?"

"How did you guess it was me? Oh, right, my accent probably. I should tell you that I've been practicing my English accent. I'm gonna whip it out sometime and you'll be all like, 'oy! Who's the new lassie from jolly ol' England, workin' the phones?' Then I'll change back to my regular voice and say, 'It's me, Joy! I had you fooled!'"

Ember pinched the bridge of her nose and squeezed her eyes shut. "Joy, was there a reason you called me?"

"Oh, right! I'd almost forgotten. Let's see, Ami from downstairs called. I don't know which Ami, mind you, 'cause once you've met one Ami you've met them all." Joy giggled. "But yup, Ami called. She said someone was here to see you. They are waiting in the lobby, on account that they don't have the security clearance to come upstairs. Come to think of it, she didn't say who was waiting. Should I call down and ask?"

"Thanks, Joy. I'll head down there now." She hung up the phone, even as she heard Joy continue talking. Ember grabbed her purse and her satchel, then made her way to the elevator. Joy was on the phone when Ember walked past. They smiled and waved at each other.

She hoped it might have been Alarik coming to see her. A scenario of mutual apologies played in her head, followed by an awkward but manageable return to how things were before Saturday morning's fallout.

Instead, waiting for her in the lobby was a tall, curvy changeling woman with dark blonde hair midway down her back. "Hi, Ember. I thought maybe I could take you out to lunch?"

Ember nodded, "Hello Anna. I'm...not really very hungry."

"Okay, then how about we go for a walk in the park?"

The Malvern woman thought about using work as an excuse. She was feeling ashamed for how she had treated Alarik, and the prospect of talking about it with the man's sister seemed too uncomfortable to endure.

"Come on, let's go." Anna's gaze flitted to the door a moment before her head turned in the same direction. She wasn't giving Ember a chance to bow out. "I'm parked in a loading zone."

Anna drove them to Roosevelt Park—the verdant acreage near Ember's apartment building. She jogged the park multiple times in the mornings since arriving in the Magic City. Today, the park was filled with young families, clustered around booths in the open fields. The saccharin caramel scent of hot kettle corn wafted from one of the vendors, mingling in the air with children's laughter. A small stage was set up, from which a polka band played enthusiastically to a crowd of older people.

"It's a Scandinavian heritage Arts in the Park event," Anna explained. "Nothing like the Norsk Hostfest later in the year, of course. Let's stick to the paths away from the crowds so we can visit."

"A hoost-fest?" Ember raised her eyebrows as she pronounced the strange word. "Do I even want to know what that is?"

The broad-shouldered woman noticed a twig on the ground and picked it up. She studied it for a moment as they walked. "People know how to party in Minot. We've got the State Fair in July, the Hostfest in September. It's a big ethnic festival. It's an excuse to eat too much, drink too much, and listen to loud music."

"Well I...I'm eager to discover this...hoost-fest."

"So, you'll be here then, through the summer?" Anna pulled a jackknife from her pocket and unfolded it. She began whittling the bark from the twig in her hand. She glanced at Ember as they both made room for a mother and daughter riding bicycles on the path. "I wasn't sure how long you would be in North Dakota. I thought maybe with things turning sour between you and Rik, that you might be tempted to call it quits."

"I still have a job to do. I promised your family I would help." Ember chewed on her lower lip. "What did Rik tell you?"

"He didn't tell me anything. I know my brother, though." Anna's head turned to watch Ember as she talked. "I know that he thinks the world of you. Not just for what you're doing for the family, either. I can tell that he respects you, Ember."

Ember chuckled weakly. "Probably not so much anymore."

"I don't know what happened between you and him." Anna held her palms up and to her sides, the knife safely between her thumb and forefinger along with the partially-whittled stick. "I just know that he's been a big gloom-ball since this weekend. He won't tell anyone anything, other than that he isn't going to be bringing you around again."

Ember felt her heart sink. "He said that?"

"He did. But you should know that my brother is a bit of a block-head when it comes to women. He's the sweetest man, and I love him of course, but he has a tendency of putting his foot in his mouth. Whatever he said, I hope you will forgive him."

Ember blinked. Her eyes were starting to sting. "It wasn't him. It was what I said. I was upset, and I said something hurtful to Rik."

"I see." Anna walked a few more steps before she stopped. "I know you two have only known each other a couple short weeks, but I know you've been spending a lot of time together. Be honest: do you care about my brother?"

Ember met Anna's dusky brown, serious eyes—eyes so like Alarik's. She nodded once. "Yes. I do."

"Then you need to make this right. If there's one thing I've learned from watching Arnie, it's that life is fragile. Don't wait for tomorrow to make things right, because tomorrow might never come."

Ember inhaled deeply and nodded again. "You're right. I'll call him. Thank you, Anna."

Anna gave Ember's arm a squeeze. "Good. Because if you wait for him to call you, you'll die of old age. We Schmitts are stubborn sonsabitches."

Ember opted to continue walking through the wooded paths of the park, even after Anna took her leave. She didn't feel like facing her co-workers just yet. She needed to be alone with her thoughts for a while.

The telltale ringing of a bicycle bell sounded off behind her, followed by a voice. "Passing to your left!"

Ember stepped aside to watch a middle-aged woman wave

as she pedaled past. The woman reached into her bike's basket, producing a peanut which she tossed into the weeds beneath a spruce tree. A grey squirrel bounced across the grass to retrieve its treat, and the woman resumed her journey.

Finding a bench in the shade nearby, Ember settled in and considered what she would say to Alarik when she called him. She wasn't eager to apologize, to make herself vulnerable to potential rejection. She wondered if it might be for the best if she did cut ties with him, for his own safety. Wallace had warned her that if she was ever found out by Higginbotham or his co-conspirators, they would not hesitate to hurt others to get to her.

She closed her eyes and sighed. Behind her, she heard a child babbling happily. The little girl was talking to someone in a hushed tone.

Ember turned to watch the girl and found what she thought might have been a Native American child, lecturing a trio of robins who seemed completely unafraid of her. She couldn't have been more than eight or nine years old. The girl wore a floral sundress, and she had dark, wavy hair trimmed short above her shoulders. Her skin was a bronzed tan, and when she looked up from the birds, she revealed a pair of startlingly bright eyes the color of oxidized copper.

It was the child's aura which particularly grabbed the Investigator's attention. She wasn't Druwish, but she wasn't entirely NonDruw, either. The girl's energy glowed brightly, and moved around her in an alternating pattern, at times spotted and then herringbone. Ember had never seen anything like it.

The birds took to the air in different directions when the girl cried out. She ran to the bicycle path before dropping to her knees. Gingerly, the child picked up the limp carcass of a squirrel that had been smashed beneath a careless bike tire.

Ember looked around. *Where are this girl's parents? They can't seriously be allowing this child to play with a dead animal!* Seeing no adults paying attention, Ember looked back at the girl, just in time to see her walking up to some chokecherry shrubs at the edge of Roosevelt Park.

The Malvern woman felt her heart ache when she saw how carefully the girl carried the dead squirrel. Those emotions turned quickly to disgust when she watched the child bring the carcass to her lips to kiss it before setting it on the ground at her feet.

Ember stood up and walked briskly toward the girl. *How did this suddenly become my responsibility? Where in the world are her parents? She's bound to catch some sort of disease.*

On the green turf in front of the tanned little girl, the squirrel twitched, and then it stood up. It scratched its ear with a back paw before scampering off into the shrubs. The tanned little girl squealed with glee, clapping her hands excitedly.

Ember stared at the girl, her eyes wide. The child noticed her then, and her expression instantly shifted from delight to fear.

"No, wait!" Ember shouted at the girl. She ran towards the child, but the little girl in the floral dress had already disappeared into the crowd.

Ember looked around, standing where the child had been.

She wondered if someone was playing a trick on her. The roof of her mouth tasted dry and metallic. The hairs on the back of her neck stood on end when she recognized the taste. *Copper. The air tastes like copper.*

She took a knee and touched the patch of sod where the girl had been kneeling moments ago. The oily, unusual mana residue she discovered was faint and fading fast. It was no doubt invisible to anyone other than Ember. Even she would not have known what it was if she hadn't felt it twelve days ago in a smoke-filled kitchen in a house in Makoti.

It was the same alien energy she found trapped within the disabled changeling when she had tried to heal him.

24

THEY'RE WAITING FOR YOU

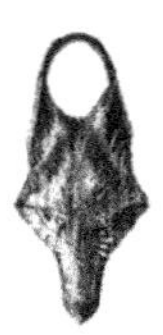

THE LITTLE YELLOW COTTAGE ON THE EDGE OF PLAZA WAS alive with activity. The blue-and-red bunting weaved into the white picket fence fluttered happily in the stiff breeze. Two young children rode their bicycles in the driveway beneath a raised American flag. An old man stood next to a black grill with smoke puffing out of its silver vents. He waved at the passing car with a spatula.

Anna tapped her car's horn twice in response as she drove past. "That's Mr. Valance. He and his wife have lived there forever—since I was a kid at least. They keep such a festive yard, always decorating for the seasons. Looks like their son and grandkids are up visiting for the weekend."

"Do you know everyone in Plaza?" Ember asked as she admired the houses through the passenger window of the sedan.

"Pretty much. It's not like there are that many people in the neighborhood, and I've lived on the farm my whole life. Everyone gets together in town whenever there are weddings or funerals, or class reunions in the summer, and for Santa Days in December. It's practically one big, extended family."

Ember looked at the driver. "Thanks for the ride. And for including me in the celebrations."

"Of course. It's the Fourth of July, after all." Anna turned the car off the paved road and onto gravel. "Did you talk to Rik yet?"

"Just briefly, to get everything set up for the meeting."

"So, you didn't make up with him yet?"

Ember glanced down. "Not yet. I will today, though. It didn't seem like the sort of thing to do over the phone."

"I'm holding you to that." The way Anna said it, Ember didn't doubt that she would.

Anna's car joined the lineup of vehicles parked in a row in the gravel yard of the Schmitt Family farm. Neighboring farmers and family friends visited in clusters outside the open doors of the cement-floor, galvanized steel Quonset building. Anna stopped to chat with an elderly couple, leaving Ember to wander unattended for the moment.

The farm equipment was pulled out from storage to make room within the arched-roof Quonset. Several banquet tables were set up, with steel folding chairs arranged around them. Insulated five-gallon jugs with spigots sat on the end of one table next to a stack of red plastic Solo cups. The rest of the table hosted an arrangement of casseroles, desserts, and salads. New arrivals to the potluck added their contributions to the buffet line.

The scent of fresh-cut grass proclaimed the yard to be recently mowed. A volleyball net was staked out on a flat patch, and a game was underway. The teams were composed mostly of teenagers and a few young adults.

Ember closed her eyes and scanned the crowd. Most of the guests were NonDruws: neighbors and friends from around the farming neighborhood. What few Druws she noticed were entirely changelings; she was the only mage.

Wings flapped overhead, and a large bird landed atop an electricity pole next to the grain bins. With her eyes still closed, Ember recognized the image on the inside of her eyelids. Standing on the post was a man—one of the changeling spies. *I was wondering when you would show up, you feckless arsehole.*

Footsteps approached and a familiar voice followed. "Hey. Anna said you wanted to talk to me about something."

Ember opened her eyes and met Alarik's gaze. She looked at her feet. "Hi. I...yeah, I do. I don't know if right now is the best time though?"

"Okay." Alarik pronounced the word slowly. "She said you asked for me, and it was important."

Ember looked past the man and caught a glimpse of Anna. She was standing near the buffet table, talking to some people, but she kept glancing over at her brother. *Thanks, Anna. I suppose you did warn me.*

"Right." Ember looked over at the spying buzzard, and then quickly back to Alarik. "Someplace we can talk?"

They walked to Anna's woodshop. Once inside, Ember paced the length of the small building, inhaling the pleasant medley of oak and pine as her heels clicked on the plywood floor. She dragged her fingertips along the sawdust accumulated in the miter slot of the band saw, drawing designs on the smooth table as she tried to articulate what was on her mind. "I wanted to apologize. Rik, it was bloody rude of me to say what I did. I regret it. You have been nothing but kind to me. I'm sorry I said what I did."

Alarik crossed his arms and nodded once, but said nothing. His square-jawed facial features revealed no expression.

"And for the containment net." Ember continued. "I just reacted. I thought you were someone else—someone trying to spy on me." She looked out the dirty window of the woodshop to verify that the changeling turkey vulture was still perched on the utility pole. The bird was still there, though he turned to watch the door of the building she was in. "There's another one of those spies outside right now. The buzzard on the tall post in the yard. I've seen him before, so there's at least two of them taking turns following me."

Alarik glanced out the window and growled low. "I see him. You're sure he's a changeling, too?"

"I am, without a doubt. He and that crow track my every move, except when you've been able to sneak me away through the tunnels. That night at the cemetery, I thought one had managed to find me. But it was you. I'm sorry I attacked you."

"I accept your apology." Alarik continued watching the large bird perched on the utility post outside. "If for nothing else, then so we can continue working together. For Arnie."

"Thank you, Rik. I didn't know how much our friendship

meant to me until I thought I'd lost you—I mean until I lost it. The friendship, that is."

He looked over his shoulder at her, though he still faced the window. "I don't want to talk about that anymore. We're just working together, alright? Nothing more than that. I've set things up for today like you asked me to. Let's not make this any more complicated than it has to be."

She felt her hopes dashed then. Ember swallowed hard and pushed her emotions aside. "That's something at least. Right, just keeping it professional then. I can do that."

"Good." Alarik turned away from her again. "Good. Then we should get back."

"Speaking of complicated, there's one more thing I need to tell you. I saw something, on Thursday when Anna and I chatted at the park in Minot."

"You and Anna visited at a park?" Alarik leaned against the workbench. "I didn't know about that."

"Yeah. Well, that's not important. What's important is that after Anna left, I saw something." Ember ran her fingers through her blonde hair. "Do you remember when I tried healing Kenny?"

"You mean when you threw up all over Peg's kitchen?"

"One of my finer moments, that. I didn't tell you what I felt —what I sensed—when I was connected to Kenny. He had a...I don't know how to describe it...a strange presence within him. Unusual mana—something alien."

"Alien?" Alarik scratched his stubbled chin. "What, like from another planet?"

"I don't know. Maybe. I can't rule anything out." Ember shook her head. "I felt something similar that day in the park. The same alien energy."

"So, you saw another one of the changelings from the Mandaree Incident?" Alarik leaned forward, and his eyes widened. "Wait, do you think Arnie's got this within him, too?"

"He might. I don't know, and I'm not sure I want to try finding out." Ember chewed on her lip and studied the squiggles she made in the sawdust. "But no. No, it wasn't a changeling. It was a little girl. Maybe eight years old. She wasn't Druwish, but she had mana. Potent mana. Rik, I saw her bring a dead animal back to life."

Alarik was silent as he studied Ember. Finally, he said, "Let's just say she did. Let's assume what you saw really happened. What does it mean?"

"I didn't imagine it, Rik. The little girl ran off, and I tried to find her but it was like she'd just vanished into the crowd. But what I saw really did happen. And I don't know what it means. It's just one more in a lengthy list of questions I don't have answers for." She rubbed fine sawdust between her index and thumb. "I don't know, but I'm going to find out."

The knock at the door startled them both. The hinges whined in protest as bright sunlight intruded. Anna leaned in and looked quizzically first at her brother and then at Ember. "I didn't want to butt in, but they've all arrived. They're waiting for you."

25

I REMEMBER SOMETHING

When Ronald and Muriel Schmitt built their house, they designed it for a large family. Though they ended up having only three children, they enjoyed hosting their extended family for holidays. The expansive family room in the basement featured a full-size pool table on one half of the room, with a stone fireplace on the other half. Between those anchors were an array of sofas and recliners along the walls. Whenever a piece of upstairs living room furniture became too worn out and the family budget allowed it, a new piece would be purchased, and the old one would be relegated to its retirement in the basement.

Every available seat in the family room was now taken, as accommodation for the ten gathered changelings.

Ember, Alarik, and Anna were the last to arrive. They stood around the aged pool table, facing the guests.

It was Alarik who started. “Thank you all for coming here today. I’ve asked all of you together because there’s someone who wants to meet you. Someone who wants to help find answers for you, for the health problems you've been dealing with. This is Ember Wright. She's an Associate Investigator, and she's going to ask you some questions."

Ember smiled and stepped forward. Before she could speak, she was interrupted.

"A goddamn Malvern?" The bald man who spoke was sitting on one end of an old sofa. When he leaned forward, a vintage orange-and-brown wagon wheel pattern was revealed on the couch's cushions. "Nobody from the Magic City ever wanted to help us before. Why would this one be any different?"

One of the other changelings grumbled in agreement. Several of the strangers glared at Ember.

"Just hear her out." Anna picked up a billiard ball and started tossing it between her hands. "Rik and I think she's the real deal. She's not from the Viceroyalty, she's representing the High Council. The Council is the one making this case."

Ember dropped the leather satchel from her shoulder and placed it on the pool table. She absently selected one of the other billiard balls from the green felt surface and held it in her hand. It was cold and heavy, this Number Seven. She looked up from the ball and tried to sound confident, in charge. "Thank you, Anna. I need to correct you though; I can't say I'm representing the Council. In fact, I can't say there's a case at all. Not formally. Ideally, I need to ask that what we discuss today not be repeated or talked about outside of this room, by any of you."

The bald man scoffed. "Is that why all the cloak and dagger?

Why we're meeting in the basement? Hiding like caged rats is what we're being treated like."

Ember casually tossed the billiard ball to her other hand, like she saw Anna doing. It felt like something that would make her appear more confident, more assured than what she actually was. Her lack of coordination showed itself as the heavy ball slipped from her hand and dropped. Number Seven dropped on her foot and rolled away, disappearing beneath a recliner. She suppressed a wince and ignored her throbbing toe, though she knew everyone had to have seen her clumsiness. "It's for our mutual security that we have to keep this among ourselves for now."

This proclamation made half of the group grumble. The bald man stood up and began to walk out of the room.

"Dammit, Roy, will you sit your ass down and shut up?" It was the gravel voice of Peggy Barth. "Ember is tryin' to help us. She met with me an' Kenny already. Hell, she tried to help heal Kenny, even."

Roy looked over at the emaciated man sitting on an uncomfortable old kitchen chair in the corner, near the unlit fireplace. "And did she? Is Kenny better?"

Kenny scratched the inside of his elbow. His gaze never rose above Roy's knees when he replied. "No. But she tried."

"Oh, that's so comforting." Roy squinted at Ember.

Arnie was sitting on the other end of the wagon wheel pattern couch. He held a red plastic cup in his hand, from which he had been sipping. His words were slurred, suggesting that the cup's contents weren't simply fruit juice. "Hey, at least she's trying to help! When was the last time any of us had anyone other than one of our family members step up for us?"

A few people nodded. Ember and Alarik exchanged knowing glances.

Roy wasn't ready to acquiesce just yet. He stepped up to Ember. Alarik's stance stiffened, and in her periphery, she saw his hand close into a fist. The bald man grumbled. "What's in it for you, mage? Why are you so interested in this?"

Peggy's rough voice interrupted again. "Dammit, Roy, she's trying to help us. Why do ya gotta think everyone's got an ulterior motive?"

"Because she's a Malvern. That's what they do." The bald man only briefly looked back at the others before he returned his glare to Ember. "They don't give a shit about changelings."

As arguments flared up among the gathered changelings, Ember tried to think of a way to salvage this meeting. *Maybe this wasn't brilliant, meeting with them all at once. I don't even know that I'll get any useful information, anything I might be able to act on.*

A shrill whistle pierced the air, followed by its source speaking. "Hey! I know as well as anyone how we've been treated by the Malverns, and especially by the Malverns in government. There's good reason not to trust them. Trust has to be earned, and it's easy to lose it." Alarik looked over at Ember pointedly. "Just give her five minutes, that's all I'm asking. You are already here, on the Fourth of July. Just give her five minutes, and then if you still don't trust her, then you can go back out to the Quonset with everyone else."

Roy still stood, his bald scalp red and his posture combative. Kenneth fidgeted in his chair, chewing his nails, and staring at the shaggy carpet at his feet. A few of the changelings looked at one another uneasily. Everyone was waiting for someone else to make a move, one way or the other.

Show time. Ember took a breath, then stepped between the flanking towers of Alarik and Anna. She walked right up to Roy. A vein in the man's temple visibly pulsed. She could smell the alcohol on his breath.

She looked into his bloodshot eyes unflinchingly and spoke loud enough for everyone to hear. "You don't sleep very well, do you? You haven't had a proper night's rest in, what, nine years, have you? You have to take medication or maybe you drink yourself to sleep, only to suffer from terrible dreams. It's the same nightmare, every time: that your animal subform is trapped, and you can't reach it. You can't help it."

Peggy Barth's ragged breathing was now the only sound in the room.

"Each of you is having the same nightmares, aren't you?" Ember walked past Roy to the center of the room. "And it happened after you came in contact with the toxic fog at Mandaree. Don't you think that's a little more than coincidence?"

She spread her hands wide, showing her palms to them. "Now I don't know what happened. There's no formal active case. But if you help me piece it together, I might be able to help find out what happened. Then, we can find someone who can cure you."

"I need to have your word that nobody will talk about this conversation." Ember made a point of looking at each person as she spoke. "There's a reason you haven't had support from your government, and I'm working to find out why that is. I can't tell you any more in part because of safety—yours and mine both—but also because at this point, I honestly don't know."

Roy turned around. His voice was subdued, no longer combative. "You're asking a lot. Asking us to trust you."

"I know I am. You've each been living with this for nine years though. It's eaten away at your health. It's taken something from each of you. It's taken something from your families. You've already lost so much. So, in trusting me, you might ask yourself: what have you got to lose?"

Some seconds of silence followed. Arnie nodded, then said, "I trust you. I promise to keep all this a secret."

One by one, each of them acquiesced. Roy returned to his seat on the orange-and-brown couch and offered a shrug.

Anna and Alarik looked at one another. An unspoken exchange happened between the two siblings. From Ember's angle, their body language looked like an amalgam of relief and surprise.

The Associate Investigator retrieved a yellow legal pad from her satchel. Ember asked similar questions to what she had asked of Peggy and Kenneth fifteen days ago, with similar responses. They were sent in to investigate the fog surrounding the town of Mandaree in February 2001. They were each told to proceed in their animal subform, and each of them had forms which were ideal for scouting unnoticed: dogs, elk, deer of varied species, and coyotes. They recalled the fog was bitter cold and tasted metallic, and a buzzing noise met their ears before they succumbed to it. When they each awoke, it was in their human forms, in early September 2001. The fog lifted around them as they struggled to figure out where they were and what had happened.

They were sent in two groups. The first four included Arnold Schmitt. They went in together at a location far north of Mandaree. Their handlers dropped them off at a trailhead, and they slipped into the quarantine zone using coulees and bullberry thickets for cover.

The second group was sent in some days later. They were six scouts, split into three pairs. The pairs entered on the same day, approaching from three different directions: north, west, and south, across the frozen Little Missouri River.

They described their handlers as the Investigators from the embassy: Duncan, Roseanne, Neal, and Jackie. Ember wrote notes on her legal pad, though she took care not to leave evidence of her conclusions. *Each of the Investigators is not-so-coincidentally under the effects of Higginbotham's Deference Spell. But is Higginbotham the puppet master? Is he doing this alone? Or is he following someone else's orders?*

When they awoke following the dissipation of the fog, they were dazed and confused. It took several hours before they were each able to realize where they were and to recall what brought them there. None could shift back into their animal subforms, and the effects of that loss were immediate.

"That's when I lost it," Arnie whispered. His red Solo cup was empty now, but he continued to go through the motion of sipping from it. His expression was distant, vacant. "I had Stephanie to go home to, and two little babies waiting for their father. That's the only thing that kept me from just bashing my head in with a rock right there in the patch of thistle I awoke in. They're the only thing that keeps me from doing that even now."

Heads bobbed in silence. Kenny gnawed on his bloodied fingernails. Anna looked over at Alarik with wet eyes. Her brother stood with his arms crossed while he stared at an empty space on the pool table.

Ember chose her words carefully. "No judgment here. Have...have you each had such thoughts since then? Of ending it?"

One by one, each of the ten changelings offered a nod. Only Roy didn't, though he was leaning forward with elbows on his knees, holding his head in his hands. His palms cupped over his bloodshot eyes, offering Ember only his trembling, pale scalp to study.

"This is what I hope to help you with," Ember said. "I can't guarantee that I'll be able to, but I will do all that I can."

She looked over her notes. "None of you remembers anything that happened otherwise during your time in the fog. Did any of the Investigators ever follow up with you when you...when you returned, in September?"

"The Senior Investigator did." Peggy coughed. "That... Duncan...Duncan What's-his-face."

"Duncan Heywood," Ember offered. "Is that who debriefed each of you?"

It was.

Peggy coughed again. "But we didn't have much to tell him. Just what we've told you today, really."

The others nodded, except Roy. He muttered something at his knees.

"I'm sorry, Roy, I couldn't hear you." Ember craned her neck. "Could you repeat that?"

"I remember something." Roy looked up at Ember. His face was pale, except for his reddened eyes. "I don't know if it's important though."

Roy gestured at the recliner and the overweight man with a mustache leaning back in it. "Marv and I, we were the pair that came in from the south. We came in from the south shore of the river—the Little Missouri. It was frozen over, so we had no trouble crossing it. Until we got into the fog, that is."

"Like everyone else, when I got a whiff of the fog, I went under, so to speak." Roy aggressively rubbed his eyes with his palms, causing a disturbing squishing noise as they moved within their sockets. "Problem was when I came to, I was in the river. Marv was too, though he was upriver from me. Ice chunks were all around me, and it was colder than a witch's tit, but I managed to make it to shore. I tried shifting into my elk form, but I couldn't. It hurt so bad, feeling that... knowing that part of me was suddenly missing."

"So, I curled up right there on the muddy shore, surrounded by cattails. I thought about going back into the icy water—I hear that freezing to death isn't such a bad way to go. But then I heard it: a woman's voice."

"My clothes were wet, sticking to me while my teeth chattered. I poked my head out from the cattails. I saw a man run down from the butte above the river. Run right past me. He kicked off his shoes and headed to the water. A girl ran after him—blonde, but darker hair than yours." Roy stuck his elbow out at Ember. "She kept calling out his name, trying to get him to stop, I think. As I told that Heywood fella, these two weren't Druws—I could smell that much. They weren't dazed, either. They were running out of the fog as if it didn't even bother them, as though it hadn't affected them."

"What name was she calling out?" Ember felt excitement bubble within her. She didn't know why exactly, but her instincts told her that these witnesses were important. "Do you remember the man's name?"

Roy closed his eyes and frowned. He shook his head. "You'd think I would, but I don't. I know I remembered at the time. I told Heywood the guy's name when he debriefed me." Roy opened his eyes. "But I remember he had a scar on his face. A curved scar that cut across his cheek through his facial hair. Hard to forget a look like that."

26

A PRICE TO COUNTERING DARK MAGIC

"So, what do you think?" Anna asked.

The ten disabled changelings were filing out of the basement. A few of them nodded at Ember as they passed by. Peggy Barth squeezed Ember's shoulder with her leathery hand, offering a weary smile before she walked up the stairs, leaving the smell of menthols behind.

Arnie was the last in line. He lingered with his siblings as they waited on Ember.

Finally, the Investigator said, "I think one of you needs to give me a ride to Minot."

"What, like right now?" Anna's eyes looked at Ember a moment before her head followed.

Arnie pointed up the stairs. "We're already late for lunch."

"I need to talk to the Senior Investigator, to find out what he knows." Ember stuffed the legal pad back into her satchel. "I need to talk to Duncan."

"What makes you think he'll tell you anything?" Alarik crossed his arms and leaned back as he watched her.

"It's called 'Investigator's Instinct.' I think I can get him to talk."

Anna began to protest, but Alarik held up a hand. "It's alright, I'll take you. Anna, you brought her here, so I'll take her back. Ma probably could use your help with the guests, anyway."

Alarik took the back roads to Minot, coming in from the west. They hadn't yet reached Highway 2 when he began grilling her.

"Tell me why we have to do this today?"

Ember pinched the bridge of her nose and squinted. "Honestly? Because I won't be able to rest until we have."

Alarik bared his teeth and began to chuckle until he glanced at her. "You're serious. You really care about this case that much?"

"I do, but it's not just that. It's that there's an injustice. I can't let it continue." Ember shook her head. "Rik, it's like I can't move on. I can't look away."

He frowned as he considered her explanation. "It physically bothers you?"

"It does. And this one is an especially big affront to the Investigator's Creed, so I guess it bothers me even more." She closed her eyes and recalled the faces of the ten changelings she had just interviewed. "However much this bothers me, it's a fraction of discomfort compared to the pain your brother and the others have been living with. For nine miserable years."

Alarik said nothing for the rest of the drive into the Magic City.

Ember imagined the conversation with Duncan, how she would need to get close enough to implement the counter-spell to temporarily lift the Deference Spell. She would have only enough time to ask one question, so she needed to get it right. The Senior Investigator was merely an unwilling pawn in this cover-up, but one who had access to those who pulled the strings. She needed to find out who those puppet masters were. *Who is working with Elton Higginbotham?* She mentally practiced the counter-spell posture and hoped she was ready.

As the cityscape emerged in the windshield, Ember recited from memory the address from the envelopes she found on Duncan's desk.

"And then what? What's the plan, Boss Lady?"

"Then I need to use magic," Ember sighed. She had to explain as simply as she could without telling Alarik the truth. He couldn't know about the Deference Spell—nor the danger of attempting to lift it. "I have to exercise a spell, to force Duncan to tell me the truth."

"You can do that?"

"I think so. That's the theory, anyway. I've never done it before."

"So, it's like you've got Wonder Woman's Lasso of Truth?"

"That would be handy. But no, I'll only be able to ask him

one question. It won't last more than ten or fifteen seconds. If he's standing when I talk to him, I'll need you nearby to catch him after I release him."

"Won't he be pissed off when you release him?" Alarik took the off-ramp from the divided highway into Minot.

"No. He won't remember anything—not the minutes leading up, nor for many minutes after." Ember thought about the lesson Barnaby had given her, how he explained that the target's memory would be a blur for the duration. *That is if I execute the counter-spell correctly.*

Alarik slowed the pickup as he approached a traffic light. "What's the question?"

"Hmm?"

"You said you have time to ask him only one question. What's the question?"

She couldn't tell him about the greater conspiracy, about Director Higginbotham's involvement, nor the suspicion she and Wallace held that others may be involved. She lied again. "I don't know yet. I'll think of something."

Duncan Heywood's residence was a white, 1960's ranch-style house with a single stall attached garage. The yard was ungroomed, with as many clumps of weeds as there was grass. An overgrown hedge surrounded the lot.

Who is working with Elton Higginbotham? Ember recited the question as she walked up to the front door of the house with Alarik.

She knocked on the door and rang the doorbell. Nobody answered.

The garage door had three narrow windows to invite in sunlight, so Alarik walked over and cupped his hands against the glass, peering into the garage. He shook his head. "No car in there. He's out."

They returned to the Ford, and Ember instructed Alarik to park a couple of houses down, facing Duncan's house. They reclined the tall seats in the pickup back, unclasped their seatbelts and waited.

"Maybe he's not even coming home tonight, Ember. What if he's out of town entirely for the holiday?"

"Then we'll wait and find out."

A scratching noise brought Ember's attention back to the driver's side. Alarik held something small and pale in his hand, and he was working it over with his thumbnail.

"What're you doing, Rik?"

It took him a moment to realize what she was asking. Alarik grinned and showed her his hand. In his palm was a slender stick, glossy smooth except for the edge his fingernail had carved. Fine, white talc powdered his palm. "It's a soapstone. I'm never without one. Tool of the trade; I use it to mark steel where I need to make a cut or to show where I need to lay a bead. It wipes off easily but doesn't melt away on hot iron."

"Mmmkay." She picked up the slender stick. It felt brittle, at once polished yet soft and malleable. She dug her fingernail into the material and drew a line, carving a tiny furrow. The residue on her skin felt like a bar of dry soap. "Is this just a nervous habit you have?"

"I wouldn't say nervous. Just a habit." He accepted the soapstone and resumed his absent whittling. "Helps me think, I guess."

As the sun set, fireworks crackled and boomed in the sky. The vibrant municipal show in the distance at the fairgrounds outcompeted scattered personal displays around the neighborhood. Ember and Alarik watched it all from the front seat of the Super Duty, windows rolled down to let in the warm evening air.

"How long do you want to wait?" Alarik scratched his stubbled chin as he peered at the unlit house two doors down. "I know you're a skinny little bird, but we just skipped two meals. Plus, I do have work to do in the morning. I'm guessing you do, too?"

Ember looked at the illuminated clock on the dash. "Let's give it until midnight, yeah?"

"It's really that important for you to talk to him tonight?"

"I think it might be." She combed her hair with her fingers and leaned back in the passenger seat. "I'm not excellent at patience, Rik."

"I've noticed. You're more than a little obsessive, too."

"I've never claimed to be otherwise."

The clock on the pickup's dashboard showed 11:36 pm when the light in the garage sprang to life and the overhead door began climbing. A white Jeep turned into the driveway and waited for the garage door to finish its ascent.

Ember sat upright. She hissed, "that's him. Follow me."

They hurried along the sidewalk, and across the unkempt lawn. She led the way, with Alarik close behind. Trying to be stealthy in the shadows proved more difficult than she would have guessed, as she tripped and took a tumble on the grass. She landed on her side, the fall cushioned by the lumpy turf. *Why didn't I let him lead? A coyote changeling would have seen better in the dark.*

Alarik helped her up, but the commotion hadn't gone unnoticed.

"Is someone out there?" Duncan's alarmed voice called from the garage.

Her cover blown, the would-be ninja stepped into the blinding floodlights. Ember squinted at the man standing next to his Jeep. The driver's side door was still open, its door-ajar chime repeating.

"Hello, Duncan. It's Ember, from work." She walked into the garage. And jutted a thumb over her shoulder. "And this is Rik."

"Ember? What're you doing here?" Duncan frowned as he silenced the chime by slamming the Jeep's door shut. "What's this all about? Who're you pointing at?"

She looked over her shoulder, then turned around completely. Alarik was gone.

Duncan Heywood may have been functioning under the effects of a spell, but he was still a seasoned Investigator. He sensed mischief. "I don't know what you're trying to do, but that's far enough. I'm going to call Embassy Security to come pick you up." He plunged his hand into his pocket and produced a cell phone.

She was still the vehicle's length away from the Senior Investigator—too far away to engage with the Deference

Spell as Barnaby had taught her. *Everything is falling apart.* She needed to act, and quickly.

A blur moved to her right. A dog—no, a *coyote*—ran into the garage. It skittered along the right side of the parked vehicle, knocking over a silver trash can.

Duncan swiveled towards the noise. His phone slipped from his grip and clattered against the concrete floor.

Ember seized the distraction and ran toward the man, but he was too quick. She saw—almost in slow motion—mana charge from his core as a glow passed up through his shoulder, down his arm and to his balled fist, all within microseconds. As Duncan's torso turned toward her, he brought his left fist up and pointed it in her direction. His fingers unfolded, and an orange charge shot out.

Though she targeted others with it before, Ember never had a containment net aimed at her. Thin tendrils of golden-orange light expanded brightly, just missing her as it passed overhead and slammed harmlessly into the rafters.

Duncan shrieked as his aim was deflected by a snarling coyote. He fell backward into a steel tool chest when the animal jumped at him. Alarik pinned the struggling Senior Investigator as wrenches jostled noisily within their sheet-metal drawers.

Ember punched the garage door button on the wall, and the mechanism complied. As the overhead door slid shut, Ember quickly initiated the movements Barnaby taught her.

She had been practicing the moves every morning and night until she was able to execute the entire series accurately within seconds. She timed her breathing perfectly, filling her lungs to hold in the air for the duration of the counter-spell. Ember lunged her right foot forward, landing on her heel with toes pointing slightly inward. She held her arms bent at the elbow at a right angle, her fingers pointed toward the ceiling. Shifting her weight forward, she used the ball of her left foot to pivot as her right foot flattened to the floor. Her fingers began to tingle as she drew attention from the shadow enveloping her target's aura.

Duncan stopped struggling. His eyes were wide with awareness, even as his body froze.

What Alarik witnessed—then in the cemetery and now in the garage—did hold some vague resemblance to Tai Chi. He may have made the observation offhandedly, but the elaborate form looked simultaneously martial and Zen. The coyote cautiously withdrew behind Ember.

Ember lifted her left leg, bending at the knee to point her toes at the floor. Her elbows remained bent as she dropped her arms down. When her splayed fingers were pointed at Duncan, she pushed them forward at the same time as her left foot crossed over her right.

Though she was a yard away from her target, Ember felt her fingers sink into the shadow around Duncan. The Deference Spell felt like fishhooks made of ice, slicing into her flesh, embedding itself to the bone. She resisted the urge to withdraw, to scream. Barnaby had warned her, but nothing he said could have prepared her for the surge of pain.

The Grand Inquisitor's gritty voice echoed in her memory. "There is a price to countering Dark Magic. It will terrify you. It will probably harm you. If you exhale, if you cry out, you will be lost. Breathe in the scent of a Deference Spell not meant for you, and it will surely be your last."

She closed her eyes and visualized her fingers plunging deeper into the murky shroud. She saw a tent made of tar paper, heavy and uncooperative as it tried to collapse around her hands. Ember saw herself parting a flap within the inflexible material.

Within the sagging tent was Duncan Heywood, frightened and awestruck. "How did you—?"

"No time." She uttered the syllables without breathing. She had only seconds to speak with Duncan before the Deference Spell collapsed, and she with it. She had been running the question of the conspiracy through her mind the entire evening, practicing what she would ask. Now that she was here, she could only think of the one question that mattered more.

"It was 2001. The Mandaree Incident. You debriefed Roy Turner. He told you about a man with a scar running out of the fog. What's the man's name?"

"Yes. I remember. There was two of them. I tracked them down and interrogated both. They knew about the fog. A lot about the—"

"Names." Ember grimaced. Her lungs burned, begged her to exhale. The weight of the shadow-tent pressed down on her. "Their names."

"Dominic Hershel and Katrina Berg. But they—"

Whatever else Duncan had to say, Ember would not hear it. The heavy weight of the dark spell closed in around her. She slid her hands back as quickly as she could, closing the imagined tent flap and blocking anything Duncan said. Reversing the earlier movements, Ember stepped backward, bringing her arms up toward the ceiling, repelling the Deference Spell from her fingertips. As she shifted her weight back, she opened her eyes and gasped.

Duncan's eyelids dropped, and his body went limp against the tool chest.

Alarik had already shifted back to his human form. He caught the Senior Investigator as the man collapsed. "What happened? Why didn't it work? Why didn't you ask him any questions?"

She felt dizzy, light headed. Ember closed her eyes and staggered, catching herself on the Jeep's door mirror. She managed to whisper, "I...did."

Alarik's jaw went slack when he looked at the Malvern woman. The pitch of his voice elevated in alarm. "Ember you...your nose. Your eyes. You're bleeding!"

As if a marionette with severed strings, Ember's knees gave out. She crumpled to the floor and her head fell forward to her chest. She tasted metallic saline when something dripped from her nose to her lips. She wanted to touch her face, to wipe away the fluid that tickled her skin, but her arms wouldn't obey. Tears of blood trickled down her cheek as she lost consciousness.

27

SHE'S TOUGHER THAN SHE LOOKS

"I THINK SHE'S GETTING BETTER. AT LEAST THE BLEEDING stopped."

"I can't believe it was coming out of her eyes. What does that mean, bleeding from the eyes? Head trauma?"

"Her nose, too, but I had that much cleaned up before you got here. She didn't hit her head so—"

"And she's been like this since talking to that Duncan guy? Passed out, I mean?"

"Yeah. But, there wasn't much talking. Whatever she was trying to do, it didn't work."

A PHONE WAS RINGING.

"Damn it, again. Can you turn that thing off or make it go silent, please? It's going to disturb her."

"I did turn it off. This is another one."

"She's got two cell phones?"

"Looks like. Think she's a drug dealer on the side?"

"Yeah, I'm sure that's it, you dork. Well, I'm awake now. You'd might as well try taking a nap. I can watch her until you wake up."

"Don't you have to work today?"

"I'll get someone to cover for me. This is more important than babysitting drunks."

"AND HERE WE GO. IT'S WARM CHICKEN BROTH. HERE'S THE spoon at your lips, Ember. Just open and swallow. Good, good. One more now."

Someone sponged the sweat from her neck with a damp washcloth.

"She's still burning up. Rik, we need to get her to a Healer."

"You heard her talking in her sleep. Director Higginbotham is one of the bad guys. Who can we take her to? What if they try to hurt her?"

"Then we'll kick their ass." The woman sighed. "Okay, then to the E.R. Someone at Trinity can at least help with the fever."

"We've given her Tylenol, but I don't think what she's fighting is something NonDruw doctors are equipped to handle."

"It's not something that a couple of Tylenol will touch,

either. We have to at least try to find her family. To tell them. What if...what if she doesn't—"

"Don't even say that. She's gonna pull through. She's tougher than she looks."

"SHE'S AWAKE AGAIN, SIS. I JUST HEARD HER MUTTER something."

"Her throat's probably dry. Here, sit her up again and I'll give her some of this."

A cold, steel spoon touched Ember's lips. She parted them and was rewarded with a teaspoon of strawberry gelatin.

A woman's voice cooed. "Mmm, it's good, right? Jell-O. Want another?"

Ember swallowed, nodded once.

"She's not a baby, Anna. You can talk to her like an adult."

Ember tried to open her eyes, to no avail. She swallowed another offering of gelatin and managed to hoarsely whisper, "Can't...open eyes."

"Oh, they must have dried shut again. I'll get another washcloth, hang on. Keep her propped up, Rik."

Water flowed from the faucet over the bathroom sink. Just as she faded out again, Ember heard Alarik saying something. Telling her something he said was important. She tried to focus on his voice, but she couldn't understand what he said.

HER EYES HURT, BUT SHE MANAGED TO OPEN HER EYELIDS AT least. Her vision was blurry as if there was smoke in the room. A figure shifted next to her bed.

"Ember? Can you hear me?" It was Alarik.

Her lips stuck together briefly, resisting as she opened her mouth. She touched her fingers to her throat and made a croaking sound.

"Here, here. Water." Alarik propped Ember up and brought a cup to her lips. He tipped a splash of water into her mouth, most of which dribbled down her chin.

Ember dragged the back of her hand over her chin, then reached for the cup. It felt heavy in her grip, but she didn't drop it. She didn't recognize her own voice. It sounded damaged, worn out. "I feel...depleted."

"Yeah, I don't doubt it." Alarik held the back of his hand against her forehead. "Your fever is breaking, at least. You had a rough day-and-a-half."

She closed and opened her eyes, reassuring herself she was able to do at least that. "Day...and...half?"

"Mmhmm. The bleeding stopped by the time I got you back here. To your apartment." Alarik took the cup of water and set it on the nightstand. He popped open a plastic cup of gelatin and placed it in her left hand. He gestured with the spoon before sliding it into her right hand. "You were burning up, bad fever. You've been a mess for 36 hours or so."

She accepted the spoon and fed herself as the memories of

her confrontation with Duncan percolated to her consciousness. "It's Tuesday?"

"Yep. Tuesday afternoon. Anna has been helping, too. She's home now, but she'll be back tomorrow morning." Alarik adjusted the pillows behind Ember's back, helping her stay propped up. "She bought some groceries. You didn't have anything but ramen noodles and crackers in your cupboards, and leftover take-out in the fridge. You eat like I did when I was in college, minus the cases of beer."

"I feel like...like I've just been danced on by a herd of rhinos."

"No offense, but you kind of look it, too. You'll be wanting a shower when you're able to get up, I'm sure."

"That does sound brilliant." Ember closed her eyes and imagined hot water flowing over her. "Could you bring me my mobile, please? I had better call sick to work before they send someone to check in on me."

"Sure." He left the room and came back with a device in each hand. "Which one? You've got two."

Some part of her subconscious flashed an overheard conversation—or was it a fevered dream? Her memories were unfocused, blurred like her vision. She selected the embassy-provided cell phone and called the spa manager's direct line.

"Hi Josette," Ember croaked. "I'm so sorry, but I'm calling in sick."

"Oh, girlfriend, you sound it! What happened?"

"Um...something I ate over the holiday, I think."

"I've never had food poisoning before, but I've heard that for the first 24 hours you'll feel like you're dying. For the second 24 hours, you'll wish you had."

"That sounds...about right." Ember swallowed.

"Well don't worry about a thing. Heal up, take as long as you need."

Ember thanked her, disconnected the call, and made a second call.

"Department of Investigation, front desk. How may I assist you?" The chipper voice answered.

"Joy, this is Ember. I'm calling in sick. I had food poisoning from Sunday." The lie sounded even more convincing the second time.

"Oh no! Ember, it doesn't even sound like you! Oh, my goodness, that's just awful. I was wondering why you hadn't come in. Yesterday was a holiday, on account the Embassy lets us have the Monday after Independence Day off, well if the Fourth of July falls on a Sunday. Which it did, this year. It doesn't every year of course. It's nice having a three-day weekend. Well, unless you have food poisoning, then—"

"Joy, I'm sorry," Ember interrupted the chatterbox. "I think I'm about to throw up again."

"Oh, gross! I mean, sorry. That's terrible. I'll mark you down as sick, it's alright. Dennis is going to be so lonely, not having you to entertain him." Joy snickered. "I kid, I kid."

"Bye, Joy."

Ember rubbed the bridge of her nose and sighed.

"Want me to help you to the bathroom?" Alarik was standing in the doorway of her bedroom. "I'll be right outside, so you can shout if you fall or need me for anything."

She accepted his assistance. The hot shower was every bit as refreshing as she had imagined it to be. She had one towel wrapped around her and she was blotting her hair dry with another when Alarik called from the other side of the closed door.

"Are you hungry yet? I'll make you something to eat."

"I am, thank you. If you could heat up a Pot Noodle, that would be lovely." Ember called out to the backside of the door. She was pleased that her voice was returning. "There are instructions on the package."

Alarik chuckled. "You're going to eat something other than ramen noodles. How about I make you some eggs and bacon? Anna bought some. Said you'd need something solid on your stomach when you rejoined the land of the living. Orange juice and apple juice, too, since we didn't know what you would prefer."

Ember smiled at her reflection in the fogged mirror. Her eyesight was returning, though not yet quite normal. Tendrils of damp, gold hair peered out from beneath the towel on her head. Her fire-blue eyes were puffy and looked as tired as she felt. The carved coyote face draped against her sternum, staring back at her from its place just above the valley between her breasts. "Thank you. Orange juice would be brilliant."

"How do you like your eggs?"

“Poached, if you would?”

“Poached? Uh...how about...over easy or sunny-side up?”

Ember grinned at the mirror. “Over easy, in that case.”

“Coming right up.” His voice was cheerful. “Take your time in there.”

She still felt like roadkill, but now slightly fresher roadkill. Ember wore her robe and a towel wrapped around her wet head. She took one more look at her reflection and marveled at the weary face staring back at her. It felt strange, letting Alarik see her in such a vulnerable state. *Judging by how I feel, he and his sister saw me looking far worse.*

When they were done eating, Ember excused herself to her bedroom and called Wallace on the burner phone. She updated him, told him about what she learned from Duncan.

“This is your idea of laying low, Ember?” Wallace was gruff. “This is an incredible risk you took.”

“I know.”

“You asked him about the Mandaree Incident, not the co-conspirators.” It wasn’t a question.

“I did. I know I should have pursued the bigger picture like you said.” Ember sat on the edge of her bed and stared out the window. “I’m sorry. I was just following my instincts.”

“You were listening to your heart, instead of your head.” Wallace grumbled into the phone. “You made a move without thinking it through, at great risk to yourself. To Duncan, too. When you’re able to, I want you to ask him about Higginbotham's co-conspirators. Be *delicate* when you do. No brash moves here."

Ember squeezed her eyes shut. "Wallace...I don't think I can do that."

"What? Why can't you?"

"I...it wasn't easy lifting the Deference Spell. I don't think I can try it again. I...Wallace, it almost got me."

Wallace hesitated, then spoke calmly. "Explain."

She told him about the after-effects of the counter-spell, the recovery. The fact that Alarik and Anna had been nursing her back to health.

"Bloody hell, Ember." Though he cursed, the anger in his voice was absent, substituted now with concern. "We can't have you try that counter-spell again. It seems you barely survived this one."

"You'll hear no arguments from me on that."

Wallace muttered to himself as he verbally recapped Ember's findings. "There's just one thing you left out. How did you lose your tail?"

"Hmm? My tail?"

"You said you and Rik left the Schmitt Farm and went straight to Duncan's house." Wallace anxiously tapped his fingernail the receiver of his phone. "How did you slip away unnoticed from the spy? From that changeling vulture you said was watching you at the farm?"

Ember's blood grew cold with realization. Her mouth opened slowly. "Oh bollocks, Wallace."

"What?" His voice went up an octave. "What?"

"I...we...I forgot about the spy altogether."

"You *what?*"

"I was just so...so fixated. On the lead. On the possible break in the case." Ember's voice wavered. She held her forehead in her hand. "I forgot about him."

"Do you know what you've just done, Ember? You've connected Duncan to the Schmitt family. To yourself. You blew your cover." Wallace's voice sounded strange.

Ember felt the room spin around her. "But I...we closed the garage door before we talked to Duncan. We...they haven't... nobody has come by to arrest me, to pick me up. It's been two days, if they knew, then why haven't they—"

"They may be planning, Ember. They may be waiting for you to be alone, to pick you up when you're away from your apartment. They might be waiting to see who is working with you."

"How could I have been so bloody *stupid!*"

"You were thinking with your heart, not your head." Her former partner sounded anxious, but if he was panicked, he wasn't letting her know that. "Do you have somewhere safe you can retreat to? Until I can get you out of there?"

"I've got Rik with me now. Here. In my apartment."

"That might be the safest place for you to be right now. They will doubtless wait for you to leave so they can make their move. I'll see if we have any assets in the colony I can trust. It might take a day or two to extract you."

Assets. Extract. Wallace's choice of words, his veneer of calm over suppressed anxiety. Ember felt the walls crumble around her as she imagined being whisked away.

"What about the Schmitt family?" Ember's tremulous voice whispered. "What about Rik? What about Anna?"

Staccato percussion vibrated across the phone line from England as the man thrummed his fingertips against the phone. "Right now, let's just worry about keeping you alive."

"I'm…I'm so, so sorry, Wallace." Her eyes burned. "I was just following my instincts like you always told me to."

"Maybe I was wrong to tell you that. Just as it was wrong for me to send you solo into the unknown. It was wrong for me to let you stay there when we discovered just how dangerous it was. You're not the only one who's bloody well messed things up."

When the call was over, Ember sat hunched on the edge of her bed, holding her head in her hands as she felt tears form. When she looked up, she saw Alarik standing in the doorway, watching her, worrying a stick of soapstone in his hand.

"I didn't mean to listen in." Alarik rubbed his stubbled jaw with the talc stick. "It sounds like things have gone pear-shaped."

Ember sniffled, then glanced away. She looked back at him and slowly nodded as her emotions boiled to the surface. "I cocked up, Rik. I cocked up bad."

Alarik wordlessly sat down on the chair next to the bed.

They sat in silence for the next twenty minutes, alone in their respective thoughts.

The doorbell startled them both back to the present.

He leaned forward and hissed through clenched teeth. "It's not Anna. She's not coming back 'til tomorrow morning."

Ember blinked wide-eyed at Alarik as the doorbell rang again. She exhaled. "They've come for me."

28

IT'S AN ACQUIRED TASTE

Ember watched from her bedroom as Alarik approached the front door.

The doorbell rang a third time.

Lacking a proper kitchen knife set in the spartan apartment, Alarik dropped his soapstone and picked up a paring knife from the dish rack. He gripped the tiny blade tightly in his right hand as he peered through the door's peephole. It would have been almost comical if the situation was otherwise.

She tried to summon her mana, to prepare a containment net for the intruder. Ember was so weakened, so discharged of energy that she could scarcely gather a faint glow within her core. Even that minimal effort made her feel faint. She was helpless in contributing to her own defense.

Alarik retracted from the door. "It's just a deliveryman." He unlocked the deadbolt and knob.

"Wait, I didn't order anything." Ember felt a wave of fear as the door swung open.

A man in a brown uniform and matching cargo shorts stood in the hallway, holding a cardboard box. "Oh good, you *are* home. I'm glad I didn't have to lug this thing back downstairs. I just need your signature." He produced a handheld computer from its holster on his hip, scanned the package's barcode, and handed a stylus to Alarik.

Alarik held the door open with his left hand and reached for the stylus. He still held the paring knife. "Oh, sorry. I was...just making supper." He tucked the knife in the back pocket of his jeans.

While he scrawled a signature, the deliveryman rocked on his heels, still holding the box. "I deliver packages to your next-door neighbor all the time. They've given us blanket permission to leave them without having to sign. If you're ever interested in that, just go on our website and set up an account."

"Thanks," Alarik murmured as he exchanged the stylus for the box. "I'll keep that in mind."

"You have a good day now."

The door closed and deadbolt latched, Alarik sat the mid-sized box down on the kitchen counter. He sniffed the package as he read its label. "It's from the U.K. From, um... Wor...Worsess—"

"Worcestershire." She sighed as the pendulum of emotions swung from dread to cheerful anticipation. "It completely slipped my mind. I know exactly what this is. It's a care package from Mum."

Ember reached her hand into Alarik's back pocket and retrieved the paring knife, which she used to slice into the box. She ripped the packing tape loose, tearing noisily through the corrugated cardboard. "You, my chap, are in for a real treat. Have you ever tasted the jam of the gods? No? Well, step right up, mister."

She tucked into a box of crackers from the cupboard and selected a happy, rotund jar from the box. It was identical to the ten others within the shipment, but she christened it as special, for its new role in satisfying her fix. A handwritten note was included, but that could wait.

When she opened the jar, Ember used the yellow, plastic lid to waft the familiar soy aroma into her nostrils. She closed her eyes and shuddered in an ecstasy that was only partially embellished. "Nothing rivals a fresh jar of scrummy Marmite."

"I can think of a few things that might." Her skeptical companion scrunched his nose.

Ember slathered a healthy layer of the deep brown, sticky paste onto two crackers, offering one to Alarik. She tapped her cracker as a toast to his as he squinted, unconvinced of what he was about to taste.

That first bite was every bit the treat she knew it would be. Her eyes rolled up and she moaned, chewing slowly to savor the salty brewer's yeast. The first taste was meant to be savored; there would be unladylike gorging later when she had no witnesses. Ember held her eyelids half closed, caught in the hedonistic dream. She chewed purposefully and watched the initiate sitting across from her.

Alarik was chewing slowly as well, but his expression

couldn't have been more unlike hers. His whole face was fixed in a grimaced expression. He swallowed, then at once went for the kitchen sink. Two glasses of water later, he sputtered, "That has got to be the nastiest thing I've tasted in my life. How can you eat that stuff? I mean, seriously, have you no taste buds?"

Ember grinned with blackened teeth. "It's good for you! Packed with Vitamin B12 and folic acid. I suppose it's an acquired taste."

"Acquired taste?" Alarik refilled his glass beneath the faucet. "No, beer is an acquired taste. Coffee is an acquired taste. Punching yourself in the face could be an acquired taste. This...this stuff is on a whole 'nother level. If we fed this to Lucky, the first thing she would do is lick her butt, just to get the flavor of this out of her mouth."

"Rik! Really!" Ember threw the yellow Marmite lid at him. It hit the edge of the countertop instead and fell to the floor with a clatter. "Speaking of a foul mouth!"

He shook his head and smirked. "Great, now the cover is dirty. Maybe it will improve the taste somehow."

"I won't need the lid anyway. This jar might not make it through the night. I just wish Mummy would have sent me more than ten."

"Seriously?" The man pointed accusingly at the opened box. "This right here is a lifetime supply. For a small army. Preferably an enemy army."

Ember shrugged and dipped a fresh cracker into the jar. "Not everyone is equipped to handle high culture, I guess. Your loss."

"High culture? If we go digging through the expired take-out boxes in your fridge, I'll bet we could find more high culture in the form of mold. I might even be tempted to eat that to help me forget the Marmite."

"Poor Rik. Too bad Lucky's not here. Then maybe you'd have another palate-cleansing option."

When evening arrived, Ember asked Alarik if he would stay the night. She was still feeling weak and his presence was reassuring. She was relieved when he accepted.

He slept on the couch while Ember sat at the kitchen table with her laptop computer. A pad of paper was covered with scribbled notes, cracker crumbs, and smudges of Marmite. She fixated on the glowing screen, following a series of internet searches for the two names she had obtained from Duncan. Her obsessiveness kept her up through the night, plotting her destinations on the North Dakota state highway map.

"I need to borrow your pickup, please." She made the request to a blustery-eyed Alarik. He had been sleeping.

He sat up on the couch, blinking as he looked at his watch. "It's not even four in the morning. Why aren't you asleep?"

"I've been up all night." Ember gripped the legal pad as she paced back and forth in front of the sofa. "I've been doing some digging online. Tracking down the names Duncan gave us."

"Huh? Ember, Duncan never told you any names. I was there, remember?"

"Right. No, he did, Rik." Ember tapped the paper for punctuation. "You just mustn't have heard it because I was inside the tent."

"Okay, now you're making even less sense." He glanced at the partially-consumed jar on the table. "How much of that shit did you eat? Is this what an overdose looks like?"

"Don't be silly. I know how this sounds, but he did talk to me." Ember pointed at the names on her notepad. "Dominic Hershel. Born in 1966. That would make him...43 now. He lives on a farm near Mott, in the southwest part of the state."

Alarik squinted and scratched his scalp. "Dominic Hershel? I don't—"

"The girl who was with him, she's Katrina Berg. Best I can find, she's about 32 years old. She went to North Dakota State University. Geology Department. Lives in Pembina, which is northeast of here, right at the Canada border."

"I know where Pembina is, sure. But why do you—"

"The towns are on opposite ends of the state, but I think I can visit both places today. I just know they will have some clues. Duncan told me they knew about the fog. A lot about it, he said." She continued pacing. "It'll be a long day, to be sure. I'll need to leave soon. That's why I woke you up."

"Ember, you want me to drive you to Pembina? Now?"

"No, I'll get there myself. I've thought about it, and I think that would be safer. If they come after me, they might still think I'm operating alone—after all, you're officially my boyfriend. So, it won't raise any suspicions that you've been visiting me. I can't let them think you're a part of this."

Alarik rubbed his eyes and yawned. "Ember, if that buzzard

did follow us to the Senior Investigator's house, he saw us together. They already know that I'm a part of this. Whoever 'they' are."

"My mistakes have already put you and your family in danger, Rik." Ember cast her gaze to her notes. "You still have some deniability, if they do question you. If I tell you more or get you even more involved by talking to witnesses then—"

"Then what? They're going to throw me in prison? For what, exactly?"

Ember shook her head slowly and looked pointedly at his sleepy, umber eyes. "Not prison, Rik. These people might kill you. And not just you, but Anna, too. Probably Arnie. Maybe more."

Alarik swallowed. "Damn. That took the wind right outta me."

"You see? If I take your vehicle, if I do get caught you can just say I stole your keys, or that I borrowed it but didn't tell you where I was going."

"What will they do with you?" Alarik was morose. "If you get caught, what will happen to you?"

Ember took a deep breath, then sat down hard on the couch next to him. She chewed on her lower lip. The silence answered for her.

He studied Ember. "Are you sure you want to do this?"

"I don't want to. I *have* to."

"Then we'll distract them." Alarik murmured. "I'll call Anna and have her park at St. Leo's. I'll make a show of leaving here, and you can go through the tunnel and take her car. She can walk to the coffee shop down the street, and I'll pick her up there."

"Brilliant. They would think I was still in my apartment, sick." Ember ruminated on the proposal. "I'll close the curtains, keep a light on and the TV blaring. Even if they break in, they won't know where I went."

"We'll stay in Minot until you get back." Alarik scratched his stubbled chin. "I want you to call me, give me updates. With that other phone of yours. The one they don't know about."

"That's really not necessary—"

"That's the deal, Ember. Non-negotiable." He crossed his arms. "I need to know you're safe. This works both ways, you know."

Ember paused as she considered his demand. "Then I'll be calling you from the road. We should probably get started. We're burning daylight."

29

HERMAN, WE HAVE A VISITOR

THE TERRAIN WAS ALMOST PERFECTLY FLAT IN ALL DIRECTIONS in the Red River Valley, creating few obstacles for I-29 to weave around. Trees grew taller here in the rich soil and were much more plentiful than their cousins in the western half of the state. The sprawling farms were populated more with sunflowers, potatoes, and sugar beets, with far fewer cattle operations.

The border town of Pembina arrived like a mirage on the windswept northern plains. As Ember turned off Exit 215, a wheat-colored tower lined up with her view. The black letters on the side of the building proclaimed, in all caps, "PEMBINA STATE MUSEUM."

She flipped open her burner phone and hit the first number in her contacts list. It rang once.

"It's me. I'm just turning in to Pembina."

"What took so long? It should have only taken four hours."

"Oh, I had to stop a couple hours back." Ember looked both

ways before she accelerated onto Stutsman Street. "There's a pleasant rest area outside of Demon Lake. Brilliant location, so said my bladder."

"Devils Lake," Alarik corrected. "I know where that rest stop is. The deal was that you would call before you stop anywhere. Anytime you leave the car."

"It was just a quick stop."

"Every time you leave the car. No exceptions."

"Yes, Father." She peered through the side window, trying to read the street signs as she slowed the car. "No, I'm sorry. No, you're right, Rik. I'll not take any chances. I'll call you after I leave Pembina. I'll need to stop for petrol before I return, anyway. There's a fill station right at the exit I just left."

"All right. We're standing by. Good luck with your interview. I hope this Katrina lady is helpful."

She flipped the phone shut and dropped it back into the open maw of her purse. The borrowed Ford Taurus idled down Second Street until she found the house she was looking for. She parked in front, then glanced over her notes to verify she had the right address.

The lot which hosted the petite, cream-colored house was well taken care of. Along the boulevard, a row of mature ash tucked their toes beneath a carpet of manicured turf, their branches creaking and groaning as they resisted the north-west winds. Songbirds chirped happily throughout the canopy, flitting overhead as they paid little attention to the blonde woman below.

There was no answer at the door. "Come on Katrina, don't tell me you're at work." Ember murmured as she stepped back from the front steps. An oblong pot of marigolds hung from an open window's sill, the vibrant flowers' aroma teasing her nostrils. She leaned against the black, iron railing while she scanned the neighborhood. The quiet town was a hardwood forest with large lots and wide spaces between residences, and very little traffic. A dog barked somewhere down the street, answered shortly by the howl of a hound a block away.

She would need to camp out in front of the house and wait for the woman to return home. Before she returned to the sedan, she walked a circuit around the house. Her feet sunk into the plush lawn, leaving evidence of her trail as she walked. Ember felt a little guilty for her trespass, given how much the homeowners obviously cared for their yard.

As she stepped around the corner, she saw a woman crouching in a nascent vegetable garden. Ember's heart rate increased for a moment until the woman sat up and held the small of her back, stretching.

The gardener was an elderly woman, wrinkled and grey beneath the broad, straw sun hat. She squinted against the bright afternoon sun and called out. "Herman, we have a visitor."

Ember noticed the old man before he computed his wife's announcement. He was trimming an arborvitae bush with hand clippers. His faded denim bib overalls were rolled up at his ankles, and he walked with a stoop.

"Hello," Ember waved cheerfully. "I'm looking for Katrina Berg. Would you two happen to be her parents?"

"Eh?" Herman asked.

"She's asking if we know Katrina Berg." The old woman approached with effort. She shouted at her husband, "This young lady thinks we're her parents!"

"I'm sorry," Ember pulled the satchel from her shoulder and extricated her notepad. "I might have the wrong address."

"You've got the right address," the woman said as she limped to Herman's side. She reached a hand over to his shoulder for support. "At least, you would have if you were visiting five years ago."

The old man moved the shears to his other hand, away from his wife. "Eh?"

The woman breathed in, then shouted, "I'm telling her that the Bergs don't live here anymore!"

"Do you have any idea where they moved to?"

The woman shook her head. "I don't, sorry. I think Fargo? Or was it Grand Forks. I don't know. They'd already moved before we bought this place. I do remember that they had a daughter though. She stopped by once, right after we closed on the house. Said she was in town visiting classmates and had to see the family house, for sentimental reasons. She was so young, maybe your age. She was very pretty, too, like you."

"Thank you," Ember smiled, though she was crestfallen. "You've been very helpful."

"Eh?"

The woman just shook her head at her husband. She smiled back at Ember. "Would you like some iced tea? It's so hot today, isn't it? We really shouldn't be in the garden when it's so hot, but it's good exercise, weeding."

"I have a long way to drive, so I can't stay. That's very sweet of you, though. Thank you for offering." Ember looked over the backyard and gestured. She spoke loudly, so Herman would hear. "You keep an amazing yard. Absolutely gorgeous."

The man's confused expression morphed into a smile. The wrinkles around his eyes merged as his lips turned up and he nodded.

"I'll be on my way. Thank you again for your help." Ember waved at the kind couple. A butterfly fluttered past her face, and she blinked for just a moment. That was all she needed to see the mean-looking man, standing impossibly atop a birdhouse high above the vegetable garden. When her eyes opened, she saw plainly what she failed to detect before: the changeling crow.

Blood drained from her face, and she stuttered in her gait. Ember quickly looked away, pretended not to notice the spy. *How did he find me? Was he watching, listening the whole time?*

She walked hurriedly to the white Taurus and opened the passenger door before she realized she was getting into the wrong side. She cursed, got back out and went around to the driver's door. Once inside, she hastily drove off.

When she turned in to the gas station on the edge of town, Ember flipped the phone open and dialed Alarik. She locked the car's doors and looked around, trying to find the spy. Semi-trucks and passenger vehicles with license plates from Manitoba, North Dakota, and Minnesota parked in front of the last convenience store on this side of the border.

Twin flag poles held colors proudly: the Canadian maple leaf on one, the American stars-and-stripes on the other.

"That was fast. Did you find her?"

"No. She doesn't live there anymore." Ember spoke quickly. "I don't know how, but one of the spies found me. The crow. He followed me, Rik."

"Shit. How could he have? We were so careful."

"I don't know. It doesn't matter now. He heard me say Katrina's name. They know I'm not under the Deference Spell now."

"The deference...what? What are you talking about?"

Ember shook her head, the phone slipping in her sweaty palm. "Forget I said that. It's all moot now. I've got to fuel up. I'll figure out what to do next. I'll stop at that rest area on the way back, and call you when I get there."

"Maybe you should stay put," Alarik suggested. "Anna and I can come get you. It might not be safe for you to be alone."

"I'm in a public place, with lots of people around. You're safer staying away from me." Ember bit her lower lip to stop it from quivering. "I should have listened to Wallace and kept my head down. Why do I keep doing this?"

"There'll be time to kick yourself later. Let's just focus on getting you back, safely."

"Right. Okay, petrol then I'll be on my way. I'll call you again in two hours."

She filled the tank of the car and paid with cash. She didn't see the changeling spy but knew he couldn't be far.

The long drive back to Devils Lake gave her ample time to think. She considered calling Wallace, but there wasn't anything he would be able to do for her. Ember knew that she was poison now, and the best thing she could do was distance herself from everyone else, lest they become tainted by association. She would need to find a place to hide until she could get a flight out of the Magic City, away from the clutches of Director Higginbotham and his cohorts.

Is anywhere safe though? Barnaby had posited that a cover-up this significant had to rise to the highest levels of Druw society. He pointed to the High Council as being suspect. Wallace shared those suspicions. She would be driving through Surrey on the way back to Minot. Maybe it would be helpful to stop by the cemetery to consult with the deceased Inquisitor.

She was startled out of her thoughts by a ringing in her purse. Ember shuffled blindly until she found the embassy-provided phone. The caller ID showed a familiar number. "Hello, Mum."

"Ember? Are you in a dance club? I can scarcely hear you over that racket."

"Oh, hang on." Ember turned the radio off. Anna's Shania Twain CD had been playing on loop for the entirety of the drive from Minot. By the third time she heard the song, "I Feel Like a Woman," she found herself singing along. What she lacked in pitch, Ember made up for with volume.

"Has your mobile been broken?" Benedette Wright asked.

"No, it's been working fine."

"Oh. Because you said you were going to call when you were with your supposed friends. That was two Fridays ago, darling."

"I know, I know. I'm sorry, Mummy. It's been frantic here."

"I'm sure you're busy. Your father tells me that the package arrived, according to the tracking number."

"It did, yesterday, yeah. Thank you, I meant to call to say that." Ember signaled and turned right onto Highway 2. "I'm driving, so I can chat now."

Mother and daughter visited for the duration of the journey. The distraction helped whittle the miles away and kept Ember's mind off her troubling situation.

The sun was blindingly low on the horizon as she approached the end of the first leg of her return trip. The four-hour drive from Pembina to Minot was bisected almost perfectly by the Minnie H rest area east of the city of Devils Lake. A single steel pole pointed to the sky at the split entrance to the rest area. The American flag shared the metal staff with a blue North Dakota flag below it. Both standards whipped in the stiff prairie wind.

The red-trimmed flat roof of the facility hung over the entrance to the building. Painted white and lined with large windows, the structure was placed in a widened section of median between the divided highway, allowing traffic to enter it from either direction of Highway 2.

She took the car out of gear and parked in front of the building. Ember groaned with relief as her cramped legs stretched out of the open door. Her locks tugged at her scalp as they caught the fierce breeze. Her mother was still talking, telling her about Cynthia and her happy little family. She knew the inevitability of the next topic before it was even mentioned.

"Do you remember Farqhar Cowie?" Benedette said. "He's an Associate Analytic and such a handsome young man. He has a promising career in the bureaucracy."

Here it comes. Ember rolled her eyes as she walked the length of the sidewalk past a whitewashed picnic table. The only other vehicle in the parking lot was a station wagon, which was now leaving, turning onto the westbound lanes of the highway.

"Emberly, you will be amazed to know that Farqhar is still single."

"That's fascinating, Mum." Ember couldn't help but chuckle at her mother's predictability.

"Isn't it though? You know, you should call him. I'm certain you two share common interests."

A wry riposte was just forming on her lips when a black bird fluttered into view. The crow landed on the concrete walkway directly in front of her. Ember blinked and saw a dark-haired man with his arms sleeved in tattoos.

She turned on her heel just in time to see a second crow land on the picnic table she had just walked past. Goosebumps formed on her skin and she muttered, "Two crows."

"What was that, Emberly?"

"I...I have to go now, Mum." She kept her gaze locked on the picnic table. Her phone was already away from her face and folded shut when she said, "I love you."

Ember's heartbeat pulsed deafeningly within her ears. Her mouth went dry, and her palms grew damp. She was acutely aware that she was alone against these foes. Desperately alone.

The bird on the table grew, its feathers shrinking into pale skin partially concealed by a cotton tank shirt and torn blue jeans. Its beak became a nose, the beady eyes no less so but now migrating from the side of its face to the front, the dull yellow replaced with tar-colored human eyes. The glint they held was malice laid bare, with a toothy scowl to match.

She didn't notice the six-foot wingspan circling overhead, descending in a spiral until the vulture emitted its distinctive hiss.

30

WHAT WOULD WALLACE DO

THE CHANGELING STANDING ON THE PICNIC BENCH SHIFTED HIS weight. *He's going to launch himself at me.*

Ember quelled her panic. She dismissed the impulse to chastise herself for not being more careful, for not being more aware of her surroundings before she left the car. There would be time for that later. Hopefully. *Think. What would Wallace do?*

His voice accompanied the answer that sprang into her mind. It couldn't be clearer if her mentor was standing there right now. She even saw his grey, handlebar mustache twitch as the thoughts formed. *Turn this threat into an opportunity.*

The plan formed in her head, in the course of two seconds: she would capture these belligerents, interrogate them, and then give them a Memory Wash that'll keep them off balance for a week. More importantly, they won't remember a thing.

Ember's inspired plan was the easy part; executing it would

be difficult. She was still drained of mana from her encounter with Duncan. She had to use more traditional means to pull this trick off.

She turned so that the other crow wouldn't be behind her. He, too, had already shifted into his human form. They both had an abundance of tattoos covering their arms and neck. They weren't gang symbols—at least not for any gang she was aware of. Both men were lean, sinewy. They had hungry, mean eyes fixed in glares. The men had the deep tans of someone who spent a lot of time outside, though with the pimpled complexions that comes from exposure to grease or other pore-clogging activities. They looked like brothers, or maybe cousins.

She noticed something else: they were both nervous. *I can use this.*

"Hang on," she called out. The wind stole her words away, so she spoke louder, with confidence. "Hang on just a second. Tell me what this is about. I'm an Investigator here by authority of the Druw High Council. Cooperate and I will not harm you." She shifted her weight onto one foot and put her left hand out. Her right hand formed a fist, ready to call on her mana just in case.

For a moment, her ruse seemed to work. The greasy-haired man on the picnic table flashed an uncertain expression at his partner. Then he laughed nervously. The man on the sidewalk mistook the laugh and joined in, jeering at Ember.

When the turkey buzzard landed on the hood of Anna's Taurus, his talons made a terrible scratch. The noise surprised Ember, and she turned just enough to see its source. The bird's six-foot wingspan was shrinking into the arms of a man, and long, dark hair remained on his angular head as feathers pulled into flesh.

The changeling on the picnic table made his move. He bent his knees and placed a foot forward, on the edge of the wood table. The table betrayed his movement, as the old, whitewashed wood creaked in protest.

It was just enough warning for the short, blonde Malvern to call on her mana. Even as she pulled upon her energy, felt it emerge from deep within her torso, she knew she only had enough for one shot. The power flowed up her shoulder, through her arm, and to her fist, which unfolded as she cast the containment net at her attacker.

The glow of bright orange light erupted from Ember's palm, racing to its target atop the table. The net expanded its gold weave, colliding with the man with enough force to take him off his feet. He was airborne for a moment, falling backward while the net closed in around him. His body made a heavy thud as it landed on dry dirt, padded only sparingly with clumps of dried brome.

Suddenly, a horse kicked her. Twice: once in the back of her skull, and a second time in her face. At least, that's what it felt like when one of the other changelings landed a fist to the back of her head, and when her face planted into the concrete walkway.

The man rained kicks onto her torso, her arms as she brought them up to defend herself. Ember's legs were watery when she tried to get up. She looked at the white sedan and thought only of escaping to it, locking herself in and driving off.

She was disabused of that plan when her attacker gripped

her blouse, ripping buttons from the red, collared shirt. *I just bought that, you bloody arsehole.*

"Yes!" The man who was moments ago a buzzard hissed. "Oh, those are the fuckin' titties I've been wanting to see. I've been watching this pretty little bitch for weeks, but seeing them up close is gonna be so much fuckin' better than watching her change clothes through the window."

Ember felt green. She tasted blood, and her lip was swollen. Her ears rang, making it difficult to concentrate.

"Shut the fuck up, Josh," the man who leered above her grumbled. His hook nose vaguely resembled the sharp beak of his crow form. "We're here to clean up *your* fucking mess, don't forget. We wouldn't have to do any of this if you would've done your job like you were supposed to."

Josh whined, "you know I had to check on the cook! I wasn't gone long. How was I to know the stupid bitch would leave a party right after getting there? I thought I had a couple hours at least."

"Yeah, well, you can fucking explain that to Mister B when we bring her in."

"Think he'll understand? I had a cook—"

"You fucking dumbass, if you even mention the cook, Mister B will stick ya in the same grave as her. Now go check on Matty."

"You would've done the same thing, Doug. If it was your shift and you had—"

"I said 'go check on Matt!' Looks like the bitch knocked him out."

Ember brought her trembling hand up to her chest, feeling the exposed skin. She found the carved coyote pendant and wrapped her fingers around it. In her dazed state, the simple reminder helped bring her some degree of calm. *Need to focus. I have to get out of this.*

"Oh, what's this?" Doug crouched over her, giving her a view up the hairy nostrils of his pimpled hook nose. "Are ya trying to be fucking modest, bitch?" A knife unfolded in his hand. "I'll just cut that bra right off-a ya. It's a long drive back to Minot, and Mister B can still quiz you so long as we don't damage your fucking teeth." He dragged the point of the knife lightly against her cleavage. The knife was sharp, as proven by the thin trail of carmine fluid it left in its wake.

Ember sucked in air through clenched teeth as the pain burned from the fresh laceration. Her whole body trembled with adrenaline-enhanced anger. *Use this.*

Doug's ugly hook nose was just above her. The man was distracted by the contrast of crimson blood against her milk-white chest. It didn't take much effort for her to grab his greasy, jet-black hair.

Ember pulled the man's skull down abruptly, just as she lifted her head. She wrapped her teeth around that pimpled hook nose and clamped down harder than she ever had in her life. Cartilage snapped between her incisors, and a stranger's blood rushed into her mouth.

The changeling's scream was an air horn, deafening and high. Doug pulled away, but Ember didn't let go. He punched her. She clawed at his eyes. Hot blood pumped over her chin, flowing like something out of a horror show.

One of his punches landed in her torso, knocking the wind

out of her and forcing her to let go. She spat foul-tasting blood and wheezed, bent over on her side as she tried to catch her breath without inhaling Doug's nose-blood.

"You fucking bitch!" His scream was high and nasal now. His chin was drenched with blood, which continued to flow freely from his nose. His dirty, white tank was becoming saturated.

Tires squealed near the entrance to the rest area, followed by the roar of an engine. Even with the wind rustling against it, the sound reached the changelings' sensitive ears, though she couldn't hear it.

"What the *fuck*?" Doug gaped to the source of the noise. He backed away from Ember, staring at the approaching pickup as he shifted into his crow form. It took him only a moment to make the full transformation. His wings flapped furiously as he lifted off the ground.

Ember sputtered and watched with confusion as the crow transformed once more: this time, into a cloud of black feathers and pink mist, splattered against the grill guard of a roaring pickup. The vehicle ripped parallel trenches through the lawn as it slid to a halt.

"Doug! No!" Josh shouted. He jumped onto the picnic bench and began flapping his arms as he shifted. Long, dark feathers sprouted from his skin, his neck became thin and elongated, and his dirty jeans faded and shrunk into spindly claws. The turkey vulture ponderously flapped its wings and began to find air beneath them.

She reached her hand toward the buzzard and yelled. Ember couldn't let him get away. She rolled onto her hip and inhaled a stranger's blood as she willed her shaky legs to support her.

The buzzard flew right past her, its wings so close she could almost touch it. She lunged for the bird but caught only air.

The carrion bird hissed and flapped its massive span as it made its escape. It was over the parking lot, several yards off the ground when a blur of feathered lightning shot from the sky and connected with the buzzard. The wind carried a piercing scream, as the black-winged bird was sent down to the pavement with a sickening crack.

The turkey vulture flailed desperately, its wing broken as it futilely tried to defend against its attacker. A golden eagle had its claws buried in its prey's back. It mercilessly pecked its sharp beak at the vulture's exposed, thin neck as it rode the buzzard through its death throes.

31

THE EASY PATH OR THE RIGHT PATH

It all happened so fast, Ember's dazed senses struggled to catch up. The crow changeling, Doug, had become little more than a hood ornament. The turkey vulture changeling was on the parking lot's asphalt, quickly being shredded by the claws and beak of the eagle who took him down.

"Stop!" She spat blood that wasn't her own. "Don't kill him! I need to interrogate him."

The golden eagle had the vulture's long neck between its crushing, hooked beak. She was shaking it back and forth. Only when the buzzard's neck snapped did the eagle stop thrashing long enough to hear Ember's plea.

The Super Duty pickup driver's side door opened. Alarik stepped out and hurried over to Ember. "Good god, Ember! What did they do to you?"

She shook her head, her blonde mane now dyed by blood and the setting sun to turn it a ruddy hue. She looked through Alarik, her dazed, fire-blue eyes not quite focusing on him. "Nothing's broken. The blood's not mine. Not most of it."

The eagle shifted into its human form. Anna wiped her mouth with the back of her hand, then picked up the carrion bird by its broken neck. The thing was a heavy mass of crumped wing and shedding feathers.

Alarik helped Ember walk, as her legs threatened to collapse. He supported her until she could sit down on the picnic table bench. On the opposite side was the changeling the others identified interchangeably as Matt and Matty.

Matty wasn't moving.

The containment net Ember had cast was weak, as she had so little mana left to send at it. It was strong enough to knock the man off the table, and the elevated position plus gravity had done the rest. The hard, packed earth where he fell, head first, had snapped the man's neck; he was dead.

Anna opened the tailgate to her brother's Ford, hefted the dead buzzard into the pickup box, then spat on its carcass. She and Alarik loaded Matt's body in alongside his dead compatriot.

A reflection in the turf caught Ember's eye, so she limped over to investigate. It was Doug's knife, the one which slashed a line on her cleavage which still wept and stung. She picked up the knife and walked over to the front of the pickup.

There wasn't much left of the crow, but for a mangled body mashed between bars on the chrome grill guard. Using his own knife, Ember picked Doug's mangled corpse free and deposited both in the pickup.

The Schmitt siblings watched Ember in silence. Maybe they sensed that she needed to participate in this posthumous exercise. Or maybe the sight of her gave them pause: red shirt torn open, white pants ripped, the clothing and its wearer entirely sullied by wet blood.

They unrolled a black vinyl tonneau cover, concealing the grisly cargo before they shut the tailgate. It would make an adequate hearse.

"We shouldn't stick around," Alarik gestured with his chin at the sporadic traffic on Highway 2 to the north and south of them. "You want to clean up before we head home? I'll back the pickup up, get it off the grass before an H.P. sees and comes to take a closer look."

Ember didn't answer. She just stared vacantly at the rear of the pickup. At what she helped load into it.

"Come on," Anna said gently. "I'll come with you."

"I'm fine."

"Ember, you're covered in blood. You've got a cut on your lip, your chest—"

"I said I'm fine." She said it more forcefully the second time. Her gaze fixated on the emblem on the tailgate. She had a strange sensation that she should be in there, alongside the three bodies, lying inert.

Some part of her consciousness became aware of Anna wiping her face and neck with paper towels moistened from the restroom sink. Gatorade from a bottle purchased from the vending machine served to rinse her sticky mouth clean. All the beverages in the machine wouldn't be enough to clean the taste from her memory, though.

She didn't know it at the time—couldn't have known it, really—but later Ember would recognize that she was in a state of shock. One moment she was talking on the phone with her mother, having a normal if comically exasperating conversation with someone she loved. The next, she was brutally attacked, caught unaware and unprepared.

Unprepared. Never again. I'm no victim, and never will be. The pronouncement was a cold fact. The heated anger she felt was still there but joined by a determinedness that seemed permanent. The switch had been flipped, and there was no going back.

Anna retrieved her cell phone from the pickup. She transferred Ember's satchel and purse (minus the car keys) from the Taurus. She would drive it home, following Alarik and Ember in the pickup.

Home. "We can't go back to my apartment."

"I know, Ember." Alarik was buckling Ember in. Somewhere along the way, her drenched, torn shirt had been replaced with his jacket, which hung heavily and too large on her shoulders. "We're going to take you to Plaza. To my place."

"The bodies—"

"We'll take care of them, don't worry."

They were driving now, though Ember didn't know how much time had passed. "I can talk to them." Her voice was monotone. It sounded like someone else speaking.

"They're dead, Ember."

"I didn't mean for them to die." She turned in her seat and stared at the closed tonneau cover, imagining the three corpses beneath. "I would have interrogated them. I could have cast a Memory Wash on them, and let them go. I didn't want them dead."

"If it's any consolation, they seemed determined to kill you." Alarik peered at his passenger with his umber eyes. "I for one am glad that they didn't succeed."

Ember continued staring at the rear of the pickup, twisted against the shoulder belt as she was. "I don't think they were going to kill me. Not until I was questioned. 'Mister B' they'd said."

"Mister B?" Alarik frowned at the windshield. "Who the hell is Mister B? The Director of Wellness is Elton Higginbotham."

Ember turned forward. Her senses were starting to return. "Higginbotham isn't in charge. There's someone else. Maybe multiple someone elses."

Alarik whistled low. "How deep can this possibly go?"

She shook her head. Her hair was encrusted with dried blood. Her skin felt gross, sticky, clogged. "They hadn't told him. Their boss, this Mister B. Whoever the puppet master is, he doesn't know that you and I temporarily lifted the Deference Spell on Duncan Heywood. They don't know that the spell didn't work on me.

"You mentioned that before. Deference Spell. What is it?"

Ember considered Alarik and his question for a good minute. "Before I tell you, I need to know how you and Anna got to me. How you knew I needed help."

"We didn't know you needed help." Alarik's eyes met hers

for as long as he dared to take them from the road. "I...we were worried about you since you said that the spy had followed you to Pembina. The rest stop was the halfway point for the journey back. You said you were going to stop there on the way, so we figured we could meet you there, and convoy back. Safety in numbers, and all that."

"But Anna..." Ember's voice trailed off.

Alarik's lips twitched up. "That sister of mine is half crazy. Get this: we were easing up to turn off into the rest area. I have my turn signal on, and she sees her car parked, and then she sees three men surrounding it. She yelled to me to open the window, then shifted into her eagle form right there in the seat." He pointed at where Ember sat now. "I barely got the window down, and she hopped up to the edge and then launched herself out. I'm just glad I had slowed down enough, or the wind would have messed her up. I don't think she even gave that any thought. She just jumped without thinking."

Ember closed her eyes and furrowed her brow. Her voice was raspy and low. "Anna could've gotten herself killed."

"My sister's tougher than she looks. And I know how tough she looks. But you're right, she could have. But she didn't."

"Her car's hood is scratched," Ember said morosely. "The buzzard landed on it. I'll apologize to her for that."

Alarik flashed a grin, then saw that Ember was sincere. His tone was compassionate when he placed his hand on her arm and gave it a gentle squeeze. "Ember, you're alive. That's the only thing that matters."

Her eyes started burning when he said that. She looked

away, determined not to let him see the tears. She didn't pull her arm away from his grip.

Ember told him about the Deference Spell, though she was careful not to mention Barnaby. She told him about Higginbotham—or what she knew about him—and how the rest of the Investigators were under his influence. She told him that there was a cover-up within the highest levels of the Viceroyalty—though she didn't tell him about the suspicion that this conspiracy extended to the Druw High Council. She didn't tell him about the Inquisitor lineage, either. Some things were just too dangerous to share just yet.

Alarik's response was all of two words: "Holy crap."

"Yeah. There's a lot I can't tell you, Rik, for your own good. I wouldn't even be telling you this much, but you're already neck deep in this bloody mess. I need your help."

"No more gallivanting off by yourself, then?"

"I think I've learned my lesson."

If she would have had enough mana—if she wouldn't have been completely drained of her energy—Ember would have brought the ghosts of the three changeling spies back to question them. She didn't have the mana for such an action though, not tonight. She would need to make time for that, later. There was never any guarantee that the ghosts would cooperate with her, and she had very little leverage over them to compel answers. It was entirely possible that all they knew, they already told her.

"A cook." Ember murmured the thoughts aloud. "They mentioned Mister B and a cook. I wonder if those are code names for people."

They arrived at Alarik's farmstead at around one o'clock in the morning. They got out of their vehicles. Ember's hip still hurt, and she walked with a limp.

The lights were on in Alarik's house, and his Uncle Boniface waited at the kitchen table. A mostly-empty carafe of coffee sat on the table. His fingers were hooked around a ceramic mug.

"Ember, nice to see you again." The changeling raised his mug and offered a wink. "You look like shit. I hear the other guy looks even worse. Atta girl."

Ember stiffened, "How did you—"

"I called him," Anna shrugged. "He's going to help me bury the bodies. Literally. Don't worry, Uncle Boni knows how to keep secrets. You can trust him."

"I don't have much choice now, do I," Ember said grimly. She closed her eyes and saw Boniface Schmitt's fox subform sitting at the table.

"Young lady, I'm gonna let you in on a secret." Boniface took a sip of coffee before he continued. "You live as long as I have, you learn that you always have a choice. You can take the easy path or the right path."

"My niece told me about what you done today for Arnie. For us. Way I see it, you've walked to hell and back for my family, and you barely just met us. Your kind is mighty uncommon to stumble across in the world, and I've done a lot of stumbling in my day. Someone who's willing to walk that hard path for me and mine, well hell, it'd just be damn rude not to reciprocate the favor." He winked at Ember.

Ember studied his aura and saw that the wily man was more

than capable of fibbing, but in this statement, there was only sincerity.

"Thank you." Ember canted her head. "I promise that I'm doing all that I can to help Arnie and the others."

"We know," Alarik said.

She waved her hands slowly in front of her, her fingers splayed as she gestured at her figure. "Now if you don't mind, I could really, desperately use a scalding hot shower right now."

She ran the water heater until it was cold, letting the pressure flow over her. Steam filled the bathroom, and she used half a bottle of her host's shampoo. The blood may have been gone, but she still felt sticky, filthy. Only the frigid shift in water temperature finally prompted her to step out of the shower. She would have stayed in there indefinitely and still not felt clean.

Ember stared at herself in the mirror. The cut on her lip was swollen but felt a lot worse than it looked. Her right cheek was bruised, but that, too, would heal. Her eyes looked grey in the steam-filtered vanity lights.

The laceration on her chest ran about three inches along the side of her left breast. It would probably scar, serving as a reminder of the evening's battle and what it almost cost her. The carved coyote face hung on its leather cord, draped alongside the new scar. She lifted the pendant to her bruised lip and gave it a kiss.

Alarik found the t-shirt he loaned her when she last stayed overnight, along with a pair of denim jeans that were way too large, even with the legs rolled up. The belt he provided would keep them on her hips, but she looked like a child playing dress up in her father's clothes.

Dressed in the borrowed, baggy clothes, Ember emerged feeling weary but determined. Her hair hung damp against her back, soaking through the loaned shirt.

Boniface and Anna were already gone. They had transferred the bodies into Boniface's pickup and left to dispose of them before daybreak arrived.

"Rik, where did they take them?" Ember asked.

"Does it matter?"

"Yeah, it does."

He raised an eyebrow. "Okay. In that case, I'll ask them when they get back. I don't know about you, but I could sure use a stiff drink while we wait for them."

"I could, too, but that'll have to be another time." She claimed his jacket from the back of a kitchen chair and slid her arms into it while he watched, bemused. "We've another long drive ahead of us."

32

ONE MORE PIECE TO THE PUZZLE

IT WOULD BE A FEW HOURS YET BEFORE SUNRISE. THE NIGHT outside Alarik's pickup was clear and cool, and the wind had calmed. The moon was a nearly perfect, full circle in the star-filled sky. Moonlight reflected on the inky, still water of Lake Sakakawea, beneath the concrete Highway 23 bridge west of New Town.

"What makes you so convinced that this Dominic guy will be useful?"

"It's just a hunch," Ember admitted. "Nobody remembered the time they spent within that fog back in 2001. Everything I find credits some sort of mass amnesia or inexplicable coma. The fact that there are NonDruws who might have been able to escape the effects leads me to believe that they can tell us what happened. Duncan seemed convinced that they knew things, anyway."

Alarik pulled a wedge of welder's soapstone from his pocket as he drove. He used the talc stick to gesture. "Do you think they had something to do with the industrial accident?"

"That thought crossed my mind."

"If Duncan knew, and if he is working for Director Higginbotham—"

"Not working for," Ember corrected. "Under the influence of Higginbotham. Courtesy of the Deference Spell."

"Okay. Then under the influence of the Director, then that would mean the Director of Wellness is purposely refusing to help Arnie and the others."

"Maybe. Or maybe he just doesn't know how to help them. He may know what caused it but doesn't have it in his power to heal them. He's a Sixth-Level Healer, but what I felt in Kenny was a different type of energy. A foreign magic, maybe." She thought of the dark-skinned little girl in Roosevelt Park, how the residue from her mana felt similar when Ember sensed it.

Traffic was heavier, west of the Missouri River. Tanker semi-trucks and heavy-duty pickups outnumbered passenger vehicles. Though it was after midnight, a steady flow of vehicles traveled Highway 23. When Alarik turned south onto Highway 22, the traffic seemed to increase even more.

"What are all those fires?" Ember gaped at the tall torches, which illuminated tank batteries and pumping equipment.

"Those are flares. Methane and Hydrogen Sulfide being burned off. We're in oil country now, and there's a boom going on. It's a modern-day gold rush." Alarik glanced at Ember. "I've had so much welding work, I've had to turn projects down for lack of time."

She scrunched her nose at the hair-curling scent of rotten eggs that drifted into the cab of the pickup when they drove past the flames. Ember stared out the window, thinking for some minutes. "I've taken you away from some of those projects, haven't I. You're losing money every time you chauffeur me around."

"I'm not gonna lie to you, yeah I've had to miss out on some nice bids. But some things are more important than chasing dollars." Alarik shrugged. "Most things are."

"You won't have to drive me around much longer. Wallace wants to bring me home, due to the potential danger."

"Ah. There it is. That's why you're being so insistent on getting to these interviews with the witnesses, huh? But if those spies didn't report you to Higginbotham—or whoever Mister B is—are you still in danger?"

"I'm going to plead that case to Wallace. It doesn't mean there's no longer danger. It might just be delaying the immediate threat."

Alarik dragged his fingernail across the soapstone. In the dim illumination from the dash panel, tiny flecks of white shavings fell onto the floorboard. Evidence of the man's peculiar habit accumulated like dandruff on the carpet. He clicked his tongue to the roof of his mouth and pointed his soapstone at her accusingly. "You're not telling me everything, are you."

Ember raised her eyebrows. "Pardon me? I've told you way more than I should have. More than I was authorized to, certainly."

"Maybe so. But you're not telling me everything. I've been thinking about this, and it just doesn't add up. Not completely."

The Ford clung to the asphalt road as it plunged down into a valley, weaving sharply through rough, wooded buttes populated by cedar and juniper. Ember let the centrifugal force push her up against the passenger door. She studied her transparent reflection in the dark glass, saw the driver watching the road as he maneuvered.

"You're right, Rik." Ember sighed. "You deserve to know more. I can't tell you everything though, not yet. I have theories, suspicions. Some of them are bloody dangerous theories, too."

"You're doing all this for Arnie though. For my brother."

Ember flicked her tongue across her lip, tasted the salty, swollen wound she found there. "I am. But there's more to this than that. More to the Deference Spells, the cover-up. I just don't know what, exactly. And believe me when I say that for now, you're better off not knowing all my theories."

"But you think talking to Dominic Hershel will clear that up."

"It might be one more piece to the puzzle, yeah. Or it might be just a wasted trip. *Another* wasted trip."

"Let's hope we don't hit any birds this time around." Alarik flashed a grin.

"That's not funny, Rik." Ember felt green as she thought of the bodies that rode in the pickup box behind them only a couple of hours ago. "I've never killed anyone before. I didn't mean for that to happen."

"I never had, either. Neither had Anna. But I would do it over again, without a doubt. I don't feel any remorse whatsoever. Those assholes got exactly what they deserved."

"I guess." Ember nodded slowly. She thought of the lecherous way the spies spoke to her. How they said they had watched her change clothes in her apartment, what they intended on doing to her on the drive back to Minot. *Did that mean they deserved to die though?*

"To the east," Alarik pointed to his left with the whittled soapstone. "That's the turn for Mandaree. We'll be crossing the Little Missouri up ahead, where Roy and Marv said they entered the fog.

Ember studied the rugged terrain with the benefit of moonlight. Atop the steep hills were flat rocks jutting out like balconies. The trees seemed to cluster on the north faces of the rough terrain, with the woods dwindling on the southern slopes. An oil drilling rig stood atop one such hill near the highway, its towering derrick brightly lit by glaring, white lights.

Exhaustion and hypnosis of the highway caught up to Ember soon after. She drifted off and slept through the rest of the journey. She awoke an hour and a half later to a bright sunrise. As she stretched in her seat, she yawned and looked over at Alarik. His face was exhausted, unblinking.

Her yawn was contagious, as he duplicated the action. "We're past Regent. You missed the Enchanted Highway.

"The...what? Enchanted?"

He chuckled tiredly. "It's a stretch of road with giant, steel sculptures done by a local welder from Regent. Fifty-foot-tall grasshoppers, a giant tin man and woman, stuff like that. I know Gary—well, I met him once. Describing his creations doesn't do them justice. You'll see on the way back."

She rubbed the sleep from her eyes and yawned again. "You must be exhausted, Rik."

"I'm gettin' there."

The address Ember found online for Dominic Hershel led them to a farmstead partway between the towns of Regent and Mott. Surrounded by fields of wheat in all directions, the farmyard was bordered with massive silver grain bins. The driveway and yard were coated with a layer of red-orange rock which Alarik called "scoria." Parked between two steel pole buildings was a blue-and-white tandem axle grain truck with its hood up.

A man in denim bib overalls was bent over the hood of the truck. He stood straight when he heard the Super Duty roll down the drive.

Ember felt her excitement turn into anxiety as they stopped a few yards away. This man was older—probably approaching his 70s. "It isn't him, Rik. Dominic Hershel is supposed to be in his mid-forties."

Alarik took the Ford out of gear and turned the ignition key vertical. "We drove into the man's yard. We've gotta at least talk to him." He opened his door and left her in the pickup.

She opened the passenger door and grimaced as she stepped down from the tall vehicle. Her legs were sore, her hips hurt like mad, and her back was cramping up. Ember guessed this must be what 200-year-olds feel like. *Maybe sitting in a vehicle for three-and-a-half hours after getting my butt kicked wasn't such a great idea. Leave it to a massage therapist.*

"Morning," Alarik called out to the farmer.

"Good morning." The man held a greasy rag and a ratchet wrench in his hands. His dark eyebrows were bushy over wary eyes, and his skin was wrinkled and tanned so heavily it might have been leather. He looked at the two visitors apprehensively. "What can I do for you?"

"I farm up in Mountrail County." Alarik offered the snippet of biography as an icebreaker. His fingertips were powdered white from worrying his soapstone through the nighttime drive. They left a pale, dusty smudge on his stubble when he rubbed his jaw. "I don't suppose you're Dominic Hershel by any chance?"

The man leaned back and frowned. Somehow, his eyebrows became even bushier. "No, I'm Fred. Dominic doesn't live here."

Ember felt her weary muscles deflate. *All this way, for nothing.*

"Nick's my son." Fred pointed with the chrome wrench in the direction of the rising sun. "If you need to talk to him, he and his wife Kat live that way, just down the road."

33

WATCH OUT FOR THE LAVA

"Did I just hear him correctly? Did he say that Nick Hershel's wife is named Kat?" Alarik waved at the elder Hershel before departing the farmyard.

"Short for Katrina. Could we be so lucky?" Ember was as surprised as Alarik. "We are overdue for a lucky break, yeah?"

They drove down the scoria road in the direction Fred pointed them. Nick and Kat Hershel lived in a modular home with Masonite siding painted a cheerful mint green. A camper was parked on the cement slab next to an attached double garage. Theirs wasn't a farmstead so much as a cozy rural property, with copses of young trees staked out around a yard built for a family. A swing set, sandbox, and playhouse with scalloped-cut shutters were surrounded by myriad plastic toys.

A younger version of Fred Hershel was seated on the front deck, soaking in the morning sun. His grey-stockinged feet were resting on the deck railing, and a white ceramic mug was cradled in his hand. He balanced the coffee cup on the railing when he stood to greet the strangers.

"Morning. It's a little early for a sales call, isn't it?" The man's voice was gruff, with a hint of antagonism below the surface. He spoke like someone who was used to solicitors pitching him, and equally accustomed to sending salesmen on their way, disappointed.

Ember's feet crunched over scoria that hadn't yet settled and compacted. She approached the deck with Alarik and studied the man. She knew it was Dominic as soon as she saw him: the dark hair, the faint, curved scar on his right cheek. He was tall, though not quite as tall as Alarik. More noticeable still was the fact that this man—this NonDruw man—had a shadow blanketing him. *Why else would a regular human have a Deference Spell on him unless he knew something he wasn't supposed to know?*

"Hi, Nick. I'm Ember Wright, and this is Rik Schmitt. We're not selling you anything. We're here hoping you might be able to help us, actually."

Nick frowned slightly. "Help you? With what?"

"We've got friends who were affected by the Mandaree Incident from 2001. It's my understanding that you were there. That you were in that fog, too."

"I was." He sounded uncertain even as he admitted she was right. "Not many people know about that. I don't know how much I can help you though. Kat and I don't really talk about that, and we don't remember much about what happened. We were in a coma, brought on by the toxic gas that we breathed in. We're lucky to be alive."

"Kat. That wouldn't happen to be Katrina Berg, would it?" Ember quirked a smile.

"It was, sure. Until we got married. How did you know that? How did you get our names, anyway?" The man was tense. Though Ember was the one asking questions, he kept a wary eye on Alarik.

"We've been doing research, trying to help our friends figure out what happened to them when they were in the...coma, as you say. Your names came up."

"Yeah, well, like I said, we don't remember much that happened. Sorry."

She saw Alarik glance at her, then to Nick. "I'm sorry to be a pain, but we just drove through the night from east of New Town. I wasn't bright enough to stop for coffee along the way, and it's a long drive back. Could I steal a cup of coffee from you?"

Nick hesitated as he considered the request. Finally, he nodded. "Sure, I suppose so. Come on in. Shoes off outside." He turned and slid a glass patio door along its track, revealing the kitchen inside.

Alarik and Ember followed, kicking their shoes off. As Ember unlaced her boots, she noticed a splatter of blood on the toe. She took care to tip the boot onto its side, hiding the speck.

An attractive blonde woman with deep blue eyes was at the kitchen stove, using a silicone spatula to melt butter in a cast iron skillet. She was roughly the same age as Ember but taller and slightly heavier. She, too, had the shadow of a Deference Spell cast over her.

Two girls, maybe seven and eight years old, were seated at the table. They were chasing the last pieces of floating cereal around their bowls with a spoon. The children had their mother's hair and fair skin, but their father's dark eyes.

"Kat, we've got company. This is Rik and Ember, from up north. They drove down to ask us about the Mandaree Incident." Nick took down two clean ceramic mugs from the cupboard and poured piping hot coffee into them from an insulated carafe. He slid the steaming mugs across the table, to two open chairs.

"Kids, why don't you run outside and play while the grownups visit?" Nick ruffled the girls' hair, causing them to squirm and giggle.

"Drink your milk first," Katrina ordered.

The command was obeyed without argument. The girls hopped down from the chairs that were too big for them, then carried their empty bowls to the sink. The older one said, "Lucy, let's see if the mud pies are done yet." Two pairs of bare feet ran out onto the deck and down the steps.

The younger one hopped from the last step, over the rough scoria and landed on the plush lawn. "Watch out for the lava, Bonnie!"

Katrina slid the patio door shut. "I was just getting ready to make us breakfast. Would you care to join us?"

Ember's stomach grumbled. She ignored it. "Oh no, we couldn't—"

"It's nothing fancy," Katrina began cracking eggs into a steel mixing bowl. "Just an omelet with chopped ham, onions, and cheese."

Alarik swallowed and raised his eyebrows as he looked longingly. His coyote subform licked its lips in anticipation.

Ember hugged her hands around the warm coffee mug. "That's so nice of you. Yes, thank you."

"I was just telling them that we don't remember much from the toxic cloud." Nick poured the last of the coffee into a pink mug on the countertop next to his wife. He filled the carafe with water from the sink and prepared another pot.

"Nothing at all?" Alarik asked.

"Wish we could help you, but that was almost a decade ago." Katrina whisked the eggs as she held the bowl. "I don't remember much about it. We're just glad we survived."

"If you don't mind my asking, how did you two meet?" Ember poured a spoonful of sugar into her coffee, stirring it slowly so the metal would not clink against the walls of the mug.

"We worked together in the oilfield as mudloggers—wellsite geologists." Nick measured grounds into the filter basket of the coffee maker. "We worked and lived on active drilling rigs, evaluating formations as the wells were drilled. In fact, we met on that drilling rig, right before the mishap that caused the gas leak. Good ol' Ensign 77."

Alarik said, "Ensign 77? I think I've worked on that one."

"You're a roughneck?"

"No, a welder. My brother and I own Schmitt Brothers Welding, up in Plaza. We've won a few bids for Ensign Drilling."

"You'll have to give me your card," Nick said as he flipped

the coffee maker on. "I'm a consultant now, and you don't know how hard it is to find reliable welders right now. Or maybe you do know."

Alarik produced a business card from his wallet and handed it to Nick. "I do. This boom is really building steam. I wish I could clone myself."

As the men talked shop, Katrina poured the contents of the mixing bowl into the hot skillet. She began chopping mushrooms on a cutting board, with an onion and a slab of Cloverdale teardrop ham waiting for their turns on the counter.

Ember studied the woman's back and the shadowy Deference Spell that blanketed her. *Why a Deference Spell on these people? A Memory Wash would have been more effective, easier to implement. Only an Investigator could cast such a spell, but Higginbotham has Investigators under his influence. Does an Investigator need free will to induce a Memory Wash?*

The Malvern woman looked inward, tapping her store of mana. Ember's reserves were still far too low to cast the temporary counter-spell she had used to extract information from Duncan. Even if she had the power to do so, she wasn't sure it would be worth the cost, not for answers to just one question.

Katrina laughed at something Nick said. Ember didn't hear what the others were saying. She sipped her sweetened coffee and thought about the elaborate counter-spell movements that Barnaby taught her. She visualized going through those poses now, as if she were standing in the kitchen next to the other woman, rather than sitting at the table watching her.

A strange thing happened when Ember saw through her mind's eye. As she got to the midway point of the movement, her fingertips began to tingle, just as they did when she had physically cast the counter-spell in Duncan Heywood's garage. Though her hands were both wrapped around the coffee mug on the table, she felt the Deference Spell around Katrina react. Ember could see a heavy, tar paper tent surrounding the woman as she stood at the stove.

Ember continued visualizing the remainder of the counter-spell. She was at the end point, where she would plunge her fingers into the tent, forcing a flap to form, within which she would reveal the host trapped within. She hesitated.

Her fingertips continued tingling. Ember was breathing normally, though she willed the imagined version of herself to continue holding her breath. She touched the Deference Spell's tent, and it felt real. It was stiff but pliable, like canvas. Her fingers gently ran along the side of the material, feeling its smooth surface. At one spot, she felt a tiny bump. Barely perceptible, it felt like a deformation in the Deference Spell—a knot in the canvas.

Using her fingernails, Ember imagined plucking at the bump, teasing it until a thread came loose. It was such a little thing, this single thread, but she pinched it between her fingers and began drawing it away from the tent. The thread became a string, and it grew. She willed the dark string loose, pulling it steadily as the material forming the tent fell away.

Katrina began humming a happy tune as the Deference Spell came apart and evaporated into the air. Ember imagined stepping backward through the counter-spell. She gasped aloud.

Everyone stopped talking and looked at Ember.

"Sorry, the coffee's just hot." Ember shrugged. She looked at Katrina to find her aura clean and unblemished. The Deference Spell was completely removed.

Ember wanted to jump up and down, wanted to dance on the table right then, shouting "I did it! I removed a Deference Spell! Not just temporarily, but completely!" Instead, she cleared her throat and imagined giving herself a fist bump.

She repeated the movements on Nick. Instead of forcing the mana to her will, she was able to gently guide and redirect the energy, even while seated. The man didn't freeze at any point, didn't even seem aware that anything was happening to him. None of them were.

When the dark tent fell away around Nick's aura, his smile became brighter, his expressions more vibrant. He set the table with four plates and forks, but not before giving his wife a kiss on the cheek. "Love you, Honey."

Katrina was all but glowing. Her disposition wasn't unpleasant with the Deference Spell in place, but with it gone she was appreciably happier. The woman purposely bumped her hip against her husband's thigh and continued humming a song nobody else knew.

Alarik watched the exchange, then looked away, self-conscious to be observing such a tender moment among strangers. He suddenly found interest in the crayon drawings pinned with magnets to the refrigerator door.

Ember closed her eyes and smiled. The sugar-laced coffee certainly helped perk her up, but the real rush was in doing what she technically should not have been able to do. She expended so little mana in lifting the Deference Spell, too. She felt refreshed, ready to take on the world. *Or at least those in the world who stand in my way.*

Katrina's omelet smelled and tasted like it was made in heaven. The melted cheddar held together diced onions, mushrooms, and ham within the scrambled farm-fresh eggs, toasted to buttery perfection on the skillet. *Today's secret ingredient is victory.*

"Are you sure you don't remember anything from your time in the fog at Mandaree?" Ember asked cheerfully between bites.

Alarik was wolfing his breakfast down like a hungry coyote. He stopped chewing long enough to raise an eyebrow at Ember. The eyebrow reached higher when Nick Hershel responded.

"Huh. You know...I said I didn't remember anything about it but...but now I feel like it's all coming back to me."

Katrina blinked and looked at her husband as memories surfaced. "Wow, me, too. I'm getting a serious case of déjà vu here."

Mr. and Mrs. Hershel continued looking at one another, an unspoken message passing between them.

"I wouldn't even know where to begin," Nick murmured.

Ember steepled her fingers. She rested her elbows on either side of her plate and leaned forward. "A good place to begin would be the beginning. When did you first come into contact with that fog?"

Nick shook his head slowly. He turned from his wife and settled his gaze on Ember. “You wouldn’t believe it if I told you.”

“You’d be surprised. Try me.” As she talked, Ember began gently willing the two NonDruws to relax. It was a skill she learned from apprenticing with The Legend himself, an ability exclusive to practitioners of the Investigator Track of magic. It wasn’t a spell so much as a refined interrogation technique. Wallace had explained it to her: “*Think of it as a coin. One side is a carrot, the other side is a stick.*” The carrot was so much more pleasant to use than the stick—for everyone involved.

The gentle nudge must have worked because Nick sighed and leaned back in his chair. “It was just before Christmas, 2000. We were drilling on the reservation, south of Mandaree and just north of the Little Missouri. Kat and I were mudlogging, and she was on tour when the drill bit ran into...something. It was in the Three Forks formation, I think.”

“Middle Bakken, wasn’t it?” Katrina tilted her head. She, too, had stopped eating.

“Yeah, I think you’re right. Bakken formation. Anyway, we hit something that resembled metal. Bronze or something.” Nick shook his head and looked from Alarik to Ember. “Not something that was supposed to be down there.”

Ember continued willing the Hershels to relax, to feel comfortable sharing their story with her. “So, what was it?”

“This is where things really started to get weird,” Katrina said. She slid her hand over Nick’s and weaved her fingers between his.

The man squeezed his wife's hand. He swallowed and met Ember's gaze in an effort to show his sincerity. "You won't believe it, but we drilled into this thing that shouldn't exist in the real world. But it's very much real. It's a sort of...pipeline that carries energy. Magic energy. It's called a Ley Line. We ruptured it, and brought Hell to Earth."

34

LEY LINE MAGNET

"What do you mean, Hell came to Earth?" Ember showed no reaction to the mention of a Ley Line, though with that one new clue, gears in the Investigator's mind slipped into place.

"It wasn't *literally* Hell," Katrina offered an apologetic shrug on behalf of her husband. "At least, not after we found out what had happened."

"Which was..." Ember let her voice trail off in expectation of an answer.

"Well, it's like this: the magic pipeline—that Ley Line, as it's called—has a casing around it. That casing is made of a bronze-like metal—"

"The Ley Line Shell," Katrina interrupted her husband.

"Right, the Ley Line Shell. That's the stuff our drill bit broke into. When that happened, it made things go all kinds of catawampus." Nick inhaled slowly until the words could find their way to his lips. "I know all of this is going to sound like we're crazy, but I'm telling you the truth."

He was. They were. Ember sensed the sincerity, not just in their body language and voices, but in the way their unblemished auras moved. NonDruws such as these two people had faint auras compared to Malverns and changelings, but the colors and movement of their auras reacted to lies and deception in ways that Ember easily recognized. Nick and Katrina were telling the truth. "I believe you. Please, continue. When did the toxic cloud come into this?"

"Not long after we drilled into the Ley Line, I guess. The rig's pumps were still circulating for a couple of hours to clean out the hole. My guess is that it took time for enough drilling fluid to bring the energy from the Ley Line to the surface." Nick looked at Katrina for confirmation. "It might've been that when enough hydrostatic pressure accumulated, that energy reached a tipping point."

"I don't think there's a proper formula we could use to calculate that, but it makes sense, I agree. It wasn't a toxic cloud, though." Katrina ran her fingertip along the edge of her pink coffee cup. "It had a taste to it—metallic, like copper maybe—but it wasn't poisonous."

"The buzzing, too," Nick added, using the index finger on his right hand to gesture at his ear. "I've got tinnitus, but the fog made a buzzing noise. Kat heard it, too."

"That's right, I'd forgotten about that." Katrina nodded as she stared at her coffee. "The hellish part was that everyone disappeared. Everyone but us, I guess."

Ember gripped her coffee cup in both hands. Though its contents were hot, she felt a chill run through her. "What do you mean, everyone disappeared?"

"Disappeared, disappeared. I mean Nick and I were the only humans left. All the equipment was dead, vehicles wouldn't start, anything electrical—even flashlights—all dead. And every single soul was missing, without any footprints to show them walking away. Nothing."

Nick squeezed his wife's hand, whose fingers were still weaved together in his left hand. "Animals were left behind. Wildlife, cattle, dogs. And monsters."

Ember glanced at Alarik, who was leaning forward just as she was. Neither of them said anything.

Katrina looked at the guests sitting across the table. "He's telling the truth. Giants, from another dimension. Another planet or something. They stalked us, chased us. Two of them cornered us, and almost killed us. We barely got out of there alive."

"But you did get out alive," Ember stated the obvious. "How?"

Nick chuckled, though there wasn't any mirth in his tone. "We just walked out. We kept walking until we got out of the fog."

Katrina pulled her hand back from Nick's, slowly. She reached for the coffee pot and refilled everyone's mugs. "That's when we found out that three months had passed, although to us it only felt like three days. We were questioned by some government goons, told not to talk to one another, and sent home."

Nick winked at his wife. "Neither of us are very good at taking orders, though. We talked, and we decided to go back into the fog."

"Why? Why would you go back in when you barely made it out alive, as you said?" Ember continued holding her coffee mug without sampling from it.

Katrina and Nick looked at one another. Another of those unspoken messages passed between them, as only happens in relationships tempered by fire. Katrina answered, "neither of us could sleep. We both had the worst nightmares when we did sleep. It was the same thing, too: we dreamed of the people who disappeared. They were stuck in the ground, calling at us for help, but we couldn't get to them." She stared directly at Ember, her blue eyes cold with fear. "Nick and I had the exact same nightmares. Only, they weren't just dreams. It was real."

Alarik and Ember exchanged startled glances. His mouth was open, and Ember realized hers was, too.

Nick shifted in his seat and took a long draw from his mug. "We both knew we had to go back. We had to try to help them, somehow. So, we went back into the fog."

"Déjà vu again," Katrina said. "I remember telling all this to someone, years ago. Two someones. A couple of Federal agents."

"Oh yeah!" Nick nodded as the memory surfaced. "I forgot about that, too. I didn't like those guys. Especially the one agent, the older man. He didn't say much, but he had an arrogant way about him. I've worked in the oilfield my whole life, so oversized egos are nothing new to me, but that guy, he was just a *dick*. He smiled a lot, but you could tell he was full of shit."

"Elton." Katrina tapped a finger to her lip as she called on the memory. "That was his name, Elton. I remember he had a blue gemstone tie pin. It just seemed out of place for someone who worked for the government. The other agent, the one who asked most of the questions, his name was Duncan. I remember he had a buzz cut like you see on soldiers. I can't believe I forgot about them."

Ember saw Alarik glance at her again, but she kept watching the couple. The Deference Spell repressed their memories for nine years, but with it lifted their memories were rushing back. She subconsciously reached for the coyote pendant, touching the carved face between her fingers. "How do you know all this, about the Ley Line. Why were you two the only people who could come and go into the fog without disappearing?"

"You'd better do the explaining, Honey." Katrina squeezed her husband's forearm.

"His name was Tresden," Nick sighed, swallowed another gulp of coffee before continuing. "He was another one of those...monsters, I guess. But a good guy, it turned out. That pipeline we'd drilled into—the Ley Line—well, it was somehow connected to this other dimension. Aedynar, they call it."

"So, when the atmosphere of Aedynar mixed with the atmosphere of Earth, it caused some sort of reaction. It had something to do with the magic of the two worlds. He had a name for it, I can't remember what it was."

"Mana," Katrina offered.

"Right, mana. Well, when the mana from Earth met the mana of Aedynar, it caused the fog that the media kept calling a 'toxic gas cloud.' It wasn't toxic, but it did make everyone who entered it, well...it made them disappear."

Katrina murmured, "but not us."

"Right, not us. Tresden said it was because we were the only two who touched the Ley Line Shell itself. Being mudloggers, we handled the drill cuttings that circulated up the wellbore. Those tiny pieces of bronze, well we were the only humans to ever touch them. So, when the fog settled in—I mean really settled in—then we were the only ones who weren't trapped. Everyone else was trapped between dimensions—not on Earth, not on Aedynar."

"Trapped between dimensions," Ember repeated. Another gear in her mind slipped into place.

"Yeah, I know how strange it all sounds." Nick shook his head. "It's all so fucked up. Or it was, anyway. Tresden was able to get the Ley Line repaired, with our help. He was able to get it repaired and returned things to how they were, more or less. The creatures from Aedynar went back to where they came from, and all the people from Earth became unstuck. None of them remembered being gone though. Kat and I were the only ones who remembered a damn thing."

Katrina slapped her palm on the table. Ember was so engrossed in her thoughts, that the sound made her flinch. Katrina slid her chair back and stood up. "We know how crazy this all sounds, but we have proof."

Nick frowned. "We do, Honey?"

"Yeah, we do. I'll be right back." Katrina left the kitchen for a few minutes. When she returned, she was carrying a cardboard box. She began shuffling through its contents at the table. "I can't believe that we haven't even talked about this for, what, a decade almost? I even forgot we had...this."

Katrina pulled out an off-white, unbleached cotton bag closed with a drawstring. The bag was no more than six inches long and had an unmarked yellow tag sewn into the seam. Something heavy was in the bag.

The hairs on the back of Ember's neck stood on end. She *tasted* the energy before the bag was opened, before she saw what was inside. It was powerful, alien, and had the same oleaginous mana that she had felt living within Kenny's aura, in place of his animal subform. It was the same mana that the little girl in the park exuded when she brought the squirrel back to life.

The object Katrina pulled out of the mudlogging sample bag looked like it was made of brass. It was shaped like a leaf, hollow in the middle and with five small spheres attached along one side. The relic was infused with an impossibly strong mana that glowed so brightly, it hurt Ember's eyes.

She squinted and looked away, but noticed that Alarik continued studying it. *He can't see the mana. None of them can.*

"Tresden had a name for it, but we called it a Ley Line Magnet." Nick accepted the heavy object from Katrina. He handled it before passing it over to Alarik. "I forgot we even had this. I think he accidentally left it with us."

"No beads, no brazing marks. It's like this was cast whole,

somehow." Alarik held the magnet close to his face as he admired the shape. "What was it used for?"

"He made it to help us find the pieces of the Ley Line Shell." Nick drank the last of his coffee in one gulp. "When we drilled into it, it shattered the casing around the Ley Line into dozens of tiny pieces. We used this like a magnet to fish those pieces out of the reserve pit. It was a pretty tedious process, but in the end, we got enough for Tresden to work his mojo, to put it all back together again."

"And the nightmares went away. The real ones and the dream ones." Katrina smiled and squeezed her husband's hand.

Alarik handed the leaf-shaped metal to Ember. She reached instead for the cotton sample bag and gave it to him.

"You didn't tell those agents about this magnet?"

Nick and Katrina both shook their heads. The curved scar on Nick's cheek flexed as he clenched his jaw. Katrina was the one who answered. "No, we didn't. Those two men made our skins crawl. I guess we just felt like they didn't need to know about this part of the story."

"But you trust us." Ember picked up the bagged relic from the table. Even through the fabric, she could feel the oily mana, as though the forged brass was coated with thick grease only she could see or feel. "I think this may be helpful for our friends. Unlike you, unlike everyone else, they continue to suffer from those nightmares. I think there might be a way to use this magnet to help treat them."

"If you think it could help them, somehow," Nick looked at his wife, who nodded. "Then by all means, please borrow it.

Only just...only if you promise not to tell anyone where you got this from."

Katrina walked over to the patio door to watch her daughters playing in the yard outside. There was an edge to her voice when she said, "our little family is happy and safe. Please don't do anything that might change that."

35

FISHERMAN'S DREAM

After breakfast, they exchanged phone numbers with the Hershels. As frosty as Nick's reception was just two hours earlier, he and Katrina now treated Ember and Alarik like old friends.

When he shook their hands, Nick told them, "I hope this helps your friends. I wouldn't wish those nightmares onto my worst enemy. And they've been living with it since 2001? That's brutal, just brutal."

To Ember's surprise, Katrina gave her a hug before they got into the pickup and left. They left the gravel road for pavement and drove north on what Alarik referred to as the Enchanted Highway.

"Rik, did we just make new friends?"

"I think we might have." He pointed at the cotton bag riding on the center console between them. "Do you really think that thing can help my brother?"

"I think it could, yeah. We'll need to find a competent

Healer who can figure out how to tap into this magnet's mana. Its energy feels just like what was tormenting Kenny. Just like the sort of magic that the little girl in the park was using." Ember glanced at the sample bag and sensed its strange energy. She didn't fear the talisman, but the memory of Kenneth Newman's damaged aura made her shudder.

Alarik said nothing for some time. He gestured with his chin as they drove. "Up ahead to the left, is that tin man I told you about. A farmer, his wife, and their child."

He slowed down as they approached the giant steel sculptures to the west of the road. The 30-foot-tall woman stood closest to the highway, holding a blue basket of flowers in front of her. She wore a buff-colored dress with a matching hat, all made of steel. Her hair was black and looked to consist of a tangled mess of cables, also painted black. Her face was cheerful, with a cartoonish smile shaped like a wide, red-lipped "U." The farmer stood next to her, holding a pitchfork in his right hand. His body was built out of a large cylinder, painted to look like blue bib overalls with a red shirt beneath. Their fifteen-foot-tall child stood nearby, facing the road and licking a huge pink lollipop.

"Wanna stop in and say 'hi' to them?"

"Um...no, that's fine, thanks anyway." Ember chuckled nervously. "They're impressive, but honestly, kind of creep me out a little. What if they come to life and stomp on us?"

Alarik grinned and applied pressure to the accelerator. The Ford responded with a guttural burst of horsepower. "The next one, then. You'll like this one."

He wasn't wrong. "Fisherman's Dream" it was called, and it consisted of seven massive fish, painted to look true-to-life.

A life-sized person sat in a boat, with a fishing pole cast in the water. Before him, a towering monster burst from the waterline, snapping at the tail of a six-foot-long dragonfly.

"Northern pike," Alarik pointed at the elongated fish as he parked the pickup on the scoria byway. "And those over there are walleye and catfish."

"That's beautiful." Ember gaped from the passenger seat. "The artist who made these put a lot of time into it. I can't even imagine how many hours. Do you think we could walk around here for a few minutes?"

"Of course."

The grounds were well-maintained, with no litter to be found and the prairie grass trimmed neatly around the base of the sculptures. Lake-bottom plants reached for the sky, their steel leaves painted in natural shades of ochre and aquamarine.

The July morning was warming up, but the breeze was minimal and there were only a few clouds in the sky. Meadowlarks sang their inimitable songs. On a gravel road in the far distance, dust followed a moving grain truck like contrails to a jetliner. Ember breathed in a lungful of fresh country air.

"You can see for miles from this hill. Maybe twenty miles in all directions," Ember marveled. She turned a full circle as she paced. The oversized t-shirt she wore rustled when it caught the breeze.

"Penny for your thoughts?" Alarik was watching Ember. "What do you make of what Nick and Kat just told us?"

Ember strode below the giant fish, looking up at their pelvic fins and painted bellies. "They were under the effect of a Deference Spell. Same as Duncan Heywood. It had all the fingerprints of Elton's spell."

Alarik followed, a few steps behind her as she wandered. "But then why did they tell us all that they did?"

"Because I lifted the spell." Ember felt a rush of pride. "I lifted the Deference Spell. Not just temporarily, but completely."

"How? You didn't do the...the whole dance thing like you did with Duncan."

"I did and I didn't. I projected the counter-spell. I imagined doing the movements and made it happen. Then when I was touching the Deference Spell, I figured out how to pull it apart."

She spun on her heel and faced him, her face emblazoned with elation. "Rik, I dissolved Higginbotham's Deference Spells. Two of them, back to back, and it hardly took any effort. Can you believe that? It's all so surreal."

"I...I really don't know what to say. I didn't think that was possible."

"Nor did I. I just trusted my instinct, and it happened." Ember resumed her circuitous journey around a set of steel cattails. She had a joyful lightness to her step, despite the sleep deprivation. "I trusted my instinct. You know... throughout all these past few weeks—ever since I arrived in North Dakota—I followed my instincts. So many of those times, it seemed like I made the wrong choice. I thought I was making mistakes. I'm fairly sure Wallace thought I was, too."

"But you weren't, were you." Alarik leaned against the stalk of one of the steep cattails. "Your gut led you down the exact path that brought you to all these clues."

"Yeah. We've been taught, we Investigators, that we need to summon our mana and bend it to our will. I didn't have enough energy to do that back at the Hershel's place. So, I...I glided along a subtle touch of mana, gently guiding it as I needed, but working with it instead of forcing it." Ember pointed at a sedan-sized walleye and spoke excitedly. "It's like trying to cross a river by swimming with the current instead of against it. You can still get to the other side, but without it being so exhausting."

"Huh," was all Alarik said.

"So," she continued, "what we learned. I have a theory now. It's good that I can talk this through with you, Rik. I'll need to report to Wallace, but I can think aloud now."

"Happy to help," Alarik grinned. Ember's excitement was infectious.

"There have been no reports to the Druw High Council regarding the Mandaree Incident, or the discovery of a new Ley Line. The Council didn't sanction any of his actions, so Elton kept it off the books. He had to have recognized the existence of magic in the presence of the fog, to know that it may have been caused by something powerful like a new Ley Line. He found out that animals could safely enter the fog where humans couldn't. But he wanted to learn more about the source of all that strange energy. So, Elton sent in your brother and the nine other changelings, in animal form."

"Only, the reaction between our world's mana and that of

Aedynar's caused unpredictable results. Humans who encountered the fog became trapped between dimensions —that was the explanation for Nick and Kat's nightmares. Changelings are unique of course; they bridge between human and animal form. That the ten scouts are having nightmares of their subforms being stuck in quicksand, and the reality that they cannot shift into their animal form—"

"Their subforms are trapped between dimensions. Still trapped." Alarik looked pale.

Ember nodded slowly. "I think so, yes. It makes perfect sense when we put these pieces together."

"We need to un-trap their animal subforms then." He made a fist and wrapped his other hand around it. "And you think the Ley Line magnet could be used as, what, a key to unlock the door?"

"That's a good analogy, yeah." Ember ran her fingers through her hair. "We need to figure out *how* to use the artifact, but yeah, it contains magic from Aedynar. I think it could help unlock the door, to release the trapped changeling subforms, somehow."

"Why would Higginbotham want to keep all this a secret though?"

"Think about it, Rik. An entire Ley Line, all to himself. He and his cronies would have access to nearly limitless mana. They've already shown themselves to be power-hungry."

"They? Duncan is under the thumb of the Director, isn't he?" Alarik pulled out his soapstone chalk and began playing with it.

"Not Duncan." Ember breathed in and stared at the square-jawed man. "Rik, Higginbotham isn't working alone. He might not even be the one in charge of this cover-up. Duncan and the other Investigators are all just pawns, being used by Elton as puppets to a greater effect."

"You said those three spies mentioned a Mister B. You're thinking it might be someone other than Elton?"

"Possibly, yeah." She flicked her tongue over her wounded lip. "Someone who Elton Higginbotham is working with. Or working for."

Alarik pursed his lips and blew a long whistle. "And let me guess, you don't know who the other baddies are yet?"

"Elton has co-conspirators, I'm sure of it." Ember's excited energy transformed into dogged determination. She rapped her knuckles against the steel cattail to punctuate her pledge. "I don't know who they are, not yet. But I'm going to find them and make them answer for their corruption."

36

SOMEONE MISSED THEIR TURN

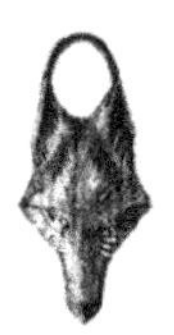

THE WHITE SUV SLOWED DOWN AS IT DROVE PAST THE Fisherman's Dream sculpture. The vehicle crested the hill as its brake lights lit up.

Alarik and Ember were walking back to the Super Duty pickup as the SUV whipped a U-turn on the Enchanted Highway. "Someone missed their turn," Alarik chuckled. "Good thing he's got a little Jeep. I'd never make such a tight turn in my pickup."

White Jeep. Why does that vehicle look familiar? Ember furrowed her brow as she searched her memory. She stood watching with her hand on the door of Alarik's pickup as the Jeep pulled into the sculpture's gravel parking lot. She remembered where she recognized the vehicle from, right before its driver's door swung open.

A barrel-chested man with a salt-and-pepper crew cut stepped out, his olive drab eyes fixed in a glower. A gruff smoker's voice rumbled loudly. "What are you doing out here, Wright?"

"I might ask you the same, Duncan." She kept her voice calm, though she felt the hairs stand on the back of her neck. "I'm just taking a tour of the countryside with my friend—"

"You're lying," Duncan said. He cast a contemptuous glance at Alarik. Though he closed the distance to Ember, he made a point of keeping both of them in sight. The dark shadow over the Senior Investigator's aura swelled like a growing storm cloud. "I need you to come with me now, Wright."

In her periphery, she saw Alarik stiffen. Ember's pulse quickened but still she maintained a calm tone. "Alright, I'll see you back at the embassy this afternoon."

"Unacceptable. You're coming in with me. *Now*."

"There's no need to be testy, Duncan. We're going to be—"

"I said *now*, Wright. That's an order."

Alarik spoke with a growl through clenched teeth. "What's this about?"

The shadowy cloud surged around Duncan. His glare challenged the other man. "It's none of your business, changeling. Don't interfere unless you want to get injured."

Alarik growled again, this time more beast than human. His lip curled up in a snarl and he took a step forward.

"Rik, no!" Ember shouted.

The Deference Spell may have inhibited his ability to cast Memory Wash spells, but it did nothing to slow the mage's senses or response time. Duncan Heywood was a peer to Wallace Livingston—The Legend—and had over a century of experience identifying and neutralizing threats. The coyote changeling was fast, but Duncan was faster.

Time seemed to slow as Ember watched the surge of mana erupt from Duncan's fist. The blinding, yellow light expanded from an orb the size of a softball into an ever-widening weave of energy. The Containment Net enveloped Alarik, knocking him to the ground. The net immediately began closing around him, tightening in its inescapable grip.

Bruised, sore, and drained of mana from last night's fight with the three changeling spies, Ember's options were few. She couldn't cast a Containment Net, and even if she could she doubted she'd be fast enough at this close distance. She had no weapon, but she might still be able to surprise him.

Without giving it any thought, she put her head down and launched herself at the Senior Investigator. *If I can just knock him over.*

She did catch him by surprise, but the Laws of Physics weren't in her favor. He was at least twice her weight and eight inches taller. Ember punched at the man's face, only to meet air.

Duncan's hand made a wide arc and connected with her cheek, whipping her chin sideways to her shoulder. Her eyes rolled up as a shockwave of synapses misfired through her brain. She staggered and swung her fist blindly, missing again.

He caught her wrist and squeezed like a vise. She cried out in pain and was answered with a back-handed slap that made her vision blur and her voice stop short.

Ember dropped to her knees and spat blood onto the gravel. Colorful, giant steel fish swam around her as the blackout arrived.

HEAVY BREATHING AND GRUNTS SEEPED INTO HER subconscious. She couldn't have been out for long, as Duncan was still loading Alarik in the back of his Jeep.

"You bastard! Let me out of this thing and fight me with your fists. Think you can take me in a fair fight?"

Duncan huffed, "I did warn you to back down, changeling. Now you'll be charged with interference with High Council justice."

"Justice!" Alarik snarled like an angry coyote. "Whatever it is you're doing, it ain't that."

When the Senior Investigator returned to her, Ember flirted with unconsciousness. Her head felt like it had been bashed in by a hammer. Salty fluid met her tongue as her swollen lip split open anew. Duncan rolled her onto her side and something cold slid over her wrists. The ratcheting clicks told her that it was a set of handcuffs.

Her lips parted and a single syllable escaped as a whisper: "No."

"What did you say, Wright?" Duncan's breath smelled like an ash tray when he exhaled into her face. He hefted her from the ground to stand on wobbly legs like a rag doll with too little stuffing.

"No," she repeated. Defiance tasted salty and metallic, the

words mingling with her own blood. "No, this isn't really you. I can help you, Duncan. I know the spell you're under."

The dark shroud of the Deference Spell swelled around Duncan Heywood. Ember saw a faint glimpse of the man within—the Senior Investigator who dedicated his life to chasing down criminals and fighting corruption—now struggling against the corruption that infected him. The opaque figure reached for her.

Ember tried to speak to the man within the spell, tried to encourage him, but she couldn't find the words. She gasped for air, finding none. *Why can't I breathe?*

Somewhere distant, Alarik's voice found her ears. He sounded desperate. "You lousy fucker, you're choking her! Let her go!"

The bound changeling rocked back and forth within the Jeep, pounding his shoulder against the glass, shouting. She saw Alarik's mouth move, his rage and desperation tangible. But she could no longer hear his voice.

Involuntary tears trickled out of bulging eyes, threatening to pop out of their sockets. Ember's face turned purple as Duncan's rough hands squeezed around her neck. She felt a thin, grotesque, squishing sensation from her constricted esophagus. *He's squeezing the life out of me. He's not letting go.*

Her vision narrowed and darkened along with her thoughts. *I said I'd not be a victim. Not a day ago. Yet here I am. My last fight. Nobody's coming to rescue me. Rik will be next. Just another victim. No heroes left.*

Need to be my own bloody hero.

Then she was floating. Dancing. She belatedly recognized it

was the dance she'd learned from Barnaby—the counter-spell. With what little awareness she still held, Ember realized she was instinctively imagining the movements of the counter-spell. The mage focused her energy on these movements, ignoring the fact that she could no longer see or breathe. In complete darkness, she felt the tar paper tent surrounding Duncan Heywood and found a rough thread. She drew upon that thread, pulling the tendril carefully, quickly. The thread loosened around her target's aura.

Ember's vision exploded with light and the sound of her own gasping coughs. Her forehead hit the ground as she heaved, her hands clutching gravel as her whole body wretched.

The throbbing of her neck told her that she had been released. Blood flow resumed its course and she coughed repeatedly, spitting blood from her broken lip to splatter against the gravel bed she crawled on.

Duncan staggered from her, dropping to his knees a few paces away. The barrel-chested man wheezed like a drowning man tasting air. He reached for the hood of the SUV for support, his back rising and falling with heavy breaths.

Ember watched the tar-colored threads of the Deference Spell unfurl and evaporate harmlessly into the atmosphere around him. She sucked in air between ragged coughs, her fire-blue eyes blinking into focus to find the Senior Investigator staring back at her.

His brows arched over olive drab eyes as confused surprise morphed into realization. Duncan's lips silently formed the question, "you?"

She answered with a single, affirming nod.

Duncan stammered as his cleft chin swayed, his quivering lips trying to find the right words. An involuntary sob erupted from his lungs and tears of inimitable gratitude began to flow.

For nine years, he had been forced to break his lifelong oath to the Investigator's Creed, to obstruct justice, and to serve a corrupt man. He had been Elton Higginbotham's puppet.

At a roadside attraction named Fisherman's Dream, Duncan Heywood was at last awakened from his nightmare.

37

NOT ENTIRELY SOLO

HE FLICKED TWO FINGERS UPWARD AT THE COMING VEHICLE. Alarik drove with one hand situated at the top of the steering wheel, seemingly for this exact purpose.

"That's the fifth person you've waved at, Rik. Do you really know that many people?" Her throat was hoarse, like she was coming off a bad chest cold. She felt like she was doing a decent job of hiding that fact.

"Huh?" He and his coyote subform looked at her with shared bewilderment. "I don't know *any* of these people, Ember."

"Why are you waving at them, then? And why are they waving back like they know you?"

He grinned and shook his head. "City girl. This is rural North Dakota; we wave at one another when we're driving. People here are friendly. We'll be back on the Interstate soon, but this is waving country for now."

Ember thought of the Hershels. They were probably wavers,

too. It was just over a month ago when she landed at Minot International Airport. Her coworkers were so rude to her—well, most of them anyway. Since then, she had stumbled upon a local cover-up as well as a potentially global conspiracy. She had had not one but two brushes with mortality in the past 24 hours. It was charming to find that the regular people who lived in this state weren't like that. These denizens shared a quaintness that echoed simpler times, where neighbors knew each other and strangers took the time to greet you—or even feed you a hearty breakfast when you show up unannounced.

Alarik interrupted her musings. "I still think you should've let me clock him. He almost *killed* you, Ember."

"Yeah, but he didn't," she coughed.

He winced, his fingers balling into a fist as his body language contradicted his calm tone. "That sounds rough. Your neck is already starting to bruise."

She retrieved a bottle of water from the pickup's cupholder, taking a sip. The coolness was a salve to her injured throat. "I'll heal. You know that wasn't him. I mean, not really. It was the Deference Spell that forced him to act that way. To attack us."

"I guess. Do you think it was alright leaving him alone like that?" He was studying the shrinking hilltop sculpture in his rearview mirror.

"It's what he wanted," Ember's fingers combed through her hair. "I think if you or I were in his position, we'd probably want some time alone to gather our thoughts, too. He feels bloody rotten for what he did to us. That's a lot to take in.

Anyway, he's going to continue pretending that he's under Elton's influence. He knows he has no choice for now."

After freeing him from the Deference Spell, Duncan Heywood had been simultaneously grateful and morose. He had spent the better part of a decade as a slave to Elton Higginbotham's whims. He described being in a state of seeing his actions, hearing himself speak, but unable to break through the spell. Sudden freedom from mental bondage was a lot for a man to process.

"He said he didn't know who that Mister B is." Alarik's gaze shifted to his passenger. "Do you believe him?"

She nodded. "I do. I'm disappointed of course, but I'm not altogether surprised. Director Higginbotham isn't dim. He and his co-conspirators—assuming they even exist—probably didn't let Duncan witness anything they truly wanted kept secret. To them, Duncan was just a puppet."

"A puppet," Alarik repeated. "That's a creepy way of saying it."

The rest of the steel sculptures along the Enchanted Highway were impressive, but Alarik didn't stop at any of them. They had a long drive ahead, and both driver and passenger were exhausted. Ember offered to drive a leg of the journey, and to her surprise, Alarik agreed. It spoke to how tired he was, that he would let someone else drive his pickup, especially in her own injured state.

"We'll take a different route back then," Alarik said as he took the ramp eastward rather than west on I-94. "It's not much longer, but way safer than making you drive through bumper-to-bumper oil patch traffic in the middle of a weekday. I'll hand the wheel over to you when we get to Mandan. That'll be about the halfway point."

"That's appreciated. I might accidentally take the left lane and kill us both. I can blame it on my Britishness, driving on the wrong side of the road, yeah?"

"Not. Funny." Alarik pronounced each word with emphasis, though his lips quirked a smile.

"I'm going to call Wallace while you drive if you don't mind. I need to update him. A lot has happened in the past 24 hours."

"You ain't lyin', sistah."

"Alright, I know you must be tired when you start sounding less like a farm boy and more like a daytime talk show guest."

"Word, yo."

She smirked and shook her head as she flipped open the burner phone. It was good to hear the mirth return between them after what they had just been through. "Brilliant. Right, I'm dialing the mobile now, so silence in the carny tent, please."

He pinched the air right before his mouth and drew a horizontal line along his lips, mimicking a zipper.

Ember muttered and looked away, trying not to encourage him. Wallace answered on the third ring.

"Wallace, it's Ember. I'm with Rik. We're driving."

"Is everything fine? What's wrong with your voice? Are you in trouble?"

"I just have a sore throat. Everything is brilliant, Wallace. So much has happened, and I need to catch you up. I think you'll adore this status update."

Though it had only been 36 hours since they last spoke, she did have so much to tell Wallace: the fatal encounter with the changeling spies, what they said before they died, and the findings from Nick and Katrina. Above all, the fact that she had lifted three Deference Spells, including that of his friend's. She diplomatically elected to leave out the part where his friend nearly throttled her to death.

Her mentor was not impressed with how close she came to kidnapping and worse. But even hard-boiled Wallace Livingston, The Legend, got excited when Ember told him about lifting the Deference Spells.

"You're right to give him some space, I think." Wallace practically stumbled over his words, so uplifted he was with this news. "I'll give him a call next. He needs to understand how important it is that he maintains the perception of being under the spell."

"I think he understands, but it wouldn't hurt to hear it from an old friend." Ember closed her eyes and swallowed, suppressing the nagging tickle in her throat. "I could see that he wanted to help. He'll be an important ally in the effort to root out the corruption in the Magic City colony."

"I concur. Duncan has his oddities, but he's a reliable Investigator. I'm in your debt for rescuing him from this terrible fate." Wallace sounded emotional, but he recovered his tone, even if it was tinted with excited energy. "You're sure the spies didn't report your blown cover to their handler, this Mister B?"

"Affirmative. Had they gotten away, that would be another matter. The Schmitts saw to it that they wouldn't get a chance to muck things up for me. For all of us."

"That family is proving to be an asset, Ember. You were right to trust your instinct. I was in error to call that into doubt."

Ember felt a lump growing in her throat, independent from the injury. Wallace didn't often hand out compliments, and he apologized with even less frequency. Granted, he didn't usually have much reason to apologize. Sleep fatigue threatened to make her emotions bubble to the surface, so she changed the topic. "The disabled changelings, the scouts from the Mandaree Incident. What can we do to help them?"

"This artifact from Aedynar sounds intriguing. I'll see about finding higher-level Healers we can trust, who might be able to figure out how best to utilize that Ley Line magnet. Your mother is a Fifth Level Healer, is she not?"

"She is, but...I'd really rather not get her involved if we can help it." Ember flicked her tongue against her swollen lip. "If I could keep Mum out of this mess, that would be for the best."

"Understood. I'll see who else I can find. We also need to get you better prepared."

"How so?"

"All that time you apprenticed with me, I didn't teach you how to defend yourself. I coddled you. This negligence almost cost you your life with those spies."

"I was just drained of my mana, Wallace. Had I a full reserve I would've—"

"You would've still walked into their ambush, that's what you would have done." His reproach was sharp. "You were caught unaware, and no amount of spellcasting would have changed that. You need to work on your situational awareness."

He wasn't wrong, and she knew it. Ember had been caught by surprise multiple times in the past month, in part due to her single-mindedness and ignorance of her surroundings. A cough forced its way out, punctuating the thought. She touched her incisors to the wounded bottom lip and winced at the sharp pain. *A bloody good reminder.*

"Yes, Wallace. Maybe Duncan can help guide me in that respect."

"If he cannot, we'll find someone who can," Wallace breathed into the phone. "This is just the beginning, and *when* Elton Higginbotham and his cohorts realize we're closing in on them, they won't fade gently into the night. These are dangerous people with the means to strike hard when threatened."

"That would be my assessment, too. Keeping low and moving cautiously will be the modus operandi." Ember absently touched her coyote-face pendant.

"Doubtless. One last thing, Ember."

"Yes?"

"You've done superlative work. Not half bad for a mere month in the field solo. Now, get some rest so you can get over that sore throat."

"Thank you, sir. But I'm not entirely solo." Ember looked purposefully at her driver as she ended the call.

She was tired but feeling optimistic. There would be challenges ahead—probably greater challenges than she could even fathom—but Ember wasn't facing them alone. She had friends, and she knew they would pick her up if she stumbled.

"You didn't tell Wallace about Duncan choking you," Alarik said.

"I know." She drew another swallow of cool water. "I didn't want him getting overly concerned. He might've been tempted to distrust Duncan."

"I don't see a problem with that. Wouldn't he be right to be wary?"

"We're surrounded by who-knows-how-many bad guys. We need to have allies when things start unraveling." She thought about the way she countered the Deference Spells by supernaturally unweaving them and couldn't help but smile at her unintended pun.

"If you say so. We need to gas up," Alarik said as he steered his Super Duty toward the off-ramp of Exit 147. "I could use a bite, too."

"You're hungry again, coyote? Didn't we just have breakfast?"

The look he flashed her, Ember swore he was on the verge of whimpering. "That was two whole hours ago! I'm a growing boy." He patted his stomach.

She laughed. "We can't have you starving in that case."

"Right on. So, this truck stop has a great little café. It's the Rolling Hills Restaurant, and they serve the best knoephla."

She scrunched her nose. "Knoephla? I've never heard of it. Can't I just have a burger and chips?"

"You gotta try the knoephla. I'm tellin' ya, you're gonna love it. It's infinitely better than Marmite. Trust me." He chose a parking space and shifted out of gear. Alarik turned to his passenger, extended a fist over the console, and said, "do you trust me?"

Ember tilted her head, offered a smile, and touched her fist to his. "More every day, my friend."

BONUS #1 - FREE PREQUEL NOVEL!

Keep reading for a bonus preview of *Ascending Mage 2: Changeling Hunter*.

But first, would you like to know more about Nick and Katrina's role in the Mandaree Incident?

Read the prequel novel *Fog Over Mandaree* for free, exclusively at go.frhurt.com/fom

Bonus #1 - Free Prequel Novel!

BONUS #2 - PREVIEW OF ASCENDING MAGE 2: CHANGELING HUNTER

It had been such a perfect summer day, right up until someone shot him.

A brisk breeze was coming from the northwest, making the expressionless faces in the nearby sunflower field restless. Thin cirrus clouds raced as streaks high in the periwinkle sky above the Missouri Coteau.

It was Saturday morning and Evan and Brandon were tending their salsa garden, each on his hands and knees as they worked to finish the chore of pulling weeds while the day was still reasonably cool. Water seeped from black, rubber soaker hoses laid out in snake-like spirals around the plants in the garden, bubbling and hissing fine droplets of cold drink to turn the rich soil dark.

By afternoon, the temperature would be sweltering, but they would be on their way to the lake by then. The housemates had banked up, and were cashing in, two weeks' vacation from the lignite mine where they worked. They would be spending that hard-earned downtime camping and fishing at Lake Sakakawea.

Evan had worried their flourishing garden would suffer in the unforgiving July sun while they were gone, but Brandon insisted that the plants would survive. They compromised by pledging to drive home every few days to turn on the hydrant and check their mail. It was only an hour's drive from their rural property outside of Underwood, North Dakota to the cabin they rented near the south shore at the park district.

Evan's iPhone rested at an angle atop a nearby fence post, the better to catch the weak Wi-Fi signal from the house. Pop music streamed from the tethered Bluetooth speaker, filling the air with last year's big hit from The Black Eyed Peas. Honey bees hovered among the tomato blossoms, undeterred by the "boom-boom-boom" lyrics of the catchy song.

"Another one of the Sun Golds is ripe! Want this one?" Brandon was holding a deep orange cherry tomato between his thumb and forefinger, a bright grin reaching his eyes.

Evan looked up from the habanero plant he was kneeling by. "Did you get one yet?"

"Not today," Brandon admitted. "But there'll be more when we get back from Beulah Bay next week. You can have this one if you want it." The willowy man stood up and stepped between the galvanized wire cages. When the chorus came on, he swiveled his narrow hips and snapped the fingers on his free hand to the beat.

Evan shook his head and admired the show. "You're going to get stung by one of those bees if you keep that up."

"No way! Them chickens won't copy my swagger." Brandon dropped the tiny fruit into Evan's outstretched hand, then danced back to the tomato plants to resume weeding. "I'm so three-thousand-and-eight."

"What does that even mean?"

The cherry tomato was not quite crimson, but this variety would never get fully red. Evan studied it only a moment before he popped the orb into his mouth. An explosion of sweet flavor burst across his taste buds when his teeth crushed into the juicy flesh. "Oh my god, that really *is* great, isn't it? You really can't buy tomatoes this sweet."

The other man grinned at Evan and nodded, though he was too focused on lip-syncing to the song to voice an opinion.

Fergie had just started belting out her portion of the lyrics when the phone exploded. Tiny pieces of metal and plastic shrapnel scattered across the garden.

"What the fuck!" Evan spun around to see the top of the post splintered where the phone used to be. "I think my iPhone just overheated!"

"Woah. Do you think we left it out in the sun too long?" Brandon picked up a shattered remnant of the smartphone's innards. He stood up and pulled out his own phone from the back pocket of his jeans—the phone was a twin to his friend's—and held the two side by side. "Look how deformed it is!"

Without the music to mask its report, the second gunshot was unmistakable.

Brandon's phone flew apart from his hand and shattered before it hit the ground. Blood sprayed at once from a wound that went clear through his palm, exposing splintered bones. He stared at his mauled hand, mouth agape as his mind struggled to compute what his stunned nerves prevented him from feeling.

Then he screamed.

Evan didn't have time to think, only to react. He pulled his t-shirt off and wrapped it around his friend's hand. Blood already began to soak through before he had a knot tied around Brandon's wet, slippery wrist. "Keep pressure on it! I'll get the car!" He started to run toward the house but stopped mid-stride.

A figure was approaching casually toward the garden, dressed from head to toe in hunting camouflage. A black AR-15 rifle was in the hunter's hands, its muzzle pointed at them.

Confusion threatened to paralyze Evan as he tried to make sense of what he was seeing. The stranger's face was veiled in a pattern matching the rest of his full-body camo. A strip of burlap was woven around the firearm, breaking up its unmistakable shape. Evan turned back to Brandon, who was clutching the cotton mitten around his right hand.

"Run!" Evan had to shout it three times, and even then, his friend stood like a beanpole until Evan grabbed the man's forearm and pulled him away. They ducked behind the wooden fence at the edge of their property and ran into the neighbor's sunflower field.

The sunflowers weren't tall enough this early in the season to hide them, but there wasn't any time to think of a plan, just to react. Someone was trying to kill them. Why anyone would want to murder them was beyond Evan's comprehension.

"Why?" Brandon breathed the same thought aloud as they ran. "Why did someone shoot me?"

"Probably some junkies," Evan guessed. "Some meth-heads trying to rob us. They probably didn't think anybody was home."

The breeze was stiff on their faces as they ran, hunched low. The main road was up ahead a quarter mile, and they would follow it until they got to the Gappert's place. Richard and Darlene Gappert were their nearest neighbors, about three-quarters of a mile down the road.

The collective daisy-like faces of the plants shunned the intruders. The sunflowers were only interested in following their illuminating god as it chased across the southern sky. Despite their apathy, one of the plants managed to trip Evan as he ran bare-chested through the bristly leaves.

A bee stung his exposed shoulder and some part of him wanted to laugh at the absurdity of it all. Only minutes ago, he had been chiding his best friend about upsetting the bees, and now he was the one who attracted the stinger. After they got to the Gappert's and called the McLean County Sheriff, he knew Brandon would get a laugh out of that little irony.

When they got to the ditch along the road, they were both sucking air. The makeshift bandage around Brandon's hand was seeping with a steady flow of blood. His own shirt and jeans were splattered with dark streaks. He had been exerting himself, increasing the blood flow when he should have been trying to keep his heart rate in check.

Evan thought back to the safety training they received at the Falkirk Mine. "We need to keep your hand elevated. Keep applying pressure. And we have to slow down your heart rate."

"Kinda hard," Brandon wheezed, "when we're running."

"Okay, then sit here in the ditch. I'll run over to Dick and Darlene's and come back for you."

A rusting, corrugated culvert jutted from an approach between the road and the section line trail that bordered the sunflower field. Brandon parked himself on a patch of curlycup gumweed, using the steel cylinder as a backrest. He laid his arm on the culvert and placed his uninjured hand over the blood-soaked knot of cotton. His face was pale and sweaty, and he was breathing hard.

Evan glanced back across the sunflower field to their house in the distance. Not more than a couple hundred yards away, a camouflaged figure stalked the trail they had cut through the flat field.

He dropped down and began to crawl over to Brandon. Evan felt sweat drip down his arm and when he placed weight on his right hand, a wave of pain burned from his shoulder. Only then, did he realize that it was blood and not sweat that trickled from a wound in his shoulder. Some part of his mind remembered stumbling minutes ago and feeling a bee sting.

"You've been shot too!" Brandon groaned.

Among the flat prairie fields, there weren't many options for concealment, and they would never outrun the shooter.

"He's following us," Evan hissed. "We need to hide! Can you shift?"

"It's been a while," Brandon admitted. "But I think so. Think we can both fit in the culvert?"

"You will for sure. Do it."

Evan watched as his friend grimaced. After a moment of concentration, his lean body began to shrink, and his face became narrow and flared. Brandon's ears migrated to the top of his head as they became triangular. Hair and skin and clothes were replaced with short, ruddy fur across his backside, white fur along his front. The stylish skinny-jeans that minutes ago had been shaking to hip-hop were now a bushy tail. The blood-soaked bandage melted away, and his damaged hand was replaced with a paw to match the other three, though this one was bleeding.

They hadn't considered the injury, and Evan had already donated his shirt to form the bandage. He would need to kick off his shoes and use a sock to aide his friend. He picked up the fox to help him into the culvert where he would be safe. In his fox form, his friend weighed maybe 25 pounds and was easy to slide backward into the rusty cylinder.

Brandon looked past Evan toward the sunflowers and his fox-eyes grew wide with alarm. A half-second later, a hole appeared between his eyes and his body went first rigid, then limp. Black matter and red fur splattered the yellow gumweed growing along the embankment.

Evan dropped his best friend's body and fell backward. His mouth opened in a silent scream as he looked up at the silhouette leering above him.

The hunter's Mossy Oak head cover concealed everything but a pair of rage-filled eyes. A hint of gun smoke escaped the muzzle brake of the rifle before the wind stole it away. The barrel was pointed at him.

Evan squeezed his eyes shut and waited for the trigger to be pulled. When he closed his eyes, he saw Brandon's face. He opened them and blinked up at the killer. "Why are you doing this to us?"

The hunter said a word, but the head cover and wind conspired to muffle his voice. When the killer took his hand off his rifle's foregrip to pull down the mask, Evan seized his chance to escape.

He launched himself at the stranger, catching him by surprise. The man fell backward, swinging his rifle like a club and barely missing Evan's head. The hunter fell into the sunflower field. Evan ran up and over the road to the ditch on the opposite side.

As he ran, Evan focused his thoughts on shifting. He and his best friend didn't practice their abilities as changelings often, choosing to live their lives full-time as regular humans. Their families never understood their lifestyle choices, but he and Brandon understood one another. They had that, at least.

He grunted as his bones creaked and slid. Coarse fur sprouted from his skin as his body morphed from its human form. He was on the north shoulder of the gravel road when he dropped to all fours. Evan would be able to run fast, to get away then. His senses became sharper, his eyesight just a little better, his nose more focused, his hearing more acute. He knew that even in human form, changelings had elevated senses when compared to NonDruws, but in his animal form everything was more primal, more instinct-driven.

If only he would have practiced his shifting, he might have been fast enough to get into his coyote form and run away. He was too slow, though, and no sooner was he transformed into a coyote did he smell the hunter. He heard the rifle's action and a deafening crack.

The bullet crashed through his rib cage and dropped him. Evan rolled twice down the ditch and came to rest as a crumpled heap, his neck twisted beneath his body. It hurt to breathe. A strange texture confused him. It felt like a fire was alive in his chest.

The growing haze of pain made it hard to make sense of the human who approached from downwind. Before Evan inhaled his final breath, he thought of his salsa garden and how they had left the water on. Those sweet tomatoes would be ruined with rot.

ASCENDING MAGE 2
CHANGELING HUNTER
FRANK & RAELEA
HURT
GENUINE MODERN FANTASY

AUTHOR NOTES

It seems as though every time I'm about to admit to a mystical experience, I preface the admission with a statement: "I'm not a mystical person," or "I don't believe in mysticism." You might be surprised that someone who writes fantasy fiction proclaims any semblance of rational thought, but it's true. That's my claim, at least.

So let me just offer this disclaimer before I continue: I don't believe in mysticism.

And yet...

It was on a drive to Minot when RaeLea and I began brainstorming the next story we were going to write. We always knew that *Fog Over Mandaree* would serve as a prequel to what we hoped would blossom into a wider series, but we weren't entirely sure of the form that series would take. Somewhere on Highway 83 near Washburn, we realized that our protagonist—who we decided would be an up-and-coming sorceress—should be from somewhere other than North Dakota, though nevertheless English-speaking.

Having her from, say, the United Kingdom, would allow our readers to discover the rural landscape of our state even as our main character did.

Wanting her hometown to be somewhere other than London, we randomly selected a community called Great Malvern. It wasn't until we started reading up on the surrounding district that we learned how one of the earliest Ley Lines—the pseudoscientific term for what possibly is a geologic fault line—exists in Malvern Hills.

We learned that the ancient Druids considered this area holy, and later generations built healing spas in the area. One of the more recent such spas was constructed right around the time Minot was founded.

Foreshadowing a bit, later in the series you'll find that other such magical connections exist around the world, and not-coincidentally that's where you will find other Druwish colonies.

Speaking of the Druws, we came up with that term as we wanted our magical beings—changelings and mages (who are also known as Malverns for their original source of magic)—to have an umbrella term that was unique but rooted in historical reality. As the Druids were famously present in Great Britain, it made sense that their descendants would borrow from that identity. Thus, they became "Druws."

RaeLea wrote the first draft for the opening scene in the book we would eventually name *Ascending Mage 1: Changeling Justice*. She had a vivid image of Ember running through an aged cemetery, with Wallace splitting off from her as they enter the gates. Within the graveyard, they would encounter a giant who happened to be a ghost. RaeLea searched online for graveyards reasonably near Great Malvern and found a photo of the Blackburn Old Cemetery. The photo matched the description and layout in her mind's eye. Further research found that a real-life giant had lived in that community—the tallest man, according to the Guinness Book of World Records. One Mr. Frederick Kempster.

That was a nice coincidence.

Stateside, Minot's nickname—we were reminded as we drove into the city limits—is the Magic City. What better setting could we hope to have for a modern fantasy story than a place that literally has "magic" in its name?

Wandering around Minot, we had an idea of what we wanted the Druwish embassy to look like. As she lived in Minot for over a decade, RaeLea knew of the iconic Parker Building downtown. When she showed me the eight-story structure, it was hard not to imagine secret offices hidden behind the thick masonry facade. Wouldn't it make sense for this building to sit atop a Ley Line? The ground floor would contain a spa, within which the local Druws could recharge their mana—just like they do in Great Malvern.

As a cover story, Ember would work in that spa. As a licensed massage therapist, RaeLea is able to provide realistic insights into that career, so it's a nice fit.

In later research, RaeLea found a century-old photo of some prominent-looking men standing in downtown Minot. Wouldn't you know, in the background was a construction site identified as the Parker Building.

I get chills even now, thinking about what an eerie coincidence this is.

We had our cover artist include that photo in the background for *Ascending Mage 4: Nothing Broken*. You'll see in the story that we identify some of the individuals in the photo, and you might not be surprised to learn that they'll be familiar to you by that point.

We needed a place for Ember to stay that was within walking distance of her workplace. There aren't too many residential areas in downtown Minot, but wouldn't you know there is a three-story brick building renovated from its original purpose as a plow factory. It, too, was one of the earliest structures in the Magic City. On its ground floor was a bakery. The Sweet and Flour has sadly since closed its doors, but it was open during the time the Ascending Mage series takes place. As Ember has a penchant for sweets, this, too, seemed like fate.

We learned that connecting many of these downtown buildings is a network of old utility tunnels—the perfect route for a changeling and a mage to bypass spying eyes.

There are so many other coincidences like these, though I have to be careful not to give away the plot and characters you'll be meeting throughout the series.

Our motto is "Genuine Modern Fantasy." It's easy to be authentic when there are so many real elements which align with our fiction.

But like I said, I'm not a mystical person. This isn't magic; just multiple coincidences. Right?

Frank Hurt

ACKNOWLEDGMENTS

We are incredibly fortunate to have a fantastic Alpha Team. These folks pick through our stories, proofread, and help find gaps in the plot and prose. The novel you just read is much stronger thanks to their efforts. Special thanks to:

- Robert Severson
- Jackie Hope
- Lucy Hurt
- Muriel Hurt
- Bonnie Olson
- Benedette Knopik
- Joy Vasquez
- Ian Cowie
- Stephanie Sapp
- Ronald Colbert
- Luke Hurt
- Gloria Warner
- Jolene Briles
- Boniface Knopik
- Elizabeth Key

Finally, a huge thanks to everyone who reviews our novels on Amazon and Goodreads!

Did you leave a review yet? If so, send us an email so we can thank you properly!

Our email address is frank@frhurt.com or use the contact form at https://frhurt.com

CPSIA information can be obtained
at www.ICGtesting.com
Printed in the USA
FSHW010719100520
70105FS